THE DIPLOMAT'S DAUGHTER

WILLIAM KINSOLVING

The Diplomat's Daughter

N A N   A.   T A L E S E

DOUBLEDAY
NEW YORK
LONDON
TORONTO
SYDNEY
AUCKLAND

PUBLISHED BY NAN A. TALESE
an imprint of Doubleday, a division of
Bantam Doubleday Dell Publishing Group, Inc.
1540 Broadway, New York, New York 10036

DOUBLEDAY and the portrayal of an anchor
with a dolphin are trademarks of Doubleday,
a division of Bantam Doubleday Dell
Publishing Group, Inc.

Book design by Paul Randall Mize

Library of Congress Cataloging-in-Publication Data

Kinsolving, William.
The diplomat's daughter/William Kinsolving.
p.   cm.
1. Middle East—History—20th century—Fiction.   I. Title.
PS3561.I58D55   1993
813'.54—dc20   92-34385
CIP

ISBN 0-385-41931-7
June 1993
First Edition

1   3   5   7   9   10   8   6   4   2

For Lucie

PROLOGUE

1960

MOMMY, MAY I go over to Noorna's house?" As she often did, Lily started her question in the hall, concluding it only after she'd opened the door and run into her mother's bedroom, usually without knocking. This time what she saw stopped her progress as suddenly as a wall. Her mother, dressed in a radiant white slip, was holding one of her bottles of perfume and applying the stopper between her thighs. One leg was raised, the foot propped on an ottoman. "We're going swimming," Lily said, transfixed.

Her mother glared at her. *"En français,"* she commanded as she put her foot down and turned to her dressing table.

Lily was an obedient child and repeated her request in French. While her mother responded with an impatient permission, including an often repeated litany of manners to be remembered, Lily listened but was much more interested in why her mother had put perfume there, between her thighs. The girl knew about applications to wrists and neck, which was where she put it when she secretly played with her mother's cosmetics. The perfume, the lipstick, the powder, even the black kohl eye shadow, which was the only Egyptian item her mother had allowed in her life—Lily applied them all on nights when her parents were out, or, as was more often the case, when her mother was out and her father worked in the study doing embassy business while Bach played on the phonograph.

Recently, Lily had dared to put on all the makeup, even using her mother's henna in her hair and invading her mother's closet for a dress. After a long examination in the mirror of the results—she was quite startled with how glamorous she looked, even at ten—

she presented herself in costume to her father. Adjusting his plastic-rimmed glasses with one hand, he looked up from his papers and laughed, the rolling kind of roaring laugh he had when truly happy. He called her Miss Garbo, changed the music on the phonograph, and danced her around the study before hurrying her back to her mother's room to clean up everything. That had been one of their "Cairo secrets," as they called them. Recently there had been many more.

"Allez-vous en," her mother said, apparently irritated. Lily was not surprised by the half-packed suitcase on her mother's bed, for she often took overnight trips to Alexandria. Lily hurried out of the room and down the narrow staircase. She couldn't wait to tell Noorna about putting perfume between the thighs.

Wearing a white summer caftan and red pointed slippers, Amir, the old Sudanese *boab* who looked after the house, opened the door for her. The scars on his face from deep cuts, indications of virility, made Lily's flesh crawl. He had told her strange and fantastic stories of his youth in the southern desert that may all have been lies, but they were good stories. He also taught Lily a great deal of Arabic that no one else at her school had ever heard. Lily's mother couldn't stand him, an attitude the old man suffered silently, knowing she needed him to make the house work. It was a small house, although her mother always called it a villa. Nevertheless, it was old and many things broke or stopped working. The *boab* could fix anything, not permanently, perhaps only for five minutes; nevertheless, Madame McCann's life, as imperfect as she constantly reminded everyone it was, could go on.

Lily picked up the bicycle lying under the single banyan tree on the front lawn, and pedaled down the street. She knew how unhappy her mother was, but Lily didn't like to think about it. They lived in Zamalek at the north end of Gezira, the largest island in the Nile. The community was dotted with more than fifty embassies and residences, as well as with apartments and villas occupied by diplomats and their families. The United States Embassy, where Lily's father worked, was located in a nineteenth-century mansion across the Nile in downtown Cairo. Each day, wearing his old Panama hat and a light linen suit, he would leave just before Lily went off to school. Backing out of the driveway in their well-traveled Renault, he would wave to her, and soon after, Lily was picked up by a bus for the trip to school. She kept the seat next to her free for Noorna, whose home was the next stop.

Noorna el-Sadim's house was a true villa, surrounded with jacaranda trees, formal flower beds, and a resplendent lawn that led down to the bank of the Nile. Built in opulent Ottoman style, with intricate tiles around its commanding windows, massive portico, and front door, it was one of the most stately buildings on Sharia el-Swissri. Only two blocks from Lily's house, it became her refuge from what she recently had begun to accept was her own unhappy home.

She loved her mother and father, but their unhappiness with each other saddened her profoundly. For as long as she could remember, she'd wished she had a sister to talk to about it. Once, she made one up, a girl who had her father's brown hair and long straight nose and her mother's wide green eyes. Lily spent many hours in her room conversing with this invisible sister, whom she named Suleda, after a girl she'd known in Beirut during her father's last posting. Some of the questions Lily asked made her cry, and of course there were no answers forthcoming, so Suleda quickly faded. The questions did not, and for a long time Lily had to make her mind jump away from them whenever they occurred to her.

When the family went out together, as they did often, for Cairo was a hospitable city with an active social life, Bert and Helene McCann appeared to be a particularly lively and attractive couple. Lily loved the parties because her parents seemed so happy. In the house, her mother and father never argued, except late at night when they thought Lily was asleep, and then only for a few angry phrases before she heard her father go downstairs to his study. Other than the arguments, they barely spoke to each other when they were alone, managing to live nearly separate lives in the small house, eating meals separately, seeing Lily separately, sleeping separately except when some of his friends from college or other Foreign Service people showed up to stay in the guest room. Then they had to sleep in the same room, but one morning when Lily went in, she saw a pillow and blanket on the chaise longue.

Only her father would tell her stories about the past, of how he'd met Helene Ducroix and had to learn French in order to propose.

Pemberton McCann, known to his friends and colleagues in the Foreign Service as Bert, was a natural linguist, having been brought up by missionary parents in South America, where he learned both Spanish and Portuguese along with English. After graduating from Yale and joining the Foreign Service, he'd been sent to several North African posts during the Second World War and become intrigued by the Arab world, its history, culture, religion, and language. He had volunteered to learn Arabic, one of the three languages, along with Chinese and Japanese, regarded by all as the "hardest of the hard." Subsequently he'd become proficient enough to gain an S-4/R-4 rating for reading and speaking from the State Department, surpassed only by the S-5/R-5 of official translators.

Lily knew her father was proud of his linguistic accomplishments, although he always played them down. "You can't make a diplomat out of a good linguist," he said, "but you can teach a good diplomat to speak almost anything." He loved to speak Arabic and did so as often as possible, continuing his study of the language he described as "powerful and beautiful beyond the understanding of any speaker of the Latin derivatives," which Lily didn't understand except the power and beauty part. Her mother, on the other hand, had steadfastly refused to learn a single word of Arabic, and because Bert learned French so quickly, she gave up on English early in their marriage.

The story Lily most loved to hear was about their wedding. She often hauled the heavy book of pictures down from the shelf in the study and begged her father to tell about it. It had taken place in the cathedral at Algiers. Bert was a junior political officer at the consulate and had met Helene Ducroix during his posting there. Her father was a colonel in the French army. Four generals attended the ceremony, along with seven ambassadors and most of the diplomatic corps, for the pictures showed that Bert McCann had many friends among his colleagues; he had sixteen groomsmen from all over the world, including four of his Yale classmates. His widowed father, the Reverend Doctor Horace McCann, known in missionary circles as McCann of the Pampas, came from his retirement in the United States to give his blessing, which the local Roman Catholic archbishop graciously allowed. Helene's dress was silk and lace, and its train trailed eight feet behind her. Two rows of officers in dress uniform stood at attention outside the cathedral, making a canopy of crossed swords under which the newly wed couple processed.

Her mother never listened to the story; she left the study if Bert gave in to his daughter's pleas. Lily believed her mother was the most beautiful bride in the world, with her huge eyes, her long fair hair piled high under the lace veil, her bemused smile, as happy a one as Lily had ever seen. The pictures made her wonder what had happened to make the couple so unhappy. Recently she'd concluded, although she would never say it out loud to anyone, that she thought the reason was her. The wedding had taken place in 1948. A year and a half later, they moved to Cairo. On January 10, 1950, Lily was born. She didn't know how or why, but she believed that the anger her mother and father had for each other must have started on her birthday.

Once, she was so convinced of it that she felt she should move out of the house. She asked Noorna whether it would be all right for her to move into the el-Sadims' villa. Noorna was delighted with the idea, but her mother, a very grand woman in Lily's eyes, dismissed the suggestion, although with a look of sad understanding.

The two girls had played together when they were infants, but Lily couldn't remember, because the McCanns left Cairo when she was three. In the seven years since then, she'd lived in Oman, Damascus, Washington, D.C., and Beirut, but hadn't liked any of them as much as Cairo. After her return, she and Noorna became such close friends that they had celebrated their tenth birthday together at a large party the previous January. She urged her father to ask President Eisenhower to make him the ambassador to Egypt so that they could stay in Cairo forever. When she got no action from her parent, she wrote to the president herself. Miffed at the insipid reply from some White House assistant, she decided to become a Democrat and wait for the next administration to further her request.

In early summer, she and Noorna spent the afternoons by the pool at the Gezira Sporting Club, the single large open space left in the environs of Cairo. They swam, and later, when the temperature cooled, they sat at a table in wicker chairs under the shade trees around the clubhouse, watched the croquet players dressed in their immaculate white, and were served Coca-Cola by the servants in their dark blue-and-gold *galabiyyas*. Later in the summer, Noorna accompanied her family to their villa on the beach at Alexandria or went to Europe. Lily also visited Europe or traveled to America with her parents on leave. When the two girls returned to Cairo in the fall, they immediately met at the club to exchange tales of their summer and discuss a growing list of curiosities which the two girls found hilarious or desperately secret.

Going to the club with Noorna was a great convenience, for she had a car and driver always at her disposal. Although the club was only a short distance from their homes, arriving in a car was more fun than biking or walking past the guards stationed at the entrance to keep nonmembers out. The organization had originally been called the Khedival Club. It was created by the British officers who arrived in the 1880s at the invitation of the khedive, the Turkish viceroy, in order to collect his taxes. The British soldiers remained to become the de facto rulers of Egypt in what was called the Veiled Protectorate. In those days, the club had seven polo fields, two houseboats on the Nile, a golf course, and a racetrack for its three hundred British and half-dozen royal Egyptian members. What the two world wars had not altered about this exclusive bastion, President Nasser had eviscerated five years before, once his group of fellow officers had overthrown King Farouk, the last faint remnant of Turkey's long influence over the country. There were now fifteen thousand members of the club, mostly Egyptian. The polo fields had been expropriated and turned into public soccer fields. A small golf course remained, as well as a deteriorating racetrack used for exercising horses.

When the McCann family returned to Cairo, Lily's father had resisted joining the club because he believed it was still too elitist and exclusionary. Her mother had furiously insisted but, once admitted, never went there; *"c'est trop sale et bourgeois,"* too dirty and common. Unaware of the history and social currents of the place, Lily was content to be the only McCann to use the family's membership.

With a sure sense of survival over the traffic, she pedaled across Sidky Square and streaked down Sharia el-Maakad to el-Swissri, eager to see her friend and be off to the pool. But as she approached the high iron fence that surrounded the el-Sadim villa, she sensed that something was wrong. There were no people around the house. Usually there were gardeners watering and weeding the flower beds, servants carrying trays of drinks to grandly attired guests in the gazebo, a doorman in livery directing chauffeurs around the circular courtyard. When she braked to a stop in front of the iron gates, she saw that they had been swung across the driveway and locked.

Lily had never seen them closed. To one side, there was a pull chain that rang a bell in the house. Lily leaned her bicycle against the gate and pulled the chain. There was no response. Wondering whether the el-Sadims had gone to Alexandria, she thought perhaps she'd overlooked the date of their departure. But even then, the gates wouldn't have been closed, and someone would have answered the bell. She rang again, this time at length, and thought she saw a curtain move slightly in one of the windows of the grand salon on the ground floor. But no one came, and after a few minutes Lily went back to her bicycle and prepared to ride away.

Suddenly she heard the front door open, and Noorna called out "Lily!" as she ran down the front steps and across the stone courtyard to the gate. Her tears reflected the hot sun and her red eyes looked as if she had been crying a long time. She reached through the gate with both hands, and Lily held them as her friend said breathlessly, "They took my father away." She spoke in Arabic, as the girls always did when they were together. Their school classes were taught in French, but both fathers encouraged them to speak the native language as often as possible.

"Who took him?" Lily asked, uncomprehending. Mr. el-Sadim was a very powerful man who owned thousands of *feddans* of the little fertile land there was in Egypt, as well as two factories employing thousands of workers. The el-Sadim family was one of the oldest and most prominent in Cairo, "a flying buttress of the upper-class power structure," Lily's father once described it.

"Nasser's people!" Noorna blurted and began to cry in earnest, squeezing Lily's hands convulsively.

"Why?" Lily was confused, because she knew the el-Sadims had been strong supporters of Nasser in his overthrow of King Farouk and had been hosts of the new president numerous times at the villa. Lily's parents had met him there.

"Because he's going to take our land, he's going to take the factories," Noorna said, a tone of hate quenching her tears. "Lily, we may have to move away."

The two girls stared at each other through the black iron gate, Lily unable to comprehend what her friend was saying.

"Tell me what happened."

"Two men, in *suits,*" Noorna said angrily. "They came at two in the morning, carrying briefcases as if they were on business. But there were three cars and a truck full of soldiers who got out and surrounded the villa. I saw them." She glanced over her shoulder at the deserted gardens, and when she looked back at Lily, terror had come into her eyes. Still she held on to Lily's hands. "Papa argued for hours. We could hear him through the doors of the library, demanding to see Nasser, demanding his lawyers, and finally asking only to say goodbye to us. They refused even that."

"Where is he?"

"We don't know."

The front door of heavy glass and ironwork opened, and Lily saw Mrs. el-Sadim holding the knob. Lily thought it was probably the first time the usually majestic woman had ever touched it. She seemed suddenly bent with age, and called to them in French, "Noorna, come back at once! Lily, go home! Immediately! Go home!"

The urgency in her voice prevented the two girls from embracing through the iron bars. Each started to run, but when Lily reached her bicycle, she looked back in time to see Noorna climbing the steps of the villa.

"Noorna! It'll be all right," Lily yelled.

Her friend stopped. "No, Lily, it won't!" She waved, then disappeared into the house.

Lily watched through the bars for several moments until she realized that she was afraid. She pedaled away from the el-Sadims' feeling as she had never felt before on the streets of Cairo. Nothing seemed to have changed, but every vehicle that drove by, every pedestrian, seemed a danger. When she reached Sidky Square, she found no reassurance even in the police, who lounged there in the shade of the single palm tree. If someone like Mr. el-Sadim could be taken away in the night, no one was safe. As she hurried on, Lily tried to think of everything she remembered about President Nasser in order to make sense of what was happening to her best friend's family.

He had led the officers' revolt that overthrew the corrupt Farouk. He had nationalized the Suez Canal in 1956. Two years later, with Syria, he had formed the United Arab Republic, which presented the concept of a unified Arab nation running from the Persian Gulf to the Atlantic. Lily's father called the idea "the incipient nationalism created by centuries of misdirected and oppressive colonialism." He had used these words often enough for Lily to remember them, though she was not sure what they meant. Abruptly, she wanted to know. When her father came home that evening, she would ask him to explain everything.

Lily leaned her bicycle against the banyan tree and rushed into her house before Amir could open the front door for her. As she entered, he looked up from the cane chair on which he sat all day, moving amber prayer beads through his fingers.

"Is Mommy still here?" Lily asked, poised at the bottom of the stairs.

Amir shook his head, as he did when he chose to avoid unnecessary talk. He pointed upward and gravely said, *"Khamsin,"* indicating that the hot summer wind which blew in from the Sahara was approaching. He was justly proud of his skill at predicting this change. Lily thought he looked more severe than usual. She hurried into the study to call her father at the embassy and ask him to help Mr. el-Sadim. Several times she tried to dial the number, but the call didn't go through. She succeeded only in getting static and, on the last try, an alarming repetitive clanging noise she'd never before heard.

She was about to hang up when she saw an envelope on her father's desk and realized she had been smelling her mother's perfume since coming into the study. *Bert* was written on the front in her mother's distinctive rounded hand. As she held the telephone, Lily picked up the envelope in her other hand to smell it and saw that it wasn't sealed.

She dropped the note, thought of hiding it, remembered her

mother putting the stopper between her thighs, the luminous white lace slip, then heard the telephone still clanging in her ear and slammed it down on the cradle. The quiet that followed seemed to echo an electric current. She heard the Renault turn into the driveway and stop in front of the house. The car door slammed. Lily couldn't move. She stared at the white envelope, then coughed, her breath caught in her throat by the perfume.

When she heard her father greet Amir in the hall, she rushed to the door of the study, still choking for breath. Her father saw her there and, noticing her expression, smiled warily and said, "Hello, darling. Amir says a *khamsin* is coming."

"Daddy, they took Mr. el-Sadim away last night, with soldiers and . . ."

Strangely, her father looked relieved as he adjusted his glasses on his nose. "Oh, so that's why she called," he said as he absentmindedly took her hand and went into the study. "Your mother phoned the embassy and left a message for me to get home immediately. No explanation at all. I'd have been here sooner, but some *fellahin* had driven their sheep onto the Twenty-sixth July Bridge, and the traffic . . ." Then he saw the white envelope.

He stood quietly a moment, holding Lily's hand. "Lily," he said, his voice taking on the calm, measured tone he used when he spoke to anyone at the embassy, "will you let me work in here alone for a little while?"

She began to cry, and he went back to close the study door. "Have you read it?" he asked softly.

"No," she said, trying to stop crying, "but I think I know what it says."

"Me too." He hugged her.

He was very tall; her head rested against his stomach. He held her firmly and stroked her hair. Lily tried hard to control her sobs, but the tears kept falling down her cheeks. "Daddy, what are we going to do?"

"Well," he began but didn't continue for several moments. "I'd say we're going to hurt a little while, and be very brave about it, not showing how we feel to anyone except each other. Agreed?"

"Yes." Her voice quavered too much for her to go on.

"With each other, we won't hold anything back, we'll tell each other when we hurt and how we hurt. And whenever either of us needs the other, we can ask. We'll drop everything else and get to each other, if for nothing more than just to sit quietly together. Agreed?"

"Even at the embassy? Even school?"

"Even school, even the embassy."

Still in his hug, Lily could hear that he was having a difficult time speaking. "Agreed," she said. "But how long . . . ?" Lily couldn't finish the question ". . . will the pain last? Will we miss her? Will it take a long time to forget?"

"We shall see," he said, as he always did when he didn't want to answer. "I suppose we'd better read it." He let Lily go.

"Maybe it's personal," Lily offered.

Her father went around the desk and, still standing, took the single sheet from its envelope. He read silently, then read it aloud.

" 'Mon cher Bert, I am a terrible wife and a worse mother. I cannot stand this life we live, full of lies, all mine except for the biggest one, diplomacy, which you infected me with from the beginning. I ask no forgiveness of you, only of Lily. I am not a good mother for her. Perhaps sometime in the future somehow.

" 'I'm leaving with Sami Shalabi. We'll sail in the Aegean this summer, then live in Paris. I'll get the divorce there, and work through the embassy.

" 'For both of us, I regret the time we have lost with each other.' "

He turned the paper over to see if there was anything on the other side, then held it out to Lily. "She wrote it in English," he said, trying to smile. "Even with all the crossed-out words, she did pretty well."

"Daddy, please don't do that." She knew how good he was at covering when something was wrong.

He stared at her a moment. "Sorry. No cover-ups. I'm not sure you'll see a grown man cry, but you're seeing one who hurts, as I'm sure you do. I really want to get out of here, and I hope you'll come with me."

She nodded and he reached for her hand. Together, they left the study. Amir jumped from his chair and barely beat them to the front door. *"Khamsin* coming," he warned again, as he held open the door.

"Amir, when Madame McCann left, did a car pick her up?" Bert asked.

The Sudanese's eyes hooded sadly. "Monsieur Shalabi's Mercedes."

Bert looked at Amir, then, holding Lily's hand, hurried to the sidewalk.

"Close the shutters," he shouted back at Amir as he and Lily felt the sudden change of atmosphere. They walked silently into the gentle gusts signaling the approach of the great wall of desert wind and fine sand that would soon cover the city. When they reached Oum Kalthoum, the road along the western side of the island, they dodged the traffic and ran across to the retaining wall overlooking the Nile. There, they watched men in two rowboats pull in a net stretched between them. The muddy river, divided by the island on which they stood, flowed steadily between the unremitting life of building, traffic, bathing, and laundry along its banks. People beat clothes against rocks; others washed themselves modestly at the edges of the current. On the opposite bank, as well as behind Oum Kalthoum, the rough roads were crowded with speeding diesel cars and trucks. Construction work was evident at the edges of the traffic, the jute-tied poles of building platforms forming rickety perches for the workers.

"Tell me what you heard about Mr. el-Sadim," Bert said. The gusting breeze had blown his pale green striped tie out of his tan linen suit. He reached up automatically to stuff it back to its proper position.

"Noorna was so frightened," Lily began.

"I'm sure she was. Did you see her mother?"

"Only from the gates. They were locked. I think she was scared, too. They took him away in the middle of the night, with soldiers surrounding the house. They don't even know where he is. Noorna said they might have to go away." She looked up at her father and suddenly could see what he would look like when he was very old. It surprised her, for nothing about his usually handsome face had changed from that morning. She said, "Daddy, tell me what's going on in Cairo. I want to understand about politics or diplomacy or whatever it is, and I'd rather think about Nasser than Mommy."

He turned to her, and she saw the slightest trace of a smile beneath his sad eyes. But he started talking with a relieved seriousness. "Well, first of all, politics and diplomacy are two very different buckets of bait. You mustn't ever confuse them. Politicians on occasion have been known to be diplomatic, and diplomats sometimes play at politics, but once you fall into either bucket, you're usually not very good for much else. What's going on with Mr. el-Sadim is pure, unadulterated politics, and Egyptian politics at that, which are at the moment as murky and curlicued as politics can get. In this circumstance, diplomacy is like juggling mercury."

"What are you going to do to help him?"

"Nothing, I'm afraid."

"What?" Lily said, stepping back, her hand moving out of his. "They're our friends; you and Mommy go to their villa all the time; they've come to ours; Noorna is my best—"

He was shaking his head. "If I made inquiries, even visited their villa, it would make it worse for him. I might very well become persona non grata and get shipped out of here."

"You mean diplomats can have friends, but they can't *be* friends," she said sadly, challenging him.

"Officially, no. It's part of our immense talent to practice friendship in other intriguing ways." He smiled quickly at her. "But, Lily, officially I'm not a friend; I'm here as a representative of the United States, and no country will tolerate another country's meddling in its internal politics. The other thing that you have to remember is that Mr. el-Sadim isn't just your best friend's father. He's the past; *that's* what Nasser had to steal away in the night, even though the man himself was his friend. Come on, let me tell you what I mean."

They started walking south, keeping the Nile to their right. She hoped her father would talk and talk about anything except what had happened with her mother. The men in the rowboats had drawn in their catch, only a dozen fish between them. Their women were waiting on the bank to clean the fish. The banks descended in a steep drop to the river, and except where their were private clubs or houseboats, the area was covered with litter and building debris among the weeds and shrubs that struggled for existence. "Definitely not the Seine," her mother had observed with distaste nearly every time she and Lily passed by the river. Lily brushed some hair back from her eyes and felt dampness from the heat. Already a fine grit of sand was on the wind.

"Noorna's father," Bert began, "was known as el-Sadim Pasha until the revolution in 1952. It was an honorary title granted by the king. Mr. el-Sadim brought irrigation to all the wasteland south of the city. Besides, the el-Sadim family is one of the most powerful in Egypt—or was, under the old regime. The power and privilege came from generations of the family's proximity to the rulers of Egypt. You have to remember, Egypt has had foreign rulers for centuries—English, Turks, Mameluks, even Napoleon for a couple of years. Nasser is the first honest-to-God Egyptian to run this country since Alexander the Great conquered it in 332 B.C. A lot of the rulers have been corrupt, remaining above the people, oblivious of their incredible problems. Farouk was simply the very fat Turkish straw that broke the emaciated Egyptian camel's back."

"But Mr. el-Sadim hated Farouk," Lily argued. "I've heard him say that. And he helped Nasser."

"Yes, that's true. He was the first one I know of who disclaimed the imperial title of pasha. Even before the revolution, he fought the outrageous dishonesty on which the monarchy was based. He detested Farouk for his weakness, his corruption, and because the king—who hated the British for always telling him what to do—was chummy with the Nazis during the war. So when Nasser came to power, el-Sadim backed him financially and influentially with his upper-class friends, many of whom looked down on this mere army officer with no social credentials."

He sighed and Lily thought he'd lost interest in the subject. But, to Lily's relief, he went on.

"Friendship, though, is just as tenuous in politics as it is in diplomacy. Nasser is moving way ahead of his people. They wanted a change, any change, and with that mandate he's rushing ahead, not only to change Egypt but to change the attitude of the entire Arab world from subservience to pride, and there's an overwhelming hunger for that. To do so, he can't have any of the trappings of the old world order. So old friends, old anything is at risk."

"But it's worse than that," Lily stated. "Noorna said they're taking away the el-Sadims' land, their factories. That's stealing, isn't it?"

They walked a short way before Bert answered her question.

"Getting rid of an old world is different politics from the politics of creating a new world. Both are a kind of revolution, but shaping the new world isn't quite as sudden or dramatic as overthrowing a king. It's slower, less obvious to the people, and unfortunately is often accomplished with little seizures made at night. I'm afraid Nasser's new socialist world doesn't include upper-class landholders of the el-Sadim variety."

Her father sounded angry. They walked under the Zamalek Bridge and its thundering roar of traffic. As he often did when irritated, Bert shifted the conversation to something completely off the subject.

"You know, there used to be a tramway, a trolley car that went across this bridge. It went all the way from the center of Cairo across Zamalek and out to the Pyramids. It was the best ride for a nickel this side of the Staten Island ferry."

For no reason, Lily suddenly missed her mother and thought of their "villa" without her in it. She squeezed her father's hand but didn't dare look up at him. Keeping her eyes straight ahead, she stared out of the dark shadow of the bridge. The familiar row of sycamores lined the sidewalk that ran along the top of the riverbank. She realized the *khamsin* had come. As far as she could see, down the Nile and across it to the western bank toward Agoura, the view was washed in a gentle yellow haze of powdered sand. Instinctively, she ran her other hand over her hair, feeling the grit already settled there. Along the sidewalk, the dusty sycamores provided shade from the sand-filtered sun as the gusty wind continued to blow from the west. They passed several private bankside clubs, where the waiters were rushing about the open terraces, folding down table umbrellas.

Lily and Bert came to a sycamore that seemed engorged with sparrowlike white birds swarming through its branches, the volume of their mating calls creating an insistent, high-pitched cacophony. Father and daughter stopped for a moment to watch the phenomenon, a common one along the river's bank in summer, usually at sunset. That day the strange nether light of the *khamsin* had provided the birds with an earlier stimulus.

"What would you think about moving?" Bert asked as they stared up into the branches of the trees.

"You mean away from Cairo?"

"No. Just somewhere else. To be honest with you, Lily, I can't imagine going back to that house. Your mother's all over the walls."

"Where'll we go?"

"I have an idea," he said and started to walk again. "A different kind of house. We'll go see it. Right now, yes?"

Although he spoke pleasantly, Lily heard a desperation in his voice. "Are we going to move in tonight?"

He laughed. "Maybe," he said, "maybe we will. Come on."

For a good distance, he strode along with an expectant air, Lily stretching her stride to keep in step with him. But then he began to slow down to a distracted amble. Lily looked up at him. His face was sad.

"Daddy, you said something a little while ago that I don't understand."

"I'm sorry, what was it?"

"You said that diplomats wanted to keep a consistency, stay the course or something. But what do they do if things change around them, like a revolution or a war? How do you stay the same?"

He thought a moment, then chuckled. "I suppose the image we have of ourselves is a pillar of pure marble standing in the middle of the conflagration, while debris and ash collect around our feet. Well, the fact is that when sudden change occurs, the good diplomat doesn't stand around. He's as fast on his feet as Fred Astaire. The consistency is our country, which we represent. No matter what happens in the field, we do stand for what the country stands for, whatever the consequences. That's where the fancy dancing comes in, to limit the consequences to the United States of any local change, cataclysmic or not."

"What's cataclysmic mean?"

"Like a violent upheaval of some sort."

"Oh. Well, what happens when America is the one that changes its mind or isn't consistent? You got pretty angry once or twice when something back home went wrong."

"Really? I never should have revealed that reaction, even to you." He squeezed her hand affectionately. "You remember the quote I have in that little frame in the study? 'In the end, it is only right principles, consistently applied—not the gift of prophecy nor the pride of insight—that achieve the best results.' 'Right principles, consistently applied,' is the best definition of diplomacy I know. But when the home country changes policy, the diplomat may have the dance floor fall away from under him. Then he has to dance on thin air. It does happen, more and more, I'm afraid. Rather than being a solid marble pillar, the American diplomat is becoming a weathervane, pointing in the direction of any wind that blows his way from Washington. And in Washington everybody and his Great-aunt Tilly is making foreign policy, usually for their own political purposes, self-serving as they may be."

His stride was again at a fast pace and Lily wanted to keep it that way. "But hasn't it always been like that? You always say that an ambassador is his king's puppet."

"Yes, but it should be a puppet without strings, a puppet who knows his king's unchangeable will and can depend on it. That's all we can ask for, a consistency we can depend on when the strings are cut and we're sent out to do our dance. Then it's up to us, or should be. But now there are a lot of Foreign Service officers, ambassadors as well, tying their strings back in knots so that they'll be able to sense the subtlest changes in the puppet master, whoever *he* may be, king, president, foreign minister, legislature . . ."

"Or Great-aunt Tilly," Lily threw in, making her father laugh.

"Exactly!" he said, then stopped walking and looked down at her. The happiness drained from his face, and he said, "We'll get through this, Lily. Together we can do anything."

"Yes," she said, noticing that his suit was a shade darker from the fine sand clinging to it. She looked down at her skirt, which was similarly streaked along its pleats. "But I think I'm going to need a bath pretty soon."

"Don't worry." He started walking again. "If this place doesn't work, we can always go over to the new Nile Hilton."

"Do you think they built it just in time for us?"

He smiled bitterly. "It's occurred to me that your mother thought of everything, but I don't think she could have arranged that."

They walked quietly for another hundred yards, stopping before a small locked gate in a section of wood and wire fencing running along the river edge of the sidewalk. Through the wire gate they could see the stairs leading down to one of the *dahabeahs*, two-story houseboats, moored on the banks of the Nile.

"What do you think?" Bert asked.

"This is Monsieur Moran's," Lily said, astonished by the idea.

"He's trying to sell it; been reassigned to Baghdad. He came by the embassy today to say goodbye."

"Can we buy this?" Lily asked.

"I can request a housing allowance from the embassy. They'll be quite happy to have our Zamalek . . . 'villa' back on their list." He paused but gave no other indication of the memory. "I've saved a little money, and God knows Moran is eager to sell. He'll give it to us for a song." He gazed at Lily. "And we'll keep it. We'll keep it as our home, so that no matter where I get assigned . . ."

"You mean no matter where you're ambassador," she interjected, a prediction with which she often kidded him.

He ignored it and went on. "Or where you go off to school, this will be our place. If it's practical, we can always meet here, in Cairo, the Mother of the World, as they say. You can bring your friends, and we might even have the thing towed up river to Luxor or somewhere, if it doesn't sink."

Just then, a felucca came gliding past, its crew hurrying to bring in its slanted sail before the *khamsin* blew it out of their hands.

"And by the way, I'll never be an ambassador, Lily."

"Why not?"

"I'm too . . . consistent." He laughed, this time at himself. "But no matter. Every Foreign Service officer ought to have a home. You know, I've never really had one, raised in all those South American rectories."

"A floating home," Lily said. "It's wonderful! Thank you, Daddy. Do you think we can stay here tonight?"

"I'll go down and see whether Moran's here. If he is, he's packing. If I buy the thing, I'm sure he'll put us up. We'll send a cab

back to the villa for a change of clothes and overnight things, and
tomorrow I'll have Amir and the movers . . ."

He rang the bell beside the gate, and they heard Monsieur Moran yell up from the dahabeah. As they shouted greetings back and
forth and the Frenchman hurried up the steps to let them in, Lily
looked down at the boxy houseboat, painted white with neat green
trim around its windows, deck, and doors. She remembered, from
the times she'd been aboard with her parents, that the rooms were
done up as elaborate desert tents, with Arab carpets and pillows on
the floor, each room festooned with billowing material of intricate
pharoanic or Islamic design on the walls and ceiling. On the bottom floor was a sitting room, kitchen, and bathroom—so that water didn't need to be pumped upstairs—and a large sun room with
a wall of windows, on the river side, that ran from floor to ceiling.
Up the steep stairs, she recalled, there were three bedrooms, two
with views over the Nile, and a small workroom, which Lily realized would be her father's new study. One room on the river side
had turquoise and red tent sections patterned in hundreds of ara-
besque configurations. It would be hers.

She wondered what it was like to own a home. Having never
lived anywhere but embassy housing or State Department rentals,
she thought now about having her own room, permanently, a place
that would be hers always. She let out a sound she'd never made
before, an excited cry that startled the two men, talking nearby.
Smiling, Lily greeted the French diplomat, and they all descended
the stairs to the short gangplank that led directly into the sun
room.

As she stepped aboard, Lily remembered Noorna running back
into her villa, saying things were not going to be all right. For a
moment, Lily saw the parquet floors of the el-Sadim entrance hall
shining under the lights of the massive brass chandeliers. And then
she saw her mother standing there, resplendent in her favorite
green water taffeta ball gown.

Yes, Lily thought, it's better to have a floating home so that you
never forget how easily it can sink.

PART ONE

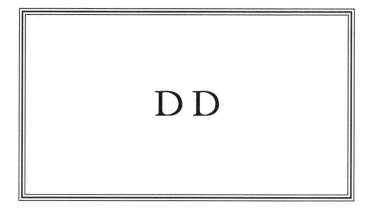

DD

May 1970–May 1972

ONE

THROUGH THE OPEN WINDOWS of the Yale lecture hall, Lily could barely hear the bullhorns from the New Haven Green. The demonstrations for Bobby Seale and the thirteen other Black Panthers accused by the FBI of the torture and murder of a fellow party member continued throughout the day. For reasons Lily didn't understand, the members of the radical group were on trial in this city, an event that had drawn their sympathizers from all over the country.

Lily stared out the window. For the last five weeks, she had been unable to sleep through the night. An undergraduate sympathy strike for the Black Panthers' cause had effectively closed down eighty percent of the classes. The governor of the state had brought in the National Guard, which was stationed outside the city limits. Kingman Brewster, Yale's president, had stated that he was "skeptical of the ability of black revolutionaries to achieve a fair trial anywhere in the U.S." and was "appalled and ashamed" that such a situation had developed. His statement had sparked the idea of a huge New Haven rally over the May 1 weekend. Lily read in the press that Brewster was "barricaded" in Woodbridge Hall, figuring out some kind of strategy, but she had glimpsed him striding through the Old Campus with a group of undergraduates, making them laugh. Lily couldn't laugh and couldn't sleep, yet she felt utterly distant from what was happening around her. In spite of four years of boarding school and three years of college in America, she felt like an outsider watching a country fall apart around her.

"So what else is new?" Mimi Peters had said in response to the crisis. "All of nineteen sixty-nine was a goddamn revolution. Why not have a little insurgency in the spring of seventy?"

She and Lily shared a room in Wright Hall, but both were hoping to move to Branford if, in the words of a university spokesman, "the logistics could be worked out." This meant plumbing—toilets and showers. It was the first year that Yale had admitted female undergraduates. Mimi's comment was "The thought of us boys and girls taking a shower or a shit together gives alumni this strange disease where they can't write checks." The Old Boys who had showed up that year on campus, full of curiosity about how coeducation would affect Old Eli, inevitably revealed, through excruciatingly delicate questions, their major interest and concern: sex on dorm.

If they only knew, Lily thought. Aside from the contempt and constant insults of the Yale men toward the "cows," as many referred to the first year coeds, Lily had never worked so hard in her life. There hadn't been time for sex, on dorm or anywhere else, and her virginity was still annoyingly intact. Since her transfer from Swarthmore, she'd kept her grades consistently high in order to hold on to her partial scholarship and work-study job at University Dining Hall. However, her study load, the waiting on tables, and the constant friction and scrutiny that came with being among the first undergraduate females in Yale's history made any idea of languishing between dormitory sheets or a quickie in the shower fairly remote, at least for her.

A breeze came through the classroom window, barely warm from the spring sun. Carried by the breeze, the sound of the bullhorns grew louder, although Lily could not hear the words. She glanced at Mimi, who sat next to her, listening attentively to the lecturer. Lily, having studied too late, was tired as usual, worried about final exams, only weeks away, about whether there could even be final exams and whether the semester's credits would be given in spite of the campus strike, about money and what Yale was costing her father, and about her dream of law school, which seemed to her ever more unattainable. With the various demonstrations against the war in Vietnam all year, and now the Black Panthers and the threatened trashing of the university, Lily even had doubts about the possibility of having a senior year.

And June was coming, an anniversary she dreaded. She admitted that what had occurred three years earlier probably had more to do with her state of mind than anything happening around her in a fractured America. The memory of the event was indelible, both consciously and in nightmares, which the State Department psychiatrists had promised—wrongly—would go away. Fear had become a part of her life, on a daily basis.

It had happened in June of 1967. Lily had just graduated from Madeira, third in her class. Accepted by five universities with scholarships, she had chosen Swarthmore in anticipation of Yale's rumored coming acceptance of female undergraduates. Her father had gone to Yale, and Lily hoped to transfer there in her junior year. When she returned that summer to Amman, Jordan, where her father was chief political officer at the embassy, Lily began her job as a volunteer counselor at a refugee camp for Jordanian children.

Because she was embarrassed to be seen by the rest of the camp's staff arriving in an embassy car, Lily usually had her driver stop a half kilometer away from the camp's entrance on Amir Hasan Street. That morning, her driver refused on orders from her father. The embassy was on alert. The previous April, there had been a dogfight between Syrian and Israeli planes over Damascus. Nasser had expelled the UN's peacekeeping force from the Sinai and blockaded the Strait of Tiran, thus closing the port of Elat, Israel's only access to the Red Sea. Syria was supporting Palestinian guerrilla raids against Israeli settlements on the Golan Heights, and Israel was responding with commando raids against Palestinian West Bank villages under Jordanian rule.

The Arabs seemed to want war, but then so did the Israelis. Both had talked of war ever since Lily could remember. There had been a war in 1956, when Israel, France, and England tried to capture the Suez Canal from Egypt after Nasser had nationalized it. But in 1967, the threat of war felt considerably different. In spite of vacation visits with her father and keeping up with the newspapers, Lily sensed that her instincts about what was in the air were not as sharp as they had been.

In Amman for less than a week, she'd spent most of her time catching up with her father and starting her work in the camp. The Jordanian dialect was different from her Egyptian Arabic, but the few days she'd spent with the children, and some quick tutoring from her father, brought the language back to her. Ever further from the classical majesty of phrase found in the Koran, the vernacular of the streets and camps fascinated Lily. Because she spoke three languages—English, Arabic, and French—Lily planned to study linguistics at college as part of her prelaw courses. That was what she really wanted to do, go to a good law school. The future seemed very exciting to her, very certain.

That morning in 1967, she stepped out of the embassy car and hurried away from it, disowning it in case any of her colleagues at the camp were watching. Unlike the huge refugee camps for Palestinians on the outskirts of Amman, the camp for Jordanians was not fenced or guarded by troops. It was more of a hostel for those Bedouin Jordanians who might need shelter, food, or basic medical care. Many children were left there each morning while their parents tried to find work or food. Lily's job was to supervise the eight-year-olds, of which there were eleven that day, seven boys and four girls.

After watching the raising of the Jordanian flag and singing a patriotic song in praise of King Hussein, the camp children broke up into groups, and Lily led hers to the far end of the dirt playing field along Amir Hassan Street. It was going to be another hot day, so before the sun was too high she wanted them to run off as much energy as possible. They measured off a small soccer pitch and marked its boundaries and goals with mounds of sand. Some of the children remained wary of her because she was an American and because she spoke Arabic. That combination usually meant a spy or at least someone dangerous, but their hesitation was quickly forgotten in the excitement of the game. Lily had noticed that the counselors of the ten- and eleven-year-olds had a much harder time. With them, games didn't work; the children were too old to forget.

When the score was tied, three to three, she saw an old Mercedes diesel truck coast to a stop on Amir Hassan Street next to the playing field. Cursing hard, the driver got out and propped open one side of the hood, spat, and started to work on the motor. The soccer game continued, and Lily, as referee, was kept busy. The sun rose higher and the ground began to bake, sending shimmers of heat into the air. In spite of the dark glasses she wore, Lily was forced to squint through the glare. The sky seemed white, and she thought of ending the game. Then a fight broke out between two of the boys and she hurried over to intervene. The other children gathered around, yelling, and no one noticed the five men who suddenly appeared around them. They wore black clothes, black boots. They were carrying guns and knives. Without hesitating, they silently grabbed the two screaming boys and, holding them by their hair with one hand, slit their throats with the other. Lily saw blood pouring on the ground around her. As the shrieking continued, she grabbed two girls to protect them, but they were torn from her arms and she was kicked back onto the ground. From there she saw two of the boys running toward the camp center; then a gun fired rapidly. The boys lifted from the earth and crumpled back to it. Lily saw the smoking gun three feet from her. She leaped up and attacked the man with her hands, going for his eyes. He hit her with the gun butt to her cheek and his elbow to her ribs. On the ground, her glasses smashed; she felt blood on her face and intense pain in her side. She tried to get up again; there was more gunfire. A boot kicked her down, and she heard screams from the center building but none nearby. Her hand touched the wet, lifeless body of a boy just as someone grabbed her hair and yanked her away. Lily's arm shot forward and she tore the cloth from the man's face, scratching his cheek and drawing blood. He yelled, but said no words, revealing crooked rotten teeth. His large wet eyes were furious, and he quickly covered his face again. But he knew that she had seen him, and he pointed the gun at her head.

He hesitated, saw that he was alone, and ran back, following the others to the truck. It started moving away even before all the men were on board. Lily looked around; her children were dead, their bodies broken, covered in blood. She crawled toward them and, finally managing to sit upright, held two of the girls on her lap. Nearby, she saw two brass bullet casings glinting in the sun and grabbed them with one hand. People came, yelling at her, wailing in grief, trying to help. She stared at them, not allowing them to touch her or the children she held. There were bells and sirens; trucks drove onto the field; then a flashbulb went off, and another, and she was angry. It seemed a desecration. She furiously reached for the camera and was blinded by two more flashes as the heads of the girls rolled lifelessly from her lap. She sat on the hot ground, staring at them as the screams around her became deafening. A fly landed on one girl's open mouth.

In a matter of hours, when the shock wore off, Lily talked to everyone, describing the terrorist's face, which instantly took its place in her dreams. She swore to find him one day; she threatened him. She was obsessed with him. For a single day, the atrocity captured the attention of the international press. The instant though unsubstantiated conclusion was that the perpetrators were Israeli commandos repaying the Palestinian terrorism along their border. Who else would slaughter Arab children? A photograph of Lily with the dead children in her lap, her arm raised in fury, appeared on the front pages of newspapers throughout the world.

The next day it was forgotten as Israeli planes and tanks pre-emptively struck against two fronts, its air force destroying the aircraft of Egypt and Syria on the ground. After six days, the Israeli Defense Force had captured the West Bank, Jerusalem, Sinai, the Golan Heights, and threatened Cairo, Damascus, and Amman. During that period, Lily was arrested twice by Jordanian police for breaking curfew. Totally oblivious of the war, and convinced that the terrorists who had committed the atrocity were still hiding in Amman—their truck and black clothing had been discovered several miles away from the camp—she stole out of the embassy compound to search for them. Her father had to assign a marine as well as the staff nurse to keep her in her room.

Over the following months, the CIA was able to trace the shell casings to a firm in Springfield, Massachusetts. Similar American ammunition was supplied regularly to Israel. No official charges were made, because the United States and Israel were irretrievably bound by the war. Lily's obsession faded even as the atrocity itself had been subsumed by the conflict and its aftermath.

But each year in June, on the anniversary of the event, a letter arrived from the terrorist whose face she had seen.

———————

Mimi's elbow jabbed Lily in the ribs. "He's reading your paper," she whispered. She knew whose it was because she and Lily edited each other's essays. They had taken this particular course together because it was a hot class taught by a campus star, and Lily knew a lot about the subject, Near Eastern History. Therefore, both women depended on a fast A.

The class, which met twice a week, was one of the few that continued as scheduled throughout the strike, although attendance was sparse. The instructor, Associate Professor Cotesworth Deloit, had a thin body easily surpassing six feet, a quick wide smile, and a noticeably large head with wavy, dirty-blond hair that did not get messed up when he drove through campus in a maroon Austin-Healy convertible. "I hear he has a yacht in Old Saybrook," Mimi had informed Lily. "He sails on weekends with a crew of as many or as few women as he wants."

Lily knew that, along with carrying out his teaching duties, he had written two books, *The Price of Democracy in Postwar Asia,* which evolved from his dissertation, and *Arab Economics: Oil,* which stimulated editorials around the world. He wore tweed coats over sweatshirts to class, and she'd caught sight of him several times walking toward the gym with a squash racquet.

"That son of a bitch has everything a rich, brilliant Wasp could have," Mimi had summed up.

Lily watched him as he read her familiar words. She felt hot with embarrassment and gritted her teeth, hoping he wouldn't publicly identify her.

" '. . . and it is impossible that the Kurds, a people whose civilization is traced to two thousand B.C., can be denied the title of "nation." Of course, being a sovereign state is another reality, often decided in this century by the whims of convenience, which passed for diplomacy in the peace treaties following World War One.' "

He looked up and smiled around the banked rows of students in the lecture hall. "Note the author's editorializing—good editorializing, but nevertheless . . ." He read further.

" 'Today there are some nine million Kurdish people populating an area spread over northern Iraq, northern Iran, and southern Turkey, a seventy-five-thousand-square-mile region, about the size of Oklahoma, or twice the size of the nation-state of Jordan.' "

He smiled again. "Nice point, Mr.—" Turning back the pages, he looked at the name on the title page. "I beg her pardon, '*Ms.* McCann.' "

In the still sensitive atmosphere of the campus's sexual integration, his emphasis produced a laugh. He acknowledged it with mock surprise, then went on with the paper. Lily pressed back in her chair and shielded her face with her hand.

" 'Without the support of a major world power, the Kurdish nation's cause languishes. History therefore forces the question: If the Jews make historical claim to Israel, if the Palestinians claim their part of Palestine, if the Hashemites can claim Jordan and the Saud family the whole of Arabia, do not the Kurds have a claim to their state?' "

He put the paper down on the lectern. Lily glanced under her hand at the other students, who were listening attentively.

"An interesting question," the professor said. "And yes, of course the Kurds have their claim. But so do maybe a hundred or so other beleaguered minorities around the world. Granting any such claim opens the can of worms called giving up sovereign territory, which most existing states will go to war to prevent." He checked the paper again. "Deserving, on its own, seldom changes the map. Ms. McCann, will you please stop by here after class?"

Lily didn't move as his eyes went quickly over the room. He continued his lecture.

"Glib son of a bitch," she muttered, drawing a bemused glance from Mimi. Not hearing a word of the rest of the lecture, Lily composed brilliant rejoinders to his easy deflection of her hypothesis.

When the class ended, she headed directly for the exit. Mimi, realizing her intention, said, "Hey, Lily, don't be a nut bar. The guy wants to see you. Big chance time."

Lily didn't hesitate. "Yeah, sure, to be one of the groupies who ooze up to his lectern after every class. Hell with that."

"Ah, come on, so he didn't give you Oklahoma for the Kurds. He liked your paper enough to read it to us."

"To allow him to make his simplistic—"

"Look, he gives good grades. Bottom line."

Lily sent her a dirty look, acknowledging the point. "Wait for me."

"Okay, just remember how gorgeous you are and if he asks you to go sailing or anything, you can—"

Smirking, Mimi hurried out with the other students as Lily went to the front of the lecture hall and waited while a clutch of earnest coeds asked questions meant to impress. He answered them with an amused distraction until he noticed Lily standing behind them. She was wearing a grubby plaid skirt and a sweatshirt, to which she hadn't given a thought until that moment. Lifting her book bag in front of her, she wrapped her arms around it.

"Miss McCann?"

She nodded, noting the private use of "Miss" in place of the public use of the modish "Ms."

"Excuse me," he said to the others as he picked up Lily's paper and stepped down from the dais. Behind him, a teaching assistant gathered up the books he'd referred to in his lecture and stacked them in a canvas boat bag.

"If you'd be willing to rework a small part of this," he said, watching her with eyes so pale blue they were almost gray, "I'm pretty sure I could get it published for you." He held the paper out to her, and Lily saw a large A+ written in red on the title page.

She couldn't quite make herself reach out to take it. "It didn't sound as if you liked it much."

He lifted his head as if to see her from a different angle, then looked at the title page and held the paper out again. "Obviously, I did."

She took it. "Rework which part?" she asked, noticing the elegant length of his nose and his broad brow.

"The emotional part," he answered. "It gets in the way."

She smiled and bowed her head to cover it.

"Is that amusing?" he asked.

"I'm sorry. That's something my father always says about . . ." Hesitant to drop her father's profession, she stopped.

"I think if I'd seen that smile in class before, I'd have remembered you," he said. "Look, your paper's very good. You should expand the history, particularly the Kurds' revolt against Atakurk in nineteen twenty-five, when he liquidated all their leaders. And more recently, about Israel's training Kurdish rebels, and the shah's financing their struggle against Iraq. Bring us up to date. But your conclusion can't be an undefined *cri de coeur* about a homeland for the Kurdish heritage. It's all right to play God; give them whatever you want. You have to base it, though, on international law and current political realities. Now," he said, shifting the weight of his body from one leg to the other. He was wearing a tan cashmere tweed jacket, dark brown corduroys, and a dark green sweater, all of which Lily registered as he asked, "How do you know so much about the Middle East? There were little hints of intimate knowledge in just about every paragraph."

"I grew up there."

He took a step closer. "Where?"

"All over."

"Army brat? FSO brat?"

She nodded. "DD—Diplomat's Daughter. My father's a Foreign Service officer, in Tripoli right now."

"Tripoli? They just had a revolution last year. He must be having fun." Then he switched to Arabic. *"Hahl tatakaliyama al-arabi?"* he asked intently.

She nodded. *"Nah'am."*

He smiled at her and continued in Arabic. "Where did you learn it?"

"Cairo," she answered, already aware of his skill with the language but noting his difficulty with the glottal stop used in the middle or at the end of words.

His enthusiasm, however, carried him through as he continued. "That's great; that's the dialect I learned at the Monterey Language School. I found a Moroccan on campus, but I couldn't understand a word she said. How am I doing?" he asked, doubt clouding his face.

"Very well," she continued in Arabic. "You slide through your words without the stops, which can confuse emphasis and change meaning, but I could get everything."

"I know," he said. "May I give you a ride somewhere? My car's right around the corner." He took the canvas boat bag and put his other hand on Lily's arm to guide her out the door. She was very aware of the touch and wondered whether he was, even as he intently pronounced his Arabic. "I really want to get this right. Not just good, but sublime. I went through Monterey with the highest rating they give, but I know I still sound like a tourist. I want you to make me into a native."

They went into the hall, where Mimi was waiting. When she

saw the situation, her mouth edged into a wry grin and she turned away to examine the mortar in the nearby brick wall.

As they passed Mimi, Professor Deloit said in English, "Listen, I have a nifty idea. Are you busy Saturday? Maybe you can come sailing with us."

He did not take any notice of Mimi's giggle as they reached the hall steps and proceeded out of the building. Lily walked along, still conscious of his easy grip on her arm, listening to his fast though flat Arabic but more concerned about Saturday. She had to work in the dining room, she had to study, she had no idea what to wear or who "sailing with us" referred to.

"You think you can make it?" he asked as he helped her into the Austin-Healy. The top was down and the seat's leather was warmed by the sun.

"I don't see why not," Lily said, wondering if the invitation represented any interest beyond his desire to speak better Arabic.

"Terrific." He dropped the canvas bag into the space behind the seats and folded himself into the seat beside her. "Is your father an ambassador or what?" he asked as he started up and pulled out of the lot into the street. "Where am I taking you?"

"Oh, the Co-op will be fine."

They were moving down a one-way street. Around a corner a block in front of them came a crowd of two dozen hippies carrying placards and chanting along with several bullhorns. Behind them a campus police car was following discreetly. Professor Deloit stopped instantly, threw the gear into reverse, and started to back up. He had only ten yards to go; a panel truck braked hard behind them. The best he could do was pull over to one side to allow the police car to pass. The demonstrators saw the sports car and started to run toward it, urged on by the bullhorns. The police car flipped on its flashers and followed quickly, but with no siren.

One of the men with a bullhorn leaped on the hood. He wore a pair of pants made out of an American flag, a sleeveless Levi's jacket with Harley-Davidson insignia on its back, and, around a wild mound of black curls, a hairband that read MAKE ME, NOT WAR.

"What do we got here?" he yelled into the bullhorn as he smiled happily. The Austin-Healy was surrounded with demonstrators, many of whom were leaning on the car or standing with one foot on the fender. "I'll tell you what we got here. We got the hope of America here, the shimmering hope of America, with its tweed and fancy sports car and Ivy League education and enough privilege to float a motherfuckin' yacht. You got a yacht, man?"

The demonstrators laughed and yelled, repeating the question. Lily was as angry as scared. She looked over at Professor Deloit.

"The damn thing sank," he said with such ingenuous charm that the hippie hooted a laugh into the bullhorn and leaped down beside the car on Lily's side. Bending over her, he put his face close to her ear and said, "You want to meet me later? I mean, he doesn't even have a yacht!"

"No, thank you," Lily said as firmly as she could, although her hands were trembling as she held on to her book bag.

The hippie moved so that she had to look into his face. He was no longer smiling. "You have it all, don't you, honey? Well, don't blow it, hear?"

"Have what?" Lily said, anger winning out. "What the hell do you know about having or not having? You're just having a good time." By then, she was talking into the hippie's face. "Would you be so brave if you knew you'd get hanged for it?" She saw a campus policeman step out of his car.

The demonstrators started to move in and shout, but the hippie said into his bullhorn, "She's right, folks, we're having a real good time here, at least a lot better than any poor drafted sum-bitch in Saigon, or any black man in whitey's jails. So let's leave America's hope sitting here—in their sports car. And hey, ssh, don't tell 'em, but pretty soon they won't be able to recognize the place!" A bellowing cheer went up, and the demonstrators followed the bullhorn down the street, the campus police car trailing behind them.

Professor Deloit pulled the car out from the curb and quickly drove away. "Are you all right?" he asked.

"He should see what clowns with bullhorns get in Syria."

"As in every worthy cause, there's a hell of a lot of narcissism at play in the antiwar movement."

"I'll never get the American perspective right," she said.

He drove without speaking for a while, not going in the direction of the Co-op, she noticed although she said nothing.

"What's your first name, Miss McCann? I've forgotten."

"Lily."

"I'm called Worth. May I offer some advice?"

"Yes."

"Never show anger or fear in public. Either one tends to reveal vulnerability and stimulate a reaction, usually unpleasant, mostly unmanageable."

"Fear? Did I—?"

"Your hands were shaking."

"I'm sorry."

"No need to be. It's over."

"Is it better to joke with them?"

"When there are, say, twenty of them and two of us, the best distraction this side of a howitzer is to make them doubt their hate. Humor often works."

"But what about what they say?"

"Nothing anybody says means anything anymore. The only substance is in the situation; words are for performance. Whatever that energetic jerk who ran around on the hood in his Keds said surely won't be remembered by anyone, except maybe you. It had no effect, unless he scared you or made you angry, which he did. Your reaction gave his performance the substance it didn't deserve."

Lily turned to look at him. He was laughing quietly, at himself, she thought. "Did you just make that up?"

"I don't much trust the power of words."

"That's too bad. You're pretty good with them."

"Yes, so I've been told . . . Where am I taking you?"

"Here's fine." They had driven by the Sterling Library. He stopped the car and got out to open her door.

"I have to give you my address. Can you get over to Guilford? That's where I live, and we can drive over to the boat from there."

She stood facing him after he shut her door. "I'm sorry, but I really can't come. I'd like to, but I have to wait on tables and study and, well, I don't think I have anything to wear on a boat."

He looked as disappointed as she could have wished. "Proves my point. I talked so much, the situation changed. Goodbye, Lily." He went back to the driver's side, stepped over the door, sat, and put the car into gear. "I hope you'll rewrite that paper," he said and drove away.

On Saturday, Lily was busing tables when she suddenly remembered that this was the day she had been asked to go sailing. Looking up through the high windows of the dining room, she saw a few billowing clouds move swiftly across a burning blue sky, and wondered who was on the boat with him, whether it was cold on the water, and what they were wearing. She hadn't studied much; because of the strike, there might not be exams. She wished she'd gone, then smiled to herself as she piled dishes into a busing tray and said, *"Malesh."* She had picked up her father's favorite Arabic expression, a combination of "so it goes," "it doesn't matter," and "never mind." Usually said with a shrug, it indicated an acceptance of Allah's will.

Thousands of people had arrived in New Haven over the previous days. Meetings and spontaneous marches continued through the day and evening, leading up to the rally planned for Friday night, May 1. No one on campus knew what would happen. Mimi was covering the demonstrations as a stringer for a national magazine; Lily hadn't seen her for two days. The roommates had barricaded the windows of their room on the second floor of Wright Hall, which stood across the Old Campus and through the University Gates about two hundred yards from the green where many of the demonstrations were taking place. The women had locked up whatever they could in their closets and hidden anything that would be tempting to smash. Everyone they knew had done much the same thing; some had packed up what they owned into a car and parked it on the outskirts of New Haven, out of harm's way. The rumors grew that the National Guard had moved closer and that tanks were involved. The university's police force and the New Haven police were on full alert and had been in evidence on and around the downtown campus, some wearing riot gear.

The word went out from President Brewster's office that the Yale campus would remain open at all times and that each of the twelve resident colleges would make every effort to feed demonstrators in need and care for any infants among them; the gates of the university would not be closed. The city of New Haven adopted a similar stance, and the emotional basis for any destructive reaction was effectively diffused. Mimi was responsible for breaking the story that the National Guard, although present nearby, had no tanks and was not on full alert. Lily volunteered to work extra hours at University Dining Hall to feed any people who came in from the streets.

Then on the Thursday before the planned rally, President Nixon announced a military "incursion" into Cambodia, thus expanding the Vietnam War and betraying his frequent pledge to end it. The national reaction was instantaneous; demonstrations took place all over the country, and a strike of the nation's universities was proclaimed. The rally at Yale the next night was attended by thirteen thousand people. It took place peacefully, broken only by a relatively small crowd that went on a stone-throwing rampage on the New Haven Green three hours after the rally. It was dispersed by tear gas, and the campus remained calm.

By Saturday, any threat of a campus "invasion" was gone. The demonstrators' attention was focused on the nationwide student strike against military operations in Vietnam and Cambodia. The crowds of students returned to their own campuses and the atmosphere at Yale took on the buoyancy of relief.

As Lily turned to wipe off a table, she saw Worth Deloit come into the dining room. He was wearing jeans and a heavy black turtleneck sweater. After showing his ID to the woman behind the check-in table and handing her an envelope, he looked out over the room and spotted Lily immediately, standing with a rag in one hand, staring at him. Embarrassed but unwilling to pretend she hadn't seen him, she smiled the question of what he was doing there. He came over quickly. "Hello, Lily."

"What happened? I thought you'd be sailing."

"I lost my crew. May I talk to you a minute?"

"Sure, as long as nobody gets up from a table."

"I need your help."

"You do?"

"I've been asked to go to the Middle East this summer with some congressmen on a junket over there, as a kind of professor, guide, *and* translator. You have to get me up to grade."

"Me? I, well, I don't know if there's time—"

"Hey wait, I'm not that bad."

"No, I mean I don't have—"

"You work three hours a day here, at least when there isn't a revolution going on. If you gave this up for the rest of the school year, I'd want only an hour and a half."

"I couldn't do that; I'd lose my work-study program if I—"

"Lily, don't underestimate me." He was still looking at her pleasantly but there was a compelling edge to his voice. "I've talked to the work-study office *and* the dean of students *and* your tutor. The financial situation was worked out—today, as a matter of fact. The office was open because of the strike. Everybody agrees this would be advantageous for you and an enormous help to me. Will you please put down that rag and say you'll do it?"

She dropped the rag on the table. "I'm not a teacher. There must be other—"

"And I'm not a student." There was a slight frown on his face through which he forced a bare smile. His voice was deadly calm. "I'm a bit beyond Berlitz, and besides I don't have time to travel to some rabbit warren school to learn *'Aheenah ahtahwahlit?'* I know how to learn, Lily, and know what I need—someone who speaks the language idiomatically and who can correct what books can't teach."

"When do you want to start?"

"As soon as you can finish here."

"Today?"

"Do you know where my office is?"

"No."

"Room seven-o-four, in the Graduate School tower."

"I'll come as soon as I can."

He took a step back, and Lily realized that at some point he had moved in very close to her. "Lily, that's the best news I've had all day. Now, what do you recommend for lunch?"

"Anything but the tuna melt."

"What's wrong with it?"

"I heard the tuna isn't tuna and it melts before the cheese does."

He laughed, surprisingly heartily, and walked over to the cafeteria line. His presence was acknowledged by the students, with whom he began an animated conversation; he went with a group of them to a table, where the talk continued.

Lily quickly cleared a table and wiped it clean as a few more

students and demonstrators sat down. It was after two, and the line
for food was growing sparse. She went to her supervisor and started
to explain, but the supervisor had already been informed by
Worth's just-delivered letter from the work-study office. Lily
looked back at Worth Deloit, surrounded by students, arguing a
point and entertaining them as he did so.

No, she thought, don't underestimate this man. She didn't know
whether he had the slightest interest in her beyond her Arabic, but
admitted to herself that she was flattered and would rather be used
for tutoring than for busing dishes.

After hanging up her apron in the locker room, she washed her
hands and checked her hair in the mirror. Pulled back in a ponytail
for work, it reached down her back, all of a honey-brown color, the
highlighted sun strands from last summer in Tripoli grown out and
dulled by the long gray New England winter. When not working
in the dining hall, she usually wore barrettes, dividing her hair so
that it framed her face. It was much more becoming, and she
thought of changing the ponytail but then decided against it. He'd
spot the effort and would draw the right conclusion. She tucked in
her blouse and smiled at herself. Throughout boarding school,
she'd wished she hadn't grown so tall, but it wasn't so bad in
college, and Professor Deloit was a good five inches taller. He'd said
something about her smile—less a flirtation than a courtesy, but
others had commented on it. She had her mother's green eyes and
"lush lips"—her occasional nickname at Madeira. Her father had
warned her that she was beautiful, but Lily didn't believe him. As
she assessed herself in the mirror, however, she hoped she was. On
the other hand, Professor Cotesworth Deloit didn't seem to care
much what his Arabic speaker looked like. She scowled, turned,
and banged through the door.

He was still sitting with the students, arguing, a look of amused
challenge in his eyes. Lily went over to the coffee urn and poured
herself a cup, then added a spoonful of instant coffee to it. American coffee wasn't strong enough. She sat down at a table near his to
wait for him to finish. When he saw her, he excused himself,
picked up his plate and glass of juice, and came over.

"Obviously I talked too much to eat. Sorry," he offered as he
took a bite of his sandwich.

"That's okay."

"You said something the other day that was very interesting."

"Oh? What?"

"That you'll never get the American perspective right; something like that. Don't you consider yourself American?"

"Well, legally at least; my mother's French."

"Really? Then you speak French as well."

"Yes, but it gets pretty rusty between visits with her." She saw the question in his expression. "My mother and father are divorced. She lives in Paris."

"Ah, now I see. The diplomat's daughter, raised in embassy residences, surrounded by an Arab *cordon sanitaire,* with occasional visits to Paris for—what? Holidays, summer vacation?" Lily shook her head. "Twice a year? Once?" She nodded. "And between your father's diplomatic tours of duty, you returned with him to the rarefied bubble of State Department Washington."

Lily laughed at that, agreeing with the apt description.

"When you were growing up, were your schools and friends Arab, or did you go around with the other diplomats' children?"

"Well, both, but my dad would send me to an Arab school if there was a good one. I went to one some of the time in Cairo, and in Beirut, too, but not in Tunis. And my best friends were Arab."

"I'd say you haven't had much chance to get into this country."

"I see what you mean, but . . ."

He looked at her as if reaching a conclusion. "There's only one solution, as far as I can tell."

"What's that?"

"I'm going to seduce you with America." He gazed at her a moment, took a large bite of his sandwich, and laughed, looking off toward the windows. "How would I say that in Arabic? The congressmen could use that, for sure."

TWO

ALL RIGHT, CAIRO," Worth said in Arabic as he gazed up at the mainsail and turned the wheel to correct a slight luffing. "Tell me everything."

"Nobody knows 'everything' about Cairo," Lily replied, correcting his pronunciation of *koll' sheh,* "everything." He continued to rush through the phrase and miss the stop.

"I don't mean *everything* everybody knows," he said expertly, "but why you love it so much."

"Well, the obvious answer is that Cairo was my first home . . . and I guess the last, too. We happened to be back there when my mother left. We've been moving ever since."

Worth continued to watch the sail. "Yes, you said something earlier, something about the luxury of permanence."

Off the stern was Fishers Island, where earlier they'd anchored and rowed the rubber dinghy to a beach that belonged to friends of the Deloit family. A wide lawn led up a slight rise between the beach and the immense old shingled Cape with its screened porch running the length of the front. There had been sixteen for lunch; a staff of three served it on long planks set up under two apple trees near a tennis court. The family and their friends were informal, animated, and graciously hospitable to Lily.

"It is a luxury," she said. "I feel real envy when I'm with people who've lived in a place and had friends there for a long time."

It was warm enough for Worth to be wearing shorts and no socks with his worn-down boat shoes, but not so hot that he could avoid a sweater. Leaning back on the cockpit cushions a few feet from where he stood, Lily noticed the rock-hard muscles of his legs covered with a fine down of blond hair, then quickly looked over

43

the port side at the wave of foamy lace that the keel cut from the water. According to Worth, the forty-two-foot genoa-rigged sloop was making fifteen knots in the westerly breeze.

For the last five weeks, they had worked for an hour and a half every day speaking only Arabic to each other no matter the circumstance. Most of the time they met in his office, but occasionally, if the spring weather was particularly fine, they walked around campus or went out to the playing fields to jog. In spite of the informality of the arrangement, their work was intense. He often took notes, and Lily was impressed by his progress from one session to the next. On the other hand, he had not expressed the slightest interest in her other than as a teaching machine. But at the end of the exam period, he asked her once again to go sailing on the day before she flew to Tripoli. This time she did not refuse, was comfortable enough to ask what to wear—white slacks, blue sweater—and was pleased to learn on her arrival at Old Saybrook that they would be sailing alone.

"My father used to say," Lily offered, "that being in Cairo was like living in the middle of a huge heart, rather dark, usually damp, with life pouring over you every second, a variety of passions in the hidden corners, and the friction between eternity and death supplying the intensity of the place."

Worth laughed. "What an image! I look forward to meeting your father. I agree with him, except for 'dark.' When I was there, I could barely open my eyes outside, the sun was always so bright. I wanted to shoot it out of the sky."

"I think that's the point. Everyone stays inside in the dark to escape. Do you remember the soft, filtered light coming in through the wooden *mashrabiyyeh* screens? Shade all day long, latticework over interior courtyards? There's no darkness as subtle as what you can find in midday Cairo."

"Yes, yes," Worth responded while tacking the sloop around. As the boat heeled over, Lily shifted and let herself fall into the seat across the cockpit. "I remember when I first saw the place," Worth said—"this was five years ago, no, six—I thought you could paint a picture of the whole city with one tube of burnt sienna. The entire place was that single brownish color, except the Nile Hilton. It was blue."

"How long were you there?"

"Well, you know, the Egyptian Museum, the Pyramids, and a fast felucca ride up the Nile. Then we went exploring around several monasteries in the desert for a week."

"That's not enough. I wish I could show you . . ." She hesitated.

"Yes, maybe we'll be there together sometime."

She turned to face him, but he was still watching the sail. Then he said, "By chance, I heard about what happened to you in Amman, just before the Six Day War."

Startled, she asked, "How'd you hear about that?"

"I get occasional calls from people in the State Department. I happened to ask about your father; the story came up."

"Oh. Well, yes, it's my split second of fame." Her mouth had gone dry and she had to cough.

"A pretty horrible split second."

She didn't answer and thought of going to the head in order to avoid the subject, but he spoke too fast and switched to English, which seemed a sudden intimacy. "May I ask you about it?"

For more than two years, she had not mentioned it, only with her father and two psychiatrists she'd been sent to at State Department expense. She didn't know how she would respond to Worth, even if she could. The terrorist's annual reminder had arrived the week before, and she was still shaken by it.

"I'm not sure I can say anything, but go ahead and try me."

"I've heard that things like that usually get repressed. Memory can't seem to deal with them."

She thought a moment. "I still have nightmares occasionally, but I'm not driven the way I used to be."

"Driven to do what?"

"To find the people who did it. I was a little crazy at first about revenge, until the fear set in."

He sounded concerned. "Is that still there?"

She watched a seagull fly lazily over the bow. "For a time, I wanted to kill them the way they'd killed those children. But even if I had the chance, I doubt I'd be able to, though I still get caught up in the fantasy from time to time. Yes, I'm afraid—not enough to keep me from walking around, but I know he's out there. I'm the only one who saw him, and he knows just where I am. It keeps me looking back over my shoulder a lot."

"I think you're safe at Yale," he suggested.

"Oh, really?" she replied testily. "The letter I got from him last week was postmarked New Haven." She wasn't supposed to tell anyone about the letters, and never had before.

Worth's surprise was revealed only by his slightly lifted brow. "He writes you?"

"Once a year, on the anniversary." She hoped she could trust him, hoped he'd ask more.

"What does he say?"

"I'm not supposed to talk about that. I send the letter to the State Department security people, they send it on to the CIA, and it goes in my file. They'll never find him." Unexpectedly, tears welled up and fell onto the wind, which carried them overboard. Embarrassed, Lily said, "Damn."

"Let's drop it," Worth said.

Lily shook her head. "The last one—they're all short—it said, 'To the diplomat's daughter'—they all begin that way, in English, typed in English. 'You remember my face. I remember yours. Perhaps we'll meet again. I always know where you are if I want you. Each minute. But if you ever see me, pretend you are blind. Or you will be.' That's all." She took a deep breath, amazed by her sense of relief.

"Do you think he was in New Haven to mail it?" Worth asked incredulously.

"I doubt it. He probably has access to someone who'd get it there. But I find myself watching people on street corners. I do that all the time."

"How does he know where you are?"

Lily smiled bitterly. "I'm not sure. But if he has access to the Mossad, it'd be pretty easy to track any diplomat's family in the Middle East."

"You think he's with the Mossad?"

"I don't want to think that, and the Mossad has denied it from the moment it happened, denied that the terrorists were even Israeli. But the weapons they used were American-made, the ammunition traced to a sale to Israel. Besides, who else slaughters Arab children in Jordan on the eve of a war?" She was angry again and looked away at the Connecticut coastline.

"Arabs kill Arabs all the time," Worth pointed out, "for all kinds of reasons."

"Yes, but not the day before a war, not children."

Worth concentrated on sailing the boat before he asked, "What if he were caught?"

"I hope he'd rot in a small cell for the rest of his life."

Worth chuckled. "And the Arabs do jail so much better, or worse, depending on your point of view. As I remember, there's a prison in Cairo where they say the screams of the prisoners peel the paint off the walls."

Lily gazed up at the sails. "I wouldn't wish that on anyone."

"What would you do if you actually saw him on a street corner one day?"

She hesitated. "My father tries to convince me to do nothing except find a phone. But when I imagine it happening, I usually see myself going after him—to confront him, if nothing else. I doubt if I'd be very rational."

"Do you think, if you confronted him as you say, you could possibly make him feel any remorse for what he did?"

Worth was across the cockpit from her, standing at the wheel, watching her with a sidelong scrutiny. "Of course not," she answered, suddenly alarmed by the old anger, an anger that used to take over her life and last for days. "Look, what I think is rational as hell. The guy probably had all the motives anyone would need. But emotionally, viscerally, it's not so clear. I probably couldn't kill him, but sometimes I feel my fingers around his throat." Her voice was clutching.

He stepped across the cockpit and held his hand out to her, a simple gesture of concern. Anger made her hesitate, but she took it. He sat on the helmsman's seat, holding the wheel with his other hand. Lily turned away and watched the keel's spray again as the boat rode the backs of swells and gently slid down their faces, the breeze behind them, filling the mainsail and genoa, making them taut, straining against the tall aluminum mast. Their hands stayed joined for some time. Nothing was said; no pressure was applied. He withdrew his hand to tack leeward and asked Lily to move to

47

the winch. Together they pulled the halyard to firm up the mainsail. He tightened the winch as she held the wheel; they exchanged places and she sat down again.

"I may see you this summer," Worth said. "I think my gaggle of congressmen want to see the shores of Tripoli. You'll be able to check if my Arabic is still working."

"You'll do fine. When will you be coming?"

"I think July."

"Hot."

"Yes. Maybe we'll be seated together at the inevitable welcoming dinner."

"I never go to those unless my father has to give one."

"Make an exception?"

"Of course."

"Good. By then, I'm really going to want to see you again."

Lily didn't move but was aware of a new heat in her face and hoped she wasn't blushing. She spoke quickly. "When you talked with your friends at the State Department, what did they say about my father?"

His response was preceded by a significant pause. "As far as I could tell, the people in the Bureau of Near Eastern Affairs think that Bert McCann is one of the best in the field, and you know those Arabists. They regard themselves as the only real professional 'dips' in the diplomatic business. Your father's considered the purest of the pure and, as such, a little old-fashioned, but one of the best out there."

"Is that the word they used?" Lily demanded, instantly irritated. "Old-fashioned?"

"One did."

"Well, he's wrong. My father's kind of diplomacy works. He makes his contacts and gets their trust, no matter whether they're friends or enemies. Then he can start to communicate. What's old-fashioned about that? I suppose they want him to connive and mislead and throw around the weight of American money and power. Show me one place where that's done any good."

"Please don't kill the messenger," Worth said with an arm up to ward off blows.

Lily laughed. "Sorry. He and I have both heard that word before."

"He's deputy chief of mission now?"

"Yes, and he's been lucky. Being number two at an embassy is a terrible job if you have a bad ambassador—you know, some rich friend of the president's who wants the title or has a wife who likes to give parties. 'Sam, go buy me an embassy'; that kind of thing. Daddy's ambassador, even though he's a polyp, has been terrific." She leaned forward and knocked wood on the teak cockpit table.

"Polyp?" Worth asked.

"Political appointee, pol-ap, polyp."

He smiled, then said, "Your father's going to be chargé d'affaires this summer."

"How do you know that?"

"I can't reveal my sources, but the ambassador's coming back to Washington for consultations, so number two DCM will be number one chargé for a while."

Lily was astonished and delighted. She was well aware that a strong performance by a DCM as chargé in the ambassador's absence spoke loudly in Washington. Bert McCann was fifty-seven, about to be given his final post before mandatory retirement at sixty. By tradition, a last assignment was usually a reward posting. More than that, she realized that each day her father was in charge, his salary was increased by half the difference between his own and that of the ambassador's. And Cairo! He'd requested that his final posting be there. They'd be able to go home to the dahabeah on the Nile. For three years, neither had visited the houseboat because of scheduling and "obligations of State," their code excuse to each other for anything that the world scene or the department required to ruin their plans.

So exhilarated was she that she stood up, grabbing hold of a halyard to steady herself. Over the bow, she could see the inlet of the Connecticut River where they would soon be docking. Impulsively she turned and said, "Thank you for telling me about that, and for all this, Worth. I can't think of a better day."

He was standing behind the wheel and again reached out his hand to her. Unhesitating, she took it, and he pulled her toward him. When she let go of the halyard, she became dependent on him

49

for balance as he gently drew her closer, then put his arm around her waist. For a moment, they held on, watching each other's eyes. Lily saw no yearning or even desire, more an examination and a decision. She started to pull away, but before she had a chance, he kissed her. It was a long, deep kiss, broken only when the sails began luffing and he had to look to the sloop.

Staring up into the sails, he turned the wheel and brought the boat around while still holding Lily. She did not try to move away but kept an arm casually around his waist, her hand flat on the side of his torso. "Did you hear what I said a minute ago," he asked, still watching the sails, "about really wanting to see you again?"

"Yes, of course I did."

"You didn't respond."

"I didn't know whether you meant me or your Arabic teacher."

He seemed surprised and a bit vexed. "Lily, there are forty-three undergraduate and graduate students at Yale who speak Arabic. A number of them are natives. I met with a lot of them, but I chose you. The work went as well as I expected, but the pleasure in it was you."

"I didn't see any sign of that."

He held her gently with his arm, his legs braced against the boat's pitch. "You'll learn, or at least I hope you will, that I'm somewhat demented when I have to accomplish something. Single-minded, compulsive, driven—I've been called all those and worse, but it's none of those things. I simply can't stand to waste time. I do whatever I do as completely as I can do it. You know the T. S. Eliot line: 'Distracted from distraction by distraction'? I don't allow a distraction. What I do or choose to do is what I can and must do totally, such as teaching, such as sailing or writing a book, or learning a language."

"So that when we were working, if I were anything more than your Arabic dragoman, I'd have been a distraction."

"Yes, during that time. But before that, when I found you and set out to get you to teach me, I went about it with a fairly dogged determination, as I think you'll admit. And since we've finished our tutorial, I've been just as determined to let you know how I feel about you."

They hit a swell, and Lily had to put both hands around his rib cage. It was awkward. When she let go, she lurched back to the halyard.

"Why?" she asked, facing him as the boat regained an even momentum. "And believe me, I'm not fishing for compliments or reassurance. I just don't understand why I'm getting this much notice in a life like yours."

He looked at her for a long moment, then said, "You don't know yourself, Lily. You don't know how smart you are, how impressive you are standing up to a smart-assed intimidating professor, how wise you are about a lot of things you've no business to know about at twenty. I'll bet you don't even know how lovely you are." He checked the sails again. "I'd say about the only thing you really know about yourself is that you're your father's daughter. Forgive the cheap psychology, but I'd like to show you more of who *you* are, and I'm conceited enough to think that I may have observed a good deal about the subject."

"I don't know what you're implying with that mini-analysis, whether it's Electra and Freud or what, but I think I know enough about myself, father and all. And whatever else there is to find out, I'll get to it sooner or later. Thanks anyway." She was angrier than she wanted to be.

"Sounds pretty defensive," he said coolly.

"Well, under the circumstances, that seems appropriate," she answered, forcing her tone to be as calm as his.

"There's no need to be. I'm not attacking. If I ever do that, I promise you'll know. Look, let's take one of those calm diplomatic breaks while we bring the boat in. Grab that halyard on the port side of the mast, will you?"

"Right side?"

"Left."

They brought down the sails and, with the help of the auxiliary engine, moved the boat into its slip. After tying and bagging the sails, they washed down the deck with fresh water. Lily helped him attach the blue nylon protective covering over the cockpit. Finally they stood on the dock to take a last look at the sloop. Weaving his fingers through hers, Worth clasped her hand.

"I'm glad you came today," he said.

"So am I, despite the defensive outburst."

He laughed, let go of her hand, and picked up the two canvas boat bags they'd carried aboard.

"We have a choice to make," he stated as they walked up the dock toward the parking lot.

"What?"

"How far along are you with your packing?"

"Done, except for what I have on."

"Then the choice is, I can drive you back to New Haven now, maybe stop for dinner on the way, or we can have dinner at my place and you can spend the night. I'll get you to the airport in time for your flight, I promise. And Lily, this is not a proposition. There are several things I still want to ask and say, so I'd like the day to go on as long as it can."

Lily didn't answer until they'd reached the Austin-Healy and Worth had dropped the two boat bags behind the seat. When he faced her across the car, she said, "I don't take it as a proposition, although I have to admit I wonder how often the choice has been offered before." She smiled to make certain he knew she was not concerned.

"No comment," he said, "and no defense."

"Your attention is something new for me, and I'm having a hard time believing it, which I'm sure is my problem. So I'm going to turn down what has to be one of the more intriguing offers I've ever had, and hope that with a little time for my—what? the sociology people would probably say my 'acculturation'—you'll ask me again."

He smiled and opened his door. "I will, at least five times between here and New Haven. But I don't depend on the future, Lily. You never can trust it. The situation always changes."

———

Forty-eight hours later, Lily was eating a tuna fish sandwich in the kitchen of her father's apartment in Tripoli. It was three in the morning and her hunger had awakened her. In spite of jet lag, she was grateful that the State Department, which paid for the twice-annual trips of diplomats' children back and forth to school, had at last agreed to join the rest of the world by allowing jet travel rather than insisting on the less expensive and much longer prop flights. Then she remembered her father railing that jet planes would be the ruin of the professional diplomat, allowing the almost instant appearance at a crisis of amateurs or higher-ups from Washington. She smiled at his rejection of the modern convenience, which made her wonder if he really was old-fashioned, which in turn made her think of Worth Deloit and wonder why she had been so crazy as to refuse his offer.

Her father came down the hall and stood in the doorway in his robe and slippers, wiping his glasses on his pajama top.

"Did I wake you up, Daddy? I'm sorry."

"No, no. I think I'm just excited that you're here. How's the jet lag?"

"The usual oatmeal in the veins and a stake through my skull." She stood up and went over to give him a hug. "I'm so glad to see you. Tell me everything. I couldn't think when I got off the plane, and I forgot whatever you said to me. When will we know about Cairo?"

"Any time now." She sat again and he went to the refrigerator and poured a glass of bottled water. "But before that, it seems I'm going to be chargé around here, and you're going to have to play hostess for me."

He looked at her proudly for a response. She smiled and bent down to fiddle with the remains of her sandwich. "Daddy, that's wonderful," she said, devoid of surprise.

"When people talk to their food, there's always a reason. That's about the most muted reaction I can imagine."

Lily laughed and took his hand as he sat down opposite her. "It is. I know. It's just that, well, oh, Daddy, it really is wonderful. That should mean Cairo for sure."

"We shall see. Nothing is sure in this business. But what was all that well-oh-it's-just-that stuff? You're looking as guilty as a cat with a fish tail in its mouth."

"Oh no, not guilty. I wish I were. Anyway, I knew about the chargé business."

"How on earth? I just heard about it a week ago."

Lily took a deep breath and let it out. "Well, his name is Cotesworth Deloit, and he's coming here next month."

They talked over the kitchen table for nearly an hour, but the conversation kept drifting back to Worth and his impending visit. Lily was yawning, but her excitement kept her at the table.

"Yes, well, we've been warned about the congressional junket," Bert said. "They come every two years, the summer before the elections, to get their picture taken in foreign climes with heads of state, which apparently gives voters the impression that their congressmen have something important to do with foreign policy. If they don't like the local ambassador, if he doesn't provide them with every comfort of home, from their favorite bourbon to their choice of hours at the local PX—and often other comforts that home does not provide—they go back to Washington and bellow about incompetence to the department and the press. I hope your friend Mr. Deloit will be kind in translating our humble efforts to his charges, although I must say he sounds as if he has his own ambitious agenda."

"I think he does," Lily admitted, "but if he didn't, it'd be a waste. Daddy, he's so damn brilliant."

He assumed what she always called his diplomatic mask: brow lifted, eyes hooded, nostrils dilated as if picking up familiar scents. "I haven't heard you go on about a man like this since that pimpled Lothario from Saint Albans took you to his spring formal. Should I regard this as something serious, a Cairo secret?"

"Yes. No. I don't know yet. No. Maybe." When his eyes rolled heavenward, Lily started to laugh. "I've got to go back to bed. I can only tell you this. I'm not in love with him, but I could fall in love with him in about five seconds. I don't know what's stopping me, except that I don't know him very well, and I don't want to be another project for him to conquer before going on to the next one. Daddy, you're not going to check up on him at the State Department, are you?"

Bert stood up and put his glass and her plate into the sink. "My darling, *he's* already checked on *me*. If I sent cables asking about him, don't you think the boys in the bureau would have a good laugh? Also, State Department profiles seldom reveal what really counts. I've always depended on meeting the man, which in this case I look forward to."

"Daddy, you'll be nice."

"As always."

"No, I mean really nice, not digging for dirt under his finger-nails while you give him your famous ministerial manicure."

"I'll promise you only that he'll think me a fine fellow, and I'll tell you exactly what I think of him. That is, if you want me to."

Lily looked at him doubtfully for a moment. "I'll let you know."

THREE

WORTH WROTE ONCE from Washington, on a thick Cartier card with his name engraved in plain block letters.

> You really made me look good—or sound good. I've been tested three times to make sure I can speak Arabic. I even corrected one guy on his glottal stops. I loved our day sailing. Is there anything to see in Tripoli? Saints' hearts, ancient sites? Everyone's curious about Qaddafi. See you soon (currently July 21; don't depend on it).
>
> W

The W was twice as big as the other letters. It neatly filled out the card, which Lily propped up first on her work table in the apartment, then put in the frame of the mirror over her chest of drawers, where she read it daily.

Lily wrote four letters in return, but sent only one, a short note on an embassy card embossed with the Great Seal of the United States, care of the State Department. She hoped that the congressional affairs office would get it to Worth before he left on the junket.

> You are officially invited to visit Tripoli on July 21, give or take seven days either way. This invitation admits one and is not valid for anyone but the addressee. Activities will depend on scheduling, but tours of ancient parts (heads, hearts, spleens) are offered, as well as other diversions. No sailing is available (alas). Come soon. On arrival, call 112838 to confirm special arrangements.
>
> Lily

When the military transport landed at Wheelus Air Force Base, Worth was one of the first to descend the stairs, staying close to the two senators for whom he translated introductions to the Libyan welcoming party. Lily and her father were next in line to greet the visitors. As Bert welcomed each congressman, Worth stood aside, next to Lily. "Miss McCann, I believe, official guide to saints' spleens?"

"At your service," she said, and took his hand. He was about to kiss her on the cheek, but one of the congressmen called out, "Deloit!" Smiling his regret, he hurried over to ease the awkwardness between the representative and a loquacious Libyan second minister of airport arrivals. The limousines arrived on the tarmac, and in minutes Worth was gone.

The congressional party was lodged during its scheduled three-day visit at the Grand Hotel on the waterfront. Outside its front entrance was a large construction site of indeterminable purpose, at the time producing nothing more than clouds of dust amid the grinding roar of numerous generators. Within hours of their arrival, the two senators and four representatives let it be known that they expected the chargé d'affaires at the American Embassy to halt whatever was going on outside their windows until they left.

When Bert did not succeed in shutting down the work, their disdain for an embassy where the ambassador was absent became overt. The truth was that Bert had barely tried to plumb the labyrinthine depths of the Libyan Department of Interior Affairs, since he regarded the congressmen's request as outrageous as their demand for a masseur's twenty-four-hour availability.

"We have a betting pool at the embassy," Bert fumed on the afternoon of the junket's second day as he and Lily climbed the front steps of the Ambassador's Residence, "how many of the six will request an excursion to see the last belly dancer in Tripoli, of course as an example of the fast-disappearing local culture under the new leader." Libya, having overthrown a king the previous year in a bloodless coup, was at present controlled by a twenty-eight-year-old officer in the military, Muammar el-Qaddafi.

The mansion was a magnificent Victorian, crumbling, ready to be abandoned for a new one, depending on future relations between the two countries. Bert and Lily went into the kitchen to greet the Residence staff and go over details of the evening's dinner. Bert's apartment was too small for a large party, and if the congressmen weren't shown the Residence, they might regard their Libyan visit with even greater distaste.

When they returned to the ambassador's armored Cadillac limousine, Lily said, "Daddy, we'd better get some more flowers in there."

"You're right. Will you have time to do that? The staff's pretty busy."

"Drop me at the apartment. I'll change and pick them up on the way back. What time does the party start?"

"We'll arrive as soon as our audience with Colonel Qaddafi is done. The Libyan guests are asked for eight. Have you had a chance to see your young man?"

"At the airport. He called the apartment last night, but I missed him. The whole group is exhausted. This is their fifth stop in two weeks. Did you like him?"

"I spoke two words to him, I can't remember in which language. He looks fine, certainly has a good tailor. I'd say he's the most prepossessing of all that lot's staff. I'll try to speak with him at Brother Muammar's—no titles in the new Libya."

"Please don't say anything about me."

"What would I say, except that you've been mooning around Tripoli for the last several weeks in a gooey fog, waiting for him to arrive."

"Daddy."

"Trust me."

It had been maddening, the evening arrival, the imperious insistence of the congressmen to get to the hotel, the missed phone call later that night, then the visiting party's tour of two local Italian factories recently "liberated" and being run by Libyans. Worth, as the party's primary translator, had to stay with the congressmen at all times. Lunch with some of Libya's military, a tour of the harbor, and a meeting with the head of state before dinner meant that Worth had been in town for almost twenty-four hours and Lily had barely spoken to him. If something didn't happen that night, she planned to invade his room at the Grand.

After Bert dropped her at the apartment, Lily bathed and changed into the gold-and-pink caftan she'd been planning for several weeks to wear. While brushing her hair another hundred times, she telephoned the florist to have the appropriate flowers ready for pickup. When she arrived back at the Residence, she made herself busy with arranging and placing the flowers, refolding the napkins at the dinner table, turning the serving plates so that the Great Seal was exactly right, checking the seating and making certain that she was next to Worth, and reviewing the serving order with the staff. From a list prepared at the embassy, she made sure that each congressman's alcoholic preference was available and that the new Greek bartender understood about jiggers and American adoration of ice. In the drawing room, she found a trace of dust on the piano on which stood the silver-framed pictures of the absent ambassador with President Nixon on *Air Force One* and together with wives at a formal dinner. Rather than interfere with the staff, Lily found a dust cloth and was cleaning the piano just as the cars drove up. The butler hurried across the entrance hall to open the front door. Lily stuffed the dust cloth under a sofa pillow and went to greet the guests.

In the middle of introductions, instant calls for drinks, and requests for the washroom, Worth came in. When he saw Lily, he stopped and gaped. The caftan had done just what she'd hoped it would do. He was wearing a buff-colored linen suit, a light brown shirt, and dark brown tie, and looked so handsome that she was sure she too gaped. Bert was busy leading the congressmen into the drawing room and satisfying their demands. She made her way through the group of politicians, introducing herself to those she hadn't met, until finally she was next to Worth.

"Welcome to Tripoli," she said in Arabic for privacy.

He continued in Arabic. "I've never seen you dressed up before."

"I was the one in the green dress at the airport."

"Maybe you do know how lovely you are. I have so much to tell you. We are seated together, aren't we?"

"Yes, and maybe afterward you'd consider taking the tour I call Lily's Late-night Tripoli. There's one space left on the bus."

Before he could respond with anything more than an anticipatory grin, the butler opened the front door to let in the first of the

Libyan guests. Both Worth and Lily were pressed into translation duty, although fortunately several Libyans spoke English. At dinner Lily and Worth spent most of the time conveying other people's conversations. When they spoke to each other, they could not depend on Arabic for privacy or on having any time to complete a thought.

"How's the trip been?" Lily asked during a pause.

"Madness; exhaustion," Worth answered. "Every Arab wants another war with Israel and all my congressmen get campaign money from the Israeli lobby. It's been skipping rope on a razor blade. Lily, when can we—?"

The senator next to Lily interrupted. "Miss McCann, ma'am, would you please explain to this lovely Libyan lady what we're doing in Vietnam? I can't make her see . . ."

Lily couldn't speak to Worth until the next course.

"Lily," Worth said during another lull, "I wanted to tell you about your scholarship. Have you heard from Yale?" "No." "You should soon." "Tell me." "Well, I . . ."

"Deloit," a representative called across the table, "could you tell this fine gentleman here that I have a company in my district in Georgia that makes the best goddamn tractors in the world . . ."

As the main course was being cleared, Worth again leaned toward Lily. "It doesn't look as if I'm going to have much chance to talk about this, but I've missed you. After you left New Haven, I kept waiting for you to show up every day for my hour and a half."

Then, without noticing how it had started, they both heard an argument progressing at the other end of the table between a Libyan minister in the new government and a senator who, Lily had learned, was on the Foreign Relations Committee. Bert and the Libyan minister's wife, who spoke no English, were between them.

The senator was saying, "The Israelis don't use terrorism for political purposes."

The Libyan minister, with a smile, responded, "What was the intention, if not political, of the massacre in Dir Yassin a month before the State of Israel was proclaimed? Arab civilians—men, women, and children—were lined up by the Irgun and shot. As a result, tens of thousands of Arabs fled their homes. Surely that

massacre had a political purpose. And surely the Irgun was a terrorist organization."

"That's rather ancient history and out of historical context," the
senator replied patronizingly. "The Irgun was suppressed as soon as
the State of Israel was established. You can't blame a country for
the zeal of its supporters."

"You can for what it does or doesn't do with them when they're
caught," the Libyan continued, aware of the room's attention.
"What about the Stern Gang's offer to make a deal to fight for
Adolf Hitler, of their assassination of the UN's peace negotiator on
Palestine, Count Folke Bernadotte, of the British minister for the
Near East, Lord Moyne? The Stern Gang was another terrorist
group, some of whose members today are sitting in the Knesset."

"The State of Israel chose to regard them as patriot fighters
against the British and the Arabs during the struggle for its existence!" the senator barked.

The Libyan replied calmly, "If you justify their terrorism, you
justify the PLO for shooting up the Zurich and Munich airports
this year. Palestinians have the same reason as the Jews—desperation—for their people, their homeland, their 'existence.' "

"I'm not sure," Bert interrupted before the senator blew up,
"whether those examples are commensurable, Minister. But I think
we can all agree that terrorism isn't an appropriate device of government under any circumstance."

"Then we must define terrorism," the Libyan said. "Would you
regard the saturation bombing now taking place in Cambodia as
terrorism, or does being thirty-five-thousand feet above it remove
the onus of the crime from the pilots and those who gave them
their orders?"

"That's a policy of war," Bert said, "and whether we agree with
it or not, I doubt that we can surgically isolate terrorism from war
tonight." He smiled and raised his glass, hoping for an impasse.

"When you're in a war, sir," the senator stated truculently to the
minister, "you do what you have to do to win it."

The Libyan leaned forward to reply, but Bert spoke first to avoid
further confrontation. "The problem with that, Senator, is that
those nations, or dispossessed peoples who can't afford F-Fifteens,

might think that you were justifying their doing what they had to do by using what they *could* afford, which is often terrorism."

"I'm not justifying terrorism, McCann."

"No, sir, of course not. I think everyone here is aware of your rider on the foreign aid bill this year preventing funds from going to a country that in any way harbors terrorists. It's an example of United States consistency on this horrendous problem, a policy we can all be proud of, and one that the new government in Libya has expressed interest in emulating."

Bert raised his glass informally to toast the senator, but then thought better of it, many of his guests being Muslim and forbidden alcohol. The senator lifted his glass briefly but also didn't drink. He smiled murderously at Bert, who turned to the minister's wife beside him and began to speak to her in Arabic.

Worth and Lily exchanged a worried glance before both were again recruited to translate for their other dinner partners. The attending Libyans, many of whom could be expected to report the conversation, were barely able to contain their anger at the senator's remarks. But within minutes, the table was awash with animated conversation, and soon after, the butler announced that coffee would be served in the drawing room.

Lily escorted the Georgia congressman, translating his tractor encomiums to a Libyan couple who were eager to visit his state, or said they were. As others passed them, Worth whispered quickly to Lily, "Your father's terrific, but politically suicidal." She smiled, though the argument still worried her.

As the afterdinner drinks were passed and the conversation stayed comfortably clear of area politics, Lily noticed one of the congressman cornering each of the others in a short private conversation. He then summoned Bert and Worth, who, when they heard what the congressman said, looked at each other with careful smiles and discussed the situation briefly. After they broke up, Bert began to circulate around the room; in passing Lily, he said, "I win the pool!"

Soon after, the senators rose and asked the translators to express their regret at departing, and to explain that the demands of their itinerary were great. Worth was at last able to speak with Lily only as he was following the honored guests out the front door.

"It seems we're going to see a belly dancer named Astonishia in her last-gasp appearance before Qaddafi's pure veil of Islam falls over the land. Is the telephone number you gave me still good? I called last—"

"Yes. I'll be there."

"It may be late."

"Doesn't matter. No one else is scheduled for the late-*late*-night tour."

He touched her arm, then hurried into one of the limousines. Lily stood at the top of the steps as the entourage drove away, preceded and followed by security vans. As any ambassador in the world would do, Bert had assigned several of the embassy's middle-level FSOs to accompany the party in case there were problems or in case one of the distinguished visitors "went too far." The FSOs who drew the duty were on their own. It was a field test of their adroitness.

"Your young man is quite impressive," Bert said as he approached Lily on the steps. They were alone for a moment and remained to take advantage of it.

"I knew you'd think so, but tell me why."

"As you say, he's very bright. I spoke with him briefly at the Defense Ministry before Qaddafi came in. Speaks Arabic *pretty* well" —he chuckled his emphasis for the teacher—"and he's very clever at not showing his hand. But listen to this. After Colonel Qaddafi was there a while, ducking any questions the political boys could get their teeth into, he requested that my new friend on the Foreign Relations Committee accompany him into his inner office. Rather than taking any of the other congressmen, the senator insisted on having your Mr. Deloit with him. That is a tall compliment."

Lily was pleased. As they turned to go back into the Residence to talk with the guests who remained, she asked, "What happened?"

"They were in there about twenty minutes. When they came out, they all looked grim but said nothing, which the senator enjoyed because it made the other congressmen as envious as boys outside the circus tent. But the moment he could do so without attracting attention, Worth came over to me and said, 'I'll submit a memcon to you as soon as I can.' I told him I wasn't sure the senator would be pleased if he did, and he said, 'Well, Mr. McCann, I'm here at State Department expense and the senator hasn't told me not to. Besides, I don't see that he's going to know about it, do you?' Now that's the kind of pure gall that either destroys you or takes you very far. It's not exactly vaulting ambition, but an absolute certainty that he's entitled, because of who he is, to the best the world offers. However, he impressed me, which I'm sure is what he wanted to do, under the present circumstances." He gave Lily a knowing look as they returned to their guests.

———————

The phone call came at two-fifteen. By then, Lily had changed clothes twice, settling on a blouse and linen slacks. She grabbed the phone after the first ring.

"Hello?"

"Astonishia lived up to her name. Where are you?"

"Ten minutes from you. Are you at the hotel?"

"Yes."

"I'll come there. What's your room number?"

"Meet you in the lobby. I have a USIA roommate, of course, who snores."

"Of course. I'll be right over."

She hung up the phone and said, "Damn!" Obviously the congressmen's staff would be doubled up, so the United States Information Agency was interfering with the one night Lily might have had with Worth. The congressional party was scheduled to fly to Tel Aviv the next evening after another hectic scheduled day, and if the luck of the logistics didn't change before then, Lily would not see Worth alone.

As she sped across the empty, brightly lit streets of Tripoli in her father's Fiat, Lily tried to think of solutions and wondered whether she dared suggest them. Her asking for his room number had surprised her. She hadn't planned on it. Could she suggest that they take another room or go to another hotel, even though it was two-thirty in the morning? On the phone, he seemed as disappointed about the roommate as she was. Maybe he'd already taken another room.

She drove up to the hotel's main entrance and parked at the

curb. There was no doorman at that hour. Hurrying into the seedy, dim lobby, she saw Worth standing at the reception desk, still in his linen suit. When he caught sight of her, he smiled, then looked pointedly across the lobby at four Libyan men in suits. Surely they were members of one or another of the government's intelligence organizations, collectively known as the *mukhabarat*. They were sitting separately on sofas and chairs, trying to look as if they were idly passing the time. Worth walked toward her, holding out his arms. Lily did not hesitate to hurry into them. He held her briefly and said into her ear, "We are now a recorded couple."

"I don't think the *mukhabarat* arrests foreigners for this."

"No, but I'd just as soon get out of here."

"The car's outside," she suggested, still holding him.

He shook his head. "I'd say they'll follow us. I mean, what else do they have to do? Maybe if we take a walk, they'll give up."

"I doubt it, but let's try."

Hand in hand, they went out the glass doors and began walking down the street. When they looked back, two of the Libyans were following. They saw one signal to a car down the street, which pulled up behind Lily's car to pick up the two men.

"Damn," Worth said.

"You know, I don't care what they see," Lily stated quietly.

He took her into his arms and kissed her. Behind them, they heard the car stop and its doors open and close, but nothing mattered. A diesel truck roared by, and a motorcycle started up in the construction site across the street. Somewhere in the distance, the siren and bells of an emergency vehicle sounded, became louder, then was muffled in the motorcycle's whine. Still the couple kissed, speaking in phrases before they stopped each other with another kiss.

"Lily, I have a wake-up call in four hours."

"I know your schedule by heart."

"Can we go somewhere?"

"Yes."

"Is there another hotel around here?"

"Why not go back——?"

"I've already asked. It's full of Italians and American oil men who're trying to make deals with Qaddafi."

She pulled back to look at him. "You've already asked?"

"Yeah. I had hopes . . ."

Delighted, she kissed him again as the motorcycle passed by. "Come on," she said, leading him by the hand toward a hotel she knew of only a block and a half away. It wasn't a very good hotel, but it wouldn't be full. Ahead of them, the motorcycle stopped to let a passenger off, then sped into the dark. In the purple-tinted light of the street lamp, Lily saw the man's face for an instant before he turned to walk away. The shock weakened her knees and she stumbled.

"It's him." She gasped and impulsively started to run after him.

"Lily, wait!" Worth called and grabbed her wrist.

Conscious of nothing but the terrorist strolling away from her, Lily tried to pull loose. When she couldn't, she wound her other arm back, hit at Worth, and started running. He fell and yelled, which caused the man to turn. He saw her coming as well as Worth on his knees, trying to get up. Behind them, the car that had been idling in front of the hotel lurched into gear, tires screeching.

Lily saw the terrorist reach straight up into the air. She looked for a weapon in his hand, and rushed to grab his throat. His gesture distracted her; when she reached him, she was not able to stop. He ducked, gut-punched her, and let her body's impetus carry her over him, sending her sprawling onto the sidewalk. He looked down at her, smiled contemptuously, and ran down the street into the first alley, its high, narrow opening instantly blocking out any light from the street lamps.

Lily came up on her hands and knees. She couldn't breathe. The car roared up beside her and stopped. Three Libyans jumped out with automatic weapons drawn as Worth staggered to her and stooped down. Blood was pouring from his broken nose. In the car, the fourth Libyan was yelling into the car radio for reinforcements and an ambulance.

Gesturing in the direction of the alley, Lily gasped for air and shouted in Arabic, "Israeli terrorist—down that alley!" Still struggling for breath, she saw the confusion of Worth and the Libyans. She shouted, "Israeli terrorist! He got off the motorcycle. Jew! Jew! Don't you understand?"

Two of the Libyans ran into the street toward the alley. The third stood guard, surveying the street, as did the man in the car, who stepped out holding his own automatic weapon. Lily struggled to stand. Through the dark, a number of emergency vehicles approached. She started to move toward the street to follow the Libyans, but the man guarding her shoved her back. Worth grabbed her to cushion her fall. The Libyan moved in as if to make sure she didn't try to get up again.

"This is the daughter of the American chargé d'affaires," Worth said pointedly in Arabic. "I'm a special representative of the secretary of state. We request your assistance." He held out his diplomatic passport. This stopped the advance of the Libyan, who then exchanged brief glances with his colleague. He slid back into the car and began speaking again over the radio.

Lily saw Worth's bloody face as she tried to get up again. "I've got to go after him!"

"Lily, stop it!" Worth ordered, grabbing her wrists and pulling her down. "These guys aren't letting you go anywhere. And don't try to hit me again."

Military vehicles began to arrive from all directions. Two truckloads of troops in full battle gear pulled up in front of the hotel. The soldiers piled out and surrounded the building. The first cars stopped long enough to get directions to the alley, which they invaded, their spotlights and the strip lights on the roofs of the cars illuminating their way as even the noonday sun could not have done. In the street, military officers appeared through the glare of headlights and conferred quickly. One of them approached.

"Miss McCann," he said in heavily accented English, "you and your friend can please to step to the ambulance?"

Without taking her eyes from the alley's entrance, Lily let herself be led to a nearby ambulance. She held her hand over her solar plexus and limped on her left leg, but was not aware of pain. Hearing shouts from the alley, she watched the lights play over the buildings' balconied windows, most with their shutters closed. A Red Crescent nurse spoke to her. Her leg and right hand were bleeding, the skin scraped off from the fall on the street. The nurse sat her down in the side door of the ambulance. Behind her, lying on the stretcher, Worth spoke Arabic with a doctor who was examining his nose. Still watching the alley, Lily gradually began to hear what they were saying.

". . . so I can't spend much time with you, Doctor."

"It will have to be set. Otherwise—"

"Can't you stick it full of Novocain and do it here?"

"No."

"Well, you've got a little less than four hours."

Lily turned to look at him. The bleeding had stopped and another Red Crescent nurse had cleaned up his face. His suit, however, was blotched with blood all the way down to his knees.

"Worth," Lily said. "Oh, my god, I'm sorry."

He turned his head only far enough to see her and grimaced slightly. "The nose we can fix, but do you see what you've done to the suit?" He tried to smile, but the bleeding started again and he had to turn away as the nurse worked gingerly around his nose.

Another car arrived, moving slowly through the others, escorted by two Libyan soldiers on foot who explained its presence to those who questioned it. Lily saw the diplomatic plates, and recognized the embassy duty officer when he stepped into the headlights' glare. His name was Harris, she recalled. Her father liked him. He came directly to Lily and asked calmly, "Are you hurt?"

"I'm all right."

"Can you walk?"

"Yes."

"Your father's on his way to the embassy. I'm to take you there."

"No!" Lily said, standing up. "I have to stay here in case they catch him."

"Lily, you're in the middle of a very tricky situation," the officer said quietly but firmly. "I'm here to get you away, and I want you to come *now*."

"Lily, go," Worth called from the ambulance. "If it was your Israeli terrorist, what do you think he was doing around here, with an American delegation at the hotel?"

One of the Libyan officers who were listening came forward to speak to the embassy officer.

"When will I see you?" Lily said to Worth.

He gave a quick laugh and said, "I don't think it's our night, Lily. We'll make up for it. Now get out of here, will you?"

The duty officer took her by the arm to direct her to the car. To Worth he said, "Mr. Deloit, the consul general's on his way."

"I'd prefer a plastic surgeon."

As the embassy car backed through the trucks and military vehicles, one of the marines in the front seat radioed the embassy that their mission had been successful. Lily watched Worth in the dim light of the Red Crescent ambulance; just as the car turned, she leaned forward to look into the alley. It was lit from the dirt street to the top of the four-story buildings that formed it. Troop transport trucks were parked at its entrance. Shutters opened and people yelled at the soldiers who appeared at windows with bayoneted rifles, signaling down to their officers in the alley. Lily saw two soldiers shake their heads before pushing their way back into the buildings to continue their room-to-room search.

Sitting back in her seat as the car gained speed, Lily knew she'd done everything wrong, that the Israeli would get away again because she hadn't known what to do when she saw him. Why hadn't she told Worth and then followed the man, finding help somehow, and capturing him? Instead, she'd warned him, broken Worth's nose, and caused an incident that would probably embarrass her father.

At the embassy, Harris—she couldn't think of his first name—escorted her directly into the DCM's office. Her father was there with several officers of the embassy, including Jim Gage, the senior security officer, Art Randall, the political officer, Paul Howard, the CIA station chief, and one of the communications officers whose name Lily didn't know. They all stood and filed out quickly, some smiling a greeting to her, some not. Jake Streeter, the public affairs officer, wanted to say something as he always did, but thought better of it and gave her arm a squeeze instead. When they were alone, her father came around his desk to hug her.

"You're all right?" Bert asked.

Looking down, Lily saw that her hand and leg had been bandaged by the Red Crescent nurse, which she hadn't remembered.

"I'm fine, but Worth's hurt . . ."

"We have a doctor waiting for him at the hospital, trained in London. What happened? Did the fellow you were chasing hit him?"

"No. I did."

Bert took a step backward in reaction. "Not knowing any details, I can only be intrigued. When the security people talk to you, I think you can safely keep that particular fact to yourself, unless you are asked directly. Now come sit down. We have to work quickly, because the Libyans are worried that someone may be trying to hurt their American guests. Apparently you told them the man you saw was an Israeli terrorist. Was he the one in Amman?"

"Yes."

"You're sure," Bert pressed.

"Positive. There isn't a face in the world I know that well."

"We've already notified Washington to send the composite you worked up with the Jordanians. They'll want you to update . . ."

Seated across from Bert at his desk, she looked distractedly around the office as he talked.

"What's the matter?" Bert asked.

"I called him a Jew."

"Isn't that appropriate?"

"The Libyan agents wouldn't go after him, so I called him Jew, Jew, knowing it would make them hurry. I played on it."

Bert paused, then said, "I don't think your labeling the man, whatever he is, Jew or Methodist, can be construed as a prejudice, my darling. You have a certain justification, which anyone would understand, probably better than you can. You have a tendency to find fault with yourself about that incident. You needn't, I assure you. We'll talk later. Right now, I have to let Jim and Paul back in here—if you think you're up to it."

She nodded. Bert rose to open the office door. When the security officer came in, he said to Bert, "Just heard from Washington. They concur with the Libyans."

Bert nodded and explained to Lily. "It seems that Colonel Qaddafi is anxious about the possibility of congressional blood on his sand. The Libyans have suggested that the party be sent on to Tel Aviv later this morning."

Lily suddenly felt exhausted. "When can I see Worth?"

Bert smiled diplomatically. "We'll go to the airport to see them off. Now I'll go get us some coffee."

Throughout the interview, Lily fought fatigue. She liked the CIA chief and the head of security, and they were considerate of her. The embassy doctor appeared and looked her over. She drank coffee with aspirin for the pain in her ribs and the headache that had developed. During the questioning, which took place in an alcove of the office, Lily overheard her father and Art Randall arranging for the congressional party's departure and its early arrival in Tel Aviv. At one point, Bert interrupted Lily's interview to say, "We've just heard from the hospital. Mr. Deloit is doing well and sends his regards to you."

"May I go there?" Lily asked.

"We'll see him at the airport," her father replied. "I promise."

When the questioning was over, Lily was told to rest on the couch; there wasn't time for her to return to the apartment. A staff assistant arrived with a change of clothes. She tried to sleep, but in spite of an aching fatigue, she could only lie with her eyes closed, asking herself questions that she knew couldn't be answered. What was the Israeli doing in the construction site across from the hotel? She'd overheard Art Randall saying the Libyans were already searching the area. Were the terrorist and some accomplices planning an assassination of the Americans to embarrass Qaddafi, to further enrage the United States and solidify its support of Israel? Why wasn't he armed; if he was, why didn't he kill me? And why did he get off the motorcycle at that particular spot, barely a block away from the hotel where the American party was staying? Was it by chance? Did he know there was security there? And in response to my bungled attack, what would he do to me now?

Her father stood above her. "Lily, it's time to go to the airport."

In the back seat of the limousine, father and daughter sat silently. Although he had displayed his usual ease with the embassy staff and courtesy to doormen and drivers during the crisis, Bert seemed distracted. Nevertheless, when they reached the perimeter of the military airbase where the United States Air Force plane was parked in a remote area, he snapped on his diplomatic mask, ready for all eventualities.

As they stepped out onto the tarmac, the string of limousines carrying the congressmen and their staffs arrived, along with ten Libyan armored vehicles serving as their escort. The congressmen, looking grim, offered Bert little thanks and perfunctory goodbyes before hurrying aboard the plane. Lily stayed close to the embassy car, almost crouching beside it.

From another direction an ambulance streaked across one of the airbase's runways. It stopped near the tail of the plane where the staff members were overseeing the loading of the luggage. Worth jumped out of the front seat, wearing a clean suit, and was greeted with a cheer from his colleagues. On his face was a T-shaped metal brace. The crossbar was taped to his forehead, the vertical taped over his nose. He acknowledged his reception with an airy wave and a rejoinder that Lily couldn't hear but that made the other staff members laugh. Then he saw her standing alone near the limousine and walked toward her.

They hesitated to embrace, both sensing the formality of the occasion. She saw that both of his eyes were black and blue. He reached out and they shook hands, but held on as they spoke.

"And so we bid goodbye to beautiful Tripoli," he said.

"Will you be all right?"

"The doctor said I could have either a Nasser nose or a Golda Meir nose. I went with hers."

"I'm so sorry. About everything."

"Don't be. The State Department thinks I'm a hero. They'll give me a Purple Heart or something. Did you tell anyone that it was you who hit me?"

"Just Daddy. Nobody else asked."

"Terrific. I'll make up some impressive stories. How are you doing?"

"Fine," she said shakily.

"Promise?"

He stepped forward and gingerly kissed her. As gentle as it had to be, they held to each other's lips a long time, until a staffer called from the plane.

"That's not much of a kiss," Worth said, still holding her. "Will you just consider it done, as well as anything else you want to imagine might have happened last night?"

"I can't stand this. Where are you staying in Tel Aviv?"

The staffer called again; Worth waved at him and turned back to Lily. "You have my address in Guilford?"

"Yes."

"Write to me. Come early if you want to. Yes. That's it. I mean it." He held her hand a moment longer, then hurried to the loading steps. Bert was there, having bade farewell to the congressmen and staff. The two men shook hands, exchanged a few words, and laughed. Then Worth hustled up the steps and was gone. Immediately the steps were rolled away, and the first jet engine began to whine. The many vehicles around the plane began to move out of the way as Bert helped Lily into the limousine. The driver shut the door behind them and ran to his place to start the car.

"It seems that Mr. Deloit will survive," Bert said.

"I'm going to marry him."

"Good gracious! I wouldn't have suspected he'd just proposed."

"He didn't," Lily said, without smiling. "I just know. I'm not sure when, and it won't be easy getting there or staying there. But we'll be married one day."

FOUR

THREE WEEKS LATER, Lily returned to the apartment to meet her father. In the mail was a notification from Yale. Based on her academic record, her scholarship had been expanded to cover just about all her expenses. No more University Dining Hall! She was sure that Worth had made it happen, and, in her euphoria, she called the embassy's travel coordinator to arrange for her return to the United States a week before classes began.

When Bert didn't arrive for tea, Lily called the embassy to make sure he was still there and left a message saying that she was on her way. After folding the letter from Yale into her shoulder bag, she left the apartment. For the first time since the incident with the terrorist, she chose to walk, and found herself full of fantasy about accepting Worth's invitation. Only twice did she stop to check a doorway or watch a group of people at a bus stop.

At the embassy, she hurried out of the elevator on the third floor into the reception area. The ambassador's office, empty at the moment, was to one side, the DCM's office to the other. The door opened, and Art Randall, on seeing her, gave a sweeping bow: "Please enter the sanctum of the future desk officer for the Middle East in London." He gazed at her to note her reaction.

"London?" Lily repeated. She walked into the office, where she saw her father leaning back against his desk with a drink in his hand, his diplomatic face in place but looking slightly skewed. "London?" she asked.

Before Bert could answer, the CIA station chief Paul Howard, who was sitting on a couch with the FSO named Harris, said, "Yes, if we can convince him not to tell Personnel and the secretary to sink into the Foggy Bottom in which our current Department of

State wallows." Jim Gage was there, as were Mr. Dorton, the head of the AID program, and Jake Streeter, who jumped up to offer Lily his chair. Lily noticed the three-quarters-empty bottle of bourbon on the coffee table.

"This started out as a celebration, Lily," Art Randall said as he ambled over to a leather chair by the window.

"This embassy is as leaky as the Tripoli sewer," Bert said. "I'm having Jim give you all lie detector tests to see how this vitally unimportant news swept through the halls of the place within an hour of its arrival."

"Are you going to London?" Lily asked, aware of her father's well-covered disappointment.

"No," Bert said quietly. "That's what they offered. I plan to turn them down."

As they faced each other, there was a chorus of disagreement around the room.

"Don't do it, Bert," Jake Streeter said. A usually quiet man with a penchant for bow ties so small that they seemed mere knots of paisley, the public affairs officer spoke with a tipsy fervor. "London's a great place to be."

"Have tea every afternoon at Brown's Hotel," Harris added.

"And you can be fitted for that beautiful suit," Randall rumbled; "you know, the one you'll be buried in. I'd suggest dark blue, pinstripe of course."

Streeter abruptly thrust his glass before him. "Here's to General Dan Sickles, the only foreign service officer who got out with appropriate style."

"Who the hell was he?" someone asked.

"The great one-legged hero of the Civil War; became our ambassador to Spain," Streeter proclaimed, warming to his subject. "His love of conflict drove him to help start a revolution against the king. When he was declared persona non grata, he withdrew to Paris, where he continued his flagrant affair with the recently deposed nymphomaniac Spanish queen."

There was laughter, and the men glanced at Lily, who said, "Should we amputate the left or the right one, Daddy?" He kissed her on the forehead as the others laughed and the bottle was passed.

"How did this happen?" Harris asked seriously.

Seeing his concern, Bert answered succinctly. "No one in the Department of State likes to have a senator on the Foreign Relations Committee breathing fire down his neck. I obviously displeased one such senator."

"Let's get out of here," Jim Gage suggested, "so Lily can talk some sense into that aging head over there."

The men finished their drinks, several offering last words of advice, and filed out of the office. Harris held back and asked, "What are you going to do?"

Bert stood up from the desk he'd been leaning against. With a glance at Lily, he answered, "I'm going to demand, as one demands —pleasantly—a post in the NEA field at any rank, my hope being that such dedication will shame them into giving me, if not exactly what I want, then at least something interesting to do."

Harris nodded, but clearly was disturbed. "How can they do this? You're one of the best people out here. Everybody knows it."

"For the benefit of your career," Bert said as he walked Harris to the door, "that's an opinion I urge you to keep to yourself. But I'm grateful for it." Harris smiled but left the office shaking his head.

"That's why we're starting to lose our best people," Bert said after he closed the door. "They see the diplomatic future and it's too short and too crowded."

"What if Foggy Bottom turns you down?" Lily asked pointedly as her father returned to his desk and searched for something.

"Perhaps I'll go live on the dahabeah and become a dragoman at the Egyptian Museum for intrepid blue-haired ladies."

"Daddy, don't try to defuse me. What will you do?"

He sat back in his chair. "I won't go to London, not out of spite or bitterness, but because I'm not needed there. If I can't really serve for the last couple of years I have, then I don't want to be thrown the fish of London. I joined the Foreign Service a long time ago with the perfectly respectable idea of service, and I've been bound to serve ever since. I don't want to end my work in London; I know and they know that's a placement just to keep me comfortably out of trouble. No. No." He spied what he'd been looking for, an envelope, and handed it across the desk to her. "The travel coordinator dropped this off a little while ago."

Seeing by his professionally neutral but attentive expression that he already had concluded what the plane ticket meant, she opened her bag and handed him the letter from Yale. "I'll trade you."

She watched while he read it. A smile spread and his eyes blinked rapidly behind his glasses. He looked at her. "I'm very proud of you," he said, his voice wavering.

"Well," she said, "I have to admit that Worth Deloit probably had a lot to do with it."

"I doubt it. The scholarship committee isn't that easily manipulated. I think you can give yourself the credit."

"I'll try."

"We must celebrate." He stood and came around the desk. "Where are we supposed to appear tonight, do you remember?"

"I forget their names. He's the head of the concrete factories."

"Ah, at the Salmans'." He took her arm. "They'll have champagne, I'm sure . . ."

"Daddy, I thought I'd go back a week early."

"I see," he said without breaking stride to the door.

"I'll be staying with Worth."

"Um-hmm" was his only response except for a slight hesitation before he turned the knob.

"Wait, Daddy." She held the door shut. "I don't have to go if you'd rather have me here. I called for the ticket before I knew about London."

"No, no, that's not it at all," he replied, shaking his head. "How can one be a diplomat with a daughter?" He sighed hopelessly and laughed at himself. "I was using all my skills to keep from grabbing you and saying, 'Is he good enough for you? Will he be kind to you?'—all those questions that fathers drive themselves crazy with, heightened in my case by certain traditions of my youth, like virginity until marriage and, until after the ceremony, dire secrecy about any physical contact above the elbow."

Lily laughed and kissed her father on the cheek. "He's an amazing man. I'll be fine."

He smiled affectionately but, as Lily noted, without agreement. " 'Amazing' is not a quality that reassures fathers," he said and led her out the door.

Worth rolled over and propped himself up on his elbow. Lily didn't move to cover herself. Behind him the light flowed unevenly through the several original glass panes remaining in the twelve-on-twelve windows, refracting sunbeams into occasional rainbow spots on the sheets and walls of his bedroom.

"Worth?"

"Um?"

"I love you." She'd never said it before, and so she said it again. "I love you."

Once again, his eyes went over her body as if he were memorizing it. "Not counting your time as my tutor," he said, "we've spent about three days together."

"I know. Just think how I'll feel next month."

"By then you'll know me better and may hate my guts."

"You're warning me again. You do that a lot."

He moved over to her and kissed her. She wanted him again and put her leg around him to let him know. Her original diffidence and their combined ardor had given way to a languorous intimacy, and they made love again taking more time with each other, exchanging smiles and sounds for pleasures given and received.

"There aren't any neighbors," he said. "You can make as much noise as you like."

Lily was embarrassed by how much she made, but it seemed to delight Worth, who always noted the cause of her pleasure and repeated it until again they both lay motionless, sweating and gasping for breath.

"I really like this," Lily said slyly.

"As much as you thought you would?"

"It must be better with you."

She turned over and looked around the room. She was delighted with the two-hundred-year-old salt-box house. There was a warm, easy comfort among the Shaker furniture, Japanese electronics, and photorealism paintings with which Worth had filled the rooms, displaying surprisingly good taste with the eclectic mix. In the two days she'd been there, he'd revealed himself to be ever meticulous, restlessly moving an old pitcher back and forth to find its exact spot on a hall table, rewiring a speaker so that the angle of sound in a room would be better, fretting over a crack in the study's plaster-and-lath walls not yet spackled and painted by the caretaker.

"How the hell did you stay a virgin through the sixties?" he asked.

"I moved a lot, and in the Middle East, the sixties was about Nasser, not free love and pot."

She reached up and ran her fingers delicately over his nose. There were still traces of discoloring, but otherwise it seemed completely healed. "I think I did you a favor," Lily said. "It looks *much* better."

He laughed and kissed her. "Are you still worried about that guy?" he asked.

"Yes. Actually fighting with him—not that I scored any points—made him less a phantom, brought him down to human scale. No nightmares, either. But I don't think I'll ever stop being afraid of him."

"Did they ever figure out what he was doing there that night?"

"Just theories. The Libyans found explosives and Uzis in a construction shack and, as expected, accused Israel of planning an assassination attempt on the congressmen. But our intelligence people don't believe that; they think the Israelis were there stockpiling for the future. Qaddafi seems to want to get under Nasser's cape, and who knows when the Israelis might want to do something about him. Of course, Israel denies the whole thing, and Qaddafi went a little crazy."

Worth grunted a laugh. "How well I know," he said. "Did your father tell you about my memcon?"

"My father is very discreet."

He propped himself up on his elbow again and gazed out the window. "Well, it's no big secret now. The Foreign Relations Committee discussed the meeting I translated with Qaddafi in open hearings, and nobody paid much attention, though I understand your father sent my little note on the subject as a FLASH cable, which got it a lot more attention than I'd ever hoped for. It was passed up to the secretary of state, who sent it over to Henry Kissinger at the White House."

"Oh, well, if Henry knows, you can tell me about it, can't you?"

He glanced at her and acknowledged the sarcasm. "In our meeting, Qaddafi wanted to know what the U.S. would do if Libya helped the Palestinians in Jordan overthrow King Hussein."

Lily sat up. "That's incredible. What'd the senator say?"

"He was pretty good. Said he could speak only as a senator and not for the president, but that in his opinion, if there were a threat that the Palestinians would take over Jordan, Israel would be forced to declare war. And the United States would back Israel to whatever degree was necessary."

"What'd Qaddafi say?"

"Nothing. He nodded once. But I think he was pretty angry. Like every other Arab, he hates having foreigners telling him what he can and can't do. This guy sees himself as anointed by Allah, coming out of the desert with the flaming sword of Islam. He's got the charisma but not the smarts to carry it off. I'd say he's dangerous as hell, though at the moment, everyone seems charmed by his calm revolution and the amiable way he's taken over the oil companies and sent the American military home. I think he's got a warped sense of himself on the world stage, and that, together with all his oil money, makes him a real threat."

"Did you put all that in your memcon?"

"All that and more. Just to cover a few more bases, I slipped in a prediction that the PLO would start a civil war in Jordan against King Hussein this fall."

Lily studied Worth as he lay there, smiling his self-satisfaction, his body glowing in the sunlight. "What if it doesn't happen?" she asked. "What will Henry think?"

"Nothing," he said. "Do you have any idea how many cables and memcons and documents and papers come into Foggy Bottom every day? Hundreds of thousands of words, and how many of those get to the secretary and to Henry the K? Fifty? A hundred? And how many of those register? Maybe three sentences? For sure, Henry doesn't remember my memcon now, but when the civil war starts in Jordan, I'll bet he'll have his minions look it up. And if the war doesn't start, what have I lost? I mean, if you don't tell people how smart you are, who's going to know?" He laughed at himself, but Lily saw how much he believed what he'd just said. "The thing is, you have to be careful if you're smart, because most people in Washington want to avoid dealing with intelligence.

When they have to, they're suspicious of it, not knowing when it'll be used against them."

"It sounds as if you've given the process a lot of thought."

He reacted too quickly, just a flick of the head with a look of resentment, as if she had assumed something about him without his permission.

"Not really," he said, but Lily didn't believe him.

———

"Do you think you'd want to come down to Washington with me?" Worth asked Lily one night in December. They had planned her first ski trip to Stowe that weekend, but there was no snow, so they decided to spend the time working and studying together at his house in Guilford. As they unpacked groceries in the modern kitchen, hidden though most of it was behind paneling made of ancient chestnut floorboards salvaged from a house that had been torn down, Worth lobbed bread, lettuce, and cheese to Lily across the room.

"When would we go?" she asked, already doubtful.

The couple had several rules—never cut a class; work comes before each other; and school nights are spent in separate dwellings, she in the room she shared with Mimi Peters at Branford, he at the house in Guilford. The weekends were theirs, and they spent them together without exception.

They went to art galleries in SoHo and to the theater on Broadway, to tailgate parties and football games at the Yale Bowl, to museums and concerts in Boston, and to good restaurants anywhere within a radius of a hundred miles. They sailed as often as time and weather permitted, until rough seas set in and they battened down the sloop for the winter. Their time was planned for maximum joy and usually featured an American tradition. As the autumn weeks passed, Lily had given in happily to her seduction.

"I have an appointment a week from Thursday. I thought we'd take the shuttle down the night before, have dinner with some friends I'd like you to meet, and fly back late the next day."

"I have four classes on Thursdays," she said regretfully.

He stopped throwing things to her and carried croissants and baguettes to the crisper. "This might be too good to miss," he said. "The appointment's with Dr. Kissinger."

"He read your memcon?"

"*And* my book. Thinks I'm brilliant." He laughed and flipped the crisper closed.

As Worth had predicted, the civil war in Jordan had broken out in full force the previous September. King Hussein called on his Bedouin army to drive the seventy thousand Palestinian guerrillas, the *fedayeen,* out of Amman. During the nine-day conflict, forever to be known as Black September, Syrian and Iraqi troops moved across the northern border, ostensibly to help the PLO, but pulled back when Israel threatened to intervene and the United States alerted the Sixth Fleet. Two weeks later, while hammering out a settlement between the two warring parties, President Nasser of Egypt died of a heart attack, at the age of fifty-two. Since then, the Middle East had been in turmoil.

"I think this trip's for you," Lily said, smiling proudly at him, "but not for me."

"I think it's for us," he said, standing still for a moment in front of the refrigerator, looking at her for emphasis.

"What's that mean?"

"It's quite simple. This could be an important trip. I'd like us to go together."

"I'm missing something. Why exactly is this so important?"

"I suspect you know, or at least have an idea."

Lily put down a package of smoked salmon on the counter, then leaned back on it. "Are you telling me there may be a big change of scene around here?"

"You see, you did know."

"No, not really. I suppose that somewhere I figured Washington would be a natural for you."

"Washington isn't natural for anybody. It's just that they've been after me for years to go down there in one capacity or another. But nobody in his right mind goes without having his own horse in place, somebody who has enough power to take you along on the fast track if you can keep up with him."

"And Kissinger's the horse."

"I'd say that Henry Kissinger is going to run American foreign policy for the next six years, and influence it even longer."

"He's not the secretary of state."

"Yet. Wait until Nixon's second term. But even now he has the president's ear; his office is the best you can get in the West Wing, nice and close to the Oval Office. Proximity, not title, is what counts in Washington. A title gets you a good parking space; proximity gets you power—and a better parking space."

"What Henry whispered in that ear was to bomb Cambodia. That's a dangerous horse."

He sighed. "Please spare me the current fashionable rhetoric. The fact is that Henry Kissinger has taken the National Security Council and has turned it into *the* place where foreign policy is being made. When he came in, there was a staff of thirteen. Now there're more than a hundred and fifty. The guy goes all over the world meeting foreign leaders—"

"He sure does," Lily interrupted. "So why should a foreign leader deal with a mere ambassador when he can talk to Henry the K, who speaks into the president's ear? My father's heard a lot about Henry's fast visits. Aside from snubbing the local American diplomats, he's outrageously rude and treats them like gofers."

"Lily, the man's going to change the world."

"For better or worse?"

"If you could think for yourself and not through your father's time warp . . ."

"And if you weren't so hot to get on the fast track . . ."

They stood across the kitchen from each other, his hands jammed into his pockets, her arms crossed in front of her.

"It seems we're having a fight," he said in a superciliously calm voice, which only irritated Lily further.

"Over Henry Kissinger," she said with distaste. "And don't fight dirty by bringing my father into it."

"I believe you did that," he responded even more calmly.

Lily had the intense feeling that he was waiting, like a matador sighting down his sword, for her to charge. "If it goes well for you in Washington, what do you hope will happen?" she asked, determined not to lose her temper any further. She stepped over to wash a pair of potatoes in the sink, her back to him.

Opening the refrigerator door, he put lettuce and yogurt inside. "If all goes well, I'll go into the Foreign Service, and with any luck at all, I'll be an ambassador in ten years. After that, who knows?

Maybe national security adviser, what the hell, maybe even secretary of state. That depends on the politics and power at the time." After taking out a bottle of wine, he closed the refrigerator door.

"That's pretty ambitious."

"Yes, and presumptuous as hell, but not unreasonable."

"Ten years for ambassador? Most take their whole careers to get there, if at all."

"It's possible these days, particularly if you go into the NEA Bureau with any expertise. In that little Arab area, there'll always be the Israeli threat, and the conflict will keep bubbling over. That means fast-shifting sands, diplomatic hot seats, quick little wars. There are thousands of Russian experts, but relatively few Arabists. Fewer frogs at the oasis."

Piercing the potatoes with a fork, Lily asked off-handedly, "And once you get there—ambassador, secretary, whatever—what do you want to do with it?"

He chuckled as he uncorked the Chardonnay. "Live a privileged life, be worshipped by my slavish staff, and have my humble words change the course of world history."

She had to laugh as he handed her a wine glass and poured. "But, Worth, isn't there just a little sense of service in there somewhere?"

Pouring into his own glass, he hesitated, then finished and raised the glass to her. "You are your father's daughter," he said, clinked his glass on hers, and drank.

And you're a son of a bitch, she thought but didn't say, and didn't drink either.

"That day in Tripoli when I interpreted the meeting with Qaddafi," he continued, "that's when I knew I couldn't stay comfortable and easy in academe anymore. I really wanted Qaddafi to talk to me. I knew more than the senator, and I could have learned more from Qaddafi. I *knew* I could have. I want to be in place to have the conversations that affect the world. Simple as that. Even the senator probably convinced Qaddafi not to join the PLO in Jordan, but I'll bet I would have found out something about his plans. That's why I'm in a hurry. The best way to serve any system is to go as fast and as high as possible in that system so that you end up with the time and clout to improve it."

"What about Yale?"

"My department's been on notice ever since I took the Foreign Service exams three years ago. The results are valid for four. I can leave at the end of the semester." Hoisting himself up to sit on a counter, he poured more wine into his almost full glass. "I suppose the other question you may have is, what about us?"

"Any ideas?"

"I plan to find a house in Georgetown, and Georgetown University has a damn good law school. Unless you're devoted to dorm living, we could live together." Pleased with the plan, he peered over his wine glass for her reaction as he drank.

"What about this house?"

"I'll sell it."

Tears came into her eyes and she turned away.

"What is it?" he asked, confused.

"Nothing," she replied, finally taking a large swallow of wine.

"Lily," he said sensitively, "it just isn't appropriate for us to get married right—"

"Worth, that's not it." She began to laugh and wiped the tears away with her hand. "My god, not that at all. It's always hard for me to give up a house I love; that's all."

"Maybe we'll look around for another one when we're in Washington."

She put her glass on the counter and tore off a paper towel to blow her nose. "I'm not going to go, Worth. That better be your party. I'm not sure I'd be any good at it."

"What's that supposed to mean? Look, I called Brownell Spalding today, a Yale classmate, does corporate law for Covington, which of course means lobbying. He's lived down there all his life. His mother's old Philadelphia money, father's in the World Bank. The Spaldings know everybody, and B is going to invite some heavyweight dips and Israeli lobbyists to dinner, beautiful house on Kalorama Circle." He checked her for a response. "Lily, you ought to come. No matter what you do, or how well you do it, the right people make the big difference."

She nodded slowly. "Yes, probably." Again conscious of her anger, she tried to laugh. "I think I've lived in the desert too long. I don't want the right people to make the big difference. And I really don't want to go to law school at Georgetown. As a matter of fact, I've applied for a scholarship to study international law for a year in Paris."

"Really," he said, matching her casual tone. "When did you do that?"

"A couple of weeks ago."

"A secret?"

"Not at all. It's a long shot. I didn't see any point in talking about it until I knew something. I was thinking that maybe if you took a sabbatical, you could have come with me." She smiled at the irony.

"Once again, you're selling yourself short," he said. "I suggest that you'll get anything you apply for, including Harvard Law or Yale, Stanford, wherever. I think the idea of doing a year in international law before you go is brilliant." He smiled and reached for her as if nothing had changed. "It's just that now I'm going to have to figure out how to get to Paris between stamping visas at some sand-blasted consulate."

She embraced him, but Lily felt that their bodies didn't fit together as they had. It was probably anger, she thought, hers for what she regarded as his purely self-aggrandizing motivation for a career, his for her not agreeing to do what he wanted. He wasn't used to having anyone oppose him, and Lily had a sense that sooner or later she'd be punished for it. What bothered her most, however, was his instant acceptance of the distant geography. As soon as she'd mentioned far-off Paris, he adjusted to her future absence from his life and was already making other plans to find a small place for her.

Purposefully they made love on a favorite sofa seat built into a gabled window, then put dinner together, studied, and went to bed, with no further mention of the different circumstances in which they found themselves. As the weekend passed, they made winter plans, to go skiing in Stowe over the George Washington Birthday weekend, to visit a display of conceptual art in a New York gallery, even to schedule her commuting down to Washington on weekends. But the unknown made intention hollow, and dates were set with a surface enthusiasm but no certainty.

FIVE

WORTH, I'm not going to be able to make it this weekend."

During the time he took to respond, the wind whipped sleet against the glass of the phone booth. It was dark, and all that Lily could see were highlights of dirty plowed snow on High Street in the glare of passing headlights.

"Really?" he said with no hint of understanding. "Well, listen, I'm going to have to take someone to the dinner Saturday night. It's seated, and I can't throw my hostess a curve at the last minute."

Another warning. There had been many over the months since Worth moved to Washington.

"I'm really sorry. It's just that I have two papers, and—"

"Hey, you're talking to your former professor. First things first; I know that."

She waited, hoping for some expression of regret on his part, which didn't come. Having taken off a glove to dial his number, she struggled to get her fingers covered again while she cradled the phone on her shoulder. "How are you? How are things at the Foreign Service Institute?" The questions were small talk and she knew it. So did he.

"Pretty boring, to tell the truth. And kind of ridiculous. Economic-Commercial Studies, our big course, is taking twenty-six weeks to make us into little accountants. Then there's Negotiations in one week and Human Rights in three—count 'em—three *days*. Gives you an idea of the priorities of American foreign policy. And movies! The Area Studies courses are all movies. 'And as our boat sinks slowly in the West, we see the threat of Communist infiltration along the honey-colored beaches of Mogadishu.' " He laughed hollowly.

Lily could barely feel her feet and stamped them on the metal floor of the phone booth. She knew he was sitting in the small paneled den of the house he'd bought on O Street. Probably there was a cozy fire.

"How's the house coming?" she asked. He had not had the time or inclination to furnish it himself. The studied formality of the Early American antiques that had come from Worth's family attic was a responsibility given to a decorator who was well liked by Worth's numerous friends in Washington. The kitchen became an efficient factory, and exquisite dinner parties took place in the dining room, where there was a set of ten Sheraton ladderback chairs around an oval Queen Anne table. The Austin-Healy was replaced by a diplomatically black Mercedes, which was garaged on the first-floor level next to the living room. Although the house was on a quiet street, the traffic noise and ambulance sirens of Wisconsin Avenue were a steady disturbance through the night, unlike the rural quiet of Guilford.

"It's one room at a time now. Mother's atticful of stuff finally arrived, just after the floors were refinished. But you were here for that, weren't you?"

"Yes, Worth, I was there."

"What's the matter?"

"Stop being so casual. Of course I was there. I helped move everything from the upstairs to the downstairs, remember? I'm sure you do. Listen, I'm ten times sorrier than you are that I can't be there this weekend, but don't punish me for it. I have to do my work. I don't know what they can teach you in a week about negotiations, but acting as if you don't give a damn is a lousy technique."

"What are we negotiating?" he asked coolly.

Lily kicked angrily at the side of the phone booth, which hurt, meaning that her foot wasn't frozen. Outside, several fast-moving pedestrians bent into the wind, the sleet accumulating on their parkas and watch caps. "I suppose we're negotiating a few more crooked boundaries of this particular long-distance relationship," she said patiently, hoping to sound reasonable rather than snide.

"Lily, we sure as hell don't need boundaries. You're welcome here any time you can get down. When you can't, I miss you. It's as simple as that, unpleasant though it may be for both of us."

"It's awful," she said, hoping her agreement would make them sharers of a common regret. "And completely unreal. When we're apart, I plan the absolute perfection of our next weekend so that anything less is a bummer. When we do get together, it's all so heightened—with time pressures and needs for enough wonderfulness to last until the next time—that we can't really have a normal conversation, which we then try to have with these phone chats that become a kind of tense little ritual. Don't they?"

She waited, noticing her breath had fogged most of the windows around her.

"What do you want, Lily?" he asked, with no impatience, with even a hint of genuine concern.

"I don't know. I suppose somewhere lurking in my mind is the fantasy that you'll come up here some weekend. I've hustled down there five times already this winter."

Lily had never liked Washington. When she lived there, as a child, during her father's occasional home postings, she had always felt like a stranger, if not a foreigner. In the schools she was sent to, which she inevitably left before summer, she was shunned by the cliques of children who had known each other for years. To her, Washington was a lonely place, much like an airport where people hurried to come or go while having intense conversations before the next plane departed. She'd made few friends; most of them, like her, were the daughters of diplomats, and she had never seen them again.

"Unfortunately," Worth replied, "what I'm about down here isn't limited to the classroom. The weekends are when I can best cast my pearls around. I'll soon be sent off to some desert consulate, so I have to make enough of an impression here in the sties of power to be remembered. By the way, the wish list came through last week for us to choose our first posting. I decided, based on your reports, to shoot for Cairo. It's only three hours from Paris, by the way."

The operator came on. "Please deposit a dollar and ten cents for another three minutes."

"Oh, God, Worth, I don't have—"

"What's your number? I'll call you back."

"No. I'm freezing. I'll call you on Saturday."

"Please deposit . . ."

"Make it the afternoon; I'm playing squash—"

They were disconnected. Lily hung up and slid open the squeaky door to be met with an icy blast of sleet. She hunched down against it and, carrying her book bag over her shoulder, hurried to York Street and turned the corner heading for the Sterling Library. He had said he missed her, and that was the straw she clutched. The rest was facts and frustration. His dedication to his weekend activities, apparently his most serious course of study, infuriated her.

Seated at the head of the table opposite Worth, she had acted as hostess on those Saturday nights when she was in residence. But she was as much a guest as the others. They were inevitably involved in foreign affairs, as journalists, State Department people, Worth's Foreign Service Institute classmates, or staffers from the Hill or White House. Worth had found a caterer who planned, prepared, and served the entire evening from pheasant consommé to Montecristos and Calvados. Lily's French and Arabic seemed to impress the others, and she often noticed Worth proudly looking down the table at her, giving her an intimate smile, then turning back to the conversation at left or right hand.

Those looks were what she thought of in New Haven when she recalled their weekends. More than their time alone, either talking over breakfast or making love, those glances in public through candlelight and cigar smoke seemed to be the most intense and clear statements of his love for her. Their conversations were about who was who in Washington, struggles with studies, and the logistics of finding time to be together. When she was there, Lily inevitably found Worth in the middle of his aggressive social routine, surrounded by his classmates, who were bound by their common experience of having survived the Foreign Service entrance exams, tolerating the boredom of the Institute, and sharing the anxiety about Personnel, which would soon decide their immediate futures. In spite of the group's obvious appreciation of her, Lily felt like an outsider all over again.

She gave in to the jealousy of wondering who would be sitting in her place at dinner on Saturday night, and how long the evening would last. At least she wouldn't have to do her hair. She'd been wearing it in a massed lion's mane, which took a long time to prepare. Instead, she would be typing a paper that night on "The Linguistics of Despair: The Language of Law in Vichy France." How appropriate, she thought.

––––––––

At the agreed-upon time on Thursday, one of three routine appointments the two lovers had established during the week when she would call the O Street house and he would make every effort to be there, Lily hurried to the familiar phone booth around the block from the library. It was a beautiful spring morning, early enough for her to catch Worth at his breakfast before he drove over the Key Bridge to the Institute, in Roslyn, Virginia. Their Thursday conversations usually had to do with the confirmation of their weekend plans.

"Hello," he said with his usual morning determination to get the day started.

"I have some news," she offered with no preliminaries.

"So do I. Tell me yours first."

"Paris. I got the scholarship to study international law."

There was a pause before he said, "Rabat," with no indication of his reaction.

Lily was wary. "Are you pleased? Should I say congratulations?"

"It's not exactly Cairo, is it?" he said acidly. "Those bastards in Personnel decided to cut me down to their puny size; want to see whether I can swallow my pride and serve with the requisite humility. It's so damn boring, their silly psychology."

"I'm sorry, Worth. But it's only for a year, isn't it? What's your position there?"

"Vice Consul."

"My god, Worth, that's not so bad, and Morocco's pretty good. You'll show them what you can do. Vice consul postings are on the ambassadorial track; you know that. Administrative experience and all that."

" 'And all that,' " he repeated bitterly, and for a moment Lily thought his disappointment was turning on her. "Well, speaking of all that, I'm afraid our weekend plans are shot. Can you come next weekend instead? It looks as if it'll be my last one."

The relief that Paris had offered Lily suddenly collapsed into her missing him intensely. "That's pretty fast, isn't it?"

"The vacancy came up. God knows I'm ready to get out of here."

He didn't go on. There was an awkward silence.

"Yes, sure," Lily said. "I'll come down a week from tomorrow. What's happening this weekend?"

"Three of us are assigned to Morocco. There's a visiting scholar at the Institute from Rabat who knows the scene and can bring us up to grade with the Arabic they speak there. We're taking him off to the Greenbrier for the weekend. Will you call me Monday?"

"Yes, of course. I'll miss you. And remember, Cairo this summer. Will you be able to take a leave? Daddy's leave starts in July, so we'll be there—"

"Why do you think I wanted to be in Cairo?" he asked, sounding irritated again—Lily hoped not with her. "There'll be a day when I'll remember those bastards in Personnel. Call me Monday. I'll miss you, too. Oh, and congratulations about Paris. I never doubted you'd get it."

"Thanks."

"Goodbye, Lily."

"Goodbye."

She hung up and stood with her hand on the phone for a moment, not willing to let it go. Then she left the booth and walked back to the library, oblivious of the day, disappointed about the weekend, and feeling more uncertain about Worth Deloit than she had ever been. Trying to distract herself, she thought of her scholarship, Paris, international law—living with her mother, another problem she didn't want to consider.

She'd done all of her homework in anticipation of being away for the weekend. Mimi planned to visit her parents in Manhattan, so the room would be empty. Because she was away from campus so much, Lily had not involved herself in any extracurricular activities. She thought of taking the train into New York, and remembered there was a concert of some sort at Woolsey Hall. More and more depressed, she was crossing the library lobby when she thought of the sloop, still berthed in Old Saybrook, waiting until

Worth had time to sail it south to the Chesapeake and up to Potomac, Maryland, where he planned to keep it. They had planned the trip, talked of it, and now she wondered whether it would ever happen.

SIX

LILY WOKE to the familiar sound of an argument outside the dahabeah on the Nile. Men were screaming at one another through the early heat of the summer morning. She rose and opened the *mashrabiyyeh* shutters on one of the three windows of her room. In the early light of dawn, a felucca was drifting by on the current. Except for a man at the tiller, the crew surrounded two colleagues on the deck who were intent to fight. One man picked up a wooden mallet and started for his opponent, but another crew member, bald and with a crippled leg, grabbed the mallet-wielding fist, held it hard, and then kissed it. A pause in the yelling followed, the mallet was dropped, the two antagonists shook hands and embraced, and the men went back to their work on the felucca.

Lily smiled. The old man was a true diplomat, waiting for the perfect moment to kiss the fist. The white slanted sail was raised, and the felucca moved silently north. Up and down river, a morning mist rose pink in the early light. Already the automobile traffic roared from the western bank.

"Lily," her father called from downstairs.

She had slept naked, so she slipped on a *galabiyya* and hurried to the top of the steep, narrow stairs. "Good morning, Daddy."

"You wanted me to wake you. Coffee's on the stove; I'm off to get the papers." He was wearing linen slacks with a new striped cotton shirt, one of several he'd ordered the first day he arrived in Cairo from Beirut on his vacation. Without a tie or jacket, he looked thoroughly at ease. A battered straw hat was in his hand to protect him from the sun's glare, which would be uncomfortable by the time he returned. His circuit was the paper stand, street-side baker, and a favorite hubbly-bubbly shop where he would eat 'aish, unleavened bread with honey, drink thick coffee, and talk to the Arab men smoking their *nargilehs*. The water pipes, provided by the establishment, diverted the men before they faced their day of work or, as was more likely, idleness. In Cairo, unemployment was chronic.

"I like your shirt," Lily said.

"Yes, rather natty." Bert grinned. "When will I see you?"

"I'll be back after my run with Noorna."

He adjusted his glasses and, all innocence, asked, "I believe it's four days to W-Day?"

"Go get your papers." Lily laughed as she went back to her room to change into her running clothes. Worth would be arriving in four days. She checked her body in the full-length mirror opposite the tented bed, thinking of them both on it, exciting herself with the image, then getting dressed with impatience at having to wait so long. He'd be there a week. In the ten days she and Bert had been in Cairo, Lily had planned every hour of her time with Worth, several times, then thrown out all itineraries. Her father was going on a trip to Aswan for the first five days, leaving the dahabeah to them. She'd thought of sex in every room, amazed at how completely desire succeeded in smothering her other concerns. Worth's letters from Rabat had been funny and affectionate, but with more bravado about his triumph over consulate bureaucracy and Moroccan reticence than with his longing for her. Their last weekend in Washington had been tense; they were distracted by their separate plans. It was the last time she'd had sex, and it was what she chose to remember. Throughout their relationship, Lily had seldom allowed herself to conjecture, much less ask about any other sexual relief Worth might have found. Both of them had that opportunity; she made her own choices and didn't wish to know about the ones that Worth did or did not make. He would be there in four days; they would have a week. That was enough—at least to think about that morning.

After her coffee, she ran up the steps from the dahabeah to the street, locked the gate behind her, warily checked the sidewalk, and hailed a taxi. "Gezira Sporting Club, the west gate," she said in Arabic to the driver and sat back as the ancient black-and-white cab careened into traffic, spewing smoke and emitting gear-jamming noises that surely caused metal damage. As the vehicle gained speed, the driver casually propped a book on the steering wheel and began to read. Lily had grown up with the practice; her driver was studying an engineering text. Nasser's leftover promise to guarantee employment for every college graduate in Egypt had created an ever-expanding pool of the best-educated taxi drivers in the world, not to mention the Ph.D.s, who were given desks in the enormous government bureaucracy but sat all day with little to do except to make that little last. President Sadat, having recently emerged from Nasser's shadow by surviving a coup and signing a friendship treaty with Russia, seemed more interested in getting Russian weapons than in helping the educated underemployed.

The taxi passed one of Zamalek's many embassies, surrounded by piles of sandbags left in place after the 1967 War. Egypt's defeat was still regarded as the national shame, a shame so profound that it was believed to have killed Nasser. Israel's occupation of the Sinai rankled in the Egyptian soul. Yet Lily had sensed a spirit of optimism since she arrived. In spite of the massive Russian presence in Zamalek and all over Egypt, the oppressive socialism of the Nasser years had been lightened. Sadat had declared an end to the arbitrary seizure of property and the wiretapping of phones without a court order. Many of those who had fled the country in self-imposed exile were returning, including the el-Sadims.

At the invitation of the Nasser government, Russians had taken over their villa on the bank of the Nile. The el-Sadims had bought another in Zamalek, not as grand or as conspicuous but still impressive and convenient to the club. For reasons of security, the new villa was not on the river and was surrounded by a high stucco-and-brick wall. Its iron gate was kept closed except when a car entered or departed. There was a garden within the walls, which Noorna and her mother tended; the gardeners had been replaced by guards posted at the gate and front door. Ten years of exile in Morocco had not relieved the fear born in the el-Sadim family on the night Noorna's father was taken.

Mr. el-Sadim had spent five months in Cairo's Central Prison and, as soon as he was released, fled the country. His family had preceded him. Within a year, he was successfully operating a number of cement factories in Morocco. In spite of financial success and the contentment the family found in their villa outside Casablanca, they began packing a week after Nasser's funeral in anticipation of their return to Cairo. They came as soon as they were sure that Sadat had secured his power as president over the Nasserites who tried to overthrow him. When Lily and Bert arrived that summer, the el-Sadims had been in residence a scant two months.

In addition to several celebratory dinners, Lily had seen Noorna every day at the club, early in the morning so that they could exercise before the summer heat became too intense. They met at the west gate, a small break in the high circular wall that surrounded the club's remaining land. As Lily paid her cab driver and wished him luck with his studies, she saw Noorna approaching around el-Gezira Street on her bicycle, ignoring the toots of horns from the vehicles that roared past her. The old limousine in which the girls had been driven to the club more than a decade ago was in storage. Mr. el-Sadim was still wary of any such display of wealth.

"Oh, Lily, you cannot leave Cairo, ever. I can't talk to anyone else. Everyone in my family is impossible. My brothers think it's indecent for me to go out alone like this. My mother is afraid even to weed the garden, and my father is usually depressed, which he has every right to be, because every day he discovers more that we've lost, more terrible change in the country . . . And how are you this morning?"

They talked faster than they ran. Each morning, they managed to circle the two-kilometer dirt track three times, running and walking, keeping out of the way of the early morning horseback riders who trotted or cantered past them. In spite of the hot weather, they both wore outfits that covered their arms and legs in deference to Muslim custom. Noorna wore a scarf over her long black hair, at her mother's insistence, in order not to attract any undue attention, although few women at the club bothered to cover their heads.

Noorna had changed beyond Lily's imagining. When she was ten years old, she'd been short and plump with a round fleshy face that seemed to submerge her twinkling brown eyes. She'd grown into a svelte, five-and-a-half-foot beauty whose prominent cheekbones curved to accent kohl-rimmed eyes that flashed with both humor and anger. She had kept her hair thick and coiffed it in a massive frame of black waves. Her face was accented with dimples and her wide smile was outlined in burning red lipstick. A passing look from her had caused a number of sleek male equestrians to lose their self-absorbed concentration.

"Will you be with me at my wedding, Lily?"

"If you'll be at mine."

They had told each other everything about their romantic hopes and joked about much of it.

"I don't think I can put it off much longer. It's been arranged since before we left."

"I know, Noorna, but that was a long time ago."

"Lily, I was promised. Perhaps if we hadn't come back, it could have been forgotten. But here I am. And it was he who brought us so much of what we might have lost."

"You mean money?"

"And jewelry and so many other things, which, if he'd been caught, he'd have been imprisoned for. We are very much in his debt."

"Yes, but why are you the one to pay it?"

Noorna laughed as they stopped running. "Will you be my lawyer and get me out of this?"

"Absolutely. During a wedding, doesn't the Koran allow the woman to refuse the marriage?"

"That only happens in the movies. What applies here from the Koran is that obedience to parents is next in importance to obedience to Allah. They arranged the marriage. I could never disobey them."

"But would they want you to be unhappy?"

"I'm not sure I will be. He's a good man, a doctor from a notable family. I'll be cared for, as will my children. I just might not be ecstatic, but how many women are? How happy will you be with this Worth, whom you say you love so much?"

Lily walked silently before answering. "You can be your own lawyer. Whose side are you on? How old is the guy?"

"Forty-three," Noorna said grimly. "As many say, old enough to be my father. He's very nice and very dull. I'd as soon go to bed with a tree trunk. But I'm a good Muslim woman and I'll do what's expected of me."

"I can't argue against the Koran," Lily said. "Just remember verse thirty-four of the Fourth Surah."

"Thirty-four," Noorna said, then recited, " 'Men are in charge of women because Allah hath made the one of them to excel the other . . .' How did you discover that one?"

"In class. It goes on," Lily said, trusting Noorna's memory better than her own.

" 'So good women are the obedient, guarding in secret that which Allah hath guarded. As for those from whom ye fear rebellion, admonish them and banish them to beds apart, and scourge them—' "

"Scourge means whipping, lashing," Lily said.

"That verse only illustrates that the Prophet Muhammad, may His name be ever blessed, was a man."

Lily laughed as they jogged again and passed under the Sixth October Bridge approach that was built across the club's grounds. Their laughter echoed against the arched concrete, and as they came out of the overpass, they saw the enlarged red ball of the sun filtered through the city's dust and pollution, rising above the apartment houses surrounding the open space of the club's grounds.

"How did you ever memorize the whole Koran?"

"My brothers had to, like all good Muslim boys. They said a girl wasn't smart enough to do it. I beat both of them by a month. It wasn't hard. The writing is magnificent, and what else is there to do in exile? Race you to the break in the fence."

The two friends sprinted twenty meters to the opening in the three-boarded white rails through which riders and their mounts entered the track. Lily won by a foot, and pranced a few steps beyond, then leaned against the rail next to Noorna, breathing hard.

"Your legs are too long, Lily. I should get a head start."

Catching their breath, they watched the sun, a rider who came cantering by, the bridge traffic. Even at the early hour, it barely crept along, emitting above the drone of a thousand cars futile beeps and a visible cloud of exhaust, which rose as high as the Cairo Tower before the slight breeze from the western desert dissolved it. The friends could smell the night-blooming jasmine that grew on the walls around the club.

"I'm so glad to be back," Noorna said and took Lily's hand.

"So am I."

"It is our home, isn't it?" she asked, looking up at Lily for reassurance. "Even though we've spent more time away than here?"

"I don't have any other," Lily said. "Do you?"

Noorna shook her head and watched another pair of joggers passing by. "I will marry him, Lily, but I'll find a way to live my life, I swear to you. This place we love is in such terrible trouble. Do you know there are thirty-four million people in Egypt and the land can feed only nineteen million? I plan to do *something . . .*" She squeezed Lily's hand, then released it. "Let's go. If I'm not back soon, my brothers will call the police."

They walked toward the west gate. "When does your Worth arrive?"

"He's not mine yet, but Monday."

"And you'll bring him to dinner on Wednesday? That should give you time to settle down a bit." She gave Lily a quick smile. "And will we be jogging on Tuesday morning?"

"I hope to hell not."

They both were laughing when they heard Bert yelling, "Lily! Lily!" He was standing at the west gate, waving urgently for them to hurry. When they reached him, he handed each a newspaper and showed that he had a cable. "Good morning, Noorna. Lily, there's been a coup attempt in Morocco. Worth was involved but is fine. The cable's from him."

"When?" was all she could say as she tried to answer her own question with the copy of *Al Ahram* her father had handed her. She'd never read Arabic as well as she spoke it, and repeated her question insistently. "When?"

"Yesterday at two o'clock. King Hassan gave himself a birthday party of golf and feasts for a thousand people at his seaside castle at Akhirat. Worth apparently cadged an invitation. Just as the main course of the luncheon was being served, fourteen hundred rebel soldiers attacked. They killed four hundred and fifty people."

"Oh, god!" Lily exclaimed and felt Noorna's hand on her shoulder. She reached for the cable and read it quickly, allowing Noorna to see it.

DON'T WORRY MANAGED TO SURVIVE STOP ARRIVAL ON MONDAY
INDEFINITELY POSTPONED AS LOCAL INVESTIGATION PREVENTS MY
LEAVING STOP VERY VERY SORRY STOP MORE NEWS THROUGH EMBASSY
STOP WILL CALL WHEN ABLE WORTH.

"We missed it on the BBC last night," Bert reminded her, "because we were out. The local news of course said nothing until this
morning."

"Where did you get the cable?" Lily asked, horrified, relieved,
and deeply disappointed all at once.

"I went back to the dahabeah as soon as I saw the papers, but
you'd gone. A messenger had just left this under the gate."

"We have to find out more," Lily urged.

"The taxi's waiting," Bert answered and started for the west
gate.

"Call me when you get back to the dahabeah," Noorna said.

Because of the traffic, it took twenty-five minutes to reach the
office building where what was now called the American Interests
Section was located. The embassy had been formally closed when
Egypt broke off diplomatic relations with the United States because of its support of Israel in the Six Day War. The American
diplomatic outpost occupied a large suite of cluttered, badly lit
offices in a building off Tahrir Square. A skeletal staff of FSOs and
communications people ran the place, many of whom knew Bert
personally or by reputation. The head of the section, Bill Griffin,
seated father and daughter in his office, offered them Cokes, and
filled them in with professional alacrity. Griffin was a large, world-
weary Southerner whose smile was wide to distract from his cunning eyes. Going bald from front to back, he did nothing to cover
the void. On each side of the room a large fan blew, ruffling the
papers on his desk. Griffin also wielded a fan made of palm leaves.
Still he sweated through his already wilted shirt.

"As you know, Bert, the picture won't be clear for a couple of
days. The attackers were kids, military cadets following a particularly charismatic officer. King Hassan had apparently insulted this
officer in public somehow. Anyway, His Majesty wasn't harmed in
the coup, and order's been restored, though fifteen army generals

have been arrested." His glance slid over to Lily. "I understand you have some interest in one Cotesworth Deloit."

Lily nodded. "Yes, sir."

Griffin smiled. "Well, that boy must be something. Bert, you'll appreciate this. The shooting takes place at about two in the afternoon, right? Takes three hours to mop up, so that's five o'clock. Then the army comes in, and police, and there's questioning. So that's nine, say, or ten, enough for one day, wouldn't you think? Well, this gentleman Deloit not only manages to whip off this long, elegant cable to Foggy Bottom describing, among other things, his derring-do, but the son of a gun manages to get it routed to every damn post in the Middle East for our morning reading. How's that for *chutzpa?* Oops! I know we're bugged here and it's not such a good idea to use Yiddish." He shouted to the ceiling, "Sorry! *Malesh!*" and benignly went on fanning himself.

"May I read the cable?" Lily asked.

"Classified as usual, ma'am, but I can tell you most of what you'd want to hear about."

"Please."

"Well, apparently Deloit was seated off to one side. I mean to say the entire ambassadorial corps was there, so it's not surprising he wasn't sitting at the king's right."

"He'd have preferred it," Bert interjected, earning a brief glare from Lily.

Griffin chuckled and continued. "When the attack began—now we don't know yet if it was indoors or outdoors or on the eighteenth green—but anyway, Deloit said he ducked under a table and soon had a couple of dead bodies on top of him. He stayed put until there was a pause, and when he looked out, he saw that most of the cadets had run off after the king and the ones who were left to guard the party were pretty uncomfortable with so many dead and wounded. So as he was helping the wounded, he talked to the cadets and convinced some of them, who convinced the others, they'd better put down their guns, which they did. When the king's troops arrived, this Deloit character was standing there with a couple of dozen cadets negotiating the terms of their surrender. And who heard about it? King Hassan, who let it be known—just in time for the cable to go out—that he was personally grateful. Bert, I'd say we better keep an eye on this boy."

"I think that's just what he'd like," Bert responded as both men smiled at Lily, who politely smiled in return. "But we don't have to worry, Bill. By the time he's running the bureau, we'll be long gone."

Griffin agreed and fanned himself. "How do you like Beirut, Bert? Like sitting on a hand grenade that's been doused in French perfume, isn't it?"

"When were you there?"

"In 1958, when Eisenhower sent in the marines and interrupted all the sunbathers on the beach."

"It's different now."

"I hear. Wall-to-wall Palestinians. Don't seem to fit in with the chic shops and restaurants, somehow."

"And more on the way, I'm afraid."

Lily was not interested in diplomatic shop talk about Beirut. She wanted to return to the dahabeah in case Worth called. As the two men chatted, she saw the papers on the desk fluttering in the fans' breeze and wondered whether Worth's cable was there. Suddenly slumping back in her chair, she realized he wouldn't be coming in four days or six or twenty, probably not while she was still in Cairo. Maybe she'd stay over. She knew Bert wouldn't; already he had to consider going back early because of what was happening in Jordan. King Hussein's army was driving the Palestinian refugees out of their camps and across the border into Syria, from where they were hastily directed on to Lebanon.

Damn diplomacy, she thought, and began to feel uncomfortably hot in her running outfit. Why didn't the fans rotate faster? The dismay of wanting to show Worth "her" Cairo and losing the chance was depressing. She closed her eyes and heard her father say, ". . . and the fifty different PLO groups are running the asylum. Arafat can't control them. He tries to play them off against one another while he struts around, imitating a world statesman. But terrorism's the name of his game, and no rules apply. The PLO is accepted in Lebanon; they're having uniforms made; taking on grandiose ranks and titles. And they have money, lots of it, from the Saudis and the Gulf States, who want them to do the fighting against Israel. Money and status pollute purity faster than sin."

"That's a pretty fine analysis, Bert," Griffin said. "You ought to write it up and send it in."

Bert smiled self-mockingly. "Let me tell you about my cables. You know the fifth-floor communications center at Foggy Bottom, those ten CRT units where the cables come in and the specialists push keys to direct who gets them? I've been told that each unit has a special McCann key that sends my stuff directly to the trash."

"Right next to the Griffin key, except that now with all these Russians around here to write about, Foggy Bottom will read anything I send them. What you need in Beirut, Bert, is some Communists."

Standing, Bert said, "I'll try to find a few. Thanks, Bill. Will you let us know anything you hear about this Moroccan thing? You have my phone number."

Bert and Lily left the building and walked toward Tahrir Square, looking for a taxi. Once in the back seat, they rode silently as the taxi sped down to cross the old trestle bridge next to the newer concrete span of the Twenty-sixth July Bridge. There was a delay because a herd of sheep was being driven across. Lily shifted impatiently in her seat, imagining the phone on the dahabeah ringing.

"We'll get there," Bert said, touching her hand reassuringly.

She tried to relax. "When I heard what happened," she said, distracting herself from the delay, "I have to admit the idea occurred to me that Worth staged the damn coup for his own benefit."

Bert laughed. "You should have told Bill Griffin that. He'd have loved it."

"If Worth doesn't make it, would you like some company on your trip to Aswan?"

"I'd be delighted. But don't be discouraged; he may make it yet. You know, you can stay over here this summer until you go to your mother's in September."

Lily nodded but she knew Worth wouldn't come. He'd try to, even want to, but she understood all too well his instinctual reaction to such an extraordinary event and how he would take careful, precise, but nevertheless complete advantage of each opportunity presented by his highly visible role in the affair. Already his cable had been sent to every post in the Middle East. Lily wondered how many of the diplomats who read it had reacted with the deflating awareness that Bill Griffin had. But she realized the reaction made no difference; the impression was made, and made again at Foggy Bottom and probably at the White House.

Four hundred and fifty innocent people were killed, by cadets—boys—in thrall to their innocent vision of masculine and probably holy glory. The cadets would be shot, imprisoned for life at best. Worth would probably gain more from the event than anyone else. Lily wondered if he had ever been innocent, and imagined him at seven or eight in short pants, fighting and crying to get exactly the bike or boat he wanted; then his realizing by some chromosomal program suddenly released in him that manipulation worked much better than pure emotion. She was sure he'd lost his innocence very early, had torn it out of himself as an unnecessary weakness in his life.

SEVEN

MOMMY!" Lily said in surprise, then carefully spoke French. "You look—sensational."

Helene McCann stood presentationally in the doorway of her Paris apartment, wearing a dark green Chanel suit with the requisite ropes of pearls around her neck and gold bracelets around her wrists. Her highlighted blond hair was drawn back into an elegant chignon, as always without a single loose wisp. Still lovely at forty-six, with a rigidly controlled size-six body, her face nevertheless was changed since Lily had visited her the previous year. There wasn't a wrinkle to be seen.

"You aren't supposed to notice," her mother said haughtily, then leaned forward to kiss Lily formally on each cheek. "And if you do, it's very gauche to comment. Come in, darling. Are all those bags yours? Of course that witch of a concierge didn't help you. I'll call Matilde."

"No, no, I can get them," Lily said as she began to lift her bags across the threshold into the foyer. "When did you decide to have a facelift? Will you tell me about it?"

Her mother watched Lily's exertion but did not help. "I decided the moment I knew that I'd have a twenty-one-year-old daughter living here with me. In Paris, there's considerable difference between being a woman and being a mother. I have no doubt that we'll be seen together, by your friends and mine, inviting the inevitable comparison. One must prepare for such scrutiny however one can. Come, leave the bags there. Matilde has made tea. How was your flight? *Matilde!*"

Her call was a bark of command. She guided Lily into a sitting room filled with chintz-covered furniture, side tables covered with biblots from Greece, and plaster walls on which were hung oil paintings by obscure artists of the Renaissance and other periods. There were three tall windows overlooking the Seine, which flowed by four floors below across Avenue de New York. Placed before each of the three windows on a platform built for the purpose was an immense white filigreed bird cage, each with a unique design of parapets or cupolas, each overwhelming its single feathered occupant. None was larger than a canary. Their size belied the volume of song of which they were capable, and on Lily's appearance, they chorused a full-throated example.

Lily went to each cage and, with soft whistling, greeted the birds. She was relieved to see that they were the same ones that had been in residence on her last visit. Her mother, untrusting of Matilde, had little hesitation if invited to travel to put the birds out the window and buy new ones on her return.

"I suppose I should have met you at the airport," her mother said as she sat in a chintz armchair and prepared the table before her for the tea tray. "But, as you know, I can't bear crowds."

"That's okay," Lily said as she approached her accustomed seat at one end of the large sofa. Just then Matilde came in with the tea tray, placed it before Madame, and, while emitting whimpers of welcome, greeted Lily with trembling hands that appreciatively touched the young woman's face, an exchange tolerated by her mother.

After Matilde left, Helene said, "Silly old fool." She poured the tea into a Sèvres cup.

"But faithful," Lily offered idly, then regretted it instantly.

Her mother banged the teapot down. Still holding the delicate cup, she said, "If we are going to co-exist in this apartment for the next ten months or however long it is, I will not have any of your snide references to my former relationship with your father. Do you understand?"

"Mother, that wasn't intended," Lily responded without apology.

The two women watched each other, taking instant measure of the space each needed and calculating whether the apartment could possibly be large enough. In the hall, Matilde was heard shuttling Lily's bags to her room. After a moment, Helene picked up the pot again, finished pouring the tea, and added hot water to the cup to make the correct strength.

"What do you take in your tea? I've forgotten."

"Sugar, or honey if you have it."

"Oh, yes. Honey. I remember. Matilde will get some tomorrow." She put sugar in Lily's cup and held it out to her. Lily rose and took it, noting her mother did not meet her eyes but went on busily pouring her own cup.

Taking her place on the sofa, Lily stirred her tea and said, "Mommy, I'm very, very grateful to you for letting me stay here this year. I probably couldn't have afforded to come . . ."

"Matilde!" her mother called, and immediately there were the shuffling steps, an order for the petits fours, the abject apologies, and retreat to the kitchen. Archly continuing the conversation, Helene said, "I owe you an important part of your life, the part I'm told only a mother is able to give. I'll never be able to give it, I know that, not only because the time for it is past, but because I'm a selfish woman, as I'm sure you must realize by now."

Matilde returned with a plate of petits fours and prayed for pardon from Madame, who dismissed her with an executioner's look. Helene continued, "If you don't know that, then you'd better accept it before you unpack your bags."

"As I said, I'm very grateful and glad to be here," Lily stated simply. "I'm sure I can stay out of your way."

Helene gazed at Lily a moment as a droll smile spread, then was contained, apparently a well-practiced control against stretching certain muscles. "I see you've learned the diplomatic reflex, I wonder where." She took a sip of tea and spoke matter-of-factly as she stared into the cup. "I was a rotten mother to you, even before I left your father. I offer no excuses. It's too late for those to have any meaning. But I do want you to understand that I know. And I hope that during this stay, I perhaps may discover some way to be a mother, although I think the role was never mine."

"Thank you for telling me this," Lily said. "There were a lot of times when I wished you were—well, with us. But I'm not aware of ever holding it against you. The first few years were the worst because I felt you'd rejected us, but you've always been generous to me, and I guess I just accepted you for what you were."

Her mother's eyes flashed up from the cup. "And what was that?"

"That you were a woman who could live only her own life, which didn't include—me."

Helene searched Lily's face for any sign of dissembling, then sat back in her chair and let her eyes glide to the windows. "Ever since I found out that you were coming, not for a visit but for a stay, I've planned this conversation. For reasons I can't fathom, it's important to me that you understand from the very beginning who I know I am. We mustn't use the usual controlled courtesies or deceptions that mothers and daughters so often impose—and accept—in order to preserve their terrible semblance of affection." Oblivious of the effect on her face, she scowled. "We've been locked in that game for too long. I have set certain rules, and you've obediently played by them. I do not want that any longer. No more diplomacy between us!" One high-boned cheek quivered with her intensity.

"I've always wanted to know as much as I could about you," Lily said, "as much as you'd let me know. I'm not sure what you mean about diplomacy, except that I guess it has something to do with Daddy."

"Of course it does," her mother said deep in her throat. "That's what happened to us, him and me. By the time we met, he was a diplomatic animal. All his instincts, emotions, everything he did, was blocked and chopped and strained through that fine iron sieve of diplomacy. I could not reach him through all of that, no matter what I did. At first, I tried surprise, the unexpected; I went on to shock him, then make him hate me. Nothing. Always his calm acknowledgment, the reasoned patience, and the endless negotiations that followed. I wasn't a nation; I was a woman. He should have declared war." She glanced at Lily to see whether humor was appropriate.

Lily smiled obligingly. "I've always thought he believed that if he'd started a war, you'd have left us even sooner."

Helene sat without motion, her back straight, her green eyes wide.

"You mean it was inevitable," Helene stated.

"We've all agreed on that, haven't we?"

"Because of what I am," her mother continued.

"And because of who he is. War is a failure to him, on an international or a personal level. Remember? 'It's a breakdown of civilization,' he says, 'of every value the human race struggles to keep in place.' Besides that, he's dedicated, 'bound to serve,' as he says, standing for American ideals that most Americans would as soon shoot down around him. He can't help himself, but that's who he is. I don't think the two of you would have ever been happy."

Helene reached forward to pour the hot water into the teapot. "I'm not asking for forgiveness," she said.

"I wasn't offering it," Lily replied steadily.

The stream of hot water wavered once; then her mother said, "Would you like more tea?" and replaced the hot water pot on the tray.

"Please."

As she poured the tea through a small silver strainer into Lily's cup, Helene relaxed her face into its comfortable repose of slightly lifted brows and a bare smile. "My father also was dedicated to his country's ideals, and we all marry our fathers in one way or another. Be careful of that, my darling. His duty came first, his men second, and his family a distant and, for him, irritating third. He turned my mother into a wrung-out, desolate woman, alone on those Algerian bases, bleached to the bone by the sun and to the heart by his lack of care. I was not willing to put up with such a life."

"Daddy cared," Lily said.

"Yes," Helene admitted, "I know I hurt him very much. But as I've said, I am a selfish woman. I could not stay with him. Or, as we've seen, with any man for long." She did not look up as she refilled her own cup.

Instead of sitting, Lily strolled over to the nearest bird cage and sipped her tea. The tiny bird, startled by the close attention to its song, flitted from perch to perch. Lily hoped that, by breaking the scene, she might cause her mother to change the subject. The conversation, although a welcome relief from their usual courteous but distant dance, seemed dangerously volatile. It was too soon in her stay for such intensity.

Her mother also left her seat and walked over to the window in front of the bird cage to fuss with the curtains. "When does your school begin?" she asked. "Which one is it? They've changed everything since 1968. I must show you the Métro stop."

"They're still changing, but two of the newly organized campuses are at the Sorbonne. Most of my work will be there and at L'École Nationale de Sciences Politiques—or Science Po, as we natives call it. And I know the Métro, Mommy," Lily said patiently.

"Of course you do," Helene responded, looking critically at her daughter. "You're very much a woman now. I can see that. No more the little girl I never knew. Perhaps . . ." she began, but hesitated and turned back to the window to straighten the curtains again. "I must tell you of my present circumstances."

From past visits, Lily knew that this meant the current man in her mother's life, whom she had always been forbidden to see, or to be seen by, with instructions to remain in her room as long as the gentleman remained in the apartment. Occasionally this had meant overnight, and breakfast became a farce of urgent whispers, grabbed croissants, and slammed doors, without either mother or daughter later referring to the incident.

"Who is he?" Lily asked boldly in the spirit of their new relationship.

"There are two," her mother answered in the same spirit.

Lily laughed and her mother allowed a precise smile.

"And since I must presume you're now a woman, I'll tell you a story you must never betray," Helene began. "One of them is a German manufacturer. Of an automobile. Mercedes." She quickly glanced at Lily to see if her daughter was impressed. She was. Helene went on. "The other is an Italian count who was a little too close to Mussolini during the war and therefore must live in Switzerland, where he wisely had moved all his money. The two of them appeared in my life within a week of each other, last spring. Keeping them separate has not been easy. At a certain social level, Europe is a small bourgeois town. When the German offered me the Mercedes of my choice, and the Italian begged me to pick out some present for myself that he would pay for, I priced a convertible to the exact sous, and accepted the German's car on the same day that the Italian's check cleared my bank. Each man is extremely pleased when I pick him up at Orly in 'his' car."

"That's outrageous," Lily blurted as she laughed, overlooking the fact of her mother's frequent trips to the crowded airport.

"But they are both so happy." Helene shrugged.

"Are they nice? Do you like them?"

Her mother's brows arched at the question. She scowled frownlessly again and moved closer to the window. "You're still young enough to hope, aren't you? I must tell you another story. Down there in the Sixteenth, at Fifty-one Rue Nicolo—I walk past it often—is the house where one of the greatest nineteenth-century courtesans of Paris lived, the Contesse de Castiglione. For the ten years of her reign, she gave comfort to, among others, European royalty—Victor Emmanuel the Second, Napoleon the Third, and any number of Princes Poniatowski from Poland. I'm sure they were all very 'nice' and that she 'liked' them, of course some more than others. But then it all ended, as it does when beautiful flesh no longer withstands the many stresses of time." With a grace that belied diffidence, Helene idly touched a newly smooth corner of her mouth with her manicured fingers. "She had every mirror in the house removed, and lived there alone and wretched for thirty years until her death." Turning her startling green eyes on Lily, she said, "That is the bitter future I refuse."

Although Lily immediately wondered how, she couldn't think of a response, so she nodded. Her mother saw her understanding and closed her eyes for a moment. Then she gestured and preceded Lily out of the drawing room to the foyer.

"Fortunately," her mother said, "the miracles of modern science extend our control over the body's decay, so there is yet more time; I'd say another ten years." She stopped before the large gilt mirror in the foyer. Lily stood beside her; mother and daughter stared into the dim reflection. "Don't you think?" It was the first time Lily had ever seen her mother in need of reassurance.

"Fifteen, easy."

"No diplomacy."

"All right. Twelve."

Helene stepped closer to the mirror. "Fourteen?"

When Lily laughed, Helene's eyebrows arched again. The two women stood together looking into the mirror at each other.

"I thought you might be shocked by talk of my terrible life," Helene said quietly. "You've become sophisticated all of a sudden."

"Not at all. I still wish you'd find someone to marry."

Her mother stepped away, grumbling her remonstrances. "What, and go back to prison? Don't be ridiculous. I'll show you your room. I've had it done over.

"Let me tell you about marriage, which I'm sure you'll confront any time now. Never forget that people change completely every ten years. The twenty-year-old you marry is a completely different person at thirty, and at forty, and so on. I've had many proposals. I prefer freedom and cash. If they're invested well, both will last longer than any marriage."

Lily followed her mother down the familiar hall, which passed the kitchen, a small den, a bath. As her mother waited at the door to her room, Lily caught up to her and asked, "What age is safe for marriage, then?"

"When you wear black instead of white to the ceremony because the groom must go straight to the cemetery," she answered, without humor.

"Bitter already?"

"As any woman should be."

"A lot aren't."

"They're fools, blind from birth. Their fathers spoil them and treat them like dolls, so they're prepared for the slavery of marriage and the vapid window dressing they're expected to provide. But the unluckiest of them, the truly cursed, they marry diplomats!"

Lily smiled devilishly. "Since we're being so up-front with each other, I guess it's time I admitted that I'm expecting a visitor sometime in the fall, a guy who happens to be an American vice consul in Rabat."

The slight tic Lily had detected previously in her mother's left cheek became a quivering accompaniment to their conversation. "My advice," Helene pronounced, "is, if this man is of real interest to you, you give up your study of law and study how to cook."

"Oh, Mother."

"In the diplomatic field, you'll be judged more than anything else on your elegant little dinner parties. Any intelligence, any genuine talent you have is a negative, for it will only frustrate you at not being able to use it, or confuse those who expect the usual banal conversation. You should buy a pair of very high heels, white gloves, and a hat, then practice standing in place for hours with a broad smile of concrete on your face. And don't eat very much. Your figure is a much more vital asset than your brain."

"Mommy, it's different now."

"Oh, is it? Tell me how."

"Well, for starters, nobody wears white gloves or hats anymore."

"Ah, what liberation! But tell me this. Is not the success of a diplomatic marriage dependent on the degree to which the woman accepts her position of inferiority?"

"You could say that about a lot of marriages."

"Yes, but in the Foreign Service, the attitude is petrified. It will never change. Lily, existence for the wife of a diplomat is exile from life. She is unacknowledged by anyone except the patronizing men who judge her performance in her husband's annual rating reports. Any career you may have, any useful job, is broken off as you follow your husband to his next post. Your friendships are a kind of desperate intimacy, like those in the theater, where actors come together under the heightened circumstances of putting on a play. When the play closes, they are gone, never to be seen again except by chance in another production, where they fall upon each other, long lost friends, bound together again by the pressures of the performance."

Lily laughed. "The embassy as theater. Brava, Mommy."

"My darling, the embassy *is* a theater, where men always hog center stage. You, as a wife, will be given a pink chiffon costume but no substantial lines, and you will be applauded only for how well you bury your deepest self in your submissive performance."

On the bus to Orly Airport to meet Worth, Lily found herself apprehensive about greeting him, about what they'd say, about what it would be like to undress in front of him again. It was early November, nearly five months since their last weekend in Washington.

After the coup the preceding summer, he had not made it to Cairo. He invited Lily to Rabat, but four days before her planned arrival, he was summoned to Washington for consultations. By the time he returned, Lily had to be in school. During the interim, letters—short, often cryptic—took the place of their thrice-weekly phone calls, but regularity had been sacrificed to their increasingly complex schedules.

Who was this man? She had no doubt that Worth had been through as many changes as she had. In his letters, he expressed his affection, but as she sat staring out the bus window, peering through her dim reflection, she went through the few remembered phrases, testing them again for sincerity.

About ten minutes from the airport, someone sat down in the seat next to her, which she thought odd, as the bus was not crowded. Before she recognized the image reflected next to hers in the window, he said in Arabic, "Don't move or make a noise, or you'll die and so will everyone else on this bus." Lily felt something hard pressed into her ribs; her stomach lurched and her mouth went dry.

"I've read that you speak Arabic," he said with false ease. "I do too. We can talk with no fear of being understood. If you do anything to cause alarm, everyone here will die. A car is following. Those in it will make sure of that if I should fail. Do you understand?"

She managed a nod. His Arabic was accented with the Levant, his breath with anise. Even the reflection in the window showed the hatred in his eyes, the familiar hooked nose dividing his dusky olive face, the full bitter lips over crooked gold-filled teeth. The gold was new, as was the curly black hair—it had been straight in Tripoli—and two short, deep crescent scars on his left temple.

"Sit back now and look straight ahead," he ordered. "Say something to me in Arabic and smile so none of these frogs will worry."

Smiling was difficult. She forced out, "You speak Arabic very well."

"I was born in Palestine."

"I didn't see you get on the bus."

"I looked different when I boarded. I want you to stay calm for the rest of the trip. It's almost over."

"What is?" she blurted, too loud for him; he jammed whatever he had under his coat into her ribs again. "Careful," he said, smiling for the benefit of the man in front of them who had turned around briefly.

Lily smiled as well, although she didn't trust what her smile looked like. She tried to remember how many people were on the bus. Only three sat in front of them and she didn't dare look back. The driver was an overweight man in his sixties.

"Don't worry," he said. "Unless you insist, you'll go on living. You're much more useful to me alive than dead. Give this to your father."

He handed her an envelope. She tried not to let her hand shake as she took it. Bert's name was typed on the envelope. That terrified her more than the idea of her future usefulness.

"My father isn't in Paris."

Irritated, he said, "I know exactly where your father is. Call him. Read it aloud."

"How long have you been following me?"

"That is not your affair," he said and shifted in his seat. "But I'll tell you that one of my comrades who's been following you was fascinated with your lectures, particularly Legal Ethics. I'll give you *my* lecture on ethics someday."

The bus entered the airport perimeter, and Lily saw the runway lights in the distance. Before she had a chance to worry about Worth, he said, "The bus makes its first stop at the maintenance hangars. I'll get off there. I'll stand outside the bus, and if you move, even turn your head to see if I'm there, I'll shoot you. After the bus goes, don't make the driver stop. Go on to the next stop or wherever you wish. But be sure to deliver that letter. It will save lives. Then you can tell everyone how terrible I am." He leaned in very close to her face. "But if you ever see me again on a street somewhere, be wise and be blind. Next time I won't be so generous."

The bus began to slow down and several passengers went past them to the front door. He stood up—he was taller than she had remembered him—and leaned down as the door of the bus opened. "As the Arabs say, 'May you be the mother of a hundred sons.' *Shalom.*"

"Don't write me any more letters."

"And let you forget me?"

"I won't forget you. Ever." She said it as a threat, even though her hands were shaking in her lap.

He glared at her contemptuously. "And I won't forget you."

He went to the front of the bus and stepped off, watching Lily casually. His brown tweed overcoat hung loosely around him. She couldn't see the outline of whatever weapon he was carrying. She didn't move and kept her eyes on the bald spot of the bus driver's head. When the bus started and gained speed, she began to shake uncontrollably and thought she would faint. As soon as it was safe, she put her head between her knees and tried to control the tremors that shot through her body. The envelope fell and slid under the seat. Grabbing for it stopped the shakes, and Lily was able to sit back in her seat.

Instinctively she stood and looked back through the rear window; there were nothing but headlights as far as she could see. She thought of stopping the bus, alerting security. But what would she tell them? She hadn't seen the car, only his face and brown tweed coat. She wondered what had caused the two scars, why his hair was curly, and realized there was nothing she could do. Then her body clenched. Was he still following her? Did they know she was meeting Worth? And when would they be following her again with some new opportunity for her to be "useful" to them?

When the bus stopped at the terminal entrance, she got off and walked quickly to one of the elevators that took passengers with heavy bags or wheelchairs to the second floor for tickets or to the third floor for the restaurants. Two men stepped on with her. When she walked out on the second floor, neither followed. She ran down the stairs to the first floor. Constantly scanning the ticketing areas, she made her way toward the international arrivals, where she was to meet Worth. Twice she ducked into a ladies' room to see if anyone followed her, or if anyone waited outside. The "antiterrorist techniques" that had been taught to all Middle East embassy personnel and their families seemed useless. The terrorist, she knew, could be anywhere; his "comrades" could be anyone.

She waited outside the international arrivals barrier, hiding behind a telephone kiosk so that Worth could not see her. When he was escorted through by a French customs official because of his diplomatic passport, he was met by a driver—not one from the

Paris embassy, but a private chauffeur for the special evening Worth had planned. The driver took his two bags, and Worth looked around with irritation, the familiar pursed mouth and scowl of impatience easily visible to Lily. He was sunburned. After waiting a bare minute, he walked to the information desk at the front entrance. Sending the driver ahead, Worth talked to the attendant, and Lily heard herself paged. She watched him charm the attendant while scanning the airport, his glare of annoyance growing. He wore a dark blue suit, white shirt, bright red tie, and shiny tasseled loafers. Carrying his chesterfield overcoat on his arm, as well as a lustrous leather case, probably Moroccan, he succeeded in melting Lily's wariness about him and reminding her of how much she loved him. The familiarity of his body's odd slouch and the thick waves of dirty-blond hair almost caused her to run over to him, but she wanted to be certain that he was safe.

The driver appeared at the entrance. After one last look over the airport, Worth shook his head disgustedly and followed the driver to the waiting black Peugeot limousine. Lily moved quietly to a separate entrance. Once outside, she waited again to be sure she wasn't followed, then turned and ran down the walkway to Worth's car just as it began to pull out into traffic. She waved her arms, the limousine jerked to a stop, and the back door opened. Expectantly she leaned forward to step in, and heard Worth say, "Where the hell have you been? Get in here." When she sat next to him, he continued, in an edgy but jokey tone, "You realize what it's taken to set up this trip, and after five months you get here late?"

As he kissed her, Lily knew she wasn't going to tell him what had happened on the way out to the airport. She knew she wasn't going to marry him either. Remembering something her mother had said about girls always marrying their fathers, she concluded that girls could marry elements of their mothers just as easily, in this case, the certainty of his selfishness.

She apologized for being late. In response, he said, "Merry Christmas" and handed her a round-trip ticket to Rabat for a week over the holidays. She listened on the ride into Paris to an account of his life in Morocco and how he had further ingratiated himself with the king and his official retinue. While he talked, his desire became apparent, and, surprisingly to Lily, hers was too. Her dress was one she had purposefully chosen to allow him quick and easy access to any part of her body he wanted to touch. She did not resist him, and responded with her own sallies through the buttons and zippers of his clothes. Still she couldn't forget the deep-set eyes, the scent of anise, the sound of the guttural Arabic so close to her ear, and her intense fear of her helplessness.

When they reached the Plaza-Athenée, Lily left the limousine, suddenly anxious about the letter. In the lobby, just before Worth entered and checked in, she tore open the envelope.

The letter, typed in English on a plain piece of white paper, read:

> The hijacking of a TWA plane is planned for Christmas Eve, December 24. The origin is either Frankfurt or Rome, on a flight bound for the Middle East. Although other details are not known, the date is certain, as are the airline and the two possible points of origin. The PLO group PFLP is responsible. Their personnel and weapons are already in place. Other organizations have been alerted. Don't shoot each other and lose the fox.

Without hesitating, Lily left the lobby and found a public phone in a hallway. She fished for the required *jeton* in her bag, let the ridged token slide into its slot, and dialed the United States Embassy. By conveying the urgency of the situation with insider terminology, she managed to talk her way through various administrators until she reached a junior security officer who listened to her story with growing interest. Once she read him the letter, he insisted on a meeting, and she agreed to appear at the embassy the following morning. That, she knew, would allow them time to call up her file from Washington. She demanded the opportunity to call her father on a secure line, and extracted the assurance that the security officer would not make contact with him before she did. The officer agreed and urged her to be careful.

She was certain that the letter had nothing to do with her father. He was in Beirut, the counselor at an embassy with no connection to any of the areas involved. The information could have been sent to any official to bring about an alert. For whatever reason, they'd chosen her to deliver the message. If it was the Mossad, why would they choose such an odd channel of communication? If it was a covert Israeli terrorist group either within or without the official Israeli security system, why would they take the trouble to use her?

She returned to the lobby and an irate Worth.

"What is this?" he demanded.

"I went to the ladies' room."

"No, you didn't. It's on the second floor. I asked."

"Well, I'm a little embarrassed. I had to call my mother. She worries about me going around alone because of all the foreigners—"

"What were you reading when I came in?"

"What's the matter?"

"I'm not completely unaware of what goes on around me, Lily. And something's going on with you."

"Yes, it's the first time I've seen my lover in five months and I'm a little crazy. The letter I was reading was something I wrote to you and reconsidered. I tore it up and threw it away."

"Why?"

"It was—I don't know—too sappy."

Pleased, he laughed, then stepped forward and embraced her. Lily saw several people pass them, smiling at the display.

"Come on, we have only an hour before our reservation at Taillevent," Worth said. "Wait'll you see this suite."

"Have you stayed here before?" she asked as they headed toward the elevator.

"The hotel, yes, but not the suite. His Majesty arranged it." He turned his head just enough to see her reaction. "I'm paying, but I get it for the regular rate."

"It seems you've been meeting all the right people."

"Rabat's worked out very well. They say that most of being successful in the Foreign Service is the luck of being in the right place when the shit hits the in-box. Then it's up to you to come out smelling like an orchid."

"An orchid doesn't smell."

"Exactly. But it looks terrific."

The suite was as opulent as any château, huge in proportion, Louis Quinze in its appointments. There seemed to be flowers or baskets of fruit on every solid surface. Aubusson tapestries covered the walls in the sitting room, old oak paneling in the separate study, and brocade in the bedroom, with its heavily draped four-poster. The small kitchen and enormous bathroom were by contrast as modern as plumbing and electricity allowed. Few of these details were noticed by the occupants, however, for as soon as Worth tipped the two porters and hurried them out, he and Lily were at each other, pulling at clothing. Lily gave in to the urgency, still aware of his self-absorption, her fast manipulation of his ego to cover the letter, the wall she thought was rising ever higher between them. She let her body respond to its longing for him, which was as genuine as her love was muddled.

Worth lay back on the bed, propped up on his arms, smiling at his completely sunburned body, proudly tumescent. Kneeling naked on the end of the bed and looking down at what she so eagerly wished to enjoy, Lily was surprised she didn't remember how large he was. In the same moment, she thought of not remembering how tall the terrorist was. She climbed on Worth. His ardor matched her purpose and as they fell into their familiar rhythm of anticipation, Lily thought again that she might love him, and that she might tell him about the letter. The story was on her lips as she felt the frenzy of feelings lock her body into an aching delight.

———————

Two nights later, as Worth stood resplendent in his dinner jacket to deliver a toast at a small soirée at the Ambassador's Residence, he seemed to Lily a stranger. From the half-dozen flower-bedecked tables, his distinguished audience laughed on cue at his charming delivery. Lily noted how carefully he had worked the primary people in the room and knew that later, over cognac, he would work them again. Later still, she knew, he would tell her of his conquests and how each would benefit his future, a future of which he felt assured. But she had told him nothing of the terrorist.

As she listened to his toast, Lily wondered who he would be in ten years, other than an ambassador. The ambassador's wife, seated at the table with her, leaned to a dinner partner to whisper an exclamation of delight with the young diplomat. In the applause that followed Worth's toast, Lily thought of the terrorist, of the brown tweed coat, his crooked gold-crowned teeth, the scent of anise.

EIGHT

LILY WATCHED the Algerian in the park reading on the same bench where she'd seen him sit at other times. The Paris sun was bright and warm. As he studied, making notes in the margin of his book, a breeze fluttered a page and his hair. He looked up and caught her staring before she ducked her head back into her book. She was too embarrassed to move as he slowly approached her bench and stood before her until she raised her eyes. The bruise on his temple was still deep and purple.

The man had appeared the previous week in Lily's class on Third World Economics; she had not seen him before. He sat alone at the back of the class. His sharp handsome face, deep black eyes, and short careful beard announced that he was an Arab. He paid no apparent attention to her, and she couldn't be sure he wasn't just another student. But later the same day, she saw him twice, once near the Boul' Mich reading in the park where she often ate her lunch. As soon as she arrived at her mother's apartment, she called the security officer at the American Embassy. The next day, the Arab did not appear.

"What is it?" he demanded in French as he stood before her now, scowling.

"Nothing," she answered, but offered lamely, "I'm in the Third World Economics class."

The scowl became a frown of contempt. "I know that. I've seen you watching me before. Why?"

"I'm so sorry," she began, hesitated, then admitted, "about what happened to you."

He had returned to class two days after her call to the embassy with a pronounced limp and a large bruise on his right temple. As he took notes, Lily watched him, heedless of the lecture, aware of his injuries and how stunningly good-looking he was. When the class was over, she followed him. He went to a vendor on the Boule' Mich, where he bought his couscous, ate it, and, as quickly as his limp allowed, returned to the college. He'd obviously been beaten, probably for nothing except her suspicion.

At the apartment that night, her mother announced that some-one at the American Embassy—which she pronounced as if issuing a curse—wished Lily to call. The security officer assured her that the Arab was a genuine student, an Algerian whose parents were involved in the former French colony's government. According to the French police, to whom the embassy had referred the matter, he was a doctoral candidate in geology with an exceptional scholastic record.

The park, a small corner of green, was empty. He stood, shifting the weight from his bad leg. "What are you saying?" he asked angrily. "You know what happened to me?"

His French had the North African accent Lily recognized from her childhood years in Tripoli. His voice was very deep, very rough. He was a head taller than Lily. His thick black hair was brushed straight back from a high broad brow.

"I'm afraid I'm responsible for your being . . ." She couldn't think of the right word.

"What are you? English?"

"American."

He drew back from her as if she'd mentioned a disease. His lips contorted and she thought he might spit.

"Look, let me explain this," she asked.

He glared at her, then shrugged and sat down, painfully, never taking his eyes off her. She stayed at the other end of the bench, yet near enough for him to hear her. As concisely as she could, she explained why she was involved with his arrest, why she had sus-pected him of following her, perhaps to use her again, or perhaps worse. His questions were precise. She described to him her last meeting with the Israeli terrorist and the Palestinian plot to hijack the TWA plane, which led her to a brief description of her role in the atrocity in 1967.

"So let me say again," she concluded, "how terribly sorry I am about what happened to you. I don't know if there's anything I can do to . . ."

"You know what the flics do?" he interrupted. "They beat you *before* they ask questions. That is, if you're a dark-skinned foreigner of any shade. Particularly if you're Algerian. The ones who did it to me fought against us in our war of independence. They were filled with nostalgia, and beat me the way they used to do it there, so that it doesn't leave marks. This," he said, indicating the wound on his temple, "was a mistake they made after I reminded them that in 1962 they'd lost Algeria."

Lily said nothing; she studied her folded hands. After too long a silence, she reached for her book bag and stood up, trying to think how to leave with some kind of adequate apology. "I don't know how I can—"

"What happened to the TWA plane?" he asked.

"It was in Germany. The police arrested five members of the PFLP in Stuttgart two nights before they were booked on a flight to Tel Aviv."

He said, *"Insha'allah,"* by the grace of Allah in Arabic.

"Insha'allah," Lily repeated, looking down into his brooding but quite beautiful face.

He seemed to resent her use of the term. "You Americans will never understand," he said bitterly. "You see Arabs as dumb cattle with nothing but oil."

Switching to Arabic, Lily said, "And you see Americans as stupid infidels with nothing but greed."

The change of language astonished him. "Are you with the CIA?" he asked, continuing in an accented Arabic that Lily could barely understand.

She went back to French. "No, and that's another Arab attitude. Any Westerner who speaks your language has to be a spy."

"Many are."

"A lot aren't, including me."

He didn't respond, only glared at her. He wore jeans and a faded patterned shirt. It was opened far enough for Lily to see, under the material, the curve of thin pectoral muscle. She looked away too quickly, knowing he'd seen her reaction.

"Well, I wanted to tell you," she said. "Again, I'm very, very sorry. If there's anything I can ever do—" When he waved his hand contemptuously, she walked away, too aware of her attraction to him to stay.

"Wait," he called.

She looked back in time to see him struggling to stand. "Are you all right?" she asked.

"Yes. They kicked my knee. It locks sometimes." The severe look on his face remained, but he asked in Arabic, "Will you come here again and speak Arabic with me, please?"

"I'm not sure I can understand you," she said, doing as he wished. "Your accent is so different."

"We'll understand each other if we listen carefully. What's your name? I am Ammar Ben Ashid."

For the next several days, the spring sun remained warm, and the few chestnut trees in the park came closer to budding. Lily and Ammar sat on opposite ends of the same bench at lunchtime, telling each other in Arabic of their lives and how they happened to be in a French economics class. He'd had a free hour in his class schedule, and the economics of the Third World was important to him, so he arranged to audit. His father, a doctor, had fought with the French in World War II, then fought against them for six years in the war for independence. Since then, he had served in various capacities in the socialist revolutionary government. Currently he was in the Ministry of Energy, overseeing the state bureau that, the year before, had taken control from French companies of Algeria's oil in the Sahara. Ammar was the youngest of four children, the only one sent to France for advanced studies, about which he felt remorse, gratitude, and anger.

"I hate coming here to this country," he said after a week of lunches in the park. "The French occupied us since 1830, made us slaves. But I'm ashamed to sit here in the French sun or in those classrooms, knowing that our people's oppressors were taught there. Do you know anything about Algeria?" he challenged.

"Yes," Lily admitted hesitantly.

"What?" he demanded. "Americans know nothing about it except the Kasbah."

"My grandfather—I never knew him—served there in the French Army."

He stared at her, appalled. "You said you were American."

"My mother's French. She was born in Algiers."

He tried to spring up from the bench, but his knee caused him to stumble. When he finally stood before her, he said, "Are you sent by Satan to torment me?"

"I doubt it, and I can't apologize for my grandfather."

Looking heavenward, he asked, "What are the chances of my being in a class with a beautiful woman who has me beaten, speaks my language, and is both American and French?"

"I guess you're just lucky, and thank you."

"For what?"

"The 'beautiful.'"

"You are, and I don't believe in luck."

"But you do believe in Satan and Allah."

He paused. "Sometimes." Taking a step closer, he examined her. "Who are you, dropping into my life? I go to the mosque here not to pray, but to talk to people in Arabic. But then this lion-haired vision of a French-American woman sits next to me on a park bench, speaks to me in a honeyed accent, and tells me she descends from one who helped slaughter hundreds of thousands of my people. Does she expect me to believe that she is chance? Impossible. She must be my devil, come to force me to Allah."

For a moment Lily thought he might believe what he'd said, because he kept watching her as if she might turn into a snake. But then she saw a glimmer in his eyes as he reached out slowly and—to her enormous surprise, for even a lapsed Muslim would hardly dare to do so—touched her cheek with the back of his fingers.

"No, I'm wrong again," he said; "she is too human, too young to remember those years, and even though she can speak to me, she is too foreign to ever understand."

He let his fingers move briefly to her hair, then took his hand away. "What should I do, Lily? Ask you to have dinner with me, which I cannot afford? Or, *insha'allah,* accept you as my devil sent to give me faith?"

She let her eyes drop slowly from his, seeing again his chest through the open shirt, his narrow hips in the jeans, his naked feet in the sandals. His toes were arched like those of an animal ready to pounce.

"I think we should go somewhere else," she said. His hand slowly reached out for hers. She took it as she thought of Worth, inevitably, she supposed, but without any guilt. That would have been pointless. She'd been to Rabat at Christmas; he'd come to Paris twice since then; they'd made love, they always had a minutely planned and determined good time. And at the end of every visit, Lily felt as lonely as this Algerian, who wanted to have someone understand him in his own language. Holding her hand lightly, he pulled her up from the bench, and they walked out of the park.

Her mother would be appalled, but that didn't matter either. The two women made few judgments about each other, going their separate ways and meeting occasionally for tea. Worth had taken both of them out to dinner; Helene had been charmed, of course, but still advised her daughter against marriage to a diplomat. In the small world of the European upper class, her Italian count had come across her German industrialist at an art auction in Geneva. Once they discovered their common bond, they laughed at themselves and toasted Helene with fine cognac; each man wrote to her of the occasion, informing her that she needn't pick him up at Orly ever again. Then, as luck would have it, while skiing in Gstaad a month later she met an Englishman who owned oil tankers. Helene didn't have to pick him up at Orly because he kept a Rolls-Royce and driver in Paris as well as a sumptuous house on the Île St.-Louis. Of course he was married, with a number of children whom Helene chose not to know. Lily regarded her mother's life as both blessed and cursed, and surely one from which no judgment of others could be made.

Lily and Ammar crossed the Rue St. Jacques to the Rue Galande, then walked along Rue de Fouarre to its end, where there was a heavy ancient chain strung between two iron stanchions. Beyond was the Rue Domat. Lily had never been there and was sure there wasn't a street in Paris like it. The old plaster-and-beam buildings on either side seemed ready to collapse in the easiest breeze; the sidewalk rose and dipped precipitously. They came to a narrow black-mouthed alley that saw the sun for only thirty minutes at noon, creating the same kind of midday dawn and dusk as in thousands of Cairo alleys. Ammar paused and looked at her, still holding her hand, alert for any sign of hesitation.

She gazed into the dark portal and saw several black-draped shapes; they were North African women staring at her, the whites of their eyes reflecting what was left of the light. A glistening stream divided the alley and ran into the gutter. For Lily, the smell of sewage and garbage provoked deep memories of Cairo; they held no disgust for her. The entrance to the alley seemed an exciting darkness, and she stepped toward it eagerly.

Ammar moved ahead to lead her along one side; the two of them walked single file, still holding hands. Several children ran by, stopped to gape, and silently rushed on. The alley curved and descended toward its end, where it was blocked by a stone wall at the back of a mammoth building. In front of the last four-story hovel of crooked windows and split timbers, he paused again; then, seeing no reluctance, he ushered her into a damp hallway. From above they heard someone, a woman, singing in Arabic. They climbed the stairs, and again he had to lead her, for there was no light except from a small skylight at the top floor. Lily kept her eyes on the small circle of sky as they passed the door of the singer and continued up to the fourth floor. There, they encountered a cool smell of damp plaster as well as a grit of glass and dirt on the stairs. Finally they reached an old timber door, which was padlocked. He opened it with a key and swung it open.

In the dim light from the window that looked out on a nearby wall, Lily saw a table covered with books and two unlit candles in holders, a wooden chair, a sink, some makeshift shelves with more books, a chamber pot, and an unmade bed. A large plastic suitcase, open against a wall, contained clothes. In the Arab manner of shutting out the streets and creating a haven in the home, he kept the room immaculately clean.

"I would bring no one but the devil here," he said.

Lily turned toward him. Raising her hand, she touched the bruise on his temple. Then she pulled his head down so that she could kiss him.

He reacted hungrily, grabbing her up in his arms and carrying her into the room. He kicked the door shut and his hands pulled her clothes apart, racing over her body as if he were afraid she would disappear. She wouldn't let his mouth leave hers, biting, sucking, holding his head by his hair until he lifted her again and put her on the bed. He stood beside her undressing, but she had her clothes off before he was naked. She reached up with one hand and ran it over his chest as he crawled onto the bed, straddling her. Suddenly he was absolutely still, so still that Lily was afraid, as his eyes went over her body. Then he fell on her, kissing her where he had looked. Straight-armed, he held his torso above her, watching her as he moved in her, watching her breath quicken and catch, quicken and catch again as her head jerked from one side to another and her mouth opened to cry out, and yet no sound came, as if her mouth were open to swallow the world, which suddenly raced through her and split in two as they writhed together in the damp silent room of early afternoon sunset.

Lily stayed with Ammar until late in the evening. They barely spoke to each other, so intent were they in their passion, listening instead to the sounds of the alley, the children yelling, a cry of pain, a screaming argument, the woman downstairs singing, and a faithful Muslim calling to prayer those less faithful, as if his window onto the alley were a minaret. Lily and Ammar laughed together often, at what they heard, at their urgency for each other. When Ammar finally walked her down the stairs, out of the alley, and to the Métro, she could barely stand to leave him. They lingered at the entrance, she clinging to him, kissing him. He reminded her that they'd see each other the next day, and that gave her just enough assurance to walk away from him.

Exhausted by the time she reached her mother's apartment, she went to her room and collapsed on the freshly made bed. And yet she couldn't sleep, still craving him, wondering if she'd gone mad somehow, not believing it possible to love a man as she so quickly and so fully loved Ammar Ben Ashid.

She finally drifted off into a restless sleep. In a dream, she was searching for something, exactly what was unclear, and as she searched, she found herself in the garbage plains beneath the Mokattam hills in Cairo, rushing over the paths, climbing, higher and higher, as she sank deeper into the putrid garbage that burned around her, tripping over pigs and dogs, sprawling under the shadow of a small Coptic church. She got up and ran through the clouds of smoke. Collapsing on a hill of garbage, crouching on it, sinking her arms deep into the decomposing slime, hearing his bellows, feeling his head and pulling, pulling it up as she began to scream into the terrorist's face, his arms reaching for her and grabbing her, shaking, shaking her . . .

"Lily! Wake up! Wake up! You're terrifying Matilde and even the birds."

Lily stared at her mother, whose face was covered in a thick cream, with a firming strap running over her head and under her chin. "I'm sorry, Mommy. It was a nightmare."

"I gathered that." Helene reached down and cleared Lily's hair from her eyes. "You were very sound asleep when I came home."

"Do you check on me?" Lily said, pleased with the concern.

"If I'm alone, which I am most of the time now, since my friend has his own house here."

"How can you come home? Why don't you stay with him?"

Her mother walked toward the door. She didn't answer until she turned around. "Because I might enjoy it too much and wish to establish the habit. Such a habit would be dangerous, very painful, because it can never last. I know the limit of my luxuries. That is one I do not allow myself"—she lifted her head imperiously— "unless of course I'm on a yacht."

Lily laughed, got up, and embraced her mother. "I wish you'd find somebody," she said as the memory of Worth's sloop came to mind.

"You mean, someone to keep me company, to let me pretend I'm not alone? No. I am alone, you are alone, everyone is alone on this earth, but few can bear to admit it. They marry, have a family, in large part as their unacknowledged reaction against the terror of knowing we are going to die. And we don't want to die alone, do we?" she said contemptuously. "But how many succeed in that sad ambition, in spite of any number of husbands or wives, children, cousins? Go see the old people sitting on the park benches, devastated by how completely they are forgotten, remembered only at Christmas or when they are sick, not for affection's sake but for *ob-li-gation.*" She kissed Lily on one cheek and the other. "They are afraid to be alone, therefore they're lonely. I am not afraid, and will never be lonely. You won't have that obligation. Perhaps that's one maternal gift I can give you." She saw Lily's confused respect, nodded, and walked down the hall. "May I suggest a bath, my darling? It's a bit too obvious that you've been with a man."

"Mother!" Lily said, embarrassed and shocked.

Before entering her own bedroom, Helene looked back and gave Lily a Gallic shrug. "I'm delighted that there's an alternative in your life to that diplomat," she said and closed her door.

Lily took a quick shower, her mind working nervously through her fatigue. Her nakedness excited her as she thought of Ammar, wondering whether she could find her way back to his alley on her own and doubting it. Randomly, she pictured Worth's sloop still berthed at Old Saybrook and the trip south they'd never had time to take together, which seemed the perfect symbol of their relationship.

Lily admired her mother's individuality but recognized how abruptly it could become selfishness. She respected her father's devotion to diplomacy, but wondered how much of himself he had been forced to suppress in order to serve. And where did these two parents of disparate loyalty and selfishness divide themselves in her? She knew they were both there in ever-alternating degrees. Maybe she'd instinctively chosen law as a profession because her inherited qualities wouldn't clash as badly there as in others. Back in bed, falling asleep, she let her debate dissolve into a desire to see Ammar the next day.

––––––––––

"Americans can never understand the Arab world because they don't understand humiliation," Ammar said and kissed her on the back as she sat on the side of his bed, dressing.

Lily spent as much time as she could with Ammar, but as their relationship developed, she came to realize its double-edged nature. If they weren't making love, they argued. Sometimes their arguments spilled over into their sex, and they barely finished with it before continuing their dispute.

"Wait a minute, are you talking about Algeria, the Arab world, or Islam?"

Sitting on the chair, he angrily reversed his socks as he struggled to clarify. "I don't separate Islam from the Arab world. It would be like taking oxygen from water, leaving nothing but vapor. You in America separate your religion from your government by law. The good capitalists gain their fulfillment with money and give thanks to God once a week. The good Muslim worships Allah five times a day and lets money come thereafter, *insha'allah.*"

"There are plenty of rich Muslims who don't pray away the days and wait for money to fall from the sky, *insha'allah.* They go out and make it just as the infidel capitalist does, and nothing in the Koran prevents it." She buttoned up her shirt and took a hairbrush out of her book bag.

"The Koran does not permit the excesses of greed on which capitalism is based." He went over to make the bed.

"There you go, making scripture say what you want it to. It's like a lot of people in America saying the Bible specifically forbids Communism."

"The Koran reveres Jesus as a true messenger of Allah, and it's obvious to anyone who reads the New Testament with any objectivity that Jesus preached pure socialism."

"Well, I could read the Koran like that and conclude that Muhammad was really a Methodist."

"Don't ridicule me, and don't be sacrilegious," he commanded.

"Spoken like a true believer. Better watch out."

"I don't believe, but I respect the believer."

"Me too, but the Koran says that nonbelievers are doomed." She grabbed him in a tight embrace. "You think we're doomed?"

"You *are* a devil." He kissed her.

"Let's go."

She went to the door with her book bag. Still bothered, he followed with an armful of his own books. Outside, he locked the door; then he took her hand and together they went down the dark stairs to the alley.

Fortunately, they were able to study together, silently, in the Sorbonne's library or the physics tower to which he, as a doctoral candidate in geology, had access. She concluded that her passion for Ammar was some kind of preposterous fantasy, her Arabian Nights in Paris, which would disappear one day like a genie. But until that day, she saw him as much as possible, took her exams, and spent every moment she could in his flat on the Rue Domat.

When Worth arrived in Paris, Lily didn't go to Orly to meet him as she had on his previous visits. Instead, she waited in the lobby of the Plaza-Athenée. Her exams were over, and although she hadn't received her grades, she was certain she'd done well.

She'd been accepted to Harvard, Yale, and Stanford law schools, all with scholarships, and had chosen the last. Now she wanted her certificate from Science Po to be impressive. Her plans were to meet her father in Athens for a short visit before the two of them went to Cairo for his vacation. In late July, Lily was scheduled to fly to California, find an apartment in Palo Alto, buy a used car.

Having spent that afternoon making love to Ammar, then arguing about Nasser's failed flirtation with socialism as a harbinger of Algeria's future—the discussion had ended in enraged shouts and long kisses—Lily couldn't think of anything she wanted to say to Worth. When he walked into the lobby, she remained hidden in a hallway until he'd checked in and gone to his room. She waited a few minutes and called him on the house phone.

"Hello?" he answered expectantly.

"It's me."

He paused and she could imagine his face as he chose between accusation or indifference. "Did I miss you at the airport?" he asked in a neutral tone.

"No. I couldn't make it."

"I thought your exams were over?"

"They are."

Another pause.

"How'd you do?" he asked.

"Very well."

"That's terrific. Well, listen, I have a bit of a nice surprise for tonight. We're invited to—"

"Worth, I can't go."

"The hell you can't," he said, giving in to anger. "We've been planning something for this evening for a couple of months now. What the hell is this, Lily? Where are you?"

"I'm downstairs. I'll meet you in the bar." She hung up. It was over, she knew, but she wasn't having it end on the telephone. She wasn't going up to his suite, either.

When he entered the bar, he greeted the maître d' by name and exchanged pleasantries. He came over to Lily's booth, said a gracious hello, bent gracefully to kiss her on the cheek, and sat down beside her. A waiter appeared, and he ordered a kir royale. Lily was drinking Evian water.

"Well, here we are," he said pleasantly, "and maybe you'll tell me exactly what we're doing here."

"I think we're parting company."

He looked around casually, to see how near the other patrons were. None was too close unless he and she raised their voices. He smiled at Lily the way he used to smile when he was about to cut up one of his students in front of his class. "You might have saved me the trip."

"Yes, but I didn't really know until . . ." She stopped.

"Come on, Lily, no need to protect me from the awful truth. Until what?"

"Until you said we were invited somewhere tonight. I knew I couldn't go. I didn't want to go."

"You might have if you'd known what it was," he offered nonchalantly. "It's said that the Aga Khan gives a pretty respectable dinner party."

"Oh, perfect," Lily said. "Did you get the seating plan? I'm sure it'll be another triumph for you, Worth, and that everybody there will adore you. More of the right people and all that."

"I have no doubt that someday you'll learn about 'all that,' " he said impassively, "but it seems an odd reason to throw away what I at least have come to consider an extremely important relationship."

He took a sip of the sparkling kir and Lily watched him. "Worth, I know you so well, I already know how you're going to do this—either change my mind or shame me into thinking I'm rotten and a fool. Couldn't we do it another way?"

"What do you have in mind? I'm not an expert on such matters."

"Oh, you're not so inexperienced, from what you've told me. Let me say this. I've never loved anyone as much as I loved you, and maybe still would if we had a chance. But we don't. We haven't for a long time, probably since you went to Washington—"

"Oh, it's *my* fault."

"No. It's no one's fault. If you hadn't left Yale then, I would have left six months later for law school. If I'd gone to Washington to be with you, you'd have left for Rabat, or me for Paris. Now it's Palo Alto. Who knows where you're going to be next?"

"Well, that's another little surprise I had for you tonight. Please don't repeat this, but if Nixon's re-elected in November, as he's expected to be, then Dr. Kissinger will become secretary of state, and I'll move back to Washington to work in the executive secretariat of the department. He and I met briefly when I was in Washington two weeks ago—"

"Welcome to the seventh floor. Congratulations, Worth. You're on your way, as planned."

"Yes," he agreed tersely and took another sip of his drink. "But do go on."

Lily heard the edge of contempt in his voice. "I respect what you're doing," she said. "I'd like to think that you can respect what I'm doing. Then we can both accept that what each of us is trying to accomplish got in the way of our being together. It's sad, it's painful, but it's all right for us to go our own ways, without any blame, without any anger."

He looked at her, his brow raised in appraisal. "You're very good, Lily. You've missed your calling." He picked up his glass and finished the royale in a gulp. "Now look, if you can't make it tonight, you'll have to excuse me, because I have to find someone else to go, and I've got"—he looked at his watch—"only a couple of hours."

"You won't have any trouble. You and the Aga Khan are an attractive pair."

He laughed softly, nicely, she thought, and leaned over and kissed her cheek again. "Goodbye, Lily. I do love you . . ." he said as he slid out of the banquette and stood before her. "I suppose it's not often clear from my odd crystallizing-the-moment style, which I've no doubt is hard to take or understand. I have no regrets about what we've had."

"No regrets," Lily agreed. He walked across the bar and instructed the maître d' to charge the drinks to his room. Then he was gone. Lily sat for a moment with her hand on her glass. "My odd crystallizing-the-moment style." That was exactly it. He certainly knew himself. Everything he did burst into crystals from the intensity of his energy. But the next moment always needed to be crystallized, too. There was no keeping his attention except by repeatedly throwing yourself in his path.

At the hotel's front entrance, the doorman tipped his hat and asked whether Lily wished a taxi. She'd told Ammar she'd meet him sometime that evening, not knowing how and when she'd be finished with Worth. She decided to go to her mother's first, feeling in need of transition time. Taxis were not in her budget, but at that point the expense seemed justified.

As she stepped out of the taxi at the Avenue de New York, she noticed a black Chevrolet with diplomatic license plates double-parked in front of her mother's building. The driver was talking into a radio phone as she approached the door. The concierge glared suspiciously but said nothing as Lily passed the small window on the ground floor. She climbed the stairs to her mother's apartment, avoiding as usual the ancient elevator for both safety and exercise; above, she could hear Matilde creating a commotion. When she reached the landing, she saw her mother and the young security officer from the American Embassy. Matilde stood behind them, holding one of Lily's suitcases.

"Thank God you've come," her mother said, looking worse than Lily had ever seen her. "Your father's been wounded, badly. I've packed your bag . . ."

NINE

THE DOOR OF THE CAR was opened at the emergency entrance to the American University Hospital in Beirut. Lily hesitated to move toward it. "You can come with me if you like," she heard the French doctor say. She let him lead her with increasing swiftness as the party was escorted by hospital personnel into an elevator. It rose, and when the doors opened she saw Bert instantly through a glass partition. The sight of him jolted her and released a feeling of white-hot fury. She had to suppress a yell of rage.

The doctor had flown from Paris on the United States Air Force transport with her to consult on Bert McCann's injuries. A distinguished French professor of neurosurgery who practiced at the American Hospital in Neuilly, he sat next to Lily in the plane. With compassion but strict candor, the doctor had told her the little he'd learned of Bert's injuries and explained what he and his colleagues in Beirut hoped to do if Bert was still alive.

He was surrounded in the crisis unit by two nurses and two doctors, already dressed in surgical robes. When they saw who had arrived, the nurses moved quickly to hold robes ready for the professor. He donned them as he entered, greeted his two colleagues briefly, then moved to a wall of X-rays nearby.

Lily tried to follow, but the nurses objected until the professor told them to give her a robe and face mask. Lily thanked them in Arabic, which dissolved further resistance. She could hear the doctors conversing in French as she went over to stand by her father's bed.

Bert had been on his way to Yasir Arafat's headquarters in West Beirut to meet with one of the PLO leader's political strategists. A car bomb had been exploded by remote control in a parked Mercedes just as Bert's embassy car drove past. The blast disintegrated the Mercedes, threw the embassy car to the opposite side of the street, and killed the Lebanese driver and guard instantly. Bert's left leg was blown off, and shrapnel had entered his abdomen and skull. The last wound was the French surgeon's greatest concern and his specialty. The loss of a leg was not fatal; injuries to the abdomen, although painful and potentially dangerous, were often controllable. Damage to the brain, however, was frequently irreparable.

Bert's hair had been shaved as much as possible around the four wounds on the left side. One looked ominous, the others less so. Although he was unconscious, one of his eyes was half open. A catheter extended from his nose; IVs dripped plasma and saline into his arms. Large surgical bandages covered his stomach. A sheet was drawn up to his waist, but the absence of his left leg was obvious. Above him on the wall was a heart monitor giving off the regular high-pitched beeps of Bert's pulse.

"Daddy," she said firmly enough to interrupt the doctor's conversation. "Daddy, try to hear this; I know you won't give up. The people here are going to get you through this, and then we're going to the dahabeah. We'll go to the dahabeah." She watched his face but saw no sign of recognition.

"Mademoiselle McCann, we must begin." The professor stood on the other side of Bert's bed. Behind him, one of the doctors held a selection of the X-rays to take with them. Lily stood back as the nurses disconnected the monitor and pushed the bed out of intensive care into an operating room across the hall.

"Your father has a strong heart," the professor said; "for that we can be grateful. My colleagues have already operated on the leg as well as on his perforated intestine." He watched her carefully for the effect of his account. When she nodded, he went on as the other two doctors left for the operating room to begin scrubbing. "Of the wounds to the head, only one of the four pieces of shrapnel penetrated the skull. I'll be taking care of that. As soon as we're done, I'll come talk to you. There's a waiting room on the top floor."

Not until then did Lily notice the pair of American security men who stood by the elevator. One posted himself outside the door to the operating room; the other pressed the up button for her and followed her onto the elevator when it came.

"Is this really necessary?" Lily asked.

"Ambassador's orders, ma'am," the black man responded with a pronounced Southern accent. "You never know what else might be coming down."

She saw his walkie-talkie. "Do you think you can get us some coffee?"

"Black or white?"

"Thick. Turkish. A triple."

"Doughnuts?"

"In Beirut?"

"Ma'am, you can get anything in Beirut."

The waiting room was empty, and Lily took off the surgical gown and slung it over a stuffed leather chair. The security man stayed in the hall but had a view of the room through a window in the wall. Within ten minutes, a Lebanese appeared with her coffee and half a dozen glazed doughnuts, which the security man brought in to her. Only when she tasted the hot bitter liquid did she realize that she'd been standing in the center of the waiting room without thinking or moving, staring through a large window down at a group of children playing with a bright yellow ball in the street. They were all dressed in school uniform, white shirts and dark blue trousers or pinafores. As she drank her coffee, Lily saw a ramshackle school bus stop in the street and all the children run to get on, the yellow ball bouncing and rolling under a car parked at the curb, a Mercedes. The last boy on the street rushed over and reached under the car to retrieve the ball. Lily stepped forward to bang on the window, to yell at the child to get away, imagining the Mercedes disintegrating and a fireball rising. But the boy pulled the ball out and ran onto the bus, which lurched away down the street. Lily noticed that half of the other parked cars were Mercedeses, the line of windshields catching the ball of the sun in reflections of varying intensity.

"The ambassador's coming up," the security man announced from the door. Lily's head drooped. She wasn't up to it. Finding a ghostly reflection in a framed picture on the wall, she tried to straighten her hair. The picture was of the Roman ruins at the

Temple of Bacchus in Baalbek, the ancient city that had been sacked by each of its many invaders.

"Lily," the ambassador said when he came in. He offered his hand and was ready to hold her if she needed it. Lily shook his hand. Outside, more security people appeared, some in military uniform. "What's the latest?" he asked.

"They're operating now," she said and took the last swallow of her coffee.

"I know all those people. They'll get him through," the ambassador said with certainty. A career FSO, he had met Lily on numerous occasions during her visits with her father. He was tall and hulking, with watchful eyes in a large ruddy face, and he never raised his voice or allowed himself or anyone else the slightest pretension. "Are you all right?" He saw her nod and went on. "I had your bag taken to the Residence. We're expecting you any time you want to come. The security people will bring you."

"Thank you. I'll stay for a while after he gets back to his room. Do you know anything about who did it?"

He walked over to the window. "Quite a bit. The party involved has identified itself." He glanced back at Lily. "Are you ready for this now?"

"It'll be a distraction."

He looked out the window, but before he started talking a Lebanese officer poked his head in the door. "Mr. Ambassador, please would you mind not standing at the window? Excuse me, please, for interrupting you."

The ambassador scowled and moved back. The officer closed the door. "Arafat's got about fifty or sixty different guerrilla groups under his PLO umbrella," the ambassador said. "Some of them have different ideas from Yasir's about destroying Israel. An hour after the explosion, a group phoned Reuters to claim responsibility. The spokesman gave the details of the bomb to prove himself, then the group's name and its leader. We figure the bomb was as much a message to Arafat to pay attention to these people as it was to us."

"You mean they did that to my father for a message?"

"Terrorism doesn't have any other purpose, Lily."

"But why him? Why not . . . ?" She closed her eyes and turned away. "I'm sorry."

"Why not me? We don't know. I suppose because they knew Bert was headed their way, and an American would make the most impressive statement."

"Who are they?"

"They call themselves the Palestinian Command Group, PCG. From the little we know, we're talking about two dozen men. Their leader has named himself Abu al-Saffah, which gives us an idea of his political philosophy. How's your Arab history?"

"It's okay, but I don't know that name."

"In the eighth century, the founder of the Abbasside dynasty in Baghdad was a guy named Abul-Abbas, known as al-Saffah, which meant the Bloodletter. He was your archetypal brutal despot, but what set him off from the rest was that he'd butcher some group just to prove he owed no allegiance or respect to anyone, that the only way was his way. I think that's what this Abu al-Saffah wanted to tell Arafat, who, we hear, is hopping mad. He had al-Saffah flown off to Libya last night to get him out of here."

"What do you mean?" Lily asked. "If Arafat's so upset, why didn't he turn the man in instead of sending him off to Qaddafi, who'll give him a parade?"

The ambassador checked Lily and saw anger rather than tears. "Because in this particular circus of chaos, Arafat is the star juggling clown."

"He seems to enjoy the spotlight," Lily offered, making conversation in order not to think.

The ambassador sat down on a wooden settee and slouched sideways, his large frame supported by one elbow. "Every time I see a view of Beirut like this, I think it looks great. But it's all painted scenery, with three or four circles of hell right behind it. I'm no Arabist, you know. I've been in the African Bureau for my whole career. 'Cosmopolitan' Beirut was Personnel's reward to me for my years in the African wilds. Well, as something of an expert on jungles, diplomatic and otherwise, I'd choose the Congo over this one any day. Thank God your father took me by the hand."

Lily went over to a corner and finally sat down. She wanted to look at her wristwatch but decided not to. "Did you know my father before Beirut?" she asked.

"No. I was a year behind him at the Institute, then went to sub-

Saharan Africa, seldom to be seen again." He sent a grim smile to Lily, then said, "He's one of the best, Lily. He said the smartest thing I've ever heard an Arabist say, made sense out of this whole Middle East mess better than anything I've heard—that Israel is the Arab world's great excuse. That's exactly it. The Arabs stay in a constant state of war with the hated Jews, and therefore get to ignore or manipulate their own overwhelming problems."

Lily stood up again. "That's half the story," she said. There was a three-week-old copy of *Newsweek* on a side table. Lily had read it in Paris but picked up the magazine anyway. She riffled through the pages for something she might not have read. The ambassador stood and Lily raised her head, expecting a rejoinder. But he was looking at the door as it opened. She turned to see the French surgeon, still in his surgical robes. The door closed behind him.

"I'm so very sorry," he said.

Lily held the magazine in front of her. "What do you mean? You said you'd be able—" To the ambassador she said, "You told me they'd get him through." Before they could respond, she noticed the magazine in her hand and abruptly threw it against the window that overlooked Beirut. Her legs started to shake. "I have so many things to say to him. Can't you do something? What happened?"

"Lily," the ambassador started, then paused. "He's gone, Lily." He waited for a response. When she only stared at him, he said, "Why don't we go to the Residence?"

She shook her head. "May I please stay here alone?"

The two men exchanged glances. The surgeon finally nodded and opened the door for the ambassador, who said, "We won't be far; call for us whenever you want," and went out.

Before the doctor left, Lily managed to say in French, "What happened, Doctor?"

"There was more damage to the brain than we thought; then hemorrhaging . . ." He hesitated and shook his head.

"Thank you for coming, for trying," Lily said.

"Remember his life," the surgeon said. "Forget his death." He looked down as if ashamed. "I say that too often."

"I can't forget, but I will remember. There's so much." She managed to force a smile, which allowed the doctor to go. Closing her eyes, she stood without moving and heard the muffled discussion in the hall as the ambassador and his guards left. When it was quiet, she noticed her security guard through the hall window. He was alone again, watching her, expressionless. Lily went to the door and opened it.

"May I have another coffee?" she asked.

"A triple?"

"Please."

"Coming up."

"Thanks," Lily said. She let the door close and walked over to the window. Staring into the glare of Beirut, she wondered why she didn't cry. Below, she saw the ambassador's limousine speed down the street and around the corner, preceded and followed by military vans. The car reminded her of the limousine in Tripoli, then of a hearse. She was going to have to bury her father.

The embassy would want a funeral or at least a memorial service. Probably the Lebanese government would wish to take part in order to indicate that this was a highly unlikely event in civilized Beirut and not the beginning of its unraveling. Not being church-goers, she and Bert had joked occasionally about wanting their ashes strewn on the Nile or tossed to the desert winds from atop the Pyramid of Cheops.

He had never made much money yet had spent a lot on her education before her scholarships, so there would be little in his will. Except the dahabeah. With that image filling her mind, Beirut blurred before her and she felt tears running down her cheeks.

Dear Ammar,

I disappeared because my father died yesterday as a result of a terrorist's bomb in Beirut. I don't know how much of this was in the Paris papers, and I know you refuse to read them, so I wanted to let you know what happened to me. I'll send this to Science Po—I never learned your address. There's an embassy courier waiting outside to get this letter into the pouch to Paris, so I have to hurry. I hope it reaches you. I'd have called, but no phones in the alley.

I don't know when or if I'll be returning to Paris. I must go to Cairo, then to Washington to settle my father's legal matters. I miss you. I'd give anything to be sitting with you in our park arguing Islam or Lenin instead of walking through this nightmare. You so often infuriated me (because you were *wrong!*) and I think I loved you for it.

Somehow we'll meet again. I write in haste. Forgive me.

                                                                    Lily

   She didn't read over the letter, but immediately sealed and addressed it. Already wearing the black silk dress that had been delivered from a French shop to the Residence the day before, Lily stood up as she heard the commotion of people outside the door of the ambassador's small study. She put her hand on the knob and took a deep breath. Quick burials were the custom because of the Middle East's heat. Even though she'd had Bert's body cremated, the memorial service had to take place, as protocol demanded.

   She'd slept for nine hours, with benefit of drugs that had left a bitter taste in her mouth. The ambassador's wife had given her sunglasses; Lily decided to put them on. They were large enough to cover any unexpected reaction she might have in spite of her determination. She touched the black lace mantilla that held her hair in place against the possible sea breeze from the Mediterranean. Beirut was already sweltering; there had been no spring in the Middle East that year. When the rains of winter ended, the broiling summer began.

   She went into the large entrance hall of the Residence. Those gathered became silent. She saw the ambassador and his wife standing at the bottom of the stairs with the president of Lebanon. Lily looked around for the courier to take her letter just as the Lebanese leader approached her across the hall. Also waiting were embassy officers and military attachés in their full-dress summer uniforms. There was a movement into the formal order of leaving the Residence in the cars already drawn up outside the front entrance. Lily saw the courier, who hesitated to approach at the same time as the President.

   When she turned to receive the official condolences of the country, she glimpsed Worth. At first she thought she was crazed. He was standing alone by a potted palm, his hands behind him. A small section of his dirty-blond hair uncharacteristically stuck out on one side of his head as if he'd slept on it wrong, probably on a plane, Lily thought.

"May I please extend to you the great sympathy and regret of the Lebanese people," the president said in Arab-accented French, "as well as my own deep compassion."

Lily thanked him and shook his hand, barely able to keep her eyes fixed on him as he turned and walked to the front door. The ambassador and his wife came over to Lily and gracefully flanked her to escort her to their limousine. Deftly, the courier placed himself near the entranceway to receive the letter that Lily was still holding in her hand along with her bag. When Lily stopped to hold it out to him, she turned to the ambassador.

"Is there room for one more in the car?" she asked.

"Yes, of course," he answered and anticipated her move with a glance at Worth.

Lily walked back across the hall, and as soon as Worth was certain she was coming for him, he moved toward her. For a moment, they stood, saying nothing. Then Worth, conscious of the attention of all those waiting, reached out to shake her hand.

"Will you come with us?" she asked.

His eyes didn't waver from her as he murmured his thanks and let go of her hand. Lily observed, however, the familiar shift of posture and elevation of the chin as he readied himself to take center stage. She led him back to the front entrance, and the two couples were helped into the limousine by marines in summer dress. Worth sat on the jump seat in front of Lily and faced straight ahead. The car pulled out of the walled courtyard, following the Lebanese president's vehicle.

As the cortège formed and progressed slowly down the boulevard, no one in the limousine spoke. The ambassador's wife, usually loquacious, was silent, either from respect for the situation or curiosity about the new element. Lily wondered when Worth had arrived, how he'd heard. He shifted in his seat and, after a courteous smile to his diplomatic superior, gazed at Lily.

She leaned forward. "Thank you for being here."

"I wouldn't be anywhere else."

The four passengers stared at the city outside. Even though each had donned dark glasses and the windows were tinted, the glare of the streets cut through their air-conditioned space and made them squint. Lily used Worth's arrival to distract her from resentment about the instant ceremony, which had more to do with politics than anything else.

"What's that about?" the ambassador leaned forward to ask his driver. In front of them, the president's car had suddenly sped ahead. The driver and the guard riding next to him both shook their heads.

"Go very slowly, and call ahead to see what's up," the ambassador ordered. To his wife and Lily he said, "This is a pretty important event here. I wouldn't be surprised if there's some kind of demonstration. Not to worry."

The guard, already on the car radio, turned to say, "The PLO has shown up at the church, an honor brigade with flags, standing at attention outside."

The ambassador scowled and sighed. "A bit of local politics, Lily. Arafat's been calling all over the place, wanting to appear with the leaders at the church. He was refused, so he's showing who has the real power around here."

"How clever," Lily said, and Worth looked at her.

"Yes," the ambassador agreed. "He gets to show off, and gives the public impression, without ever saying so, that the PLO wasn't really responsible. The question is, what should we do?"

"What are the choices?" Lily requested angrily. The ambassador's wife flicked a look at her for the cold response.

"We can turn around and go back to the Residence," the ambassador answered, "we can arrive at the scene and refuse to take part if the PLO doesn't withdraw, or we can attend the service and ignore them. Any other ideas, Mr. Deloit?"

"I'd say your last suggestion is the way to go, sir, unless"—he turned to Lily—"unless Lily wants to face them down, get out of the car alone, and walk over to the officer in charge. No words, no gestures, just a silent statement of contempt."

Lily couldn't see his eyes through his dark glasses, whether they expressed concern for her or glinted in the particular way they did when he was manipulating a situation for best effect. She leaned forward and reached for his hand. "Let's ignore them, get this over with."

Worth agreed, and the ambassador spoke to the guard in the front seat. "Tell everyone that we'll drive up to the church and go in, taking no notice of the PLO's presence. If there's a disturbance of any sort, tell them to follow our lead." He sank back in his seat as the guard repeated his orders on the radio phone. "Sorry for the excitement, Lily," the ambassador said, "but I have the feeling Bert would consider it the most appropriate part of his memorial service."

Lily smiled, as did the ambassador's wife. Worth signaled his appreciation of the senior diplomat's timing.

A block away from the Anglican church, they could see the crowds gathered there. The PLO was immediately apparent. Drawn up across the street from the church's entrance were five rows of soldiers with their Kalashnikovs held across their chests. An officer in a new uniform stood at ease next to a soldier holding the Palestinian flag. Paying no attention to the crowd and confusion around them, the men stood motionless in the sun.

The confusion was caused by curious bystanders being moved out of harm's way by police. A contingent of Lebanese soldiers was hurrying to take a position opposite the PLO on the street in front of the church. Army officers dressed in their formal uniforms were seen giving orders to the soldiers as well as conferring with an obviously furious president of Lebanon. When he saw the line of official limousines approach, he issued several staccato orders; then, walking solemnly, he entered the church.

American security officers already at the church surrounded the ambassador's limousine as it halted at the entrance. When the door was opened, Worth and the ambassador stepped out first, then helped the two women and led them quickly inside. Lily was immediately aware that the nave was packed. She kept her eyes straight ahead on the altar, but the presence of so many of her father's colleagues, not only members of the local diplomatic community but those ambassadors and senior officers who had traveled at short notice to Beirut for the service, tightened her throat and almost broke her determination. Involuntarily her eyes picked out a familiar face turned back toward her. At first, she couldn't place him, then did: the young FSO in Tripoli who seemed so disillusioned when Bert was refused Cairo. She remembered that Bert had worked hard to convince him to stay in the Foreign Service. She couldn't remember his name. Harris? Then she saw tears in his eyes.

Worth seated Lily in the first pew, next to the ambassador and his wife, and went over to the side aisle to find a seat, since space for him had not been set aside. Behind her sat four American ambassadors with whom Bert had served. Lily had been told they were coming from their various posts in the Middle East.

As she tried to concentrate on the service, she became aware of a thought, one that had come to her occasionally in the past but went nowhere, crowded out by other interests. This time, the thought was firmly established and moved through her mind with urgency, wariness, and certainty, overwhelming resistance to it with what seemed a harmonious conviction.

In the moment of echoing consonance that followed the final chord of the Bach prelude, she knew she had to talk to someone about it, someone who would be able to perforate the emotion of the moment and force her to examine the sentimentality of her decision. Lily's thought was that she too would become a dip. The motives for such a dramatic decision were too obvious, too mawkish. And in a church. Who better to analyze and skewer such an ambition than Worth Deloit?

TEN

A CHINESE PORCELAIN JAR from a Beirut mortician seemed an incongruous container for Bert's ashes. Lily carried it, wrapped in a piece of black velvet, on the flight to Cairo. Worth had made the arrangements for the trip and accompanied her. Noorna met them at the airport and brought them to the dahabeah in her family's enormous chauffeur-driven limousine, recently released from storage.

With Worth standing on one side of her, Noorna on the other, and her father's favorite recording of Bach playing on the phonograph brought down from the study, Lily slowly poured the ashes out of the jar through a window in the sun room. A light breeze spread the fine particles on the surface of the Nile as it flowed past the white-and-green side of the old houseboat. When the jar was empty, Lily let it fall into the river, where the colorful porcelain, instead of sinking, managed to float along with the current.

Downriver, a felucca was making its way back to its mooring at day's end. As the three mourners watched, the gray cloud of ash on the water's surface floated past the boat, surrounding it for a moment before disappearing into the early evening shadows. As the porcelain jar bobbed by, one of the crew spotted it and reached over the side to grab it from the current. He held up his prize and yelled in triumph to his crewmates.

"Perfect," Lily said and turned to her companions. Noorna's eyes were about to overflow with tears, but she managed a loving smile to Lily and reached out her arms to hug her. Over Noorna's shoulder, Lily saw Worth also smile, but he did so to cover another wordless reaction to Cairo. On the way in from the airport, Lily had noticed his silent judgments of the city's crowds, its decay, its filthy streets, its anarchic traffic. On the dahabeah, the smell of the Nile in summer was pungent.

"You get used to the aroma around here," she offered.

He chuckled, acknowledging her observation. "It's fine. Nothing can be so bad as the Rabat goat bazaar."

Lily knew he'd made a reservation at the Sheraton and was surely looking forward to the air conditioning and a soaking bath.

"How long are you going to stay, Lily?" Noorna asked.

"I don't really know," Lily replied. "We just did what I came to do. Now that it's done, I have to figure out everything else." Worth caught the implication. She'd made it before in an attempt to talk with him about her decision, but she'd said nothing direct as yet, still questioning her motivation. "Let's have a drink of something," she offered. "No ice I'm afraid; the refrigerator's been off."

"As long as it's alcoholic," Worth requested.

"Just soda for me," Noorna said. "Why don't you stay all summer, Lily, and come with us to Alexandria?"

Lily, struggling to open the stuck door on an old rattan cabinet where the liquor was stored, replied, "I doubt if I'll be here that long. When's your wedding?" The door opened and she found a bottle of orange squash and some whiskey.

Noorna bowed her head to answer. "The high season, January, February, as late as possible."

"I'll come back for it," Lily said and poured from the bottle of Glen Morangie single malt, her father's favorite.

"Well, can you and Worth come to dinner this Saturday? My mother and father would love to see you."

"Noorna, my desk officer in Washington is already in a snit," Worth said with an amused air of contempt. "If I don't get back to Rabat like a good little boy, he'll burst. I really have to leave tomorrow." He took the glass Lily offered him and noticed the two women holding theirs, hesitating to drink. "It's his whiskey," he said, "so he gets the toast." He held his glass up toward the beginning of the hazy sunset they could see through the windows. "In the only place that you ever called home, here's to you, Bert. You had a pure purpose that everyone envied, and with it, there was no finer diplomat, no finer father, no finer man." He drank quickly.

In spite of knowing his penchant for toasts, Lily saw for the first time since he arrived in Beirut that Worth was genuinely moved. She was struck by her own memories, and swallowed the whiskey to dissolve any reaction to them. When will I fall apart, she wondered, and remembered crying as a girl just from an occasional morbid fantasy of her father's death. Or is this very sudden, very suspect ambition toward diplomacy some convoluted form of mourning, of keeping Bert alive by taking his place, or some such nonsense?

"Noorna, are you still jogging?" Lily asked.

"Every morning."

"The west gate at six-thirty? I'll meet you tomorrow morning."

"Wonderful."

"I have to talk to Worth tonight, since he's leaving so soon."

"Of course." She kissed Lily on the cheek. "Worth, shall I have your bags dropped at the Sheraton?"

"That would be perfect, Noorna. I'll walk you up. I'm glad to have met you at long last. Lily's told me a lot about you, but she didn't do you justice."

Noorna led Worth out of the dahabeah and up the steps to the street where the car was waiting. Lily went to the phonograph, turned it off, and slipped the old record back into its cover. She left the sun room and went into the tiny kitchen, taking her glass and the bottle of whiskey with her. When she heard Worth coming down the steps, she felt strangely enervated and wished he'd leave, probably, she thought, so that she wouldn't have to think about the future.

He came in, carrying his empty glass from the sun room. "Seconds?" he asked.

"And thirds if we want." Lily poured for him and, with no preamble, said, "I've decided not to go to law school."

He took the news in, then smiled thinly. "So this is it. I've had the impression you'd made some momentous decisions, which, perhaps, may not be too wise under the circumstances."

"I know. That's why I wanted to talk to you."

"Fine, but don't hope for any conclusions tonight, okay? You need time more than any wisdom I can drop on you."

"I don't want time. I know what I want to do, and I want to get on with it."

He watched her curiously, took a drink, and leaned against the wall of the kitchen. His head nearly touched the low ceiling; he stooped slightly to avoid it. "If you're going to tell me you want to go into the Foreign Service, please don't."

"I want to go into the Foreign Service."

"Jesus," he said and crossed one leg in front of the other. "You realize the obvious, don't you? That you're reacting emotionally to your father's death, that you feel you have to take up his fallen torch, follow in his footsteps, and all that fine crap."

"That's possible, as well as anger about how he was treated by the department. I may have some idea about wanting to set things right."

"What about the little item of revenge? Now you've got two terrorists to go after. You probably want to come back out here as super dip, get those guys, and set the whole Middle East straight."

"I hadn't thought of revenge. But even with all of those possibilities—none of which I think is valid, by the way—there's another reason."

"What did we miss?"

"That I'd be good at it."

"Not if you're doing it for any of the reasons we mentioned. You'd be suspect as soon as you walk into the oral exams. Even if you get through, if any sign of your anger ever comes out, they'll spot you and put you in a box. You'll become a bitter, driven neurotic who'll spend her career—as long as it lasts—pushing paper in Visa Services, or somewhere. Besides, you'd be a better lawyer."

"There are too many lawyers. They're clogging up everyone's lives making work for themselves."

"Well, there are too many diplomats, believe me, and there isn't enough useful work to keep half of them busy. Lily, eighty-five percent of the State Department are bureaucrats, and the other fifteen percent depend on who's president and secretary to find justification for their existence. The whole place can churn along for years doing nothing but gathering occasional scraps of information. Don't think you'll satisfy any high ideals of service. Bert was lucky to have come along when he did. If he came in now, he and his innocence would be in the Consulate Section in Upper Volta."

Lily took a drink. He'd said what she expected, probably what anyone would say. Stung, hurt, and angry, she wondered how crazy she was and thought about law school again. To her surprise, she couldn't imagine it anymore, couldn't stand the idea of going back to that ambition which she had never really questioned.

"Having said all that"—Worth broke the extended silence "—and everything else we said, I hope you'll consider very carefully. But after that, if you're honestly free of all the romantic baggage, then I'd have to agree with you. You'd make one hell of a good Foreign Service officer. I'd also point out that the two guys I've let stay in the O Street house will be leaving for their posts in a couple of weeks, so it'll be empty if you need a place to live while you're at the Institute."

Lily put down her glass. "What are you saying?"

"A lot of things. I'm saying you'd have a brilliant career in law. Law offers chances at many brilliant careers. The Foreign Service offers far less to fewer people, unless you're very lucky, very smart, and very determined." They exchanged knowing smiles, both acknowledging him as an example. "I'm saying that any career other than diplomacy would be better for you, so that you can walk away from these inexplicable tragedies that've hit your life, and get on with it, rather than putting yourself in a job that'll just continue to feed your nightmares. I'm saying also that I hope to marry you"—he glanced up from his drink to see her reaction but didn't pause—"that it's obvious—at least to me—that I'm in love with you, that when it really sank through my overweening pride and into my glibly rationalizing brain that I might damn well lose you, I had a sense of loss I've never felt before and don't want to feel again. By the way, because of you, the Begum Khan thought I was a real bore."

"Stop," Lily ordered.

"I have nothing more to say," he said and finished his drink, still leaning against the wall.

"I can't believe you said that. I can't imagine what to—how to —respond."

"I don't expect you to. It's pretty damned inappropriate of me even to mention it at this particular moment. But I had to, Lily.

When I turned around in the limo and watched you as we were driving to the service for Bert, loving you hit me so hard, I couldn't think, and I came up with that idiotic idea of you facing down the goddamn PLO." He closed his eyes at the thought. "That's one of those things you say and for the rest of your life cringe when you think of it. I'm grateful that you turned it down."

"That was about the time I suddenly thought about going into the Foreign Service."

"I see, a blinding flash. That neighborhood's known for it. Same thing happened to Saul of Tarsus over on the road to Damascus."

She laughed briefly, looked around the room for something to do, and opened the door of the refrigerator to switch it on. She put the empty ice trays upside down in the sink and turned on the water to clear the pipes. "Worth, I have to tell you something. I fell in love with someone in Paris."

Until the rust cleared, she stared at the running water, then turned it off and faced him.

"I see." He cleared his throat, trying to draw back into his usual disdainful control of an emotional situation. It didn't work. A pained frown slowly appeared as he gazed up into a corner. "April in Paris, I suppose," he said, the intended sarcasm lost in his broken delivery.

"That may have had something to do with it. I'm not sure why it . . ."

Without looking at her, he said, "I don't want to hear the details if you don't mind, except, well . . ." He took a deep breath and exhaled slowly. "Is he still in the picture?"

Lily hesitated. "I don't know," she answered with confused surprise.

At that, he did look at her, more intensely than Lily had ever seen, and said, "May I take you to dinner?"

"My God, Worth, don't you think each of us needs some time alone?"

"We'll have that chance for as long as we want tomorrow."

"I don't want to sit somewhere and have a tense little fencing match with you."

"No quick thrusts, I promise. We can practice diplomacy, as if we were seated at a state dinner next to the potentate who tortured us at lunch."

Lily eyed him suspiciously. "I don't know what your plan is, and I know you have one, but as you said, we can't accomplish anything tonight."

He laughed derisively. "Lily, believe me, after what I've just heard, my only hope is to avoid eating alone. As for the rest of the evening, no presumption has occurred, as my reservation at the Sheraton indicates. But both of us have to eat. And as I remember, you haven't had anything all day."

Whether from whiskey or suggestion, Lily unexpectedly felt ravenous. "All right, but let's go right now and make an early evening of it." She started out of the kitchen, and Worth followed.

"Any suggestions where?" he asked. "This is your town."

"I gather you don't like it much."

"I'm sure it's an acquired taste."

"I'm not so sure. Most people either love it or hate it in the first two minutes." She locked the door of the dahabeah and preceded Worth up the steps of the riverbank.

"Please don't regard my reaction as a test of my character."

"I don't need those anymore."

He didn't respond and went up to the street to hail a taxi.

———

The restaurant was a few stone steps down from the sandy parking lot. Famed for hammam—roasted pigeons—the open-air establishment was on the riverbank. In the tolerant Egyptian way, it was overrun by semiwild cats that made consuming one's dinner an adventurous competition. Given a chance, they would leap over the table and snatch a roasted bird right off a plate.

Lily and Worth were ushered over the pebbled dirt to a table under an awning of palm branches. Other tables were crowded with Egyptian families escaping their homes as soon as the sun was down to enjoy the chance river breeze after the cauldron of the long summer day. The aromatic smoke of the barbecue fires filled the air, as did the rich scent of dozens of pigeons being roasted on large racks over the coals.

When they were seated, they were presented with bottled water and Stella beer, pita, tahini, and baba ghanoush by a harried Nubian waiter in a long brown robe. They ate and drank without speaking, except for offering each other the various dishes. Lily said suddenly, "I've never really thanked you, have I? Except that once in the ambassador's car. I'm so grateful you came all that way, and that you're here. I couldn't have made it without you."

Worth wiped his mouth with the restaurant's paper napkin. "I'll take as much credit as I can get, and you're welcome. But you could have done it. I may have handled some details and provided a shoulder now and then, but you displayed an impressive power. The ambassador noticed it too, said you were all heart, backbone, and guts. I've never admired anyone more—and as you know, admiration doesn't come easily to me. That's above and beyond being in love with you."

Lily shook her head in disbelief. "When did that happen?" she asked impatiently. "And what was it before?"

"Before what?"

"Before you realized you'd lost me."

"I certainly loved you, but obviously it was something less, probably because I was so involved with what I was doing."

"Has that changed?"

"No, and I doubt it ever will. But I've become aware of something I want just as much, which is you. I also think we'd be terrific together, but that's another issue."

"Even if I'm in the Foreign Service?"

"Whatever, although I haven't considered that in any great detail. I hope you realize that my objections to your being an FSO didn't have anything to do with us, only you. But if you choose that way to go, it might turn out to be quite interesting for both of us."

Their pigeons came, two on a plate, split open and succulent. At the same time, two cats appeared on the low wall by their table, a third on the branches above. They watched for their chance as the two humans picked up the birds in their hands and began eating, extricating small bones from each mouthful. Only after consuming enough to satisfy their hunger did the humans speak again. By then the cats had lost interest and stolen away to search for a better opportunity.

Worth took out a cigar from a leather holder and a gold cutter.

"Do you mind?" he asked as he snipped off the end of the small Montecristo.

"If you want. It'll give the mosquitoes cancer."

He lit a wooden match that he drew from his pocket, and puffed at the cigar until its end was an ember.

"May I suggest," he said between puffs, "that you prepare, with great delicacy, responses about your attitudes which will give the hearer the clear understanding that, in spite of what happened to you in 1967 or what happened to your father four days ago, you stand above the Middle Eastern fray in a state of serene objectivity and pragmatic wisdom. There are those in Personnel, sitting on their lily pads, croaking, and eating flies, who regard the slightest hint of zeal as dangerously radical. And for God's sake don't let anyone know you're as intelligent as you are, and don't speak Arabic better than your examiner."

"Thanks for the advice."

"If you're smart, you won't use it, and you'll stay out of the quagmire."

"If it's so bad, why are you there?"

"Because it's my kind of quagmire, Lily, a place where, if a person is sleek and fast on the turns and can chew off his own leg to get out of the traps, he'll have a future. You're more of a desert animal, can go through any degree of hell and survive on nothing, but there are those deep wells of passion there, unpredictable and volatile. D'you suppose they have any cognac here?"

"Maybe some arak," she suggested while considering his analysis.

He signaled, and the waiter took the order. Lily declined. As he smoked his cigar and waited for his drink, he stared off at the reflection of the moon in the Nile. "Do you think there's a chance for us, Lily?"

"There would be, if . . ."

"If what?"

"If you weren't a mink, and I weren't a camel."

He laughed as the arak was delivered, laughed again as he took a sip.

"I don't know the answer, Worth. I need that time."

"I agree, but what I'm curious about is whether time is on my side or my rival's."

Lily sat back in her chair and stared at the river. Paris, her time with Ammar, the intense passion she'd felt, seemed miles and years away instead of a few hours on a plane, a few days. She hoped her letter had reached him. The idea of the future somehow including him, however, seemed fatuous. Neither of them had ever planned beyond their next meeting, and now there weren't going to be any more.

"The rival isn't the problem, Worth. It's just you and me."

"I see," he said buoyantly. "Well, here's to the problem, and the one sure thing we know about problems: they're conceived in order to be solved." He drank his arak, took out his wallet, and put some Egyptian pounds on the table. "Shall we go?"

During the ride back, they spoke of practical matters, lawyers in Washington, settling Bert's estate, and the house on O Street. Worth was most convincing in his argument that he needed someone living there so that it wouldn't tempt the capital's crime wave to crash through it. She could stay there for the rest of the summer while she worked on her father's affairs, and use the car to keep it tuned. In the fall, whether she chose the Foreign Service Institute or law school, she could decide to stay or leave.

"What happens after the election," Lily asked, "when you come back to take your place on the seventh floor?"

"Maybe McGovern will win and I'll be sent to Katmandu. Maybe you'll be in Palo Alto after all. That's a long time away, Lily, which is exactly what we agreed is needed. What'll you do about the dahabeah?"

"I want to keep it if I can, just the way he did, pay the license fees, hire the caretaker, fix it enough to keep it from sinking, scrape and caulk it every year. It's still my home."

"Home is where the heart is and I plan to nail yours to my wall."

"How uncomfortable, but thanks for the warning."

Worth had instructed the driver to drop him at the Sheraton first, and by the time they reached the hotel, they were laughing together. The hotel doorman opened Worth's door. Before getting out, he said, "One chaste kiss will have to do, serving as both 'I love you' and 'goodbye.' " He kissed her gently and she responded to the familiarity of the embrace. He held her a moment. "Be a lawyer. And marry me." Then he stepped out of the cab and walked into the hotel without looking back.

PART TWO

FSO

September 1972–November 1973

ELEVEN

MISS McCANN, other than some of the obvious reasons we've already discussed—I mean your background, your father—why have you chosen the Foreign Service?"

The question was asked by the senior of five men who sat across a conference table from Lily in a small bare room. The window provided an eighth-floor view of the Key Bridge and, beyond, Georgetown. Lily had been seated in the hard wooden chair for five hours, except for several breaks and a nervous lunch alone at the Foreign Service Institute's cafeteria. The questioning had been intense, with little jocularity. Two of the men were senior officers, two were retired FSOs, and one was on the staff of the Institute.

"I believe I have certain skills that suit me to serve the State Department," she said, "and if I'm successful in that, I'll have a rewarding career."

"And what exactly is your idea of success, Ms. McCann?" asked the man who seemed to be playing "bad cop" on the panel. "Considering, of course, that of the fifteen thousand who apply each year, we take only two hundred into the Foreign Service, and of those chosen, only three percent ever become ambassadors."

"I've been familiar with those statistics for a long time. None of them has had any effect on my decision to be here. My idea of success is to serve well, to learn more, and to exchange any understanding gained with others for our mutual benefit." This was one of the answers she'd prepared on Worth's advice.

"Miss McCann, your area of interest obviously is the Middle East," the member of the Institute's staff observed. "Your language proficiency is of great advantage there. By the way, gentlemen, the results of Miss McCann's language test is a rating of S-4/R-2. But as a Foreign Service officer, you may be asked to serve in any of some hundred and seventy countries where we have posts. Would you feel thwarted in your ambition if you were assigned outside your area of expertise?"

"I'd have to quarrel with the term 'expertise,' " Lily replied. "I'm certainly no expert. But if those in charge of such things thought I could do a job somewhere else, anywhere, I would trust they knew what they were doing. I wouldn't have any problem going."

"You have something of a history," the bad cop said evenly, riffling the pages in the file in front of him. "One could almost say 'fame.' Your answers to our questions today have been *au point* but perhaps disingenuous. I must wonder about a possible mind set toward the Middle East, one that would make objective observation difficult. That, after all, is the basic requirement of an effective diplomat."

"Please believe that I've wondered about the same thing, sir, not because of any 'fame,' but because I agree with you. The death of my father and the atrocity in 1967 naturally have had a complex effect on me. If they hadn't, I'd be even more suspect. But I can assure you, as I assure myself, that those matters have been put firmly into perspective. Except for an occasional nightmare, which you've read about in the psychiatrist's report and follow-ups, I don't dwell on those events. As to my biases, prejudices, or 'mind sets,' I can assure you that all I have is opinions, lots of them, not one of which is closed to change . . . based, of course, on 'objective observation.' "

Lily did not smile, but her interrogator did, appreciative of her turning his words back on him. Having known that the question would come, she had worked on the answer and was pleased with herself for using his phrase. Worth had warned her there would be a bad cop on the panel, usually the nicest member in real life. The five men were quiet and Lily thought perhaps her oral exam was over.

"Miss McCann, I'd be interested to know what in the world you think the State Department of the United States government is." The questioner was one of the retirees, a man with flowing white hair who had said nothing during the five hours. He sat slumped in his chair, seldom looking at her. Whether he was making notes or doodling on a pad, Lily could not be sure. The tone of his question was one of tired exasperation, and Lily answered with great care. "Aside from being the institution by which this country observes, interprets, and communicates its foreign policy to other countries, it's structured in the Executive Branch to help shape that policy, depending on the will of the president."

"And of course we know," the retiree said, "that if it's the president's will, we can sit on our hands for four years while he and some smoothie appointed to the National Security Council fly all over the world cutting their own foreign policy." He looked at his colleagues for some agreement with his dig at Kissinger and Nixon, but received none. "But if something came down to you in the field that you thought was detrimental to our country," he continued, "would you question it?"

"Detrimental? Yes, sir. But if it was something that I simply disagreed with, I'd seek some guidance."

"From whom?"

"Well, my starting rank would be FSO-Eight, so I'd probably try to find an FSO-Seven".

The man smiled and ran his hand back through his white hair. "That would be wise. But always question. We receive a good deal of reporting that's as elegant as literature, but it's used to disguise a terrible lack of critical understanding. Don't give in to it."

From the stoical looks on the other panel members' faces, Lily gathered that he gave a similar speech to all the candidates he interviewed.

"I'll do my best, sir."

For a moment, the men were silent. Lily was afraid she'd talked too much and perhaps had contradicted someone's opinion. They looked at one another, and the man sitting in the center said, "That will do, Miss McCann. You'll hear from us. Is the O Street address where we can reach you?"

"Yes, sir. Thank you, gentlemen."

Closing the door behind her, she walked stiffly across the reception area to the bank of elevators. The muscles in her back were sore; she could feel the impression cut by the edge of the wooden chair on the back of her legs. When she reached the first floor and went through the building's revolving door, she took a deep breath of the fresh air. A cab waited for a fare at the curb, but Lily decided to walk back to Georgetown, and headed toward the Key Bridge.

The breeze cooled the sweat of her exertion as she crossed the high span over the Potomac. For the exam she had worn a comfortable summer suit and practical pumps, all of which she wanted to change as soon as possible. It was an early August afternoon and the traffic was sparse. Several joggers sped by, and below, to the west, Lily saw a lonely scull on the river, shooting ahead and gliding, with every stroke cutting a fine V, each side of which rolled evenly on the surface toward the shore. Stopping to watch, she leaned against the railing and considered how she'd done.

Probably she had talked too much, as she'd feared, but on the other hand, she'd been aware of her need to control the tendency throughout the exam. The answers she'd prepared seemed to have worked; there had been little follow-up on the delicate issues of her father's death and her personal attitudes toward the politics of the area. Crawling through a minefield came to mind, at the same time the river reminded her of the dahabeah, and she felt again the weight of grief for Bert.

The painful task of mourning had been delayed until the sad excitement passed. Lily slept for almost twenty-four hours after she and Worth had parted. When she finally woke, it was dark, Worth had left Cairo, and Bert's death was devastatingly real for the first time. Not sure she could handle the night, she called Noorna, who came instantly and stayed with her on the dahabeah for nearly a week, cooking, listening if Lily wanted to talk, and being a silent companion the rest of the time. Finally they began running again at the club before dawn, and Lily found her determination returning. Within a fortnight, she went back to Washington and, with Worth's grateful blessing, the O Street house.

The grief had not left her, and the depression it caused came suddenly, without warning. None of the emotion had come out during the exam; she had been careful about that. And yet, by so doing, was she not misleading her examiners? She had admitted to having opinions, but not the kind of anger that, she suspected, under particular circumstances might allow her to do almost anything. She considered the idea of herself as some kind of ticking bomb that would go off under a certain combination of pressures, causing havoc in one Middle Eastern embassy or another.

Bert's murder seemed less personal, more capricious than the slaughter of the children in 1967. Lily thought that perhaps her reaction showed some kind of maturity with grief, that her response to the atrocity had been that of a teenage girl with little experience of such extremes, and that when Bert was killed, she was older and there was no longer the shock connected with such an event. As to Abu al-Saffah, he was no more than a name to her. Any anger she had was about the outrage of his being allowed to go free. She was relieved that she had not seen him as she'd seen the Israeli.

The week before, she had attended the ceremony at Foggy Bottom in the diplomatic lobby, where Bert's name had been carved in the Foreign Service Memorial Plaque. The secretary of state attended; there were many members of the media present. She did not say a word to them or shed a tear, although numerous television cameras focused on her, waiting for the slightest glistening. She was again surprised and gratified by the number of Bert's friends and colleagues who came; the lobby was crowded with them.

Pushing back now from the railing, she walked to the end of the bridge. In spite of being resolute about keeping her landlord at a precise, friendly distance—even as she lived in his house—Lily looked forward to Worth's regular weekly letters, one of which was due that day. She hadn't seen him since June in Cairo. They'd discussed by phone and letter the details of her residing on O Street. Keys had been left with the cleaning woman, who arranged to be there the day Lily arrived. Since then, Worth had sent flowers each week, and he'd alerted a number of his Georgetown pals to have Lily over for dinner. She'd turned down the invitations, not ready for the social scene and unwilling to be regarded as Worth's resident woman.

By the time she reached the black-lacquered front door with its brightly polished brass hinges and knocker, her entire suit felt damp with sweat and her feet hurt from the long walk. The first thing she saw when she stepped inside was a suitcase on the parquet floor, then an elaborately wrapped present resting on the hall table. Worth appeared from the study.

"What are you doing here?" she asked amazed.

"I was summoned for consultations," he answered, pleased with the surprise he'd caused. He was wearing a tan summer suit that looked as if he'd just put it on. His pale blue eyes took her in with obvious pleasure, and he smiled at her in the way he used to do when they were able to think of nothing but enjoying themselves. "It seems they've come to their senses and are going to put me into the secretariat."

"Why didn't you let me know?" she asked as she finally shut the door. He had turned on all the downstairs air conditioners, and Lily felt a chill.

"Because if I had, you'd have moved out before I arrived, which is completely unnecessary. I've already put my bags in the downstairs guest room, and if I keep the air conditioners going, it'll be cool enough back there." When Lily looked down at the suitcase in the hall, he explained. "That's the third bag. I travel heavy. Oh, and this is something for you."

As he started to pick up the present, Lily said. "Wait . . . wait. I'm not ready for you to be here yet."

"Shall I leave?"

"No, of course not. Just give me a minute to deal with it." She looked around as if there might be a place to go, then thought of having a drink. "Would you mind if I took a shower and changed? I had my oral exam today and I—"

"Today?" He took a step back. "I had no idea. I'll call a masseuse if you want one. How'd it go?"

"Pretty well, I think. I'll tell you about it."

"Want a gimlet when you come down?"

"I don't know," she said, remembering the good times they'd had with gimlets as well as the lethal effect. "I'll decide after the shower."

She had to pass him to reach the stairs. The hall was narrow, but they did not touch. Lily climbed two steps before she stopped and turned around. She watched Worth as he tilted his head to sight her from a different angle, a look of curiosity and of challenge on his face. A beam of sunlight from a window in the study reflected in the beveled mirror above the hall table, blinding her for a moment. She took the two steps down again. As she walked back to him, she said, "I'm so glad you're here," and was in his arms, kissing him before he had a chance to answer.

"I love you," he said as they held tightly to each other; he kissed her longingly. Suddenly the hall darkened; the sun had gone down behind the houses across the street. Lily pushed herself back.

"I still haven't caught up with this."

"Tell me what can I do to help you, because I'm way ahead."

"I really need that shower."

He backed away. "Help yourself. I hope it won't be a cold one, ha ha ha."

"Ha ha ha," she said and went up the stairs, this time not looking back. In the bedroom, she let her clothes fall in a pile on the floor and stepped toward the bathroom. He'd turned on the air conditioner in the window beside the bed, and again she felt a chill. The shower was in a gray marble cubicle with a chrome-rimmed glass door, separate from the bath. Lily turned on the water and, when the temperature was right, stepped in and closed the door. Immediately steam rose and clouded the glass. She stood under the nozzle, eyes closed, letting the hot water part her hair and beat on her face.

What the hell am I doing, she thought. She had to get out of there; this was not what she wanted. But as the hot water poured down her body, over her breasts, and flooded through her legs, she knew it was what she wanted, badly, and the consequences, whatever they were, she would have to accept. She needed him, in her bed, in her life, even though the only future she could conceive of with him at that moment was a few hours long. Quickly, as if drowning, she thought of his arrogance, his selfishness, his ambition, and knew she could never survive with him, that the cost of loving him was too much. She had to get out.

When she heard the click of the glass door and the sudden wave of cold air, she desperately wiped the water and hair from her eyes. Naked, he closed the door behind him and reached for her. She backed away, pressing herself against the marble wall of the shower. He put his arms up and pressed his hands flat on the wall on either side of her. He stared at her, an unspoken choice clearly offered, yet one impossible for her to escape, not because she felt trapped, but because, in spite of knowing all she knew about him, in spite of sensing what the unseen future would inevitably bring, she loved him.

———

When her cab stopped in front of the house, Lily saw the catering truck parked in the short driveway. In the three months since she and Worth had lived together on O Street, Lily had begun to hate that truck. She paid her driver and stepped out on the cover of new snow that had fallen in the morning. Worth's car was parked behind the truck. She wanted to tell him what had happened but dreaded his reaction, which inevitably would be cool and rational. Her own was fury, panic, and despair. She kicked the fender of the catering truck as she walked by it. A dinner party was not what she needed, particularly that night, although she was generally sick of the once-per-week regularity of the always charming functions that had occurred ever since Worth returned from Rabat. She had never before taken a cab from the Institute, preferring to walk or, if the weather was bad, take the bus. She resented having given in to the urge, but she had to talk to Worth, fast.

As she opened the front door and let herself in, Lily heard laughter from the catering staff in the kitchen. She scowled, resenting their presence. Without taking off her coat or putting down the hand-tooled briefcase that had been Worth's Moroccan gift, she turned immediately into the study, where he sat behind an antique partner's desk, sorting name cards on a seating chart.

"Hello, my love," he said cheerily. "I'm giving you Senator Buell and William Frazier from the White House, a nice guy but it's always William, never Bill."

"Tel Aviv!"

He cocked his head curiously. "What about it?"

"They're sending me to Tel Aviv."

She saw him take it in, start to laugh, then think better of it. "How did that happen?" he asked with less concern than she would have liked.

"I put down six choices on the wish list, six, in order of preference. They completely overlooked them."

"Wait a minute, that doesn't sound right. Those bastards in Personnel can be obtuse, but they aren't totally arbitrary. Must be a reason. How'd you find out?"

Lily knew her answer would give him plenty of goodies to placate her with, and she didn't want to tell him. She walked over to the wall of books at one side of the partner's desk and stared, unseeing, at the titles. "I was sent for by the director, right out of Political Tradecraft class, and welcomed into his office. With all his wiles oozing, he sits me down and tells me that our new ambassador to Israel needs a staff aide who commands Arabic because of all the peace proposals and negotiations flying back and forth over there. Can you believe it?"

"What did you say?" he asked without an iota of sympathy. "And how enthusiastically, I hope, did you say it?"

"I thanked him, said I'd think about it, and left."

"Well, that's a relief."

"I can't go to Tel Aviv."

"Yes, you can and you will, but tell me why not?"

"You know damn well, Worth."

"You mean because you're worried about running into your Israeli nightmare on Hayarkon Street?"

"You're damn right. That's pretty scary."

"Both the State Department and Israel are very aware of that situation. The Israelis aren't about to let you run into him. Tel Aviv's probably the safest place you could be."

"I knew you were going to tell me I had to go."

"Did you want me to call up the secretary and have you reassigned to Cairo?"

"Yes! Of course not. I want you to tell me how to get out of this."

"You can't. You mustn't. You offer one objection, and the suspicion about a bias will be all over your file. It'll knock you right out of NEA, and they'll probably send you to Borneo."

Knowing he was right, Lily sank down in a leather armchair, still with her coat on, still clinging to the briefcase. "I can't stand it."

"Sure you can. The first thing you should know is that Kenneth Keating, the new ambassador, is a dream to work for. He served in the Senate and went as ambassador to India with great success. Going to Israel is his shining hour. You should also know that Henry the K is showing interest in the Arab-Israeli peace process.

As National Security adviser, he feels his being Jewish would get in the way, so he lets Snake Face Haig deal with Israel. But when he becomes secretary of state—and he will; he's driving our poor incumbent nuts by running foreign affairs from the West Wing—it looks as though he'll jump into the Middle East with both feet, which is why I'm happy to be here poised on the diving board to help him."

He stood up and came over to her. "Your timing is perfect, Lily. Israel's still in mourning about the Munich Olympics. There's a lot going on—plots, assassinations, driving the PLO into the ground." Taking the briefcase out of her hands, he put it on the floor and, with his hands propping him on the arms of her chair, leaned in to kiss her. "And last but not least," he continued, "being the administrative assistant to an ambassador serving in a hot spot is nicer than stamping visas for a year. It puts you in places where you'll be noticed and will meet a host of people who can be important to your career."

"Or I'll be a gofer, translating the Arab newspapers in the basement."

"Maybe, but that's up to you, isn't it? I could have been a gofer in the secretariat, but I'm not, am I? And knowing you as I do, I'd say there's damn little chance of that happening."

She let her head fall on the back of the chair and stared at the ceiling. "I don't want to think about it."

"Then let me ask you this—again. Will you marry me? We ought to settle it before you go."

He'd asked once a week, taking her rejections with professional aplomb. She closed her eyes and sighed, then said, "Yes."

"What?"

"Yes," she repeated, looking directly at him. "Not right away. Not until I'm through with Israel. But yes."

"That might be two years. I'll be an old man."

"Thirty-four is hardly old. But I'll be twenty-five, which is."

He pulled her up from the chair to kiss her. "I've never been very good about waiting for anything, but this'll be worth it."

She smiled, trying to think of something appropriate to say, but kissed him again instead.

"Oh," he said, going back to the desk and opening a drawer, "I can at long last give you this." The small ring box was unwrapped. He held it out to her across the desk.

Unprepared, Lily walked over and took the box. "Worth, I can't wear rings. They make my fingers nervous; I'm always fiddling with the things."

"Fine. Wear it tonight, and then you can put it away . . . although it might offer some protection against the onslaughts of all those horny Israelis."

"How long have you had this?" she asked, covering her irritation at his having been so sure of himself.

"My grandmother left it to me, but my aunt kept it until I had some use for it. I asked her to send it when I came back from Rabat."

"So you've just been waiting."

"Hoping," he corrected. "See if you like it. It's pretty old."

She opened the box. The ring was spectacular, a single large diamond surrounded by smaller emeralds. "Worth, it's beautiful, but do we need this? It belongs to your family, and, well, rings aren't my favorite thing."

"I hope the Institute's taught you that you have to go along with the local customs. Just wear it tonight. Then you can use it to measure pasta or something."

One of the caterers knocked on the door to ask about the soup spoons. Worth had told the cleaning woman to polish them, but they had not been returned to the silver chest. He left the study to find them, touching Lily's arm affectionately as he passed her.

Lily held the open ring box in the palm of one hand, staring at it. Then she glanced over at the half-finished seating plan. Stepping to Worth's side of the desk, she sorted through the remaining name cards, placing them under the elastic cords that held them in place. The thought of the evening further depressed her. She considered switching William-never-Bill to the other end of the table, but knew Worth would spot it. She hated being caught in the intricate Washington web, which Worth excelled in traversing. It seemed to her that since his return, he'd spun radials all over Washington, weaving to connect ever more people in his remarkably far-flung foundation lines of influence. No one worked harder; his days were often twenty hours long. And the hub of his design were these weekly dinner parties.

Looking down at the seating chart, Lily knew something else that would happen without fail that night. Worth would propose a toast, a lovely one he'd had prepared for some weeks, to her and to their engagement. She shut her eyes but could see even better the image of him standing, glass raised in candlelight.

Engagement.

She flipped the ring box into the air and caught it.

Tel Aviv.

Better.

TWELVE

"EVERY DIPLOMAT who comes to Tel Aviv is automatically a spy, particularly an American."

Moshe Levy, smiling mischievously through a black beard that was flecked with red, looked down at Lily. A large man with the piercing hooded look of a kestrel, he had an aquiline face crowned with a widow's peak of black hair brushed straight back from his wide brow. He was dressed in sandals and an unusually well-cut buff-colored suit, and wore his pale yellow shirt open at the neck, as did most of the other guests at the embassy's reception. The Israeli businessmen had gathered in honor of the visiting American assistant secretary of commerce. When Levy had approached her across the embassy's lawn, Lily thought he looked somewhat raffish.

"I'm no spy, I promise you," Lily said. It was her first social event since arriving the week before, and she was making an effort to "mix," as her Overseas Briefing Book had advised. "Are you?"

When he laughed, she was dazzled by the expanse of white teeth. From her view below, she didn't see a filling. She also noticed that his black beard abruptly tufted white in a narrow straight line under his neck. Odd, she thought; he looked to be around thirty.

"I'm a diamond merchant," he said. "The only spying I try to do is on the De Beers cartel in London, and believe me I'm a complete failure. I was hoping you could help me."

The statistics she'd learned in her Area Studies classes clicked through her mind: Israel being the world's number one exporter of polished diamonds, which accounted for forty percent of the country's nonagricultural exports, employing some twenty thousand workers in the cutting factories of Netanya, twenty-five kilometers north of Tel Aviv.

"How could I help?" Lily asked, enjoying the badinage as well as his slightly British-accented English. She was not used to being a stranger to any language, but Hebrew was an impossible wall.

"By spying on De Beers for me."

"Sorry. I know nothing about diamonds."

"Really? Whoever gave you the one you're wearing certainly did. I noticed it all the way across this crowded lawn. Forgive me, but professional curiosity is all." His tone suggested clearly that his curiosity about the ring went beyond his profession. "Ah," he continued, "I believe I detect, yes, surely it's a blush."

Lily laughed pleasantly but with the reserve she'd learned for circumscribing flirtatious conversations with unknown men in the field. "I don't think he knew a thing about it," she said as she idly held her hand up to look at the ring. "It belonged to his grandmother."

Without a second's hesitation, Moshe pulled a loupe out of his pocket with one hand and took her hand with the other, turning her discreetly so that her back was to the crowd and the late sun was on the ring. "Very old, very nice," he said cursorily. "Blue-white, Dutch rose cut, four carats, D color, flawless." He dropped the loupe into his hand as he let Lily's go. "I'd say the man may be worthy of you."

"Were you judging the diamond or the donor?"

"Both, but I already could tell that he had exceptional taste."

She gave him a wary smile and quickly asked a neutral question. "Aren't the Israeli banks making a lot of loans on diamonds?"

"Of course," he replied expansively. "On the hour, the shekel loses its value to inflation. Diamonds hold theirs. Naturally, the thieves we call bankers would rather have the rising diamonds and lend out the falling shekels."

"If that's true, why would you give the banks your diamonds?"

He looked around dramatically and then bent down as if to impart a state secret. "Because the greater truth is that diamonds are basically worthless, their value floating precariously on the world's vanity, their price artificially propped up by that single rapacious company, De Beers. But please don't tell anyone this or I'll be out of business."

Lily laughed and surveyed the crowd. The reception was at full cry, and Ambassador Keating was busy looking after the assistant secretary. She thought she should mingle, meet more of the country's commercial sector, but she rationalized the vital national interest of diamonds and happily continued the conversation.

"When did you learn about diamonds?"

"My first conscious memory is playing on the kitchen table with diamonds and bullets. I was born in 1944. My father was an Antwerp diamond cutter. Winston Churchill had rescued him and his colleagues with one of the few destroyers he had—it was before Lend-Lease—just as Hitler overran the Low Countries. England needed the cutters and their diamonds to make precision war machines. During the war, my father learned English, made some necessary friends there, married, and as soon as he could, moved to Palestine, where he had me and my brothers and sisters, and fought to establish Israel. Once that was done, he started a small factory to polish the diamonds De Beers sent him. It's quite a big factory now."

"I presume your mother was involved."

"Most definitely. But enough about me. Tell me, how engaged are you?"

"Mr. Levy, you'll have to excuse me. I see the ambassador needs . . ."

"You can't blame me for wanting to know. Are you too engaged to have dinner with me? Strictly professionally, of course. It's vital to us in the diamond business that diplomats are aware of our many international problems."

His self-mockery was apparent, and the intimacy humorous. He seemed confident of his effect, and Lily remembered Worth's scornful phrase, "those horny Israelis." Nervously, she twisted the ring around her finger with her thumb as she said, "Thank you, but you really should see Bill Bobbitt in the Commerce Section. I'll arrange a meeting. Excuse me."

She turned to walk across the garden, but heard him say, "Lily, why am I not discouraged?"

Irritated slightly by his presumption, yet pleased with his use of her name, she hesitated but didn't turn back. She saw a familiar face from the embassy and joined a conversation. After a few minutes, she glanced back to see whether he was still nearby, but the area was filled with a group of Israeli journalists surrounding the assistant secretary. Lily looked around the garden and didn't see Moshe Levy anywhere. Aware of her disappointment, she smiled to herself, which confused the gentleman to whom she was ostensibly listening.

He, like so many others, was reciting some new detail that had come to light about the murder of the Israeli athletes at the Munich Olympics the previous September. As the Kennedy assassination had preoccupied the United States, all of Israel seemed obsessed with the crime, an obsession intensified by the knowledge that those who had planned the massacre—Black September, the bloodiest and most extreme group of Palestinian terrorists—were still free, some as close as Beirut, Damascus, and Amman.

Prime Minister Golda Meir's public stance was that of towering wrath, but she gave the ever-present Israeli sense of humor a welcome boost the previous week by paying a visit to the Pope. Every variation of the Jewish-grandmother-dealing-with-the-Italian-celibate joke made the rounds, including Lily's office at the embassy. She had a desk near three others, which were staffed by Foreign Service secretaries for the ambassador and DCM, whose offices adjoined. The secretaries, career professionals who were proud of the understanding that it was they who really ran the embassy, began each day with an exchange of the newest Golda jokes.

Lily was an appreciative audience, and for that, they quickly decided to include her in their circle. Between them, they knew everything about everyone in the embassy and made a point of keeping up with the latest developments. Their hours on the job were long, and their devotion to keeping their bosses' lives, files, and cables in order was truly impressive. After serving in numerous embassies around the world, the women could size up any ambassador in six seconds and, in the seventh, make his life glorious or miserable. In the present case, they all agreed that Ambassador Keating was worthy of their adoration.

Louella Taft, the senior secretary according to her Foreign Service rank, was a heavyset, gray-haired widow who pampered the ambassador but ordered the marines around with appropriate fierceness. She also knitted heavy wool garments when she wasn't typing. Once finished, these garments were never seen again, so she was kidded about the Yemenite she kept locked in her attic for her pleasure. It was she who had called the embassy's housing officer and implied it was the ambassador's personal wish that FSO Mc-Cann be given first-rate quarters.

As a result, Lily found herself happily ensconced in a newly remodeled one-bedroom flat, with bath and kitchen overlooking the old port of Jaffa.

Here, Lily began to love the city. Her resistance to serving in Israel was overwhelmed by the crazed excitement of the place and the raw energy of those she met. Any reluctance she had had was dissolved by friendliness. Her Arab landlord found her a Turkish coffee ladle in which to boil her morning brew; the neighbors across the alley, with whom she shared a laundry line, gave her one-phrase-a-day Hebrew lessons. By the end of the week, the baker welcomed her to his shop with a cry of "Shalom, Ambassador!"

By then, Lily knew the city had won her over. Before arriving, she had steeled herself against emotional reactions and forced a cold objectivity toward her duties. Her delight with the city and the people she met made her question her wariness; nevertheless, she kept it. The man who was the cause of it might appear at any moment.

He knew exactly where she was, as he had known in Paris. He'd therefore control any meeting. And yet, she doubted a confrontation, the obvious reasons being that she was now an American diplomat and Israel was his home country. She presumed that he and his superiors, whoever they were, would certainly prevent any chance meeting. Surely they'd send him abroad. Nevertheless, she had an absolute certainty that she would find him one day and that they would meet on her terms rather than his.

The embassy reception dwindled, and when Ambassador Keating left with his guest, Lily's duties were done. Coming around a corner, headed for the embassy's parking area, she ran into Moshe Levy and stumbled as she tried to avoid him. He caught her by the arms before she could fall and held her for a moment.

"Fate never ceases to amaze me," Moshe said.

"A collision in a parking lot stretches fate pretty far. Good night, Mr. Levy." She began walking toward her car.

"Lily, did you eat the fish hors d'oeuvres?"

"Only one," she said over her shoulder. "Didn't like the sauce."

"Fate again—I didn't either. But I know where to get the freshest seafood in the Levant, and we have to eat."

Lily stopped and turned, tempted but determined not to go. "Mr. Levy—"

"I'm not *that* much older than you. It's Moshe."

"Yes, well, I really can't go to dinner with you."

Comically, he looked up and down, left and right. "Is someone holding a gun on you—or is that ring too tight?"

When she started to walk away again, he said, "Does that mean that *he* doesn't ever go out to dinner, either? That the two of you took a prenuptial vow not to eat unless you're alone in a closet somewhere? That you'll be a gourmet celibate, shrinking your stomach for the sake of a ravenous purity? That having bones sticking out all over is the sign of virtue?"

Lily was still walking, but she began to laugh. He heard her and followed. "I'm not trying to interfere with your famished beatitude, Lily. I just want to feed you basics."

She had reached her car and put her hand on the door handle. "Moshe, I'm very engaged."

"But not dead, and therefore hungry."

Contacts, she thought. Having local contacts was one of the most important parts of being a successful diplomat. Here was a local businessman in a vital industry, one that she knew nothing about but could seriously affect the country's economy. It was her duty to go. She laughed at herself and said, "Where's this fish place?"

"Between eighteen and thirty-four minutes away, depending on traffic. Your car or mine?"

"You know the way."

He gestured across the parking area to a green Jaguar XK-E and escorted Lily to it. As they drove through the gate, they were scrutinized by the marines on duty but not stopped, and Moshe drove down Hayarkon Street. The traffic was bad until they crossed the Yarkon River and sped through Ramat Aviv on the Haifa Road. He asked the basic questions—how long she'd been in Israel, where she was living, had she been to Jerusalem yet—and gave enthusiastic advice about his country and how to make her life easier. They finally reached the coast road and both became silent as the intoxicating scent of the surrounding groves of Jaffa oranges wafted through the car. The phenomenon continued for many kilometers and Lily warned herself to be careful in all ways as she looked up at the moonless sky and out over the black Mediterranean, ending at the horizon where the stars began. This is all too pleasant, she told herself, and he's too attractive. Enjoy yourself, but go home. And stay on economics.

"Tell me about the diamond business," she said dutifully as they drove into the outskirts of Herzliya.

"I must confess something first," he responded seriously.

"Confess? We haven't known each other that long."

"I found out about you."

"What do you mean?"

"After you left me at the reception, I naturally wanted to know more. I have several friends at the embassy whom I asked about you. Please forgive me."

"Learn anything?" she asked glibly, not pleased with having been discussed but flattered that he'd asked.

"Not enough, but a little of your life, living so much of it in the Near East, of course the tragedy of your father's death. I'm very sorry, Lily."

"Thank you."

"And something else. I was a tank captain in the Sixty-seven War, fought the battles in the Sinai. I saw the newspaper picture of you and the Jordanian children there, taped in the cabins of three Egyptian tanks. Of course at the time nobody knew you were American. Those Egyptians, and who knows how many others, used that picture to inspire themselves."

"I've never heard that before."

He turned off the main highway and took several turns on roads leading up Herzliya's hills above the beach. Watching the curving road, he said, "There are things that time doesn't heal."

"Tell me about them," she suggested slyly.

He looked at her again, then began to laugh as he pulled into a driveway, lined with orange trees, leading up to a white villa over-looking the sea. "You're a very good diplomat, Lily."

"Thank you, and this isn't a restaurant, is it?"

All innocence, he said, "I didn't say a restaurant; I said the freshest fish. This is the place, which is also my home."

"This isn't what I expected," Lily said, clearly irritated.

"It isn't what Maman expected either, but I think you'll like each other."

Before she could respond, the Jaguar stopped and Moshe got out and walked around to open her door. As she stepped out of the car, lights went on around the building, illuminating the white stone of the walls and entranceway, as well as the tall cypress trees on either side. She saw a two-story villa with small windows on the entrance side, but as she went up the wide steps and in the front door, Lily could see, through the hallway and the living room, wide expanses of glass overlooking the sea. The walls were white, and the furniture upholstered in white canvas. Occasional crystal and silver objects rested on glass tables. A small dining table was set for two next to the windows, with a candle burning and wine cooling next to it.

At that moment, an elegant woman in her sixties, wearing a brilliant pink caftan and an apron, came through a swinging door. She was carrying a mixing bowl and a whisk, and she stopped short with surprise when she saw Lily. Her handsome face was dominated by a full-lipped mouth. In the candlelight, her eyes seemed black. Her gray hair was parted in the middle and pulled back in a knot at the back of her head. When she put down her implements in order to welcome Lily, her full figure gave further evidence that she liked to cook.

As if he had not surprised Lily enough, Moshe began speaking in fluent French. "Maman, may I introduce Lily McCann, an American diplomat. Her mother is French, also."

Lily looked at him, astonished by how much he had learned about her. He shrugged, pleased with himself. His mother greeted Lily with enthusiasm. "Now I am challenged. Moshe can't tell a béchamel from a mayonnaise. No, I exaggerate, but I will do something wonderful. Come, Lily, pick your fish."

She took Lily by the hand and led her through the swinging door into a modern kitchen of brushed-steel cabinetry and shining copper pots. A glass fish tank was set in one of the windows, and Madame Levy approached it with a small net. She stood poised above the tank, in which a dozen fish swam lazily in circles. "You too, Moshe. The sea bass is good, but so is the flounder."

Lily looked over at her escort.

"Fresh," he said.

They all picked sea bass, and Madame Levy hustled the couple out of her kitchen so that she could go to work. Moshe led Lily back into the living room, where he seated her. He opened the drawer of a built-in sideboard and added a third setting of cutlery and glasses to the table.

"No more surprises, all right?" Lily asked.

"I am spent, I assure you. Glad you came?"

"Very. Tell me about her."

He poured wine into two glasses and brought one to Lily. "She cooks for me once a week when I'm in the country. That's all she asks. The rest of the time, we hardly see each other. I don't often bring a guest."

"I'm honored."

He smiled, tapped his glass on hers, and sat in a chair opposite. "Maman is why we're here. Before World War Two, she was headed for a concert career, piano"—Lily looked toward the ebony Steinway grand at the end of the room—"studied with Boulanger, and then, well, France was no place for a young Jewish girl. Her parents sent her to England just ahead of the Nazi invasion; they themselves were captured and sent to Buchenwald. Maman happened to be taken in by a family that not only was involved with De Beers but was close to Sir Ernest Oppenheimer, the genius who created the cartel, and she played for him at several social occasions during the war. At one of them, my father showed up, still so poor that he wore a borrowed suit and shoes that didn't fit. Maman thought he was crippled because of the way he walked. He courted her with love and Zionism, and after independence, started his cutting factory, probably the only secular Jew in a very Orthodox industry. But it was because of Maman that he received his first diamonds from De Beers."

"I don't understand," Lily said. "You mean they sent them as a dowry or something?"

"No, no. De Beers controls almost every raw diamond that is mined in the entire world. That means they control the industry and the market. No one gets raw diamonds except from De Beers. Some get more than others; some get better quality than others. The raw diamonds have to be cut and polished; then they go to market, which De Beers stays out of, other than spending millions on advertising to create it."

"So it's a real cartel," Lily observed.

"In the best and worst sense of the word." He drank some of his wine. "I'll tell you a funny story. In Japan, people were usually married in a Shinto ceremony, with a drink of wine from a wooden bowl. Even after the American occupation, there was little concept of Western engagement rites. But the diamond mines were producing millions of carats, and they were filling up De Beers' vaults in London. They needed a new market, so they hired an American ad agency to create one—in Japan. Last year, after four years of an ad campaign showing diamond rings on Western-looking women in Western clothes doing Western athletic activities, twenty-five percent of Japanese brides had a diamond engagement ring. It'll be double that in another five years. An instant tradition. A market to rival America." He laughed and shook his head.

"Does this affect you?"

"Of course. When an industry is so tightly controlled, the slightest tremor is felt everywhere. This is something of a tidal wave."

"What about you personally, your factory? You seem somewhat skeptical about De Beers."

"Skepticism and diamonds are both Jewish bones, part of our skeleton. You have to realize that diamonds have always been a Jewish thing. Until the eighteenth century, what diamonds there were usually came from India; they were bought and sold by Jewish traders all over Europe. Cutting and polishing them was one of the few crafts allowed Jews by the merchant guilds. The Portuguese had established trade routes to India, so the cutters moved to Lisbon. The Inquisition drove them out of Lisbon; some went to Antwerp, then Amsterdam. The stone you're wearing is very old, cut in Amsterdam, I'd guess, from that period."

Lily couldn't help glancing down in amazement at the ring. "Where did De Beers come from?" she asked.

"Well, along came Cecil Rhodes and the discovery of the South African mines in the 1860s. Unheard-of reserves, millions of carats. The Jewish diamond merchants in London formed a syndicate to deal with Rhodes. Eventually they sent a young genius, that Ernest Oppenheimer I mentioned, to South Africa to look out for their interests. Through years of manipulation, international politics, and coercion—some might add piracy—he managed to consolidate the diamond fields and ended up controlling Rhodes's old company, De Beers, just in time for the world depression in the thirties to dry up the luxury market in diamonds. He had his world monopoly, with forty million carats by then and no one to buy them, not an enviable position for a cartel." He finished his wine.

Lily was enjoying herself, fascinated by the story and intrigued by the teller. "What happened?" she urged.

"Bankruptcy loomed. He seriously considered dumping a couple of tons of diamonds into the North Sea so that his creditors wouldn't get them and flood the market. But, World War Two presented itself, and suddenly all the countries needed industrial diamonds to make their weapons. Timing is all, Lily."

"But how did Israel get into it?"

"The war again. Amsterdam and Antwerp were closed down by the Nazis. A lot of Jewish cutters who escaped eventually found their way to Netanya, in Palestine. The Jewish settlers needed the industry, and De Beers, needing its diamonds cut and polished, was glad to have a pool of skilled cutters. So they sent us what're called melees, medium-grade diamonds, less than a carat uncut. They weren't gem grade—those go to the big jewelers—but they weren't bort either, the small inferior stuff that gets ground up and used on cutting tools. We did very well with the melees, and they keep sending them to us."

"Why don't they send you gem grade?"

"More wine?"

"Please."

He brought the bottle back to Lily, sat down, and refilled their glasses as he talked. "De Beers is like a country, with its own secret service, its own ambassadors, and its own royalty—the Oppen-heimer family. This nation-company makes its own treaties with other nations, one of which is Belgium. There's a large diamond mine in the Belgian Congo that De Beers must control to preserve its world monopoly. In order to have that control, De Beers has a private treaty with the government of Belgium stipulating that the mine's product will go through De Beers. In return, the cutters of Antwerp who survived the war, or went back after it, receive De Beers' gem-grade diamonds to cut and polish. We could do it cheaper in Israel, but we don't have a mine. That's fine; we can play that game. De Beers sends the gem-grade stones to the cutters in New York, in Antwerp. But we bid on them, offering immediate profit with no risks, and the cutters sell them to us. We cut, polish, give them to the banks here, and get more money to buy more stones. Sooner or later, Israel will have more carats than De Beers, and then we'll write our own little treaty."

He said it with a bitter smile, Lily noted. "There's a flaw there," she said, as his mother came in from the kitchen, carrying a large platter.

"Where?"

"You're depending on the banks to keep interest rates low, and inflation to keep diamonds as a hedge. Very chancy."

"Come, come," Madame Levy ordered in French from the table. "My sauce Mornay will curdle. Moshe, we'll need the second bottle; it's in the ice box."

Moshe watched Lily as they stood up. "You're too incisive," he said, then smiled and went into the kitchen.

"Sit here, Lily. We'll give you the view, although I wish we had a moon for you."

Lily joined Madame Levy at the table. The bass had been ex-pertly fileted and were surrounded on the platter by new potatoes and haricots verts.

"The plates are over there on the warmer, if you'd take one for yourself," Madame Levy directed, and served the fish and vegeta-bles. "So, Lily, tell me how you like and don't like this hydra-headed country of ours."

"I've been here only two weeks, so I'm still amazed. I don't like the traffic but I do like the excitement, which I suspect is a drug in the water supply. What do you mean by 'hydra-headed'?"

"Oh, this government, this religion, all these mouths yelling at one another."

Moshe returned, put the second bottle in the wine bucket, and filled their glasses from the first. "Maman has a rather heretical point of view, which is why we keep her bricked up out here as much as possible."

"Who's a heretic in Israel?" Madame Levy countered. "You believe or don't believe as much as you want. With all the variables of God and state that are possible around here, no two people believe alike, which is healthy, if they'd just keep quiet about it. But, alas, yelling about your belief—political, religious, or some cocktail of both—is becoming our heritage. And anybody who happens to be listening from the outside hears only a great deal of noise. I suppose that's what you're hearing, Lily."

"Not yet. Working in the embassy tends to keep us pretty cloistered. We don't get out that much. I haven't even been to Jerusalem yet."

"I'm one of the great guides to the holy places," Moshe informed her, "and offer my services at your convenience. Maman, the fish—sublime."

"Yes, Madame," Lily agreed. "I've heard it's the freshest in Israel."

Madame Levy beamed fondly at her son. "Thank you both. You may believe Moshe about most things, Lily, but be careful. He's very convincing."

"Warnings are premature, Maman. I just met her tonight and she's engaged to someone else."

She disregarded him and turned to Lily. "I saw your ring, but he's *very* convincing," she repeated with emphasis. "Just like his father. He convinced me to believe in the Bible so that we could leave London to come to the Holy Land, live in a swamp, and fight a war." She sat back and laughed at the memory. "I consider myself the luckiest fool in the world for coming with him—but not enough of one to continue believing in the Bible."

"Do you still play, Madame?" Lily asked.

The older woman looked askance at her son. "What have you told her, Moshe?"

"Everything. She had to be prepared for you."

"Lily, don't believe a thing he says about me. I play for the only audience I can trust—myself."

"Maman trusts no one, not me, not Golda, not Moses—"

"Of course not. You are a terrible boy who disappears all over the world, Golda is a grandmother riding herd on a stampede of crazy men going in all directions, and Moses, well, he's the creation of Jewish writers—men—who needed a hero to represent them at their very best. If you need any proof of that theory, what about their claim that he lived to a hundred and twenty and was still sexually potent? Would a woman write such nonsense? At that age, I'm sure, teeth are more important."

Moshe laughed. "How's that for tonight's Bible studies?"

"As a diplomat," Lily said, "I can only say that I agree with every word you said."

"I like this young woman, Moshe."

"But does that mean," Lily continued, "that it's those values, cultural and moral, which define the Jewish people, and not your religion?"

Mother and son considered the question carefully before Moshe responded. "You'll get a different answer to that from every Jew you talk to. The two who are sitting here would probably agree that, yes, our religion is secondary to who we are as a people. But I'd have to add that we know it was our religion that held us together as a people throughout the centuries of the Diaspora, when we needed a faith beyond our capacity to hope. Now that we're a nation, our spiritual strength comes from something more than religion."

"Lily," Madame Levy said, "religion—Jewish, Christian, Muslim, Buddhist—is conceived in the minds of human beings to answer the unanswerable. As it goes along, it takes in the culture around it. There'll always be religion because people can't stand not having answers. But Israel is such an enormous answer to us, beyond the Talmud, beyond the Diaspora, beyond the Holocaust. That's why we'll do anything to preserve it. Our religion will no longer preserve the Jewish people. It will ensure our traditions, yes, but not our future. This nation will."

"When you say you'd do anything for Israel," Lily asked, knowing as a good diplomat that she shouldn't, "does that mean anything is justified?"

Madame Levy paused, frowning in curiosity. "What are you asking me, Lily?"

Moshe interjected softly, "Lily was involved in an atrocity in sixty-seven, when, it's alleged, some Israelis murdered a number of Jordanian children."

Madame Levy watched Lily evenly for a moment, then said, "It's *possible* to justify anything, from one perspective or another. My husband was killed on the Golan in sixty-seven. And did you tell her, Moshe, before that, when you were three, three years old, some Arabs came into our hut outside Netanya and beat me until I was unconscious, cut your throat, and left us to die? I'm sure someone, somewhere, could justify it."

She smiled sadly but affectionately at Lily, and shrugged.

THIRTEEN

LILY, translate this please." Louella Taft handed Lily a single piece of paper.

"Where'd it come from?" Lily saw that the paper had no address or title, just a single paragraph, apparently written hastily in Arabic script.

"Local mail," Louella said and strode back to her desk and her electric typewriter. "Probably another recipe for falafel."

Lily worked quickly, typing a line-by-line translation as she figured out each phrase, using a magnifying glass when she wasn't sure of the script. Halfway through, she began to sweat. She used her Arabic dictionary to check two words. When she finished, she proofed her typing for errors, then read the translation again. As she held the two sheets of paper side by side, she saw that her hands were shaking.

When she went over to Louella's desk, the secretary looked up. "What's the matter?"

"Do you still have the envelope this came in?"

"In the trash. Why?"

"I think it'll be needed. I have to see the ambassador right away."

Louella held out her hand for the translation. "What the hell's it say?"

"I don't think I can tell you."

"Don't be ridi——" Louella stopped herself and stared at Lily, acknowledging her determination. She picked up the phone, spoke hurriedly to the ambassador, and with a tilt of her head directed Lily into his office.

"Good morning, Lily," Ambassador Keating said, his white hair and cherubic smile appearing over a desk filled with papers and documents. "What do you have for me?"

"Good morning, sir," Lily said and handed him the two pieces of paper.

He read the translation through his half-glasses, the smile remaining but hardening perceptibly. "Come over here, Lily."

She moved behind his desk to stand beside his chair.

"Show me on the original where 'anthrax' is."

"Right here, sir," she said, pointing with her finger. "I had to look that up. I had to look up 'pathogen,' too."

"What is a pathogen?" the ambassador asked.

"An organism that produces a disease."

"It reads as if the writer knows what he's talking about, doesn't it?"

"Yes, sir."

He studied the two papers another moment and said to Lily, "You realize the sensitivity of this. No mention to anyone."

"No, sir."

"Have a seat over there and we'll figure out how to handle this."

As Lily crossed the office to a couch by the wall, she heard the ambassador ask Louella to summon George Fairfax and tell him to bring an Arabist with him. George Fairfax was the CIA station chief in Tel Aviv. While they waited, the ambassador went back to the work on his desk.

Lily checked her watch; she had planned to meet Moshe for lunch on Ben Yehuda Street but doubted she'd make it. He would understand. Over the last two weeks, he always accepted the potential changes in her schedule when they'd plan to meet. It was probably a good idea for her to miss something. She'd been seeing him a bit too regularly to pretend to herself or anyone else that it was all about embassy business. On those days when she wasn't able to see him, she missed him.

The ambassador picked up her translation and read it again. "I'll tell you what I'm going to do, Lily. I want to find out how much, if anything, George knows about this. I'm going to tell him I have the information but not show him the letter until later. If I show it to him now and he doesn't want to admit anything, he'll say the letter's from a crank—which it may be. So play along with me, will you? You're sure of your translation?"

"Yes, sir."

"Sit tight. We'll see what happens." He handed her a pad and pen. "Take notes. I want George and the translator to see you. Where do you want to sit?"

"Where I can see their faces."

"Move that chair over."

Lily shoved the chair to an advantageous angle, and tried to relax. This is what diplomacy is about these days, she thought, making sure all the other agencies in the embassy aren't carrying on their own foreign policy agendas. Officially, the ambassador was in charge, but the Commerce Section reported directly to the secretary of commerce, the air force attaché to the Pentagon, the CIA to Langley. There could be a major deal for highway concrete, a sale of radar navigation equipment, an undercover plot to train sabotage teams for use against the Arabs—all diplomatically significant developments about which an ambassador might not be informed unless he was both insistent and careful.

The buzzer on the office door sounded, and George Fairfax came in followed by another American. Lily had not met the station chief, although she'd seen him several times in the halls. The other man was a complete stranger.

"Hello, George. Have a seat, will you?" the ambassador said without standing.

"This is Sam Marielli, Mr. Ambassador."

"How do you do, and Miss McCann, my administrative assistant, is going to sit in," Keating said, hurrying the meeting along. "George, what's this I hear about experiments at the Biological Institute at Nes Ziona?"

"I don't know. What have you heard, sir?"

"That the Israelis are beginning to produce chemical and biological weapons there, using a particularly nasty little item called an anthrax pathogen."

The station chief showed no response, either of surprise or concern. "Where did you get your information, sir?"

"Now, George, I never ask you that, do I?" the ambassador said with a broad smile.

"No, sir, but the source could give us a clue about whether to believe the information."

"I want you to be my source, George." His smile hardened. "I'm very aware that CIA's relationship with the Mossad is close to sacrosanct, and that the agencies have a pleasant little history of supplying and covering for each other. That's your business, George, and I never interfere, as you know. But if Israel is beginning to build biological weapons, that gets deep into my territory, so I'm asking you, officially and for the record, if you know anything about what's going on at Nes Ziona."

Fairfax's eyes darted to Lily, then back to Keating. "We'll look into it, sir," he said and started to rise, as did the other man.

"Unless you tell me why I shouldn't," Keating said, "I'm sending a FLASH cable to the secretary of state to alert the president that Israel is manufacturing chemical weapons. I'm sure your friends in the Mossad will assume you told me about it and will be very angry. I'm not sure how Langley will react, but I leave that to your imagination."

The two men sat down again. "May I suggest a trade, sir?" George Fairfax asked coolly. "How you received this information is very much in my territory. I'll tell you what we know if you tell us who informed you."

"I'll be glad to tell you the source of my information," Keating said. "You go first."

"No weapons are being manufactured at Nes Ziona. They're being developed as prototypes, nothing more. But the Russians *are* manufacturing bacteriological weapons at the Nineteenth Military Compound outside Sverdlovsk in the Urals. Russia supplies Syria and Iraq with weapons. Israel has always been consistent in meeting its enemies, threat for threat."

"An eye for an eye and a tooth for a tooth," Keating said as he handed the letter and Lily's translation across the desk. Fairfax stood to receive them and gave the Arabic letter to his associate.

"Who did the translation?" the station chief queried.

"Miss McCann here," Keating answered, rather proudly, Lily thought. Again George Fairfax's eyes slid over to her and stayed on her as he handed her translation to his Arabist.

"May I ask your translation rank?" Fairfax asked coldly.

"S-4/R-3½," Lily said. She'd worked hard to improve her reading of Arabic at the Institute and was pleased to have such impressive numbers.

The CIA man's look was contemptuous as he turned back to the ambassador. "And this came in the mail?" he asked, obviously irritated that he had traded so much for so little.

"Yes. Makes me wonder who sent it. Translation good, Mr. Marielli?"

Marielli looked up, surprised at being called on. "Looks fine," he muttered, then glanced at his boss, who stood up. He followed.

"We'll find out who sent it," Fairfax said. "They obviously want us to think one of the Arab *mukhabarat* services knows about the operation, but I doubt that. Probably some bleeding heart on the inside, guilty about Israel's getting into bacteriological weapons. Thank you, Mr. Ambassador. May I request that this remain classified until we get to the bottom of it? I appreciate your passing it on to us."

"And I'll appreciate knowing about anything of this nature before I have to come and ask you about it," Keating shot back through a smile. "I may be an old politician, but one thing old politicians know about is guarding turf. If you ever work mine again without explaining the incursion with diagrams, I'll be all over you."

George Fairfax smiled lamely. "May I presume that this matter doesn't need the secretary's attention or the president's?"

"You may, at this time," the ambassador said evenly. "But I'll expect a report as soon as you 'get to the bottom of it,' because we're dealing here with a little number called the Biological Weapons Convention of 1972."

With a final look at Lily, the two CIA men left the office. As soon as the door closed, the ambassador looked at Lily, his eyes sparkling. "We did real good," he said, approximating a Texas accent. "Did you get it all down?"

"Yes, sir, except the reactions."

"When you type it up, put in what you remember about those. I've always thought that what isn't said is as important as what is. If they're too much, I'll strike them." He gave her an avuncular look. "What did you learn from this, Lily?"

"That there's a gray area about who should know what in an embassy. It seems a CIA station chief, who has a pretty wide and secret leeway and isn't required to report to anyone except the agency, could very easily go his own way and run his own shadow embassy."

"Good for you. That won't happen here, because George is a good man and we have an understanding. It just needs reinforcing every once in a while. Every ambassador depends on the CIA. We need the information they provide, and quite often there are things an ambassador should not know and must not know. But the problem in Israel is more complex than that, because of the special arrangement between the CIA and the Mossad." He paused a moment. "You handled yourself very well, Lily. I'm going to ask you to take on a couple of projects for me. A couple of gray areas I want for my own background."

"Yes, sir."

"I want you to nose around—but not get anybody's attention—and find out what the Israeli public knows about their atomic history and the facility at Dimona. And I want to know about their water problems, where all the water comes from. The Mossad is very good; it feeds a good amount of information about the region to Langley. But I fear we're becoming too dependent on it, opening ourselves to manipulation." He ruminated for a moment. "I think if I were back in the Senate, I'd float a bill putting the CIA directly under the secretary of state. That would fix things nicely." Then he pulled his chair into his desk. "Thank you, Lily. Type that up, one copy to me, destroy your notes, and forget it. Not a word to Louella and the ladies," he commanded with a knowing smile. "Oh, and in your investigations, I'd stay clear of George Fairfax for a time. Don't make your life interesting to him."

"No, sir," Lily said and left the office.

The secretaries were pros. Having added up Lily's sudden meeting with the ambassador and the instant attendance of the CIA, Louella and her colleagues in the outer office not only avoided questions, they didn't even look in Lily's direction until she'd stopped typing. Only after she'd slipped back to the ambassador's office to hand him the transcript did her colleagues take note of her as she hurried to get her coat and purse, thinking she still might have time to meet Moshe.

"I'm going to lunch," she said and went to press the elevator button.

———

The restaurant was Russian, its minimalist tsarist décor enhanced by the dark room. People were leaving as she came in, and she waited for the maître d' while her eyes grew accustomed to the funereal shadows. A man appeared, but when she gave Moshe's name, he shook his head sadly and reached into his menu desk, producing a card. Under the lamp on the desk, Lily saw it was one of Moshe's. On the back he'd written:

> Forgive me. The office called, a big problem. Please have
> lunch here. It's taken care of and will be very fast and good.
> Try the pirozhki. The Philharmonic on Thursday?

It would have been difficult to be with Moshe and not discuss what had happened, but she was extremely annoyed that she'd missed him. She nodded to the maître d', who led her to a table near a corner. He spoke no English, so she signaled with her watch that she had to hurry, asked for hot borscht and the pirozhki.

The Philharmonic on Thursday. She was flying to Cairo early on Friday for Noorna's wedding. Aware of her joy at the idea of spending an evening with Moshe, she checked herself and stopped thinking about it.

"Miss McCann?"

She looked up at two men who stood in front of her table. One had a mustache; both were dressed in casual jackets and open-necked shirts. She thought they were Israeli but couldn't be sure. The man who'd used her name—young, in his late twenties, friendly—seemed to have an American accent. When she left the embassy, she'd been in such a distracted hurry that she hadn't taken the usual precautions against being followed. She looked around the restaurant and was reassured to see a good number of people finishing lunch, including two men in military uniform.

"Yes," she said.

"Ms. McCann, I'm Herschl Cohen and this is my colleague

Chaim Ben Haza. We work in the Israeli Defense Ministry and we're wondering whether you'd talk with us for a minute."

They were Mossad. The Defense Ministry was the usual identification.

"If this is anything official," Lily said, "we should arrange a meeting through embassy channels."

"Naw, this is more like, well, personal," the speaker said.

He was American or American-raised; his New York accent hadn't been acquired through study. He was brown-eyed with a somewhat feral face, his pointed teeth showed through his ingratiating smile. The other, the one with the bushy drooping mustache, was older and harder; the flat planes of his face looked as if they'd been hammered out of granite, his dark eyes gleamed under thick eyebrows.

"Personal?" Lily said suspiciously.

"Look, could we sit down here a minute?"

She hesitated, but decided she wanted to know what they were talking about. The instant she nodded, they sat down. She braced herself not to respond to anything.

The older man spoke in English with a heavy Israeli accent. "So," he said intimidatingly, "I finally get some life in my file. I've known you a long time, Miss Lily McCann." When he saw she wasn't going to ask how, he explained, "I've been in charge of investigating all these claims you've made about what you called 'Israeli terrorists' in 1967, then again three years ago in Tripoli, then Paris . . ." His tone changed to disdain. "It's a very *thick* file."

Lily was not interested in debate. "Why are you here?" she said directly. "And under what authority?"

Chaim Ben Haza looked at her irritably and gestured with his head to his companion. The one who called himself Herschl Cohen handed Lily a plain manila envelope, smiling in anticipation of sharing it with her.

She slit open the envelope with her table knife, pulled out a small sheet of photographs, and gasped. It was a series of front and side views of the terrorist, similar to the usual prison mug shots except that his head was being held in place by three hands, one twisting his hair. His mouth was wide open; he was probably bellowing. She noted the gold teeth, the scars.

"So they finally have him," Lily said, her voice catching.

Cohen started to laugh. "Yes, we—" But the older man, Ben Haza, interrupted. "Have who?" he asked, suddenly intent.

Furious, Lily said, "You're going to play games with me now? Where is he?"

"*Who* is he?" Ben Haza shot back at her, holding up the pictures.

"Don't you know?" Lily asked incredulously.

"We know who he is," Ben Haza leaned in to her. "Who do *you* think he is?"

"He's the terrorist, *your* man, the one who murdered the children in—"

She stopped because Cohen, astounded, had pushed back his seat. Ben Haza, after staring at her a moment, started a deep, bitter laugh. Through it he said softly, in broken phrases, "For the trouble you've caused me, now you'll atone. He's in a cell on a military base outside Rome. He was one of sixteen who were either killed or captured on January fifteenth, when they tried to assassinate Golda Meir at Leonardo da Vinci Airport. She was on her way to visit the Pope. They planned to blow her plane out of the sky as it was landing. The Italians have kept it quiet because they're embarrassed that they knew nothing about it, didn't even know it was happening under their noses. We did!"

"But," Lily began, "why would he—?"

"You mean why would a Jew, your 'Israeli terrorist' be involved with assassinating Golda?" He shook his head with disgust, then leaned in very close to her face. "We came here today to tell you that we'd caught the man who assassinated your father. But according to my files, you never saw who that was, did you?" He picked up the picture sheet and again held it before her. "This is him— someone named Muhammad Hassan Bashir, a *Palestinian* who calls himself Abu al-Saffah. And now you're telling me he's your Israeli terrorist, too."

He laughed loud enough for the patrons in the restaurant to turn and watch him.

FOURTEEN

THE SMALL ROOM was at one end of a deserted barracks set apart from the rest of the military base. The stench of urine and sweat closed Lily's throat. The room was dark and suffocating at first. Two space heaters glowed red under the single window. It was blacked out so that no indication of the sullen Italian winter was evident. The bare wood of the walls had once been stained green but most of the color had faded long ago.

Partly blinded by a spotlight, Lily saw only the back of the prisoner in outline. He was seated, his head slumped forward grotesquely, and was covered with what looked like a potato sack; his arms and legs were bound to each other with thin plastic cord through the metal slats of the chair. There were two men with him, one standing beside the light, the other sitting nearby with a lighted cigarette. In spite of the prisoner's apparent helplessness, her stomach churned with fear.

Behind her, Lily heard Ben Haza give an order in Hebrew. The man standing near the light approached the prisoner and did something with the front of his pants as his head rolled listlessly to one side.

"Is he alive?" Lily asked in English. Her knees felt as if they might give way.

Cohen, who'd come from Tel Aviv with them, laughed quietly. Ben Haza said, "We can keep people alive far beyond death." His contempt for her was still apparent, as it had been since their meeting in the Russian restaurant four days earlier.

Lily had read the prisoner's file. Originally the Mossad had only wanted her to identify him, but she had refused to make the trip unless she could confront him. The Mossad grudgingly had provided the file when she negotiated for her ten minutes of time. The man had entered Italy on a false Bulgarian passport three weeks before the attempt to down Golda Meir's plane. Discovered at the last moment by a Mossad agent on a road at the end of the airport runway, he had a Soviet SA-7 hand-held heat-seeking missile and its launcher set up and hidden in a food cart. The Mossad agent rammed the cart with his car two minutes before the El Al plane came in for a landing. Trapped under the crushed cart and left for dead, Abu al-Saffah had been seized by the alerted Italian police. He was taken to the military base, where he had been kept incommunicado for five weeks, except for the Mossad interrogation. The Italians allowed the agents access to the prisoner after Israeli threats to reveal their host's incompetence in overlooking such a complex assassination plot of a world leader.

"Let me talk to him," Lily demanded as strongly as she could.

Ben Haza moved in close to her and whispered so that no one else could hear his words, although his tone was clearly audible to the others in the room. "You don't give orders here. To me, you're a silly little American who's lost her excuse for fame. You have ten minutes; then you give your evidence to the Italians." He gave another order in Hebrew, walked to the door, and went out, followed by Cohen.

One of the men dragged a chair over and stood on it, adjusting what looked like a small plastic spigot attached to a large balloon of liquid hanging from the ceiling. He stepped down and wrenched the sack off the prisoner's head. The two men, dressed in several layers of sweat clothes, waited a few seconds until a short spurt of water from the apparatus fell on the back of the prisoner's neck. One of the men spoke to Lily in Hebrew as he moved the chair to a safe distance, gesticulating to her not to go near the man. They left casually, as if going on a coffee break.

There was no reaction to the first jet of water, but at the second, the prisoner lurched against his bindings, groaned in pain, and put his head back with his mouth wide open in expectation of the next spurt. His gold teeth and the trails of sweat on his face caught the light. He arched anxiously in that position, letting his eyes search the room as best he could. Then he saw her, standing to one side. Reacting not with surprise but with a bitter acceptance, he suddenly looked down at his lap, and as he did so, the water jet fell on the top of his head.

He yelled, furious. "You dog filth," he said quickly in Arabic, "do not distract me," and he put his head back to await the next water ration. "I'm trying to stay alive."

"You're getting the water because I'm here," Lily said, trying to balance fear with authority, but finding anger more useful. "The moment I leave, it'll be turned off." She moved the other chair so that he could see her out of the corner of his eye as he waited with his mouth open below the spigot. "And I'll leave if you don't answer my questions."

The water fell; obviously well practiced, he caught most of it in his mouth, the rest splashing into his eye and across his forehead. He savored what he had and swallowed, letting out a soft groan of appreciation. "I've told them nothing. Why should I tell you?" he said angrily as he again put his head back and opened his mouth to wait.

"My questions are different. They're only about you and me."

He didn't respond until he tasted the water again. "You're wired so they can hear anything I say."

"No, the Italians searched me very carefully, thinking I might have poison or some weapon to kill you. I have only questions."

"I don't care about you!" he shouted.

"You'd better," she said rigidly, and stood up to leave. He couldn't look at her long for fear of missing the water. She began to move toward the door. He yelled objections with his mouth still open for the water, which fell, and which he swallowed quickly. Then he said urgently, "What? What do you want to know? And I know they can hear us. The room is bugged."

Lily hadn't considered that, but it made no difference. She had no official duties here. She returned to the chair. "In 1967, why did you slaughter those children?"

"Don't talk to me of slaughter!" he shouted. "You don't know what the so-called Jordanians were doing to the Palestinians—ever since we fled Palestine in 1948. Ask yourself who are the Jordanians—" By then, the timing of the water drops was automatic to him and he expertly paused in his conversation to catch them.

"King Hussein and his Hashemite tribe and their Bedouin army, the great King Hussein, descendent of the Prophet!" He spat.

"I know the history," Lily interrupted, allowing him to get his water. "But you're an Arab. How could you *slaughter* Arab children?"

"Palestinian children were dying by the hundreds in Hussein's refugee camps; why not a few Jordanian children?"

"Is that all?" she demanded furiously. "Revenge?"

"No!" he shouted. "Remember what day it was. We didn't know the Jews would start the war, did we? We wanted the Arab states to start first, not be surprised and destroyed, sleeping in their beds, as they were," he said with disgust.

"You killed those children to start a war?"

He turned to her, forgetting the water, suddenly sarcastically innocent. "For those who are listening, I say that I had nothing to do with what happened in Amman that day. For you, I say that whoever did obviously knew that there was the beautiful daughter of an American diplomat working at that camp. They knew how she could draw even more attention to Jews killing Arab children, start a rage all through the Arab world. It almost worked. Your picture was everywhere. If Israel hadn't attacked the next day, the rage that incident began might have—" The water fell on his head; he bent forward so the liquid would roll down his face and he licked at it greedily.

Lily felt a sudden nausea. She hadn't eaten on the flight from Tel Aviv to Rome. It had been a rough one, bucking winter winds. Nor had she slept very much during the previous four days; she had had to clear the trip through the embassy and confer with George Fairfax, who was not inclined to be of much help. A senior political officer from the embassy who remained distant and passive had accompanied her on the trip in case there were problems with the Italian authorities. None of these reasons was why she suddenly felt sick.

"You're saying it was because of me . . . ?"

His response was a voice-cracking laugh as he leaned back for the water. It fell, and he swallowed it as if it were a cordial. "Any other questions you dare to ask?"

"Who were you working for then?" she asked faintly.

"No one!" he responded proudly. "I work for no one but my people. Others join me who believe in my way. I join others who believe in my way."

"What were you doing when I saw you in Tripoli?" she forced herself to ask.

"You didn't see me in Tripoli, but even if you did, it had nothing to do with you."

"You mean I was just lucky I saw you?"

"Yes, lucky—if it was me."

"Why did you choose me to deliver that message in Paris?"

"What message? I happened to see you on a bus."

"You betrayed some of your own people with that note. Palestinians. The ones involved are still in German jails."

"That is beyond your understanding," he said calmly, "and I'm not sure what you're talking about." He had taken enough water so that his rabid edginess had been replaced with cunning. "There is a vast difference between what some of my brothers call patriotism and their practice of power-grabbing publicity. Lessons are taught in many ways."

"Why were you involved with Black September in this operation? What happened to your Palestinian Command Group?"

"What is this Command Group? What is this September operation?" He glanced at her menacingly. "This I tell all of you." He shouted to the presumed listening devices. "There are many thousands of us who were shamed not to have been involved with what happened at the Munich Olympics! There will be many more Munichs!" He leaned back and smiled as the water fell. Catching it, he closed his eyes to savor it before swallowing. "There was no Black September operation here. I was in Rome as a pilgrim, considering conversion, visiting the Christian holy places. This secret imprisonment, my starvation, my torture, is because of the racist hate of the Jews for Palestinians, the paranoia of the Mossad, the pandering fear of the Italians. As an American diplomat, you are required to report the torture you see here to the proper authorities. I demand that you do so." He laughed again.

"I want to ask you one more thing," Lily said intensely enough to stop his laugh.

"Be certain you want to know the answer."

"Did you choose to kill Bert McCann because he was my father?"

"I did not kill Bert McCann," he said mockingly.

"No, the Palestine Command Group which you head claimed that honor. Listen to me. I'm not asking that you implicate yourself. These people have enough on you to do anything they want. I'm not asking who did it. I'm asking why he was chosen, not someone else. Was he chosen because of you and me?"

He looked over and suddenly spat at her. The spit fell on the edge of her coat. She didn't move. He pulled against his bindings but quickly relaxed. "There are edges of razors in these plastic cords. Do you see the blood on my ankles, wrists? They keep a jute bag over my head and let water fall on it which I must suck from the cloth. They leave my privates out of my pants for the convenience of pain. I suppose when you came, they zipped me up. I've eaten nothing but stale biscotti for weeks, just enough to keep me alive. And this is nothing compared to what they do to others. Can you understand this? Can you see anything? No." He leaned back just in time for the water and swallowed quickly. "The Holocaust blinded you Americans. You haven't seen anything since. Just as they stuff my balls back in my pants when you come into the room, they hide what they do to the Palestinians to prevent America from seeing the horror they make of a people's lives. You Americans turn your eyes, avoiding unpleasantness like the nation of tourists you are, passing through, preserving your thoughtless romance with Israel, paying for what they are doing to my people. How else can we gain your attention, cure your blindness"—then he yelled—"than by *killing a few fathers?*"

Lily was on her feet and her hands were around his throat as the water fell, splashing over them both before she hesitated and tore her hands away from him. She stood trembling as he watched her. With a smile, he said, "We are bound together in this life, Lily McCann. Don't ever forget what you felt and said and learned and *believed*—while you thought I was a Jew."

She wanted to leave before Ben Haza and Cohen came in to interrupt. She said, "I'll tell you what I thought and still think. Terror is no defense of a people. A terrorist is a sociopathic egoist, indulging himself, hoping to get wrapped up in some myth of heroism. There's a difference between guerrillas fighting for a cause and butchers who claim the cause as an excuse. You're a butcher."

"And tell me what gentle games you'd play if you lost your country?"

"I'd try to do what your people do in a thousand ways—suffer and fight without using the great fraud of terrorism."

She watched him take another mouthful of water, noticing the liquids—blood, urine, and water—mixing in the puddle beneath his chair. He glared at her as the water fell. Lily walked to open the door.

The long barracks room was filled with soldiers and officials— Italians, Israelis, Mossad. The two men who'd been in the room with the prisoner when she arrived glided past her and closed the door behind them.

Beyond the others, standing resolutely alone in a chesterfield coat and an astrakhan hat, was her colleague, the senior political officer. Unseen, he placed a forefinger across his expressionless lips, signaling care in what she said.

Ben Haza, his solid bulk wrapped in a sheepskin coat, approached immediately with his hands pressed deep in its pockets.

"Well?" he asked her.

Lily nodded, and saw him exhale a long breath before turning to the group of Italians and speaking to them in their language. Abruptly, everyone started moving to the far end of the room, where there was medical equipment and personnel in one corner, and communication equipment and personnel in the other. Between them were chairs set in a pattern around a woman seated behind a small black stenographic recorder. Lily was ushered to a chair by one of the Italian soldiers, and several of the officials spoke rapidly as the stenographer took down their words.

"Miss McCann, I am the official translator, certified by court order to act in that function at this hearing. Please let me know if I say something you don't understand. I've been instructed to tell you that you are not under oath, that no magistrate is present. This is merely an informal hearing, but nevertheless for the record. Is that all clear?"

"Yes," she responded, relieved to slip into an official role. "I should point out that I am here as an American diplomat and therefore reserve the right to refuse questions that in my judgment compromise in any way my mission."

This was translated and recorded. One of the Italian officials then asked a question, which the translator put to her. "Is the man you just interviewed the same man you saw commit the atrocity involving the death of ten children on June 4, 1967, in Amman, Jordan?"

"Yes," she answered. "Eleven children."

"You saw him commit the crimes?"

"Yes."

"Will you testify to this, and to the details of that event, in court?"

"If I may interrupt . . ." Lily's colleague walked purposefully forward to address the group of Italian officials. "For your record, my name is Gavin Richardson. I am a senior political officer and counselor in the United States Embassy in Tel Aviv." He spoke without a trace of emotion or drama, but stood directly in front of Ben Haza, causing the Israeli to peer around him awkwardly. "In spite of the informality of this hearing, it is not appropriate that Miss McCann be asked to commit herself to any future legal involvement." Casually, he waited for the translator to catch up, then continued. "She was invited here by the Italian government to identify a suspected terrorist. She has done so. Any further action or commitment on her part will have to be considered at the appropriate time, through the appropriate State Department channels."

Lily saw Ben Haza move around so that he could look at Richardson as an Italian official asked a question. "Will she sign a transcript of her meeting with the suspect?"

"It should be part of record," Richardson replied oracularly, "that we are surprised, indeed shocked, that a recording of her private conversation was made without Miss McCann's knowledge or permission. Nevertheless, any transcript should be submitted for her review. Only then will a decision be made as to validating it with her signature."

"Are you crazy?" Ben Haza erupted in English. "They're looking for any excuse they can find to let him and the others go." He spoke with no concern that the Italians could hear. "We have to shove all the evidence we can get up their ass—"

"If that's the case," Richardson said, facing the Israeli calmly, "if they are so determined, nothing Miss McCann can say or sign will change that."

Ben Haza exploded. "The only chance is to shame them—"

"We are not here," Richardson interrupted firmly and stopped to allow translation as well as a dramatic pause, "to shame the Italian government." He smiled thinly toward the Italian officials. "Our duty here, I believe, is done, and therefore I request that we be taken back to the airport."

Ben Haza was speechless. There was no sound but the translator's soft voice. When he was finished, there was an awkward silence while they all waited for someone to make a decision.

"Please be assured," Lily said, "that I will do anything to assist your case against this man."

Richardson's lips tightened, during the translation, but he did not look at her and gave no sign of his irritation. The Italians stood and one of them gave orders. Several soldiers escorted Lily and Richardson out of the barracks. She chose not to look at Ben Haza but saw Cohen by the door, for the first time without his smile. Outside, a car with a military driver was waiting. The two Americans climbed into the back seat and were driven away from the barracks and out of the base.

"I had to say that," Lily declared.

"No, you didn't," Richardson replied pleasantly. "In the future, don't. In such official—I should say, officious—situations, use no more words than are absolutely necessary. 'Yes' and 'no' do very nicely. 'I can't remember' is always best."

"The man killed my father."

"I know that," he said, not unkindly, "but diplomatically, it's beside the point. If your intention is to bring to justice your father's murderers, you've chosen the wrong career. An American diplomat on the stand in an Italian court accusing a Palestinian of murdering Jordanian children isn't exactly what Foggy Bottom would view as an enhancement of our mission to the Middle East."

"Then what did I come here for?"

"Aside from your purely personal needs, you came to ingratiate yourself with the Italians and the Israelis—and only to a certain degree. That's why I urged Ambassador Keating to let you come. There were those who preferred that you not."

She didn't speak for a time, then said, "We always have to be so cut and dried and pragmatic, don't we?"

"Yes," he answered. "On our smooth unruffled surface, we must be. Underneath, it's up to each of us." He hesitated, then said, "I knew your father, by the way. Years ago, I was a junior FSO when he was second political officer in the Sudan. He saved my neck once when I rather stupidly found myself in over my head with an irrigation project I was working on. He was something of a big brother to us, wholly dedicated, with that enthusiasm for what he was doing which only innocence allows. I assure you that I want that son of a bitch back there drawn and quartered." He met Lily's startled look with a tired smile. "But no one will ever know that, except you."

They rode silently to the airport and went through check-in and security without talking further. When they reached the departure area, he said, "My gate's at the other end. Have fun in Cairo."

"I'm not sure I agree with you, about the cold technique of it all," Lily said, shaking his hand, "but thanks for getting me out of there."

"You're welcome, and it's the only technique that works over time, believe me."

"You said something about my father, that he was innocent. I've never thought of him that way. I've heard 'old-fashioned,' an occasional 'antediluvian' . . ."

"He was also very smart and worked very hard. Innocence was his luxury. He could believe completely in his country, in what he was doing, in how the United States of America could help the whole world if we worked hard enough. Even then, we younger FSOs recognized—in our vast sophistication—that such a quality was no longer practical, that it was even dangerous to our careers. It was a different world for him. Innocence is impossible now. But we envied your father, and admired him for it."

She was suddenly moved. "Thank you."

He started to leave, but turned back. "I think you might prepare yourself for the possibility that they'll let al-Saffah go."

She said nothing, but her fury was obvious on her face.

"The Italians know that to bring him to trial they'll have to go public about the attempted assassination," Richardson said, again assuming a professional tone. "If they do, he becomes famous, and their own security system looks like rotten cheese. The PLO will hire translators and the best attorneys. They'll feed the press. They'll try to make it into a grand show trial. Italy doesn't want that. Even more important to remember, Italy was the colonial power thrown out of Libya when Colonel Qaddafi took over. They're very eager to placate the colonel and re-establish their vast commercial enterprise there. When Qaddafi makes an official request for Abu al-Saffah's extradition to Libya—which he surely will, with his recent penchant for terrorists—I'd bet on the Italians shipping him, and any other of his colleagues they have, out of Italy as fast as Alitalia will fly."

"That's horrible."

"That's diplomacy." He nodded courteously and walked away toward his gate.

FIFTEEN

LILY'S TRIP TO CAIRO for Noorna's wedding served well to cover her unexpected flight to Rome. Noorna was informed of Lily's delay by a CIA operative in Cairo. Her plane, delayed in Rome by fog, landed just before midnight, preventing her from attending the family dinner in Noorna's honor at the el-Sadims' villa.

Because Egypt was still in a state of war with Israel, security and customs formalities at the airport were endless, even with her diplomatic passport. Lily was exhausted, not only by the hours in flight. Because of her, the children in Amman were chosen to die. Because of her, her father had been selected for assassination. And the terrorist wasn't a Jew.

After retrieving her bags, she took a black-and-white taxi to Zamalek. She sat in the back seat staring at the road, numbed by the almost six years of accumulated pain and rage that Abu al-Saffah had generated and manipulated so successfully. She felt ravaged, used, a mannequin propped up before the world to point at the evil underside of Israel. How could she ever go back to Tel Aviv? How could she face Moshe Levy or his mother? How could she pretend to be a diplomat, having been so completely fooled, so obviously a fool?

The taxi driver helped her down the steps to the dahabeah with her bags, and, after paying him, Lily went through the old houseboat, turning on electricity and water, checking the known problems—a rotting sill in need of repair, a folding *mashrabiyyeh* shutter on the sun room window that was swollen shut. Not until she had lugged the second suitcase up to her bedroom and returned to the kitchen for a bottle of room-temperature Stella beer did she realize that in her distracted state she hadn't thought of Bert once, as she usually was quick to do when she stepped onto the dahabeah. She poured the beer into a glass, and stood leaning against the counter as she drank, uncomfortable for the first time in her life at being there.

"Lily." Noorna's voice called down from the gate at the street level.

Delighted, Lily hurried outside and up the steps. "What are you doing here? You're supposed to be asleep . . ." When she opened the gate, she saw her friend's tears reflected in the purplish light from the nearby street lamp. The women embraced silently.

"How can I pretend . . . ?" Noorna said desperately. "Oh, Lily, I can't pretend anymore. I've been panicking all day. Thank God you finally came."

Lily led her down the steps.

"I don't mean tomorrow," Noorna said. "The wedding's a pageant. I'll perform like a trained dog. But what do I do for the rest of my life?"

In the sun room, they sat down next to each other on a rattan settee. Noorna held one of Lily's hands with both of her own as if, letting go, she'd drown. She stared out the wide windows while the dull throbbing of a diesel engine announced the passing of a cargo boat, its decks crammed with large ceramic molasses jars from Upper Egypt.

"Tomorrow," Noorna said, momentarily calm, as if hypnotized by the passing boat. "Please, Lily, I ask you as my oldest friend, don't join in the *zaghreet,*" she pleaded, referring to the celebratory ululating cries of joy traditionally sounded by the guests at the conclusion of the marriage ceremony. "At that moment of what is supposed to be the happiest moment in an Egyptian woman's life, I'll need to see someone who knows it isn't mine."

"I'll do anything you want; you know that. I'll even stand up when the sheikh asks if you agree to the marriage and say no."

"Not to this sheikh. They say he can call down whirlwinds."

"That'd certainly make the wedding memorable."

Noorna laughed and wiped her tears on the back of a hand. "And perhaps the whirlwind would carry us away from everything."

Lily smiled, as taken with the fantasy as her friend.

"Oh, Lily, no one else must see what this is doing to me. I've been performing as the happy fiancée nonstop for months. Unless I can be truthful with someone other than myself, I can't go through with it. It's like the unheard tree falling in the forest. I'm not sure whether I exist, doing all this with no one knowing how I feel, who I am . . . Oh, Lily, you're so lucky to be marrying for love."

Worth. She hadn't thought of him since . . . she couldn't remember when. Surely not since she learned of Abu al-Saffah's capture. Remembering that she hadn't called him on Wednesday, as she usually did, she realized in the same moment that she wished she could see Moshe Levy, wished that he'd come walking down the steps.

"You are, aren't you?" Noorna said, catching Lily's slight hesitation.

"Well, there's no date set, but yes, when it happens, that'll be the reason."

"Where's the ring you wrote about?"

"Upstairs in my bag. I don't wear it all the time. It bothers me. You know, my nervous fingers."

The two women hugged each other.

"May I stay here tonight?" Noorna asked. "I want to tell you what I'm going to do. I must say it out loud before I'm married so that I can bind my words to the world."

"Won't they miss you at home? Your brothers will call out the army."

"I told them I was coming here. Father was apoplectic, but Mother let me come. We'll run at the club at dawn; then I'll go home in time for the *halawa,* and you can come back here to sleep until the ceremony."

"You're having the *halawa?*"

"Do you think my mother would allow me to go to my husband with one hair on my legs or arms? My old nanny will spread the lemon-sugar paste all over me, and when it's hard, she'll peel me smooth as a peach."

"You'll be sweet and smooth, but you'll be exhausted."

"It'll make my wedding night easier. Let me have a whiskey and soda and I'll tell you everything."

"Since when did you start drinking whiskey?"

"Tonight! People have been drinking whiskey and soda around me all my life—the British, the Americans, most of the Egyptian men. I'm going to have to confront so many icons, I may as well start here and now with you."

They went into the kitchen, where Lily made the drink and poured more beer for herself. Noorna told of her intentions with the fervor of a convert. "There is no greater problem in Egypt or the world than overpopulation. There isn't a single problem anywhere that isn't made worse by too many people—everything: economic depressions, environmental catastrophes, drugs, racial injustice, nationalistic politics—all are under increasing pressure because of an uncontrollable birth rate that will completely overwhelm the planet in a hundred years." She paused, literally quivering with conviction.

Lily handed her the glass. "You're asking for big trouble around here with that particular subject."

Standing in the kitchen, holding her whiskey and soda, Noorna quoted fervently, " 'If any do deeds of righteousness, be they male or female, and have faith, they will enter Paradise.' Surah One twenty-four. And remember 'Aisha, the Prophet's favorite wife, who rode her own camel into battle for the righteous cause, and of whom the Prophet Himself said, 'Take half your religion from her.' We must change the world, Lily. The men will never be able to do it in time." She turned suddenly and poured her drink into the sink. "I am a Muslim, and I believe the Prophet is my greatest support. Alcohol is forbidden with good reason. An icon confronted, an icon preserved."

"Soda?"

"Please. Lily, let me tell you the kind of idiocy we face." She started to laugh at the memory. "This Qaddafi of Libya, he came to address the Cairo Women's Union last year at the invitation of Mrs. Sadat. At the time, Qaddafi wanted to unify Libya and Egypt, so he came. There were a thousand women in the hall, and the man started his speech by writing three words on a blackboard—'Virginity, Menstruation, Childbirth'—then went on to say that equality between men and women was impossible because of our time of the month, and that women were really no more than cows to become pregnant, give birth, and suckle their young."

"He actually said that? What happened?"

"We shouted him down. He just kept insisting that he was right, and we kept telling him he was wrong. He was very angry by the time we finished. Sadat was on the stage with him, I think laughing inside. You'll probably meet the president tomorrow. He and Mrs. Sadat are coming."

"She seems to be changing a few things."

"Yes, and she's hated by many for every step she takes," Noorna said. "I will be, too."

"What are you going to do, Noorna?"

"Within three months of my marriage, I swear to you, Lily, as I swear to Allah, I will start a new family planning clinic in Cairo. Mrs. Sadat has given me her blessing and the Supreme Family Council promises to promote it. It will be for the poor, though it's more difficult with them. The men are completely dominant in the home, but the responsibility for family planning falls on the women. Can you imagine asking an Egyptian man—upper class or peasant—to wear a condom, even take a pill? The men will never do anything, and our women are not used to responsibility. The tradition is to have as many children as possible—sons, of course; sons are a man's eternity—to provide a work force and prepare for old age, and, more important, to bind a marriage and make it too expensive for a man to take on another wife and family. It will be very difficult, very frustrating, but we'll find a way."

"I'll help in any way I can, I'm not sure how."

"Just keep telling me I'm right to do this."

"You're right as long as you know what you're getting into. I can't imagine the sheikhs and *ulemas* are going to make it easy for you."

Noorna smiled sardonically. "The fundamentalists already condemn us, but we're lucky in Islam. Nothing in the Koran specifically forbids birth control. As a matter of fact, the sheikh of al-Azhar has publicly approved of it. I wonder how long it will take the Vatican to face this catastrophe. I hope not the hundreds of years it took them to accept that the earth wasn't flat or that it wasn't the center of God's universe."

The two women talked for another hour, until both could barely keep their eyes open. They went upstairs to bed, Noorna's in a bedroom across the narrow hall. For several hours Lily slept soundly, but she woke an hour before dawn. Assuming it was jet lag or some other adjustment of her inner time clock, she lay in bed, listening to the sounds of the river as it flowed by, watching an edge of moonlight from the window move slowly across the opposite wall. The previous long day dragged through her mind, detail by detail. She saw Abu al-Saffah's face as clearly as in a nightmare and remembered his saying, "Don't ever forget what you believed when you thought I was a Jew."

The ceremony included only the el-Sadim family and their closest friends, which together numbered a hundred. Lily was near Noorna with the women in the magnificent main salon of the villa, beneath a pair of enormous crystal chandeliers. The bride stood rigidly in her elaborate long white dress, refusing the empty chair placed for her, holding her bouquet of jasmine, roses, and gardenias with both hands, her lace veil falling into the gown's ten-foot train. And yet she smiled through the heavy make-up she wore, the same smile she had when she'd left her exhausted best friend at the Gezira Club's track early that morning, saying, "Because of talking with you last night, I don't feel I'm going to my marriage at all. It's my future."

Mrs. el-Sadim sat nearby, looking proudly at the scene, a straight smile beneath her iron eyes, which checked and graded every detail. The rest of the stunningly dressed women—most in European high fashion—were in a semicircle around them on one side of the salon, all with heads covered in degrees varying from the chic to the simple. It was an animated collection; the women did not keep absolutely silent as those on the other side of the room went about the business of the marriage.

There, a sheikh read powerfully from the Koran to the assembled men, who listened intently, for the sheikh knew his text and stared unyieldingly at anyone who indicated inattention. His voice was as powerful as his presence, itself made taller by his official turban, more striking by a black beard divided at the chin by a wave of white.

Only Mr. el-Sadim was a more commanding presence, in his

military uniform of an army general, a rank recently bestowed on him by President Sadat, who, it was rumored, was doing everything he could to bring Mr. el-Sadim into his cabinet. Having risen in his youth to the rank of colonel under King Farouk, Noorna's father was no stranger to the military, as his rigid spine and air of command clearly attested. Clean-shaven, nearly bald, the deep lines of his years in exile cut into his strong dark face, he let his startling gray eyes play over the assembled guests, but his gaze softened considerably as it settled on Noorna. She didn't see him looking at her at first; then she sensed it, glanced over, and, after a stony moment of recognition, raised her hand to her lips and directed a kiss in his direction. The hooded eyes of the hardened survivor of Egypt's recent history misted over with what Lily thought must be some hope for the future of his country as well as that of his daughter.

Through the closed French doors that lined one side of the room, the sounds of several hundred other guests collecting in the gardens became an increasing presence. The music of flutes, trumpets, 'ouds, and drums swelled into the room intermittently. Nothing distracted the sheikh, whose voice seemed capable of overwhelming riots of any sort. When he demanded of Mr. el-Sadim if his daughter had indeed accepted the man chosen to be her husband, Lily looked at the groom and shuddered again for her friend. He was smiling, his crooked teeth stained yellow by tobacco, his baldness not well covered by a thin thatch combed over from one side. His lids hung halfway shut, and the pouches under his eyes rimmed the lower part in pinkish-red. Gaunt and slumping, he looked the perfect aide-de-camp to the father of the bride, which he had been faithfully for many years. And Noorna was his reward.

"Yes!" she stated across the chasm between men and women. Her tone was of challenge rather than enthusiasm.

"She consents," Mr. el-Sadim informed the sheikh, who did not deign to look at the bride, but directed her father and the groom to sit opposite each other at a table. There, they clasped each other's right hand and pressed their thumbs together. After the sheikh dropped a white handkerchief over the two men's hands, those inside the salon became intensely quiet. Mr. el-Sadim intoned in a sharp bass voice, "I marry to thee my daughter, such a one Noorna, the virgin, for a dowry of ten thousand pounds."

The dowry, most often a ceremonial convention, was in this instance unusually large, and it caused a silent reaction in the room, through which the proud groom recited, stumbling over the words occasionally, "I accept from thee her betrothal to myself, and take her under my care, and bind myself to afford her my protection. Ye who are present do me honor by bearing witness to this."

The sheikh hurriedly began reciting appropriate texts from the Koran, but everyone in the room heard the quavering wail of joy begin deep in Mrs. el-Sadim's throat, like a song at first, but soon an ear-piercing cry, joined by the voices of the other women in the salon, drowning out the sheikh and announcing to those waiting outside that the marriage was done. The *zaghreet* reached a deafening volume as the French doors were thrown open and the relatives and friends burst outside to mingle with the other guests.

Noorna did not move as the crowd swirled around her, even as her husband came up to offer her his arm. She kept her eyes on Lily, who stood silently nearby. Finally the bride nodded to her friend and, without looking at her groom, walked with him through the French doors to the terrace overlooking the gardens, where the *zaghreet* reached a high level of ovation.

Lily was playfully seized by the two el-Sadim brothers, who escorted her outside following their parents. The two young men regarded Lily, a longtime friend, as almost a cousin, and gracefully included her in the family group standing before the assembled guests, musicians, entertainers, singers, acrobats, and belly dancers. Food tables and servers were placed throughout the gardens. In the circular drive stood a matched set of Arabian horses hitched to a carriage completely covered with the same kinds of flowers Noorna held in her bouquet. More guests were arriving, hurrying past the guards at the front gate, where suddenly there appeared a caravan of official limousines. The cars pulled into the courtyard, and from the rear poured uniformed security guards, one of whom hurried to open the door of the second limousine. President and Mrs. Sadat had arrived.

Their entrance interrupted the *zaghreet,* and as the el-Sadims hurried over to welcome the Sadats, the crowd's excitement gave way to a low roar of conversation. The president, wearing a resplendent white uniform, embraced Mr. el-Sadim, and Mrs. Sadat kissed Mrs. el-Sadim on both cheeks, then hugged the bride enthusiastically. When she noticed the crowd watching the scene, Mrs. Sadat lifted her head and let out a piercing ululation, which the crowd joined and continued as Noorna and her groom were lifted into the carriage.

The *zaffa* began. A traditional marriage procession, it was led by the musicians and entertainers ahead of the carriage, with the family and all the guests following, throwing coins at the bride and groom for luck. Usually a march through village streets, in Cairo it involved going once around the block, then back for the party, which would last most of the night. The Sadats and el-Sadims walked just behind the carriage, and the two brothers brought Lily along in back of them. The *zaghreet* continued as the carriage made its way through streets closed off by the presidential guard, who were stationed in force along the route.

Walking behind Mr. el-Sadim as the only silent member of the procession, Lily heard Sadat say, just loud enough through the chorus of deafening cries to be heard by Mr. el-Sadim, "You have the solution?"

"German water cannons," Noorna's father answered. "They can melt their mountains of sand."

The president continued to walk, analyzing for a moment. Then he responded, "Brilliant! When?"

"Late summer, early fall."

Sadat clapped his colleague on the back as the flower-bedecked wagon turned a corner and the procession stretched behind it. Lily and the el-Sadim brothers were separated momentarily from the line of procession, and when they caught up, Sadat had moved to escort Mrs. el-Sadim, ending the conversation that Lily had overheard. As the carriage turned to re-enter the gate of the villa, she saw Noorna look back for her. Lily held up her hand to show her friend where she was, but her mind roared with what she'd just heard: "mountains of sand"; "German water cannons." Every American diplomat posted in Tel Aviv was familiar with Israeli military positions. Because she happened to overhear the president of Egypt in such a conversation, she could only conclude that he and the father of her dearest friend were speaking of the Bar Lev Line.

"Late summer, early fall."

SIXTEEN

"WHAT IN THE WORLD are German water cannons?" Ambassador Keating asked. As usual, he sat perched behind his desk, smiling. His eyes, however, displayed a trenchant gravity.

"Very large, very powerful water pumps," Lily replied, standing before his desk. "The Israeli fortifications along the east bank of the Suez Canal—the Bar Lev Line—are sheltered from Egyptian view by towering sandbanks built up by the Israelis. These effectively prevent a surface assault by Egyptian forces crossing the canal from the West."

"But strong currents of water melt sand," the ambassador pointed out.

"Yes, sir. From the research I've done, I learned that the current from these water cannons can knock over a ten-ton truck."

The ambassador leaned back in his chair. "And General el-Sadim mentioned a specific date for delivery?"

"Not exactly. President Sadat simply asked 'When?' 'Late summer, early fall' was the answer."

"Lily, you've been back from Cairo a week. Why didn't you report this sooner?" Keating asked.

"I . . ." She hesitated nervously. "I had a difficult time deciding about it. The el-Sadims are my oldest friends in the world. I was at the wedding as a private citizen, and overheard the conversation by chance only because of the relationship. It seemed to be such a betrayal. Also, I consider Egypt something of a home."

"But you decided to tell me."

"Yes, sir, with considerable self-loathing."

"You made the right choice, Lily, hard as it is," he said. "You have to keep your allegiance consistent in this business, or you'll get lost very fast. Sensitive information heard in the most intimate situations has to be reported."

"Yes, sir," Lily replied. "I know."

"Here's what I want you to do. Write up a report and submit it to your political officer. Leave me out of it. He'll kick it over to the CIA people. Then we'll see what our friend George Fairfax does with it. And don't worry, I won't let him bother you."

———————

She submitted the report to her senior political officer, who in turn gave it to the CIA station, leaving it to the agency to decide on its dissemination. A response arrived on her desk more than three weeks later.

Memo to: Chief Political Officer, Tel Aviv
From: Fairfax [initialed]
Date: March 28, 1973
Subject: Cairo Social Life of Lily McCann.

1. Miss McCann's report was submitted eight days after her return, an inappropriate delay.
2. The names dropped are certainly impressive.
3. If I may, I will forward her conclusions to James Bond. She might note that Sadat banished his Russian technicians last year. Without them, their expertise, and spare parts, it is difficult to imagine why he would launch an offensive against Israeli military power, currently in its prime. "Water cannons" are doubtful offensive weapons, but might be useful for irrigation projects at present being considered in Upper Egypt.
4. Her friend Abu al-Saffah traveled first class on Alitalia from Rome to Tripoli ten days ago. I thought she would be interested.

Although she had expected it, Lily found Abu al-Saffah's freedom disturbing, diplomatically as well as personally. The use of terrorists in bargaining between nations was a grievous and irresponsible precedent. Her apprehension for herself was allayed by her being in Israel. She doubted that al-Saffah would dare put himself in jeopardy to the Mossad. His annual letter, however, would inevitably arrive in June, and she prepared herself for it.

Lily stayed clear of George Fairfax. In spite of the snide tone of his memo, Lily was intensely relieved that what she saw as her duty had not resulted in a betrayal of her friends. She discussed the memo with no one, not even Worth, with whom she spoke each week.

"The Israelis are too strong to negotiate with," Worth had pointed out. "And no Arab leader can take a chance on losing a war again after 1967. I mean, Lily, we get analyses coming in here that say Israel could launch an offensive against the Russian southern front."

"There's enough American armaments here to get them to Moscow," she agreed.

"The Israelis will continue to mop up Black September in revenge for Munich, and, with considerable hubris, deny they have an atomic bomb. Sadat will rattle his left-over Russian rockets, let a few Russians wander back so that his people will think he's doing a number, but there'll be no shooting match, I'm certain. So you can study the local waters in peace. Why does Keating want to know about water, anyway?"

"For his own information. He thinks Israel's vulnerable, running out of water, and has to find a way to get more fast."

There was another of the awkward pauses that Lily noticed occurred more and more often between them on the phone.

"Enjoying the Israeli summer?" he asked.

"It's awful. I tried to have an air conditioner put in my car. They just laughed."

"Well, convince yourself that it's almost Christmas," he said. "Come December, it'll be so cold in Paris that you'll wish you were back there in July. But we'll have a good time—if we remember each other by then. Oh, and listen, I don't want to stay at the Plaza-Athenée. Do you mind? Too many people, too big."

"I don't care," Lily said, then tried to sound more enthusiastic. "Wherever you want."

"I thought the Raphael on Avenue Kléber, not far from your mother's, a nifty place, has a nice Turner seascape in the lobby."

"Fine," Lily said.

"Terrific. I'll take care of it. Well," he said in the tone Lily had long recognized as the end of the conversation. She did nothing to prolong it and said goodbye with relief and with excitement about seeing Moshe Levy again after his absence of several weeks on business in London.

Their friendship was developing without any explicit romance. There were too many complications in her career and life to add an affair with Moshe. She regarded him as a test of whether or not she and Worth, while working separately in the Foreign Service, could have some semblance of a marriage. Moshe was her first temptation; if she married Worth and worked at her own career, there would inevitably be more.

Affairs in the Foreign Service were plentiful, but Personnel didn't seem to have too Calvinistic a response, unless scandal or security was involved. Divorce, however, was becoming more common in diplomats' families. Having lived most of her childhood through the damage that her parents' divorce had caused, Lily did not wish to become a part of that statistic. Making it through her posting in Tel Aviv, talking with Worth once a week, and seeing him during her leave in Paris were all parts of the engagement process. She hoped to discover whether marriage could be expected to work for her, with Worth or anyone else.

She admitted that Tel Aviv had seemed empty without Moshe. When he called on his return, she was nervous enough to excuse herself on the two occasions he asked to see her. She finally gave in when he invited her to dine again with his mother. That seemed safe.

The drive to Herzliya started with standard greetings and distracted questions about what had happened to each of them during Moshe's absence.

"You know we're in danger, Lily."

They were speeding along the coast road, and as it rose and fell, the sun seemed to bounce on the horizon of the Mediterranean, searching for its slot. "What danger?"

"We should be falling in love with each other by now."

Startled, she asked, "Is there some kind of rule?"

"Only one. Any human relationship either grows or withers. There's no leveling off, except stagnation or the hardening of the will into concrete. For friends, lovers, married people, a next step must be there and must be taken. Since we're not to be lovers, we have to find another way so that we don't have to talk to each other with this dithering kind of awkwardness, so that I don't have to take you to dinner with my mother in order to see you. I'm not sure friendship will suit us or satisfy us, but I see no alternative, do you?"

" 'Only one,' " she said, mocking him affectionately. "We could let it wither and not see each other again."

"I don't think you want that any more than I do, and I don't intend to let that happen, no matter what else is going on in our lives."

She looked over at him, reacting to his intensity, curious about what he may have implied. Through his black-red beard, his lips glistened, reflecting the sinking sun as he licked them nervously. His dark eyes followed the road, and there was a frown of frustration above them. He sensed her look and reached over for her hand.

"I wish it were different," she said, "but it isn't."

"You're sure you love him?"

"Yes," she said as automatically as she had said it to Noorna, convincingly, she hoped. She believed it technically, which she knew was a terrible way to believe.

"What we have to do," Moshe said, "is define the limits we will not cross, so that within those limits we can have a happy time. First, we will *not* seduce each other."

Both laughed. "What a good place to start," Lily said.

"What about holding hands?" he asked, holding hers up to view.

"I think so, on occasion, but no—meaningful pressures."

"Ha!" He laughed and continued, "And none of those phrases, even in fun, like 'I adore you,' or 'I want you . . . need you,' those substitute I-love-you phrases."

" 'I like you' is as far as we'll go."

"And what about kissing?"

"Which kind?"

"Well, I'm not talking about those inane pecks on either cheek that turn Europeans into so many birds. I mean, well, for instance, the casual kiss good night."

"Define casual."

"I can't."

"Dangerous, I think."

"Yes." He drove silently for a while. "Do we want to play this silly game, Lily, or will it drive us both crazy?"

"I don't see any alternative. I can't imagine not seeing you anymore. Having an affair, secret or not, would do damage, a lot of it. And I don't mean to my engagement or career. I mean to me. Friendship may be a pretty silly game for us, but at least it's possible. I'd rather go crazy than not play it."

"So would I."

They drove quietly, still holding hands, enjoying the blazing red and orange of the sunset, until the turn-off into Herzliya.

"I know it isn't fair, Moshe."

"What isn't?"

"This arrangement. I'm engaged; you're not. I have an obligation; you don't."

"That's my business. I want what we've just defined as much as you do."

Lily thought that she probably wanted it more, but didn't say so.

"Now please," he said as he turned into the driveway of his villa, "not a word of our arrangement to my mother. She'd hate the idea of being our chaperone."

And so the game was played, successfully for the most part, at least on the surface. They saw each other as often as their separate schedules allowed. Her hours at the embassy were never organized into an eight-hour day. If there were ambassadorial functions, her duties multiplied, although fortunately the ambassador's wife was not one of those who regarded the female staff of her husband's embassy as part of the local labor force.

For his part, Moshe was out of the country almost every other week on business. Throughout the summer and into the fall, he was going anywhere to buy diamonds, accumulating as large a store as possible, not just medium-grade melees, but gem-size stones as well. Within an hour of his return, he would call Lily to arrange a meeting.

"I have an ethical question for you," he said one evening over harimek, red mullet cooked with garlic and cumin, served them in a North African restaurant not far from Lily's apartment in Old Jaffa. "I ask you because you excel in ethics," he added slyly.

"Just stay on the subject, please. What's the ethic?"

"Smuggling."

"That's not ethics. That's crazy."

"Ethics often deceive. For instance, De Beers uses every pressure known to man to control the product of the African continent's diamond mines. They own them or make arrangements—political or economic—with those who do. This means that in certain African nations—not South Africa; it's a different situation there—the local ruler is the sole benefactor, leaving those who work and rot in the mines to struggle for their very existence. This is the status quo, unknown to most of those who wear the glittering product of such a system as decoration. Please explain the ethics of that." He smiled wickedly.

"You're setting me up. What's your question?"

"My question is, what if a native miner decides to take an impossible chance against all the technology, the X-rays, the strip searches, the dogs, et cetera, and somehow manages to get a good stone out of the mine? He travels overland through jungles and rivers, crosses an international border to a city where he can sell the stone, and thus provides enough food for his family to live in good health for a decade. Should I buy the stone?"

"Are you asking me as a person or as a diplomat?"

"Both."

"All right. First, here's me being diplomatically analytical. Yes, you buy it. The moral and humanitarian considerations outweigh any economic damage done either to the company or to the country in question, both of which might be condemned for practices that, if not illegal, are surely corrupt and inhumane." She leaned forward intimately. "No, of course you don't buy it. You'd be trafficking in stolen goods, which could severely jeopardize your free passage in the future, not to mention the disfavor such a practice would create at De Beers."

He reached across the table and took her hand. "Getting caught isn't a question of ethics, is it?"

They gazed at each other. With effort, each let go of the other's hand. As a distraction, Moshe pulled a handkerchief out of his breast pocket and unfolded it to reveal a small tissue-paper packet. "I have another question for you."

He opened the packet and held up between his thumb and index finger a dull, gray, thimble-sized stone. "Do I cut it into six, or do I take a chance of attracting attention and cut it into three? Or do I really act crazy and do the single? Here, take it. Look before the sun goes down. You can see through the coating. It's bad light, but you can see well enough; I've made a window. Look into its heart. It's quite perfect, I think. Blue-white, no clouds, no carbon spots, no feathers . . ."

She took the stone, using the distraction just as he was. He handed her his loupe and, although she didn't know what to look for, she examined the rough diamond. "It's very light."

"Fifty-two carats," he explained, "less than half an ounce avoirdupois. A miner hardly ever has a chance to find a rock that size. It takes ten thousand tons of ore to produce a pound of diamonds. The guards at the mine's exit passage make arbitrary selections of workers each day for X-ray. The machines are mainly used to examine the head and the hips, where the body's hiding places are. The miner also knew that if he was successful, he couldn't disappear the next day, or the security people would be after him."

Carefully, Lily handed back the stone. Moshe put the loupe in his eye and again examined his prize. "He'd been trucked in from his village in the jungle to live in a miners' dormitory and work his ten-hour shift six days a week. He sends most of his money back to his family, whom he visits for one week three times a year. But this year was different."

He let the loupe drop in his hand. "He was cutting down slag in a pipe mine with a pickax. When he saw the stone, he stepped on it so that others wouldn't see it until he had a chance to put it in his mouth, where it stayed between his teeth for several hours. Late in the day, he swung his pickax hard and precisely and made a deep gash in his calf."

Moshe placed the rough stone on the tablecloth between them. "He didn't make a sound until he'd taken the diamond out of his mouth and pushed it into the wound as far as it would go, around muscle to the other side of the bone. Then he started screaming, and screamed all the way to the infirmary, kept screaming like an animal, which irritated everyone, made them edgy, distracted them as much as all the blood did. He only stopped when they'd poured in iodine and stitched him up as if he were a cart horse. He went back to work as soon as they made him, his leg still in pain, and waited two months for his vacation. When it came, he spent one night at home with his family, then started out overland for the border and a capital city well known for illicit diamond trading. Fortunately, I happened to be enjoying the local scene at the time."

"You won't tell me where this was, will you?" Lily warned.

"Ever sensitive to your ethical standards, I won't taint your virtue," he said with a smile.

"Oh, thank you for your kind consideration. So what happened?"

"I was the fourth buyer he told his story to. No one believed it. The only evidence he had to offer was a scar on his leg. So I told him that I'd have a doctor come, give him a general anaesthetic, open up the wound, and if the stone wasn't what he said it was, I'd leave him there to bleed to death. I watched him very carefully as my translator got the deal through to him. If I'd seen one iota of hesitation, I'd have thrown him out. But he started crying and thanked me. Later, he told me that if I hadn't agreed to buy, he was going to have to cut his leg open and take the diamond out himself."

"But what happened when he went back to the mine with a new wound?"

"My doctor made his incision on the old scar. Back home, he just missed the mine bus for a couple of weeks until the scar was close enough to what it was when he left. The mine people don't keep track of what goes on in the villages. By then, he could afford the holiday."

Lily picked up the stone again. "Here's a hypothetical question," she said. "Suppose, when the doctor had done his work, the diamond that seemed so big to the unsophisticated native miner wasn't so big to you. Would you have let him bleed to death?"

"It would never have come to that. A miner, no matter his lack of sophistication, knows a once-in-a-lifetime diamond. If he hadn't believed he had one, he'd never have made it so far, and I would have spotted any hesitation when he came to me. Besides that, you know me well enough to know the answer."

"I don't know about you and smuggling. It seems that there are different ethics, no judgment intended."

"No, of course not. The good diplomat never reveals a judgment, does she?" He took the stone from her, examining its other angles as he spoke. "She just observes from a careful distance, where she can keep the rules and devise her hypothetical—surely not judgmental—questions." He smiled at her affectionately. "Rules change in a second, Lily—not ours, of course. If I hadn't bought this diamond, I'd have been not only crazy but, I think, unethical, immoral. Not to buy would have meant damning him to the system his country's leader and the diamond cartel have inflicted on him."

"Why are you telling me about this?"

He stared at her across the table. "I want you to know me so well that you can't forget, so that if one day something changes and this fiancé of yours is insane enough to let you get away, you'll remember who I am as if by instinct." He reached across the table once more for her hand.

"No guarantee about the instinct," she said, putting her hand on his, "but I won't forget."

Agitated, he took his hand away and again gazed at the diamond. "So, what should I do, cut it three ways or six?"

"What if you just cut one?"

"We'd lose a third of it to polishing and shaping. It'd be about thirty-four carats and I'd have De Beers down my throat two seconds after it went on sale. Even three diamonds of ten carats each would probably get too much of their attention. That's how closely they watch the market. Would you like to see us cut it?"

"I'd love to. When?"

"Maybe next month, if I can get a cutting plan in time."

"Why so long?"

"It's not like slicing bread. One false hit could shatter it. The cutter has to study the grain, chart every path of light through it before he touches it. He'll make a diagram of his strategy, and present it to me for approval. I'll have other experts consult on it. It's very intense. I've seen cutters cleave a diamond and faint dead away from the pressure. Come watch. You'll enjoy yourself."

Lily was one of a dozen onlookers when, in early October, the stone was ready to be cut. Madame Levy was there, as were a number of other cutters and experts who were friends or had been consulted on the project. In the Netanya warehouse that housed part of Moshe's factory, space had been cleared around a table on which the cutting mechanism was assembled. Bulletin boards on rollers held large blow-ups and diagrams of the stone, showing the planned cuts from every angle. Moshe had decided to take a chance on cutting three diamonds, one of seventeen carats, the others of ten and eight. The largest was to be cleaved from the rough stone, the others sawed by machine.

It was Yom Kippur, the most solemn day of worship for Jews. Moshe had chosen the day for the cut just because almost all the employees would be at temple. He knew which ones he could call on. The master cutter, a contemporary and friend of Moshe's father who had left Antwerp with him, stalked back and forth between diagrams, his hands jammed into the pockets of a white lab coat. It was a hot day, and he occasionally mopped at his mottled, beefy face and nearly bald head with a handkerchief. He examined the charts, studied the stone under a microscope, returned to the charts again. The diamond itself had India ink guidelines drawn on it by a specialist called a marker. Lily had been introduced to him and found him more nervous than anyone.

Moshe watched, occasionally whispering to his colleagues, smiling once at Lily, but concentrating on his master cutter, who would soon begin. Just looking at Moshe in the bright sunlight streaming in through the high windows, with his shirt sleeves rolled up and his massive head jutted forward to take in the slightest detail of the cut, made her question every resolve she had made. And yet she'd said nothing to him, given no verbal indication about how she felt, except her willingness to spend so much time with him.

"This is the moment when the money is made," Madame Levy whispered as the cutter took his seat at the table and examined the diamond again through the microscope. "I used to be the book-keeper, and I still like to watch an important cut. Between here and there, cutting and polishing, the value triples, maybe quadruples if it goes well. If it doesn't—" She shrugged. Then she reached over, took Lily's hand, and held it. "For luck," she said.

The master cutter picked up what looked like a small silver chisel and placed it into a calibrated vise over the stone. Everyone fell silent. Holding a metal mallet, he stood up and calmly shook hands first with the marker, then with Moshe. When he returned to the table, he hunched over his equipment, his back blocking the others' view of the stone. He turned various wheels to adjust the microscope and the vise.

Outside, in the distance, a siren began its steady climb in pitch and volume. Instantly, it was joined by two others, closer, more insistent. Lily saw that no one reacted, so intent were they on the cutter. At the sound of a car driving up and screeching to a stop, Lily felt her hand being squeezed hard. The cutter raised his mallet. They watched, transfixed, and just then the door opened and several people rushed in, shouting in Hebrew.

Moshe bellowed for quiet. There was instant silence except for the wailing of the sirens at their full pitch. Lily knew they signaled catastrophe.

A small crack sounded as the mallet fell, and a second later the cutter turned with a triumphant smile on his face. He yelled a Hebrew phrase above the noise and started for the door, shedding his lab coat.

Still holding Lily's hand, Madame Levy translated. "He said, 'Come. We go to war again!' "

All the other men hurried toward the exit as those who had arrived in the car shouted bursts of news. Moshe came over to the two women. "Maman, take the diamond home to the safe," he said in French as he kissed her, "and give Lily a ride to her embassy. She'll have to go immediately."

"Come back safely, Moshe, come back," Madame Levy whispered as she hugged her son; then she hurried over to the cutter's table.

"What's happened?" Lily asked, already fearful for him.

"They said the Egyptians have crossed the canal into the Sinai, and the Syrians are moving up the Golan Heights. My tank's waiting. I have to go."

They stood for a moment as if a camera shutter froze them in the pool of light that shone around them. The sirens' wail rose even higher. He said, "I love you, Lily," and with one step she was in his arms, kissing him, until he pulled back. "I have to go, and we're breaking our rules."

"They're broken, useless. I love you. I love you."

She let him go, but he held on to her hand.

"When I get back, I'll tell you many things. If anything happens to me, remember how much I was going to tell you."

"Let me know where you are as soon as you can."

She kissed him again and watched him hurry to the door. He didn't look back, and Lily slowly turned to face Madame Levy, whose tears were already falling.

"These aren't for him," she said instantly. "He'll be fine. They're for you and him. I'm a terrible romantic," and she tried to smile.

Lily didn't believe her. She knew who the mother's tears were for and went over to embrace her, but in Madame Levy's hands were the two pieces of the diamond. The women looked at them until they heard Moshe's car start up and speed away. Then they turned instinctively toward the sound, which soon was lost in the dissonance of the sirens' rising and falling wails.

SEVENTEEN

AFTER PASSING hundreds of cars on the coast highway speeding to military assembly areas, Lily and Madame Levy were waved through four checkpoints already in place in Tel Aviv. The car finally reached the embassy gates, where the marines were wearing full battle gear and carrying their weapons. The two women had spoken little on the drive from Netanya, except for Madame Levy's translation of the news on the car radio. They hugged each other goodbye, each telling the other not to worry about Moshe.

"Where will you be?" Lily thought to ask as she stepped out of the car.

"Wherever the Magen David Adom sends me," she answered, referring to the Israeli equivalent of the Red Cross. "If I hear about him, I promise I'll call."

"I will, too," Lily said, and Madame Levy quickly drove away.

Like most of the staff, Lily had a packed bag at the embassy with several changes of clothes and supplies for either an extended stay or a sudden departure. It was a fortunate precaution. She did not leave the embassy grounds for five days.

She learned that in spite of American satellite intelligence indicating Syrian and Egyptian troop movements, in spite of the evacuation of Russian dependents from Damascus and Cairo, in spite of the mobilization of Syria's reserves and Egypt's military preparations along the entire eastern bank of the Suez Canal, no one had believed that the Arabs would dare attack Israel.

As information flowed through the ambassador's office, Lily followed the progress of the war. The Syrian and Egyptian forces had attacked concurrently on Saturday at two P.M., the Syrians with new Russian T-62 tanks up the Golan Heights, the Egyptians in rubber boats and rafts across the Suez Canal under an umbrella of dense artillery and Russian ground-to-air SAM 2s and 3s, as well as the advanced mobile SAM 6. Once a bridgehead was established on the eastern side of the canal, the Egyptians breached the towering sand dunes protecting the Bar Lev Line with huge water hoses—German water cannons—then constructed pontoon bridges, across which flowed Egyptian tanks and armored vehicles equipped with the Russian-built Sagger antitank missiles. These, when fired against the American-built M-60 tanks used by the Israelis, were devastatingly effective.

Ambassador Keating gave Lily the responsibility of keeping track of all military reports. The backbone of Israel's military superiority had always been its control of the air, thanks to its squadrons of U.S.–built F-4 Phantom fighters and A-4N Skyhawk light attack bombers. Lily had seen them flying out over the Mediterranean ever since she arrived in Tel Aviv. Within the first three days of the war, she reported that Israel lost fifteen Phantoms and forty-five Skyhawks to the unerring SAM 6. On the ground, Israel recovered from its surprise, and on the Golan Heights began to reverse the Syrians' advance, pushing them slowly back into Syrian territory toward Damascus. It was a brutal battle, and both sides suffered heavy casualties. Lily knew where Moshe probably was and stayed too busy to speculate about him. On the sixth day of the war, she read that several Israeli tank divisions had left the north and sped south to join in the fight at the canal with the Egyptians. The Israeli position had become dire; the Egyptian army was encircling the Bar Lev fortifications. At that point, she gave up even conjecturing where Moshe might be.

A steady stream of cable traffic came and went across her desk to all points of the world. Much of the news was alarming, not only about the resignation of Vice President Spiro Agnew, which further weakened the Watergate-corroded presidency, but, more foreboding, the CIA bulletin that the Russians' Antonov 22s, their largest transport planes, were landing in Damascus and Cairo at regular intervals, resupplying the Arab side with advanced military equipment. Besides this, the CIA also learned that three Soviet airborne divisions in Eastern Europe had been put on full alert. The specter of massive Soviet intervention triggering an American response in kind presented the very real possibility of nuclear war.

Only because of Lily's proximity and service to the ambassador was she included in the various informational loops. In order to take his notes, she accompanied Keating when he was summoned to Golda Meir's office at the Knesset. The car was usually filled with senior embassy staff members who grew used to her presence on the drive and in the embassy office. At night, she spent hours transcribing what had been dictated. Because of her privileged access, she learned on the seventh day of the war that the United States was beginning its own massive airlift to Israel with C–5s and C–130s, and that fourteen new Phantoms with radar-jamming capabilities would be arriving in two days, ten more within the week. The superpower vortex had begun.

In spite of the heightened pressure, the embassy ran efficiently as a listening post and disseminator of information. Lily shared the inevitable esprit de corps, for the intensity of the diplomacy matched the strategy on the battlefields. There was even praise for the minimal fare in the staff cafeteria, along with a sense that the war would be over soon. Already the world community was working for a cease-fire. Henry Kissinger, made secretary of state by an already floundering president only two weeks before the war broke out, was actively trying to enlist the Russians in the peace process, at the same time trying to counter their airlift to the Arab belligerents by supplying the Israelis with at least as much.

She was working alone on her notes one night in front of the ambassador's office. The marine on guard outside admitted a man she hadn't seen before. He was about her age, wearing a suit and tie, and, on entering, he looked around the office to see who else was there.

"No one here but us . . ." Lily began, presuming camaraderie.

"McCann? Lily McCann?" he demanded tersely.

"McCann, Lily. FSO-Eight. Who're you?"

The young man advanced, unsmiling, and showed his ID under Lily's desk lamp. His name was Bret something, in the Political Section as a CIA cover.

"What can I do for you?" Lily asked noncommittally, not eager to say or do anything to bring her to the attention of Bret's boss.

"You received a memo, dated last March twenty-eight, initialed by the chief of station."

Lily studied the young man, wondering how much he knew. "Are you asking or telling me?"

"Telling you, I guess." He smiled confidently. "If you still have it, I've been told to get it back."

"By whom?"

"The guy I work for, whose name I can't tell you, but I'm sure you can figure out if you want."

"You know what the memo said?"

"Nope. Just the date and to pick it up, if you'd be so kind as to make this evening a little shorter for me."

She believed his attempt at charm was genuinely based on ignorance of the memo. "Well, listen," Lily said, fixing him with a hard smile. "Ask the guy you work for if it's the one where the station chief ridiculed my information about the Egyptians using German water cannons on the Bar Lev Line. Last *March,* was it? Think of that." She let that hang in the silence and saw the young man's face go hollow.

"Oh, boy," he murmured as he looked over to a corner of the room.

"If that's the one," she continued, "tell him I made a lot of copies, one for my scrapbook, of course, one for the ambassador's safe. The others are around here somewhere, and I'll be glad to give him one."

He stood very still for a moment of decision, then smiled again, this time with less confidence. "I'd say we can both forget this conversation if we want to."

"I'll do my best, but tell your boss that your visit sure has made an impression."

"So did you," he said and walked out of the office, passing the marine on guard without notice.

Lily was both angry and scared. She knew a station chief could very easily have a letter placed in her file at Personnel, and if it was dirty enough, no glowing recommendation from an ambassador would balance it. She felt under attack again, and remembered the maxim thrown around her class at the Institute: "If you're not paranoid in the Foreign Service, you're really crazy." Nevertheless, she went to her file cabinet, unlocked it, and found the memo. After reading it over, she took it to the Xerox machine in the corner and made copies, her anger finally superseding her fear. The copies would go into the ambassador's safe the next morning.

———

Later that night, Lily was awakened as she lay on the cot set up for the ambassador's staff in the board room down the hall from the offices. The ambassador had come in, and she was asked to stand by. She and Louella Taft waited outside his office as he and the embassy's senior staff met for several hours. At dawn the meeting broke up, and Lily noted that George Fairfax and the young man who had visited her earlier that evening left together, neither of them acknowledging her existence as they passed through the office. Then Lily and Louella were summoned into the ambassador's office to take cables and memcons.

There had been dramatic developments. Alexei Kosygin, the Russian prime minister, had arrived suddenly in Cairo. At almost the same time, Israeli General Ariel Sharon had recrossed the Suez Canal with his armored corps and, after establishing a bridgehead, driven north to the Cairo-Ismailia Road and south toward the city of Suez, only fifty miles from Cairo itself.

The same night, Henry Kissinger flew to Moscow to confer with Leonid Brezhnev on a cease-fire. The next day, the president fired the Watergate special prosecutor and received the resignations of the two top officers in the Justice Department, in what was instantly dubbed, both in the press and in cable traffic, "the Saturday Night Massacre."

Later that day, Lily accompanied Ambassador Keating to the Knesset where he met again with Mrs. Meir and delivered news of the president's request of Congress and his subsequent personal appeal to her to accept a cease-fire. As Lily recorded in her notes of the meeting, the Israeli was a tough bargainer but very much a realist. She managed to pry out of the ambassador as much information about the Watergate scandal and the possibility of an impeachment as was diplomatically possible. In the game that even heads of state played about who knew what first, it was Mrs. Meir who informed the American ambassador that Saudi Arabia's King Faisal, furious at the American aid to Israel, had slapped an oil embargo on the United States. The other oil-producing countries of the Persian Gulf quickly followed Faisal's example.

Then a FLASH cable arrived at the embassy on Sunday night, and Lily helped disseminate its contents with all speed. The secretary of state was to stop in Israel the next day on his way back to the United States. He planned to explain to the Israeli government the terms of the cease-fire that he and President Brezhnev had worked out in Moscow. Kissinger's visit would last for precisely four hours. Among the other details included in the cable was a list of his traveling party. Below the senior State Department officers on the list were two members of Kissinger's secretariat, one being Cotesworth Deloit.

With only fifteen hours' warning, the embassy went into high gear, as did the Israelis. Word of the time of the secretary's arrival on his Boeing 707 at Ben Gurion Airport was spread throughout Tel Aviv and Jerusalem. A large crowd was expected to welcome him. Lily was assigned to Gavin Richardson, the political officer who had accompanied her to Rome, to coordinate the logistics of the visit with the Israeli protocol people. Again she worked through most of the night. Finally, she was excused and returned to Jaffa for two hours' sleep and a change of clothes.

It was still dark when she reached her apartment, although dawn was already graying the eastern horizon. As she undressed for her first bath in two weeks—the embassy's available facilities were limited to stall showers—she wished again that Worth weren't coming. They had not spoken since the war began, which had been a relief to Lily. She'd had no news of Moshe; she had nothing to say to Worth. She wondered how she would kiss him, and hoped that perhaps the circumstances would preclude any such intimacy, maybe even much conversation.

But as she washed her hair and swore again to cut it to a more practical length, she accepted that no matter how well she acted, Worth would know something was wrong. There would be no time for explanations or reassurances, and Lily wasn't sure she even wanted to give them. She thought of returning his ring, but she'd put it in the security vault at the embassy, and she didn't have time to retrieve it. She put her hair around rollers, cursing them as she did so because they'd interfere with her sleep, and hoped that Worth would be so full of the triumph of traveling with the secretary of state that he wouldn't notice anything amiss.

Her phone rang ten minutes before her alarm was set to go off.

"Lily, Moshe's been wounded. Badly." Madame Levy's voice was shaky but under control.

Wide awake and already trembling, Lily asked, "What happened?"

"All they told me is that his tank was involved in the battle on the east bank of the canal, against the Egyptian Third Army. An antitank missile hit . . ." She stopped, then blurted, "He's been burned."

Lily heard her sob as she felt her own tears and blinked them away. "Where is he now?"

Madame Levy was unable to respond for a moment. "I don't know." She fought to recover a steady voice. "He was in a field hospital. They said he'd be evacuated today, but didn't know where he'd go."

"I'll come see you right now."

"No. I know you'll be busy with your secretary of state coming. I'm all right except for these mother's tears."

"When you find out where he is, will you—?"

"Of course. I'll call you at the embassy first. Goodbye, Lily. Tell Mr. Kissinger to end this horrible war."

Lily hung up and lay in bed. She'd barely taken time to worry about Moshe, somehow convinced of his invincibility. She presumed he'd gone originally to fight on the Golan Heights and conjectured that he might have been one of those whose tanks were sent south across the Sinai to the canal. "Burned." Her skin quivered and her stomach jolted. How badly? How much of his body? His face? "Moshe, where are you?" she said as the alarm sounded. She slammed it off and stood up, suddenly thinking of Worth again, wondering how she could tell him, if there was time, that their engagement was off.

———

The blue-and-white Boeing 707 landed just on time, but taxied endlessly to the tarmac area set up for the secretary of state's arrival. There were a great many soldiers to guarantee security, as well as the requisite diplomatic representatives from both the Israeli government and the American Embassy. What was most unusual was the enormous crowd waiting and already cheering behind fences between the airport buildings.

Kissinger was first off the plane and descended the ramp to greet the Israeli foreign minister and, with Ambassador Keating, the members of the welcoming party. Lily watched as the other Americans followed, a dozen in all, and finally saw Worth, uncharacteristically carrying a large, obviously heavy briefcase. All the Americans looked somewhat rumpled and exhausted. When Worth reached the tarmac, he didn't even look around, but kept his eyes on the secretary of state, who reacted with considerable surprise and then gratitude for the presence and response of the crowd. Lily thought the secretary seemed to swell with the applause.

The official greetings and photos were completed quickly and, as the group moved to the assembled cars for the drive to the Knesset building in Jerusalem, Lily was able to make her way over to Worth, lugging his briefcase.

"Worth."

He turned, surprised; then his tired eyes softened. "I didn't think you'd be out here."

"The ambassador wanted me to—"

"Yes, I hear he's become dependent on you." He smiled. "My God, it's good to see you."

Someone urged him to hurry.

"Are you coming to Jerusalem?" he asked.

She nodded.

"Find me when you can. This is a crazy visit, but we have to talk. You have a big problem." He started for his assigned car, then said, "Oh," and leaned back to kiss her, awkwardly. He smiled again, but his mind was obviously elsewhere. Someone tried to take the briefcase from him to put it in the trunk, but Worth refused, and got into the car holding the briefcase. Alarmed by his warning, Lily hurried to the ambassador's limousine and slipped into her jump seat. The long procession of military and civilian vehicles began to move through one of the gates. People were cheering on either side.

The ambassador was in good spirits, telling his deputy chief of mission and heads of section that Kissinger had referred to Keating's previous assignment in India, where a conflict had broken out with Pakistan. He had said as a greeting, "It seems wherever we send you, there's a war," to which the ambassador had rejoined, "An unknown talent of mine, but feel free to use it wherever a war is needed."

Lily didn't join in the excited repartee or the strategic speculations about who would accompany Kissinger into his meeting. She was thinking of Moshe, wondering how she could find out to which hospital he was being evacuated, then about Worth's plain and honest pleasure when he saw her, and his dead seriousness in saying, "We have to talk." She didn't want to talk, whatever the "problem" was, and hoped that the frenetic schedule and their separate responsibilities might keep them apart, except for glancing off each other in corridors.

In the prime minister's outer office and the hallway, Kissinger's party and those in attendance from the embassy were left to mill around with their Israeli counterparts. The secretary and the State Department's senior area specialists met with Golda Meir and her staff. As an aide, Lily stayed at the farthest edges of the crowd, ready to serve the ambassador if she was needed.

She saw Worth seat himself at a desk and open the briefcase. The briefing books inside he dispersed or discussed with those who appropriately requested them. He spotted Lily and, when he was left alone for a moment, beckoned her over. When she reached the desk, he pulled out a file and handed it to her.

Without rancor, he said, "You've made a bad friend and a good enemy. Go read this somewhere and then come talk to me about it."

The prime minister's door opened and an American assistant secretary called to Worth and gestured him inside. He hurriedly picked up the briefcase and disappeared behind the closed door. Lily took the file and went into the hallway, where a number of men were talking. She found a private space, opened the file, and went rigid.

To: Deloit, Secretariat, State
Routing: Langley, Roger Channel
Classification: Eyes Only
Country 2791–Secret
RE: Moshe Levy
Message: Thought the enclosed might be of
interest to you.
Signed: Fairfax, Tel Aviv.

With the cover letter were four official Mossad reports outlining, by numbered paragraphs in the coldest bureaucratese, the relationship between "Subject Lily McCann" as described by "Combatant Moshe Levy." The first described how he had set her up in a Russian restaurant to be met by *"katsas"* Ben Hazza and Cohen in connection with Abu al-Saffah; the rest described meals and other meetings, early in the spring. Paragraph 6 on the last document described in detail the terms of the agreement made between them so that they could go on seeing each other; it ended with "Subject is genuinely committed to the relationship with her fiancé. No date for the wedding is set, however."

Lily closed the file and leaned back against the wall. She tried to concentrate on what the file meant. It had been sent by the secret and private Roger Channel, a frequency the CIA used exclusively for its communications not seen by the local ambassador. It had been read only by the two encryption personnel at the Langley end, one of whom had sent it by courier to Worth. How many CIA people in Tel Aviv knew about it and her relationship with a Mossad "combatant" was unknown to Lily. Also unknown was what George Fairfax intended, beyond his dirty implication in sending the reports to Worth.

"If anything happens to me, remember how much I wanted to tell you." Was it this? She walked back into the prime minister's outer office, where Worth was working at the desk he'd commandeered.

She held out the file to him. "I'm very sorry, Worth."

"I don't want it. By chance, is this son of a bitch Fairfax here?" he asked, looking out over the crowded room. Surprised at his response, Lily held the folder at her side.

"No, he stays under a rock in the daytime."

"Pretty filthy thing to do, I'd say." He looked at her, exhausted but concerned. "I'm afraid you're in trouble, Lily."

Without conjecturing what exactly he had in mind, she replied, "I know."

"Wait. Do you understand why?"

"I think so, but tell me."

"Let's go outside." He gathered up the briefing books, put them in the briefcase, and, taking it with him, led Lily back to the door. In the hall, they walked past the others gathered there until they reached the spot where Lily had read the file. He put the briefcase on the floor and leaned against the wall, closing his eyes to rest them. Lily stood opposite him as he began to speak, softly, still with his eyes closed.

"Those four reports aren't all the Mossad has, obviously. They were selected for maximum effect on me. Beyond that, they place you in a position of extreme jeopardy. If this ever becomes known at Foggy Bottom, you'll be out of the Foreign Service."

"There's nothing in those reports or any other that in any way compromises—"

"Lily, I'm not your enemy here; you don't have to defend yourself to me. What you have to realize and accept is that there's documentation that you were involved to some degree of intimacy with an operative of a foreign country's intelligence service. And, Lily"—he opened his eyes and bore in on her—"they can make that degree anything they want, whether it's true or not."

"I didn't know he was a 'combatant' until two minutes ago. The degree of intimacy was nothing more than a friendship. I don't even know what a combatant is."

He exhaled patiently. "Briefly," he said in tones Lily remembered from his Yale lectures, "combatants are those who sign on with the Mossad and in civilian life have the freedom to travel anywhere with their profession as cover, like CIA contract agents. They aren't full-time '*katsas*' or case officers. They're sent on specific missions, often in Arab countries because they speak the language—"

"Moshe doesn't speak Arabic," Lily blurted.

"He does. Fluently. Grew up speaking it. I checked. Also French, German—and English."

She remembered Moshe in North African restaurants asking her to translate the menu. She stared at the ceiling. "God, he really did me, didn't he?" Then she thought of his burns and squeezed her eyes shut.

"What'd you do to George Fairfax to make him so vindictive?"

Lily explained as she stared dully at the floor between them. When she told him about the German water cannons memo, she heard him laugh.

"These goddamn spooks," he said; "they get crazed when they're threatened."

"I've tried to stay away from him since I met him, but with Abu al-Saffah—"

Worth was shaking his head. "It wouldn't have mattered. You heard the ambassador chew him out, and he resents you for that. The rest of it just drove him further into his rat's corner. The question is, what are we going to do about it?"

She noted his use of "we;" he seemed already involved in solving the problem. "What should I do?" she asked.

"I think you have to get out of Israel."

"I'm damned if I'll give in to—"

"Wait. We don't have much time, and we're both probably too tired to think straight. I've had the file longer than you, so let me tell you the way I see it, and you can consider it after I've gone."

Lily clenched her mouth shut and nodded.

"The file's a gauntlet, Lily. Fairfax has thrown it down and is waiting for you to pick it up and start a cat fight. These guys don't get into something like this unless they have plenty of ammunition, and the truth doesn't limit them. To him, you're a petty annoyance, but irritating enough for him to do something about. What does he want? I don't think he wants to destroy your career. If he did, he'd have sent the file to the ambassador or to Personnel, painted your picture a bit more graphically with spying and such, and ruined you so that anything you had on him—water cannons, diplomatic gaffes—wouldn't mean anything. He can still ruin you if he has to, but he'd rather not, is my guess. He just wants to impress you with what he could do, and, I think, get you out of his territory. Whether he wants that or not, you should go for your own sake."

"What am I supposed to do?" Lily said, exasperated. "This is my first posting. I haven't even been here a year."

"I'll take care of it," he said, not bragging.

Lily watched him and realized she was grinding her teeth. "I'd hate that. I don't want to be dependent on you, Worth; have you being in charge of my life. I'd hate that."

For the first time, he looked irritated. "This is *not* personal, Lily, and if you consider things carefully, you'll see that you're pretty much in charge of that part of your life. I'm talking only about your career, which is in deep trouble. If you leave, Fairfax will have his little triumph and it'll blow over. If you stay, he'll probably take the trouble to ruin you." Someone down the hall called Worth. "You decide; let me know." He picked up the briefcase and started back.

Lily walked beside him, still holding the file in one hand. "Where should I go?"

"I'd try for Cairo. Things are going to change there pretty fast. Our embassy . . . well, Kissinger has a few ideas, which is the understatement of the century."

An American official was urging him to hurry, but when they passed the guards at the prime minister's office, Worth stopped and looked at her.

"Do you love him?"

"I obviously didn't know who he was," she answered steadily, meeting his eyes with her admission.

He said, "I love you, Lily. That file made me realize how much, how I don't want to lose you."

He was called again, this time impatiently.

"Let me know what you decide," he said and followed his colleague into the prime minister's office.

EIGHTEEN

MOSHE."

"Hello, Lily." Moshe rolled from his back to his good side so that he could see her better in the dim light of the ward. "I've been lying here thinking about you."

"I'd have been here sooner, but—"

"You don't need any excuses at this bedside."

There were forty beds in the ward, all occupied with the war-wounded. From many of them, she heard groans or the labored breathing of painful sleep. Nurses followed a doctor on his rounds, their whispers the only talk other than Lily's and Moshe's. Small areas of light went on and off as the medical unit moved from bed to bed.

It was late, but Lily had established a routine of night visits to the hospital ward over the previous two weeks, since her duties at the embassy allowed her no free time during the day. Over that time, there had been two cease-fires, each broken by both sides. That had led to a worldwide nuclear alert on the part of the United States in reaction to Brezhnev's threat of Russian unilateral military action to support Egypt. Diplomacy took over, and Kissinger, on his way to China, had flown to Cairo to meet with Sadat. Their agreement concerning the cease-fire lines had led to the scheduling of direct peace talks between Egypt and Israel, a diplomatic leap in the Middle East of astonishing proportions.

"You're better," Lily said.

"I am. I think I can feel hair coming back on my cheek. Not very comfortable, but it's good to know it's there."

The burns covered two thirds of the right side of his body, mainly below the shoulders. Skin had been grafted on his right leg, hip, and side. The fire in the tank had fed on much of his hair; what remained had been shaved. The right cheek was still scabbed, which was where he felt his renascent beard. To Lily, he looked naked without it. His deeply cleft chin was revealed, as was the scar across his throat. Burns and all, he was still a startlingly handsome man.

"How do I look?" he asked and smiled as much as he could.

"It's interesting to see who you really are," Lily said with no provocative overtones. "How's the rest of you?"

"They say the grafts have taken, no rejection at all. A plastic surgeon showed up today and licked his lips with anticipation. Oh, and my mother wants to cook you a meal."

Lily had spoken to Madame Levy many times on the phone, but purposely had avoided meeting her, fearful that the mother would see something of what Lily had not yet revealed to the son. "It looks as if you'll survive," she said.

"Better than ever." He watched her, the smile slowly becoming bothered and then disappearing. "What is it, Lily?" He tried to sit up, but grimaced and remained on his side. "At first, I wasn't alive enough to notice, but in these last couple of days, I can tell that something's—different. You come in here—you're the first person I remember seeing after they brought me here—but, tell me, what is it?"

"I'm leaving Tel Aviv."

She saw his eyes blink and his mouth open in disbelief. Then a shade of realization crossed his face. "When?" he asked.

"Tonight." It was actually in two days, but Lily had resolved that the relationship should have its own ending. "The United States and Egypt have re-established diplomatic relations. We're opening our embassy in Cairo, and they need instant staff."

Bitterness looked strange on his bare face. "Were you planning to tell me, or were you just planning to disappear?"

"We don't tell each other lots of things, do we, Moshe?"

In spite of the pain, he lifted himself up on his elbow. "Who told you?"

"It doesn't matter. You didn't."

"You've come in here every day for two, almost three weeks, pretending that nothing—"

"I needed to do that," she snapped. "I didn't pretend anything."

"And now?"

"You used me, Moshe. You jeopardized my career, you set me up for the Mossad, and filled out reports about our time together. I was your project. The war came and you broke me down, because there's nothing as romantic and exciting as war, is there? It's just that you can't tell what'll happen in a war, or what someone who loves you might find out."

"I said the day I left that I was going to tell you—"

"It was too late, Moshe. I had to say that I loved you to get you to offer that. You should have told me who you really were the night we agreed *not* to fall in love, which you described to them in such engrossing detail. But you couldn't, could you? You were still on assignment."

He sank onto the bed again and didn't look at her. "Did the papers you've obviously seen include the letter of resignation I wrote to Mossad ten days before the war began?"

"Ten days," she said, wondrously sarcastic, then allowed anger. "Were you still submitting reports until then? Didn't you realize how they could be used, that Mossad exchanges all kinds of favors with the CIA, that I'd be held up to ridicule for falling in love with—"

He interrupted furiously. "I tried to get out of Mossad almost as soon as we met. It isn't easy, believe me, but I finally did it."

The man in the next bed uttered something in Hebrew, obviously demanding less noise.

"Well, I'll hang on to those ten honest days," Lily whispered. "Maybe it'll help the memory, but it won't save anything we had."

Moshe lay silent in the shadowed light. Then he said, "Two things I want to say. First, I apologize to you from the bottom of my soul. And then, I must thank you and whatever fate dropped you into my life in time for this war, because your loving me was surely the reason I survived it, the reason I crawled out of my tank and distracted myself from the pain of what had to be done to me. I *could* have stood it without you, but I remember times when I don't think I would have." He stared at the ceiling. "I know apologies and thanks can't be allowed to mean much to a diplomat. Let's just agree that—anger and frustration aside—we'll miss each other. That's honest, isn't it?"

"Yes," Lily said as she bent over the bed and kissed him gently on the lips. "Goodbye, Moshe."

She walked out of the ward as quickly as she could without running.

PART THREE

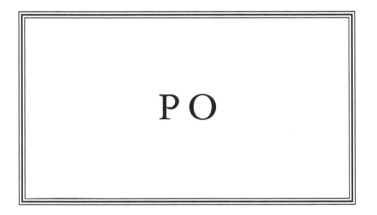

PO

October 1980–September 1982

NINETEEN

WHEN THE PHONE RANG, Lily woke up, not knowing where she was. She reached for the phone to stop the noise.

"Yes?"

"*Bonjour, Madame. Il est onze heures.*"

"Thank you," she said and hung up, just as she noticed a small gift-wrapped Cartier box next to the phone. Worth's large calling card was propped beside the box, his name crossed out, a message scrawled. Reaching for the card, she saw the bright sunlight around the edges of the draperies in the Raphael suite. Another perfect autumn Paris day.

> Happy Anniversary. Beware the seven-year itch. Please regard last night as a purely professional discussion. I love you. Maybe you'll even wear these. Be back at noon.
>
> W.

She looked over at Worth's side of the bed, at the covers thrown back from his usual explosive entrance into the day and his hurry to get it started; in this case, to arrive on time at the stables in the Bois de Bologne for an early morning ride. When he was in Washington, he'd taken to weekend riding and had joined the hunt in Middleburg. A new pair of handmade boots had been delivered to the hotel the day before. As she lay back in bed, she closed her eyes again, not for sleep but for oblivion, which was too much to hope for.

It was six years, not seven, that they'd been married. Lily thought of their hasty courtship during what became known as Kissinger's "shuttle diplomacy," the October wedding, her ivory-colored suit, the scent of jasmine from her bouquet, the kind Anglican clergyman with the halo of white hair at the British church at Zamalek, Noorna as her matron of honor, the ambassador as Worth's best man, the reception at the Residence after the hastily arranged service, and their weekend honeymoon at the Cataract Hotel at Aswan, where Worth convinced her to spend their future anniversaries at the Raphael in Paris. The hurried rituals had passed as quickly as her memory of them.

Six years. Not terrible, Lily thought, but a somewhat peculiar life for her—Cairo to Washington to Kuwait to Amman, the steady progress from FSO-8 to FSO-3 and political officer, a nice neat career. It also had been a strange, long-distance, but still neat marriage, based on twice-weekly phone calls, summer leaves together, as well as three other meetings each year, depending on their schedules. The eighteen months they'd actually lived together as a couple in the house on O Street, when Lily was posted to Foggy Bottom, now seemed, as she looked back, an oddly distant time, more distant to Lily than when the two of them lived halfway around the world from each other.

By then, Kissinger had redefined the Department of State, gathering unto himself greater control of the decision-making process of all foreign policy. Lily heard the stories of his arriving by jet for any opportunity to display this control, largely depriving American diplomats in the field of responsibility beyond bureaucratic administration. The secretary's contempt for ambassadors was well known, and this, along with the Nixon administration's inclination to deny senior positions abroad to FSOs in order to reward "polyps," had created a level of unprecedented bitterness in the Foreign Service that the Carter years had not yet allayed.

Nixon's resignation and the subsequent changes of administrations kept Worth busy treading water in the political crosscurrents of the Department of State. The time that he and Lily had lived together in Georgetown seemed to be one long strategic planning session, with an interminable number of dinner parties providing whole seasons of intramural diplomatic play. But it worked. After Lily returned to the Middle East, Worth's career during the Carter years had progressed to where he was currently the deputy assistant secretary overseeing the Northern Gulf and Arabian Peninsula as well as Jordan, Syria, Lebanon, and the Palestinians.

He'd almost had to cancel Paris for that year's anniversary. Because of what happened the night before, Lily wished he had. The Northern Gulf had exploded a month earlier in a war between Iran and Iraq, and the fifty-two hostages taken in the American Embassy the previous November were still being held in Tehran. Leaves had not been canceled, but Lily understood, as she flew in from her post in Amman, that they both might have to leave Paris at any moment.

Now, lying in bed, Lily wished intensely that the phone would ring to summon her or him away from that lovely hotel on that lovely day in Paris. However, the thought of returning to Amman and Ambassador Hooper thoroughly depressed her. In the argument she'd had with Worth, Hooper had been the catalyst. They'd gone to Le Taillevant, as they had each year on the eve of their anniversary. And, as always, the great three-star restaurant was filled with an ebullient crowd, so their "discussion" was not overheard. Only her throwing a glass of sauterne on his shirt was noticed. He had treated the gesture as an accident; he deftly blotted up the wine with his napkin and had her glass filled again.

The argument had started with Worth's impatience. "Don't you understand that I'm at a level now where politics makes a very big difference? A new administration comes in, a new secretary of state wants to establish himself as a big honcho and doesn't want somebody else's experts running the bureaus, so he cleans house. And the deputy assistant secretaries are sitting ducks. I'm damned if I want to take up ghost walking around the halls, waiting for a post. It happens, you know. The State Department's not known for looking after its own."

"Maybe Carter will win again," Lily offered.

"You've been away too long," he said disdainfully. "Carter blew his rescue attempt of the hostages. Americans can't stand that. They may know in their heart of hearts that Reagan is an airheaded mannequin, but they'll vote for someone who looks good instead of someone who's embarrassed them and failed."

"Why not have a Reagan group to dinner at the O Street house?

I'm sure you've managed to charm a contingent of Republicans at one time or another."

She'd said it off-handedly but not sarcastically as she glanced around the restaurant. His response made her snap back to watch him.

"You don't give a damn, do you? Goddammit, I've got to find some way to get to those Reagan people. They're insular as hell, and they look at outsiders the way vultures look at meat. You always did sneer at my dinner parties, but they work, goddammit, except that these California types apparently prefer barbecues or beach parties to anything in Georgetown."

"Worth," she said looking directly at him across the table, "I don't like the dinner parties, but I don't laugh at them. I know they're—useful."

"Oh, thank you one hell of a lot. That's about as patronizing a remark as I've heard from you in a long time."

"It wasn't patronizing; it was honest. You know I don't like—"

"Oh, I most certainly do. It takes about a half hour for the obligation to crack off your face."

"That's a pretty rotten remark, so I'll overlook it."

"As you overlook so many things—for instance, the effect on me of this bitchy little snit you're having with Ambassador Hooper. Jordan's my watch, you know. Hooper's a big contributor; he can get to the president or the secretary very easily. He's a major player and you're my wife. Believe me, he's aware of the connection."

"He's the worst kind of polyp," Lily responded, as angry as he. "The kind that breezes in with all the answers written in the concrete of his mind; in this case, they're based on his expertise at selling potato chips all over the world."

"Those chips come from Georgia potatoes," Worth said pointedly. "Jimmy Carter comes from Georgia, too. Get it?"

"And Wallace Hooper comes from New York with its Jewish vote and craves the Senate. Yes, I got it, and do you know what Hooper's brilliant solution to the Middle East is?" Lily asked. "Have the CIA pay off King Hussein to abdicate and establish Jordan as the Palestinian State. Then—get this—move, deport all the Palestinians from Gaza and the West Bank to their new country. How? By truck convoys! Does that bring to mind any images of the past, like boxcars?"

"Lily, Hooper's ideas don't matter. He doesn't make policy and never will. What's important here is that you're letting yourself get into a fight with your ambassador, and Foggy Bottom knows about it. It's a no-win situation. You can't beat him no matter how wrong he is, and Personnel looks on something like this as your failure; you're letting yourself in for it. They think that if you were smart, you'd figure out a way to be your ambassador's buddy and lead him out of trouble."

"I am smart, and I tried to be his 'buddy.' But it's hard to be the buddy of someone who calls you 'honey' and tells you to arrange for his shoes to be shined every morning, and who doesn't invite you to his staff meetings because—and this is a direct quote to me—'There's a position for girls over here, and I sure do hope you figure out what it is.' Aside from that, he's gained a certain fame around Amman for his series of Sheikh of Araby stories about dumb Arab men and oversexed Arab women. The ones I've heard are so offensive and filthy, I'm surprised there hasn't been an international incident."

"What the hell are you doing, tattling to the principal? You're not supposed to talk to me about this stuff."

"Oh, I'm sorry, I thought I was talking to my husband. Silly me."

"Lily, Hooper's not a fool; he's close to power; and he's on my watch. It's not appropriate for my wife, a midlevel FSO, to take potshots at him."

"Wait a minute. Amman is my watch, too. I'm a political officer there. If this potato chip king does harm to the United States in an area as sensitive as this one—suggesting that King Hussein abdicate? Truck convoys? Come on, Worth—don't I have the responsibility to do something to leash this guy?"

Contemptuously, he shook his head. " 'Leash' is a telling word. You just can't stand not being in charge, can you?"

That was when the sauterne flew from the small glass she'd been clutching so hard she thought it would break. He'd smiled with ease and chatted for the benefit of those patrons who'd seen her gesture. Dabbing at his shirt with his napkin, he raised his brow for the sommelier to refill her glass. "Well, I guess I touched a nerve. I hope you don't react this way in the field."

"No, that nerve's a personal one."

"Then let me tell you a professional truth. There've been worse ambassadors than Hooper. Not one of them has ever been 'leashed' by an officer in his embassy, but the ground is littered with the remains of FSOs who tried." He signaled to a waiter nearby for the check.

They sat quietly sipping wine as the check was delivered and Worth signed the credit card slip. They rose and walked to the entrance, where he helped her on with her coat, thanking and tipping the maître d' and coat check girl with graceful appreciation. They rode back in a taxi to the Raphael in stony silence, Lily dreading the return to their room, where, she had little doubt, his true anger would reveal itself.

As they crossed the hotel lobby, the elevator doors opened and a group of men walked toward them, their coats and hats already on.

"Good God!" Worth whispered involuntarily, but made no other gesture as he and Lily kept walking toward the elevator. Lily looked at the group of men as they passed for an explanation of Worth's reaction, but she recognized none of them. She and Worth stepped into the elevator, and the second the doors were closed by the elevator boy, Worth began to laugh, slightly at first, then so happily and freely that Lily was distracted from the gloom of dinner's end and joined him.

"What is it?" she asked.

Slowly he stopped, but a beatific smile remained on his face as he said, "I've seen the future, and it's just terrific. Come on."

They stepped out on their floor, and as they walked down the hall, he said, "You didn't recognize any of those men, did you?"

"No."

"Good. I won't tell you who they are because there's going to be some hardball, and I don't want you to get caught in the volley."

He opened the door to their suite and followed her in, still beaming. She watched him drape his overcoat on a chaise and go to the bar. "This we can celebrate. And, wait, what time is it? Yes, it's our anniversary!" He opened the small refrigerator and took out a split of champagne. "Sometimes life winds up and throws a real spitball, but by pure chance it comes right over where you can see it best and whack the hell out of it." The champagne popped and he poured into two flutes taken from a glass shelf above the bar.

"What if I told you," he said, "that one of those men in the lobby was someone of great influence on the Reagan campaign?"

"I'd have to ask what the hell he's doing in Paris three weeks before the election."

"You would indeed, you would indeed." He carried over the two glasses. "Take your coat off, stay a while. Happy anniversary, Lily. I love you more than I can say," and he kissed her, holding both glasses as she shed her coat and let it fall on a chair.

"You could *try* to say—" she suggested, taking her glass from him.

"What's the most important issue in this election to the American voter, the most emotional, the one that can change hearts, minds, and votes at the last minute, swing the election one way or the other?"

He was almost breathless with excitement, and as Lily tried to think of an answer, he started to pace the living room.

"I suppose the hostages in Tehran," she answered.

He whirled to face her. "Exactly! If they were released tomorrow, Carter might win the election. He's been negotiating like a beaver, has the Republicans really worried. But I repeat: if they're not released, Carter's a failure and loses. This is how an ayatollah is dictating who our next president will be, and the great American voter goes right along with it. Everyone's waiting until Election Day to see if Carter can pull it off. Well, Lily, my love, he won't."

He stood almost on the balls of his feet waiting for her to ask for his explanation. So she did. "Why?"

"Another one of those guys we saw downstairs was someone who's been whoring around Washington this past summer, advertising himself as a back-channel representative for Iran, mainly to buy arms. Now that Saddam Hussein in Iraq has attacked Iran, the Iranians are desperate for arms; they've let things rust since they threw out the shah. I'd say the men we saw had just completed the terms of a juicy arms deal, and I'll bet it goes something like this: don't release the hostages until after the election, and the new president will arrange to send arms to the ayatollah."

"Nonsense," Lily said, incredulous.

"Oh? Why?" Worth asked peremptorily.

"They're holding our people hostage. America is the Great Satan. You can't think they're making back-channel arms deals."

"As usual, you underestimate the pragmatic necessities of war. It'll be handled in such a way that no one who cares about where the stuff comes from will know—American or Iranian. Of course, if the wrong people find out about it, the new president might just get blown out of the water. And I found out about it, which puts me in a nifty position if the campaign man downstairs happens to become Reagan's chief of staff or secretary of state or something. So here's to President Reagan, a great American cowboy, who probably doesn't even know this is going on."

Lily tried to remember the faces of the men she'd glimpsed downstairs, but couldn't even summon up a notable feature. "It can't happen," she said, trying to remain cool.

"Why not?" he asked again, this time sounding irritated.

"Among other things—such as the fifty-two hostages—there are laws against private individuals dallying in American foreign policy. Also, the United States has an embargo against Iran."

Now Worth smiled, condescendingly. "Transshipment, Lily. The arms are sent to a cooperative country, Israel, say, which has a long history of supplying Iran with weapons."

"That's playing with those hostages' lives. They've been prisoners for almost a year."

"It's the new politics, Lily. You have to be willing to do and say anything, *anything,* to win an election, principles be damned. It's regarded by the pros as a test of mettle and manhood. That's what's respected in Washington, and the television-drugged public doesn't really care to know about it. They don't want a statesmanlike campaign; they want a bullfight. I expect Reagan's campaign people's patriotic rationale—those who know—is, aren't a few weeks or months of fifty-two people's lives worth getting the right president elected for eight years? After all, most of those hostages are only diplomats." He laughed and drained his glass.

"I hope you're wrong," Lily said, putting down her glass, still full.

"Enjoy your inherited innocence, my darling," he said expansively, "but when Reagan moves into the White House, and your husband becomes assistant secretary of state for Near Eastern and Southern Asian Affairs, you'll know I'm right. Come here and give me a kiss."

She watched him walk toward her, strangely transfixed. When he took her in his arms and pressed his lips on hers, she felt dead. When he thrust himself familiarly against her, she felt sick. Pushing him away, she stumbled backward, then grabbed her coat and went for the door. "I want to take a walk."

"Oh, for Christ's sake, Lily, when are you going to grow up? Do you really have to indulge your aching conscience this way?"

She opened the door and went out without looking back.

Once on the sidewalk in front of the hotel, she looked around, across the street, at cars parked nearby. Then she started walking, controlling her fear as she always did when she went out alone. She hadn't seen Abu al-Saffah since her trip to Rome, but his annual letters had taken on a new tone of viciousness; he blamed her for the torture that followed her visit, and swore revenge. The State Department, to which she originally had submitted the letters, gave her the perk of requesting security whenever she wanted it. She had never done so, for fear that such emphasis would eventually cause Personnel to judge her unsuitable for a Middle East assignment. For the last several years, she'd kept the letters to herself, destroying them once she'd read them, hoping to convince the department that she had been forgotten by a crank.

For two hours, she walked in shoes not meant for it. Because she hadn't brought her purse, she had no money to go into a brasserie for a coffee. Finally she started to return to the hotel, but after a few steps she stopped. Trying to think of an alternative, she looked around to see where she was and found that she was only four blocks from her mother's apartment. She walked in that direction.

Outside the building's entranceway, she wondered whether her distraught state justified waking her mother in the middle of the night, not to mention the concierge. It took five long presses of the bell to set off that woman's enraged bellows. At least she recognized Lily. After Lily crossed the courtyard, she painfully climbed the stairs, not willing to take off her shoes in the questionable dark. When she reached the landing, she stood in front of her mother's door for several minutes with the darkness roaring in her ears. Once she worked up the courage to ring the bell, she saw light appear around the edge of the door almost immediately, then heard steps. The lamp above blinded her, but she smiled toward the viewing port in the door. Her mother said, "Lily, you're not expected until lunch."

"I'm sorry, Mother, I had to come. Where's Matilde?"

"On a religious retreat." Helene sounded surly. "You'll have to wait. No one sees me like this."

"Oh, Mother, please let me in. It doesn't matter."

"It always matters." There was a pause before the locks were thrown and the door opened. Helene stood in a peignoir, a silk scarf wrapped around her neck and chin, the brim of a straw gardening hat pulled low over her eyes. "Don't kiss me; it's too late," she commanded.

Lily went in and Helene closed the door behind her. They stood awkwardly in the foyer until Lily embraced her mother, careful not to invade the area under the hat, feeling with some shyness her mother's soft flesh through the silk of her peignoir. "I'm sorry I woke you."

"You didn't. I sleep badly these days. Boredom seems to keep me at war with sleep, but I refuse to surrender by accepting some pathetic truce like loneliness. Are you hurt?"

"No, but I'd like to sleep here tonight."

A small, severe look of triumph flashed across Helene's face, apparent even in the shadow of her hat's brim. "Of course," she said, and led her daughter into the living room. Exhausted, Lily would have preferred to go down the hall to her room, but she followed her mother. Helene turned on one dim light on a side table across from the straight-backed chair in which she resolutely sat, poised expectantly.

Nothing in the room had changed since Lily's last visit the year before, not a new picture, or new material on the furniture, or a new position of a favorite figurine. The room was exactly as it had been, except that there were no flowers, and the three bird cages were empty.

"Are you going on a trip?" Lily asked, standing sadly beside one of the cages.

"No," Helene answered bitterly. "My new regimen doesn't afford 'trips.' Being celibate has not been voluntary, but, rather, inflicted by time. There's little room here for any excessive life. I put them out the window several months ago. I couldn't stand having them in here. Matilde and I have enough to put up with, with each other. She's intent on converting me to her obnoxious faith. Every day that she moves closer to death, the more fervent she is. I find her on her knees in the kitchen." She waved her hand dismissively in the air and slumped back in her chair in a way Lily had not seen before. "Tell me, Lily," she said, "what has he done to you?"

Lily stood with her hand on a cupola of the nearest bird cage and, after a moment, shook her head. "Nothing."

"Nonsense," Helene answered. "Then why are you here? I don't mean, did he beat you. I mean, how is he driving you mad?"

"I think I'm doing that pretty well all by myself."

"Ah, yes, but would you be doing it without him, or are you doing it because of him?"

Lily examined an empty perch hanging in the cage. "It's different from what happened to you and Daddy," she said defensively.

"Oh, really? Please tell me how."

"Daddy was a good man, not a son of a bitch like Worth."

"Your father was innocent; your husband is ambitious. I hope you'll allow me the point that both qualities can destroy a relationship, unless of course you're willing to be absorbed utterly into the man's point of view. For that, you're rewarded with the shiny medal of being faithful, a 'good wife.' I doubt that my daughter would accept such submission, but my husband's daughter may very well devise a diplomatic role to play. It's a choice of chromosomes, I suppose."

Lily turned from the empty cage and stared at her mother a moment. "You can simplify it like that because as far as I know you've never loved a man in your life. It gets complicated if you love someone."

"I agree. I've preferred to love myself and simply enjoy the men I've been with. It's much safer, much less stressful. What you don't know is that earlier this year I had a breast removed."

"Mother! Why didn't you—" She started over to Helene's chair, but Helene held up a hand to halt her.

"Because I'm alone and I know it!" her mother snapped. "And I know I have no right to burden you in any way whatsoever and I shall not! In any event, a woman without a breast can hardly succeed in the life I've lived. The men in my life are quite worshipful toward these twin idols we have on our chests. The absence of one is regarded as a rather repulsive blasphemy."

"Was the surgery successful?"

"You're asking about malignancy. No, there is none. The only permanent damage is that its uncomfortable for me to sit up for any length of time."

"Will you please call me if something like this—?"

"I'll consider it, but I promise nothing. Don't worry about me. I know exactly what's happening to me, and exactly what I'm going to do about it. Remember the Comtesse de Castiglione? I haven't removed all the mirrors yet. On the contrary, I have an excessive fascination with each day's ravages. Now tell me, you say you still love this son of a bitch diplomat Worth?"

Lily sat down in the place that was hers by custom.

"Yes. I have since the day I met him. There were some interruptions, but not since I married him—though it's become a long-distance affection of questionable passion."

"You've just defined marriage even for those who share the same room. Why is he a son of a bitch all of a sudden? When you bring him here to visit me, your adoration is almost sickening."

"I've been walking around Paris trying to figure that out. It's because of the kind of a person he's become . . ." She hesitated.

"What kind of a person has he become?" Helene prompted.

Lily thought for a moment. "A success," she said, exasperated. "The guy is brilliant enough to figure out what has to be done to succeed, and he does it. Can I blame him for that, even though he's a manipulative, political sociopath? As such, he's very good at what he does, highly respected, even admired. He's also very good-looking, an exciting lover still after all these years, with a stimulating mind, warped though I think it is."

"And what would he be if he weren't warped, manipulative, a political sociopath?"

"He'd probably be struggling along somewhere like the rest of us."

"As your father did?"

Lily glared at her mother but didn't reply.

"Your father wasn't a son of a bitch," Helene continued without malice. "He had a sense of honor—as maddening as Worth's qualities, believe me—and allowed his life to be contorted around his principles in order to protect them against the very profession he'd chosen. Worth obviously has different scruples, and is, as you say, a success. Perhaps it's the diplomatic life they both chose that forms the sons of bitches to serve it, and those who fit the mold best succeed, whereas those who don't grow embittered and deformed."

"I don't think Daddy was deformed or embittered. I think he was angry, but he was pretty proud of who he was and what he'd done. And I don't think you can blame the institution for what you become. That's a cop-out."

"What's this 'cop-out'?" Helene repeated the Americanism with distaste.

"A weak excuse, usually a rationalization for something inexcusable."

Helene nodded understanding and sat quietly, her eyes hidden beneath the brim. When she looked up at Lily, she was smiling sadly. In her elegant French she explained, "I believe your father became a Foreign Service officer in the days when the State Department's idealism matched his own, after the war, when America was intent on saving the world and had the power and the money to do so. Power and money make idealism a simple exercise. But when the idealism changed around him to a fearful pragmatic bureaucracy, your father was unable—or unwilling—to change accordingly. He married me with the same kind of romantic idealism, rescuing me from my military-base existence with the firm belief that love conquers all. When it didn't, and I shattered his ideal of marriage, he couldn't adjust to my reality either. I left him, but he couldn't leave the State Department, which is perhaps the greater tragedy. He was wasted there, fighting his lonely battles for the American principles he believed in and few others cared about—'consistency, consistency'; remember that refrain?—sacrificing himself to—what word did you use?—yes, what has become a truly 'sociopathic' bureaucracy, where any principle is abandoned for a quick political profit. Perhaps that's why Worth will succeed. The real question for you is, what are you going to do about it?"

"I don't know."

"Can you admit failure and leave, start again with something, someone else?"

"No," Lily replied with irritation. "I haven't failed, in my career or my marriage. Why would I leave either? Why should I? I have to tell you something, Mother. I can't help feeling that you'd like me to do what you did, that it would somehow justify or excuse, even forgive the pain you caused. Better be careful. Sounds as if Matilde and her ideas about redemption may be getting to you."

It sounded mean, and Lily regretted it as soon as she said it. She saw her mother shrink a little farther down in her chair, her face completely hidden by the hat.

"Mother, I'm—"

Helene held up her hand to stop her, and then, continuing the gesture, removed her scarf and, with her other hand, the hat. She was bald except for a slight fuzz over the surface of her head, and in the dim light, which Helene faced directly, Lily could see that she had no eyebrows. Lily rose and went to her mother's chair. Kneeling, she put her head in Helene's lap and embraced her. After a moment, she felt Helene's hand running slowly through her hair.

"I wanted you to see," Helene said quietly, "that I know exactly how I will go to my death, physically, mentally. I have no need for absolution or any other grand gesture with which religion rewards itself. My regrets, though few, are deep ones, and I must die with those. How I treated you is one of them, perhaps the greatest, and no priest, no church, not even you could ever relieve me of it, no matter the ceremony, no matter the words. I've urged Matilde with her Pope not to try, and I urge you not to, either."

In spite of her effort to control herself, Lily began to sob quietly, whether for her mother, their unrealized past, their unknown future, she couldn't tell. Her mother's hand continued to stroke her hair, catching at an occasional tangle and slowly separating it. "What a mother wants for her daughter—after obedience, of course, after the various competitions between them are dissipated —is happiness. I've seen little in you during your visits over the past several years. I assure you, I have no desire that you imitate my life in any way. Besides, you're not selfish enough to do it. I urge only that you not be drawn down and broken by despair in your determination to avoid being like your mother."

Lily slowly sat back on her heels at her mother's feet. "I can't quit just because it hasn't turned out to be what I thought."

"No? I can't think of a better reason. And if you can't fit into his life, you might do more damage by staying. Have you ever thought about what would have happened to us all if I hadn't left your father?"

Lily didn't answer, and Helene put her hat back on. "Come," she said. "I'll put you to bed."

The two women took hands and helped each other up, ending with their arms around each other. Lily hugged her mother and felt her mother hold her closely in return. They stood together for a moment until Lily said, "I'm going back to the hotel."

Helene offered no objection. "Let's change lunch to one-thirty."

Lily agreed and asked, "Can you lend me something for a taxi? I left my purse—"

At the front door, Helene said good night, then, as Lily went onto the landing, added, "If the time comes when it's too painful, too insane, too destructive for you to bear, leave him. You're my daughter; you have the courage to be alone. I want your happiness so much." She closed the door.

"You slunge! You're still in bed. What time did you come in anyway?"

Still in his new riding boots, breeches, and jacket, Worth happily leaped on the bed and, before Lily could react, kissed her. "Happy anniversary, my darling." He reached over her for the Cartier box. "I made a mistake; it's six years, not seven. I never was any good at math. Hey, you haven't even opened this. What time are we due at your mother's, and is there time for a little bed celebration before we get dressed?"

He tried to kiss her again, but she pulled away from him and sat up against the headboard. "I have to talk to you about something," she said and wrapped the comforter around her.

Seeing her seriousness, he pushed himself off the bed and stood up, still holding the box. "Yes?" he said with mocking patience.

"If what you said last night is true, about a Reagan campaign official making an arms deal with the Iranians to hold up the release of the hostages, it's more than reprehensible. It's treason. I think we have to report it."

Displaying no reaction, he repeated, coldly, " 'We'? What are you talking about?"

"You know what—"

"No, I don't. I know only that you didn't recognize any of them, can't remember them, and maybe had a little too much to drink at dinner, a fact to which a number of witnesses to your wine throwing might attest. I'm not sure that's worthy of a report, Counselor, or that this is the time for you to start practicing international law."

"Worth, you're using the hostages just the way they are."

"And do you think that if I took it public and the whole thing blew up and Carter was re-elected, the Iranians would release the hostages one second sooner? They don't like Carter. It might even be worse for the hostages. And where would I be for my trouble? The State Department regards any such controversy as akin to the plague. Officers who go public are outright fools. I wasn't involved in this caper; I intend only to respond to it. I suggest you go back to Amman and forget about it. I'm going to take a shower." He started toward the bathroom, then stopped and lobbed the Cartier box onto the bed. It landed beside her arm.

"Earrings," he said. "Happy anniversary."

TWENTY

"COME ON IN, honey. Have a seat."

"Thank you—sir," Lily said without any emphasis but the pause.

Ambassador Hooper noted the formality. He was a tall, sleek man in his fifties, with thinning gray hair carefully parted near the middle and slicked to his head. A regular dawn tennis player—with a reputation in Amman's diplomatic community for questionable calls—he was fit and deeply tanned. His broad face, blue eyes, and blinding white teeth advertised his perfect health and self-satisfaction. He wore gray suits to go with his hair; his black shoes were shined each morning in his residence and each afternoon at the embassy by a local Jordanian arranged for by Political Officer Lily McCann.

"You don't like me calling you 'honey,' do you?"

"With all due respect, sir, I think it does you a disservice."

"What's that?" he asked, smiling full force at her from his large leather chair.

"It gives the impression to the women who work with you of a patronizing indifference. I'm sure you don't mean that, and I hate to see such an attitude enforced in people's eyes."

"Well, I sure do appreciate your concern, Miss McCann. Is that what you prefer, or do you like 'Ms.'? I'll call you anything you want, but you gotta admit that patronizing indifference toward women goes down pretty damn well with these Arabs, don't it?" Affecting the Georgia redneck drawl he'd learned for the Carter years, he smiled at her, as friendly as a python.

"I'm not sure that it's a local cultural example that we should allow to corrupt us," Lily said, grinning to match his reptilian charm.

He nodded, but the glint of amusement sank beneath his eyes. "I called you in here to offer my congratulations."

She didn't know what for, but didn't want him to know that. "Thank you," she said neutrally.

"And as a courtesy, I thought I'd tell you, if you want a reassignment back to Washington and I can be of any help, I'd be glad to."

Something had happened. She'd missed a call from Worth the previous night. There'd been a message from him on her desk that morning, but the ambassador had summoned her before she could answer it. "I appreciate that, sir. I'll certainly consider it, although there are projects here in Amman that I'm eager to finish."

A familiar scowl appeared, Hooper's usual visage when he considered her, causing his thin lips to purse over his teeth. "Don't you think an assistant secretary of state could use the support of his own wife?" he asked with righteous ire.

It had happened. She couldn't hesitate. "We've always agreed that each of us would have a career, wherever we might be posted."

He glowered at her before standing up and walking to the window to look at the view of the Intercontinental Hotel across the street. The office was a temporary one; his own was hastily being made more secure. As a result of the capture of hostages in the embassy in Tehran, the theories of diplomatic security were being reassessed and reinforced in American missions all over the world.

Lily wanted to leave but could only sit and wait until she was dismissed. She stared past the ambassador's back at the hotel's façade, so different from the view commanded by his real office over the small mountain city of Amman, built on its seven hills or *jebels*. The hotel's monolithic rectangle of draped windows successfully blocked much of the view, and most of what was left was blocked by the tailored gray pongee of the ambassador's suit.

Her mind was on Worth's rise to power. The fifty-two hostages had been released in January, immediately after they and their captors heard President Reagan's inauguration oath over portable radios at the Tehran Airport. By then, they had been prisoners for four hundred and forty-four days. Two months later, Israel secretly began flying American arms to Iran, but there had been rumors of many flights long before that date. The most appalling fact to Lily was that two days after she and Worth had seen the group of men at the Raphael in Paris, the hostages in Tehran were dispersed to different locations, precluding another rescue attempt, which the Carter administration subsequently had admitted was planned. The implication was not only that a small group of private citizens had interfered in United States foreign policy, and affected the leadership of the country, but that those who had met with the Iranians in the Raphael Hotel had passed on to them information about the new rescue plan. That was treason. And now Worth was assistant secretary—ten years from his joining the service, when he promised himself he'd be an ambassador.

"Well, if you're going to stay on here," Hooper said, still with his back to her, "I want it to be real clear that you being married to Deloit doesn't mean a turd in the grass to me." He turned to face her, his lips pursed. "President Reagan himself reappointed me here to this embassy, called me on an open line, didn't give one good goddamn if our local little banty king was listening in himself. So I doubt if my newest best friend Worth Deloit is going to fool with me, no matter who he's married to." It had been reported in the *Wall Street Journal* that one week before the election, Ambassador Hooper had contributed a hundred thousand dollars to the Republican Party. The small article, titled "Chip King's Hedge," also noted that he had previously donated seventy-five thousand to the Democratic Party.

"Sir, all of that is extremely clear to me," Lily said.

"That's fine, because I want to make something else real clear. I don't want any more of your smart-mouth opinions, on memos or even floating around in the air." Having gone too far, he headed toward his chair, smiling but shaking his head. "I mean to say, honey, all I want is a little peace between us—no pun intended." He chuckled as he waited for Lily's reaction.

She gave none, considered leaving, then thought better of it. "Ambassador Hooper," she began, noticing his chin rise slightly at the title, "my job as a political officer is to serve you as best I can in relation to the situation here in Jordan. I have a lot of background in this area, a lot of experience, and I'd be delinquent in my duty to you, sir, if I didn't make available to you any useful knowledge that

I have. In no way do I want to counter your effectiveness here. I hope to enhance it. I don't ask that you agree with anything I say or write, only that I have the chance to express it—as a devil's advocate, if you will—in any form you want. To censor me—"

"Wait a minute—"

"—would be destructive."

"To who?"

"Both of us, sir."

"And I'm not censoring anyone. I just sure as hell don't need some middle-grade PO who happens to have lived here and gotten herself into a big atrocity and who's married to my assistant secretary second-guessing me behind my back."

Icily calm, Lily responded, "As far as I know, I've never offered anyone an opinion that I haven't offered to you first. Your initials are on every memo—"

"What I'm saying to you is, I don't want any more of your goddamn memos, and I don't want you sending them to anyone else. Can't you hear that, girl?"

Lily met his stare and said, calmly, "Then how else may I serve you, sir?"

"Just keep my shoes black and shiny."

"I'll do that," she said, "and I'll obey your order about the memos. But sir, I will be staying here in Amman, and I can be of use to you. Nothing said here today changes my willingness to serve our purpose here. I've been wondering whether you'd like to visit one of the refugee camps, or at least meet, unofficially, with some of the Palestinian leaders."

"We don't speak with the PLO, honey, and you better damn well not, either."

"No, sir, but the PLO is an absentee leadership living in comfort on Arab oil money in Tunis. There may be other leaders who have struggled in place—"

"I'll think on it. But you don't go back to those camps without security clearance, which I'd be willing to bet, with all this goddamn new concern for our safety, you ain't about to get."

"Thank you for considering a visit, Mr. Ambassador. I think you'd find it a vitally important—"

"Say goodbye, Miss McCann."

"Goodbye Miss McCann, sir."

She'd hoped for a smile, but he only glowered, and she left the temporary office. Instead of returning to her own, she went immediately to the embassy's security officer to ask for clearance to continue her visits to the camps. While they were discussing the details, the security officer received a call from the ambassador. Lily's clearance was not granted.

Furious, she stormed back to her office, paced for a while, started to call someone to complain, someone else to help her convince the ambassador to change his mind, a third to resign. Then she sat down and gazed dumbly at the wall, which was, she thought, exactly what the ambassador would wish her to do.

Lily had been visiting the refugee camps since soon after arriving at her post in Amman. Part of her duties as a political officer, ordered and defined by the senior officers of the Political Section, was to observe the Palestinian population and report her findings in regular memos to the staff.

The camps were a horror. Officially under the administration of the Jordanian government, they had long since been chaotically self-governed. The permanence of whole valleys of tents, raw mortar hovels, and corrugated-metal chicken coops where hundreds of thousands of people had lived for decades defined hopelessness.

After the excruciating difficulty of establishing contacts and gaining a modicum of trust for an automatically hated American, Lily was able to offer to her embassy colleagues firsthand the attitudes and often the flash points of the Palestinian refugee psyche. She walked through the fetid atmosphere created by heat, wind, and dust, the evening fires of trash, smoldering cardboard, and garbage, the open sewers, the hungry eyes of the silent children, waiting to play with an old oil can in the dust, the suspicious eyes of the women, wrapped from head to foot against the wind, as they hurried to the water drums with their empty bottles, the burned-out eyes of the men, with their gouged and wrinkled faces wrapped in *hattas,* smoking interminably, dying of shame and of untreated cancer and ulcers instead of in the battle they longed for, to regain their homes near Jericho, in Nablus, or outside Qalqiliya. After many months, she at last had succeeded in gaining the trust of some of them, who felt they could speak to her.

Now Lily sat in her office, thinking of the Palestinians she knew, of what it had taken for them to meet her, to take responsibility for her presence when she walked into the grassless dirt paths between the haphazard rows of tents and hovels. A woman alone, one who spoke Arabic, one who was an American diplomat, did not go unnoticed. Few would talk to her. Many would spit on the ground as she passed their tiny plots of onions and tomatoes laid out in the dusty soil.

Those who did talk to her, or invited her into their tin and mortar huts, believed that if an American saw how they had to live and heard their side of the argument, good might come of it. On occasion she was able to direct medical attention or other relief efforts toward a specific need in one camp or another—an inoculation program or a UN–sponsored educational project for children. For this, she was permitted to listen to the intricacies of the refugees' bitterness and the consuming dream of their longed-for return to their homes and land. Now the camps were forbidden to her.

Her phone rang.

"McCann."

"Lily?"

The connection was full of static, but the voice, even after so many years, startled her with memory.

"Yes—"

"Are you the Lily McCann who studied international law in Paris one spring several lifetimes ago?" he asked in a halting but exact English, as if he'd practiced the line.

"Yes, Ammar. How wonderful to hear from you," she said in Arabic, to relieve him. "Where are you?"

"In Baghdad, but on my way to Amman this afternoon. Can we meet?"

"Of course. Where will you—?"

"The Intercontinental. Tea at four or dinner at nine? I have a meeting in between."

"Dinner, please. They don't let us out of here before that."

"Good. We have too much to say for tea. I'm so glad it's you," he said and hung up.

Paranoia and nostalgia seemed an odd mix. How had he found her? What did he look like? What was he doing in Baghdad and

Amman? Did he call because he remembered the long afternoons in his pristine room above the alley off the Rue Domat, or because she was an American diplomat useful for his purpose? She could have requested a CIA check on him in case he was anything more than a private citizen in Algiers, but decided against it because of a certain respect for the memory. She would find out at dinner, at nine, at the hotel.

She wondered if he was married, then remembered she had to call Worth to congratulate him. She looked at her watch. It was three in the morning in Washington. She could put it off at least until the afternoon. Recognizing her reluctance to make the call, Lily was amused with herself, then went on wondering about Ammar Ben Ashid, whether or not he'd ever received the letter she wrote him after her father's death, whether or not he knew that she was married to the assistant secretary of state.

"Congratulations, Worth. I'm so happy for you."

Lily had returned to her apartment to bathe and change for her dinner with Ammar. Dressed, with hair down and perfume on, she paced as she spoke. The telephone connection wasn't as clear as it would have been from the embassy; she wondered whether she had unconsciously chosen to call from home.

He said, "I called you as soon as I was anointed, but—"

"I know. I was duty officer, so—"

"If you were duty officer, why . . . ? Never mind; it doesn't matter. I just wish you were here to celebrate."

"We'll make up for it. We always do."

"Yeah, we do, don't we?" he said doubtfully. "It seems most of our time together is making up for the time we're not. You get to wonder if we'll ever catch up."

This was odd. He seldom indulged in questioning himself.

She said, "I think it comes from wanting to have it both ways, which we seem to be having, Mr. Assistant-Secretary-in-Ten-Years."

"But not all. We don't have it all," he said wistfully.

Lily had not anticipated a serious conversation, nor did she want one. "Are you getting at something?" she asked, trying to keep it light.

"We don't have it all, Lily. We don't have a goddamn home, children . . ." He let that hang on the eight-thousand-mile line.

"Sounds like a very serious proposal," Lily said, knowing him well enough to suspect an ulterior purpose. "What brought this on all of a sudden?"

"Oh, you know. Age. Success, I suppose. I mean, don't you think it's time? Don't you want them?" The last question was slightly accusatory.

"Are you asking me to come back to Washington and get pregnant and run our happy home?"

"God, Lily, you're impossible to talk to sometimes."

"I'm sorry. I'm not sure what it is you're saying."

"I just may be saying I want more of us, and you may be saying you don't have any more to give."

"Wait a minute. I haven't said anything except congratulations."

"Well, thanks for that."

"Worth!" she said, exasperated. "You're turning this into something really mean. Why?"

He didn't answer right away. Then, "Look, I'm late. The pressures are pretty intense, as I'm sure you can imagine. I suppose I just miss you. But think about it, will you?"

"I will," she said while thinking, about what? Moving to Washington? Making the house on O Street a home? Babies?

They exchanged "I love you," a ritual reminder. They did, in some convoluted way, Lily assured herself as she hung up the phone. But what was this sudden domestic urge of his? She knew Worth well enough to know he had no sense of what having children meant. They'd talked about it on occasion over the past half dozen years, always concluding with the practical—"not the right time; keep the IUD; our lives are too separate, too frantic"—before ridiculing their imagined roles as parents.

More than that was Worth's reaction to friends of theirs who'd had children: banishment. He was bored by his formerly ambition-driven colleagues when their attention wandered to their "muling and puking brats." If one of the little monsters showed up to destroy the *objets* on low-level tables in the O Street house, Worth was visibly appalled. His usual reaction to a birth was a baby gift from Galt Brothers, then quick and total social neglect.

It didn't make sense for Worth Deloit, on the day after becoming assistant secretary, to want domestic bliss. Lily appraised herself in the full-length mirror, wondering what Worth's sudden change of attitude might mean. She was wearing a backless silk black-and-white dress on which she'd spent too much money in Paris. Her summer-streaked hair was loose on her shoulders, not quite the lion's mane she'd had as a student in Paris, but certainly more becoming than the knot she wore to the office. She turned sideways, checking the arch of back that her heels caused, the flat stomach, the still narrow waist and outline of her breasts which the dress subtly emphasized. Stepping closer she tried to see whether there was anything new about her face that Ammar wouldn't remember. There were some laugh lines around her eyes, a slight hooding of the eyelids, which gave her a languorous look in certain light, but not much more damage from the nine years since they'd seen each other. She stepped back again, put her hands on her hips, and stood with her legs apart, smiling at herself, questioning her confidence. Then she questioned her motive. Without considering any answers, she grabbed her evening bag and left the apartment.

She entered the Intercontinental's lobby and was met after a few steps by an Arab in a Western suit, who greeted her respectfully in English. "Miss McCann? Please come. The minister is expecting you." He bowed and pivoted, indicating an elevator that was awaiting them. At the door was a wary Arab with a Kalashnikov automatic rifle slung over his shoulder. Other patrons of the hotel were not allowed on the elevator. Lily's two escorts said nothing as the car rose to the top floor. Down the hall was another man with a Kalashnikov. He opened a door for Lily and followed her in with the other two men.

Lily had seen the same suite on embassy business when a senator or an ambassador-at-large had come through Amman. Ammar was sitting at a large, ornately inlaid table in the center of the room. Two men sat across the table, speaking intently, both in Arab robes and kaffiyehs. Ammar did not see Lily at first and continued his conversation. Dressed in a plain dark suit, white shirt, and dark tie, he didn't seem to have aged at all, except for the occasional white hair in his beard. Another man with an automatic rifle stood out of hearing by the windows, which opened onto a balcony.

When he saw her, Ammar didn't react, but brought his conversation to a close and escorted his visitors to the door with much ceremony. After a lengthy goodbye and the customary reassurances of eternal devotion, they left, and Ammar gestured for all the armed men and assistants to leave the room as well. The door was finally closed, and he came over to Lily, smiling as he took her in from head to foot. Then he stopped awkwardly and said, in French, "I'm not sure how we greet each other, Lily."

"First," she said, switching to Arabic, "tell me who you are and then we can figure it out."

He sighed and waved a hand dismissively at all those who'd left. "As of a fortnight ago, I am Algeria's representative to OPEC."

" 'Minister'?"

"Of energy resources, but my main job is OPEC."

"I think we have to shake hands very formally."

"If I tell you that I'm married with three children, would I be safe enough for a friendly hug?"

"Are you?" she asked, startled.

He was amused. "Yes."

Recovering quickly, she said, "Then come here," and they embraced circumspectly.

"Lily, you're still the loveliest woman in the world." He stood back from her, holding her hand. "You've been a fantasy so long, I feel quite self-conscious."

She looked up at his eyes, surprised again at their intensity. He looked strange to her in a suit; it was a costume she thought he would never wear. Involuntarily, she imagined his body.

"I'm married, too," she said.

"I know that—the new assistant secretary of state, and don't think that's why I wanted to see you. I had my own reasons."

"I'm flattered that you remembered them."

"Is he worthy of you?"

"Most of the time."

They laughed and he offered her a chair. "What can I give you to drink?"

"Petra beer would be fine, if . . ." She hesitated, wondering whether he'd become a good Muslim.

"No, no, don't worry. I love Petra beer."

He went to the bar. "The report from our embassy in Washington about Mr. Deloit included your name and location. Fate has done its work again."

"Maybe it's just a coincidence."

"Children?"

She shook her head.

He shrugged and poured the beer. "What a pity. You'd be a wonderful mother."

"I'm trying to be a wonderful diplomat. Do you have pictures?"

"Yes, they're in the other room. Excuse me; I'll get them." He handed her the glass and went across to the bedroom.

Not exactly what I expected, Lily thought, then wondered what she'd hoped for. Had she worn the revealing dress, put her hair down, used the good perfume, to preserve nostalgia or to suggest seduction? Either one was silly. Their time together—no matter how intense and wondrous—was one of those Paris-in-love escapes from reality; she'd admitted that much to herself years before.

She looked around at the opulently furnished suite, one stuffed chair costing what it would take to feed a refugee family for a year. Worth would turn up his nose at the garishness of the brass coffee implements on a table, the glittering crystal chandeliers and sconces, the whole walls of intricate Islamic designs on the drapery used to close out the desert sun. But Lily admitted that if she were going to escape again, this wouldn't be a bad place.

"The wife or the children first?" he asked as he returned.

"Both at once," Lily responded and put her beer down to receive the hinged silver frame.

"A diplomatic answer." He chuckled as he gave her the frame.

The moment she saw the pictures, tears came to her eyes. She blinked them quickly away, and shifted her back to him, presumably for better light. Her emotion was not so easily shielded. Studying the two pictures, one of three children in a rowboat, the other of their mother standing with them in front of a Roman ruin —"Four, six, and seven," Ammar said, pointing over Lily's shoulder at each child, "taken last year"—she saw a lovely woman, about her age, with large fervent eyes and a wide smile, wearing a scarf to cover her hair. She was a little overweight, had a tenseness in her face that belied the happy circumstance of the picture, and an exhaustion that weighted her body. The two younger children, a boy and a girl, were laughing adorably; the eldest was staring disdainfully at the camera, already serious with male responsibility.

"Tell me about them," Lily managed.

"The children are, of course, a joyous fracturing of the rest of our lives. Leela I've known all my life. Her parents and my parents fought the French together. We were married two years after I returned from Paris. It was the most natural match imaginable, as if each of us married ourselves, except that she's a good Muslim and I'm a very bad one, as you may remember." He laughed at himself, and Lily handed him the silver frame.

"They're all very beautiful," Lily said.

Noticing her slight reserve, Ammar closed the picture frame and put it on the table between them. "So tell me everything that's happened to you since you walked out of my life that day in Paris."

"Did you ever get my letter?"

"No."

"I wrote you the day after I left. I didn't know where to address it, so I sent it to school."

He smiled bitterly. "The French took little trouble with mail to be forwarded to Algerians. No, I heard nothing, but by chance I read of your father's tragic death, so I had some understanding of your disappearance."

"You never used to read newspapers."

"After you left, I could read nothing else. I couldn't concentrate on my studies, even novels. I began to read the papers, became instantly politicized, and here I am."

They exchanged affectionate smiles.

"I'm sorry, Ammar."

"We've survived."

Each took a drink of beer, and Lily said, "Let's agree not to examine survival too closely."

"An excellent idea. You know, I've had cause to think of you often, Lily."

"With what you've told me so far, how did you have time?"

"It's Abu al-Saffah who's kept you in my mind. I was aware of him because of what I read of your father's death. After my return to Algeria, I worked in the Ministry of the Interior and had access to intelligence and security information. Each time his name came up, and it came up often, naturally I thought of you."

Lily put her glass down. "Do you know where he is?"

He heard her anxiety and responded instantly to it. "No, but I could find out. Why?"

Lily hesitated, then said, "He sends me letters."

Ammar took in a sudden breath, disgusted. "The scum," he said.

"Not often," Lily continued. "Once a year, postmarked Paris or Brussels."

"His group has become international," Ammar noted. "What does he say?"

"Not very much; mainly reminds me of what he's capable of doing, and what I did to him. He was captured by the Italians once, and I identified him."

"I knew about his capture but not your involvement. They released him to Qaddafi. That's when we started to keep an eye on him. As you can imagine, having Libya as a neighbor keeps us eternally alert. Does he threaten you?"

"He tells me I'm still on his mind for whatever he wants, and always shows off by knowing my exact address—not at whatever embassy, but where I'm living—which doesn't make me feel too secure." She picked up the beer again and drank deeply.

"What do the State Department, the CIA, suggest?"

"They don't think about it anymore. I used to turn over the letters, but there are those who'd use them to keep me home in a closet at Foggy Bottom."

"Is that wise, Lily?"

"No, but I'm damned if I want Abu al-Saffah to run my career for me."

"Does Mr. Deloit know?"

"Of course not. He'd reassign me to Finland."

"Then why have you told me?" he asked, kindly but warily.

Lily smiled sadly. "Well, well, all of a sudden we're the minister and the political officer. I hadn't felt it until now."

"Alas," he said.

"I suppose I told you—and I didn't come here with that on my mind—because of old times, old trust, and your saying that you had access to more information than I do."

He paused only briefly. "I'll see to it that you receive any information about him that we have, but it will have to be given personally and cannot be shared with American authorities."

"Thank you, Ammar," Lily said gratefully, but added, "I'm not sure I want to know."

"That's up to you, of course. If there's anything else I can do, tell me. Terrorism is criminal enough without the sadistic. Intimidating the daughter of a man he's murdered is vile."

"I'm sure he's done much worse."

Ammar said, "He and his Palestine Command Group are for hire, Lily. He broke with the PLO, is thought to have had several of their people assassinated, and has done the bidding of those who paid the PCG the best price. It was Qaddafi for a while, then Assad in Syria, and, the last I heard, Saddam Hussein in Iraq. At whatever master's bidding, he has executed the regime's enemies at home or in Europe, blown up an Ethiopian airliner, a Turkish synagogue and a French one, attacked the Athens airport, murdering civilians, women, and children—all in the name of the Palestinian cause, of course, but directed and paid for by his current master. It's nonsense. How does that help the Palestinians? Getting them world attention? They get world revulsion."

He took a deep breath to dissolve his anger. "I've always thought that if someone does something only because he's paid to do it, he's a whore. Principles are conveniently twisted, passion is for display, ambition is for status and attention. Any purpose is lifeless. Abu al-Saffah has become just such a whore."

TWENTY-ONE

"AND YOU HAD DINNER, alone in his suite?" Ambassador Hooper asked righteously.

Around the conference table, the rest of the embassy's senior staff either watched Lily intently or looked away, embarrassed for her. Most were her friends, a few enjoyed her discomfort, but all knew she had chosen to confront rather than blend in with the ambassador's agenda, so no one would help her.

"Yes, sir, we ate there because of security considerations."

"Oh, 'security considerations.'" His implication was obvious; Lily ignored it and met his smirk with neutral silence. Hooper went on with pious ire. "And you took it upon yourself to have a private meeting with a minister of the Algerian government without informing any senior officer at this embassy. Some would call that real nervy, honey, but I'd call it downright presumptuous."

Very coolly, Lily responded, "Sir, as I reported in my memcon submitted the next morning, I did not know he was a minister until after I arrived. Mr. Ben Ashid is an old friend whom I haven't heard from in nine years. When I learned he was minister of energy resources, it seemed to me that it would be rude, if not insulting, to turn around and leave."

This prompted several friendly snickers, which Hooper cut off with a look around the table as he asked, "And just how much did your persuasive powers have to do with getting all that Saudi oil money for your beloved Palestinians?"

"Nothing, sir," she said, staying calm, but furious at the innuendo. "As I explained," she continued, mainly so that those not privy to her memcon would understand what had happened, "this was Mr. Ben Ashid's first trip as minister through the Middle East.

When he was in Riyadh, the Saudi government asked him to act as intermediary to King Hussein in order to work out a financial agreement involving funds for the Palestinian refugees. The Algerian government is eager to expand its role as mediator in the Middle East, a role it played so effectively in the release of the American hostages in Iran."

"And did your old friend give any indication of how much of that Saudi money will filter right straight into Yasir Arafat's deep pockets?" His lips pursed angrily by the question's end.

"I asked the same question, sir, though not quite in those terms. By the way, I'd made Mr. Ben Ashid aware that I'd be reporting any discussion we had of diplomatic matters, so he knew that what he said would reach you, sir. Regarding the Saudi money, Mr. Ben Ashid knows, as everyone else knows, that the Saudis' financial arrangement with the PLO is carried out directly, not by local governments. He also realizes that many Arab countries use their contributions to the kingdom of Jordan and to Palestinian relief as guilt-reducing symbols of Arab unity. I believe it's fair to say that King Hussein welcomes such financial support, whether it is a symbol or not."

"Oh hell, he'll take it wherever he can get it. The CIA's propped him up for years, and now with the Arabs' guilt money, he can afford all his elevator shoes." He looked around the table for appreciation of his humor. Several pale smiles blossomed before his eyes reached Lily again. "Well?" he shot at her.

"I'm sorry, I didn't hear a question, sir."

"There's a hell of a lot you don't hear, *Miss* McCann. But you better hear this, because there are a few witnesses here. From now on, you don't have meetings with anyone—'old friends,' personal acquaintances, anyone outside this embassy—without getting it cleared with my office. D'you hear?" He bent forward and leaned heavily on the table. "I'm putting you on a short leash."

"I heard clearly, sir."

Mollified but still angry, Hooper went on with the staff meeting, skewering several other officers with his remaining wrath before the group broke up. Outside the conference room Lily was treated to several sympathetic looks and some mordant humor. "Please try to look uglier at staff meetings, Lily," the head of the Commerce Section said. "I think the ambassador is falling in love."

Back at her desk, Lily pulled out her calendar. She'd arrived in Amman the previous September. She had a year and five months left of her two-year posting to walk on eggs, already cracked. Ambassador Hooper would be waiting for her to make a mistake, and even if she didn't, any letter he wrote for her Personnel file would be withering. She tried to adjust, to think of her remaining time in Amman as an opportunity to overcome a difficult career problem. The posting was no longer about Jordan or the Palestinian refugees, which were forbidden her, but instead was about her efforts to convince Ambassador Wallace Hooper to like her.

In an instant, she decided it wasn't worth it. Fawning for Hooper would be beneath anyone's self-respect. Abruptly, she remembered that she had used the term "leash" in Paris the past October.

" 'Leash' is a telling word," Worth had said. "You just can't stand not being in charge—" She'd thrown the glass of Château d' Yquem at him for that. It seemed a little too much of a coincidence that Hooper had used the same explicit metaphor. Was it her normal diplomatic paranoia, or could Worth have told Hooper, with ingratiating locker-room camaraderie, about her idea of "leashing" her own ambassador? Knowing Worth, Lily let the paranoia flow, realizing how sensitive he would be to Hooper's connections to the White House, and that any negative flow from their instant Republican ambassador in the Middle East wouldn't be good for a new assistant secretary. Could the two of them have established a relationship and shared wife jokes, Worth perhaps sympathizing with Hooper, chuckling over "leashing," tacitly reaching agreement that she was exclusively Hooper's problem as long as she was in Amman?

Lily found the conjecture too crazy to believe. During their phone calls, Lily didn't mention her suspicion to Worth. If it was false, he'd have laughed at her paranoia; if it was true, he'd have done the same thing, but would probably mention to Hooper that she was on to them, and the ambassador might strive to make her situation worse. For his part, Worth said nothing again about having children, and made no more overt suggestions about her returning to Washington. There were occasional hints of loneliness, as well as his old technique of describing the glamorous and powerful company he now kept, which implied numerous possibilities for her jealousy.

Lily was not jealous, but admitted suspicion. Well aware of the plethora of avaricious Washington women, she'd known from the time she was commuting from Yale that Worth would have plenty of opportunity for dalliance. Her choosing a career that guaranteed their separation was an outright dare. But Lily knew that Worth was too careful and too driven to let a petty scandal touch him. Besides that, he had an almost Puritan attitude toward those who had affairs, regarding the lying, cheating, and pain as idiotic, inferior, and pathetic. Lily never questioned him, nor he her, as if they'd both acknowledged the risk to be a silent condition of their distant marriage. Even when their transcontinental or vacation arguments reached new heights, he never used Moshe Levy against her, which Lily respected, despite her lingering remorse about the entire episode.

Believing she'd eventually hear if Worth was involved with another woman—in spite of the platitude, carved deeper in diplomatic stone than anywhere else, that the wife was always the last to know—Lily wasted no time on conjecture. She knew that her own feelings about affairs were still infected by her mother and father. As long as the relationship with Worth was alive, it was enough for her. Besides that, she'd seen too much of the wreckage from affairs in the field. Throughout her career, attractive men had made their availability known to Lily, and some of them had been intriguing. But the diplomatic affair never presented a clear temptation to her, and for that she was grateful. The male friends she made became true friends, as, frequently, did their wives.

On a walk in Amman's Old Town early in June, Lily was surprised to see a Palestinian woman whom she remembered visiting in one of the camps on the outskirts of the city. The woman, old, with a weathered, wrinkled face, was standing in a side street off Omar al-Mukhtar, one of the two broad avenues leading away from al-Husseini Mosque. She crossed the avenue to make sure Lily would see her, then waved. Dressed from head to foot in black, she was not smiling, and she gestured urgently for Lily to come to her.

The sidewalk on which she stood was lined with brown roasted chickens hanging over braziers in front of the many restaurants running the length of the street. Lily returned the wave and crossed to greet the woman, trying to remember her name.

When Lily began to say something, the woman stopped her by drawing a photograph from the sleeve of her robe and holding it out to be taken. Lily instinctively took a step back. The woman moved toward her and held up the photograph for her to see. It was close enough for Lily to recognize Moshe Levy's face, badly beaten, with a trickle of blood coming out of the corner of his mouth. He was alive; his eyes showed that, although one was nearly swollen shut. Lily reached out and took the picture.

"They followed you; they are watching us," the old woman said in Arabic. "If you do not come with me, without a pause, without a word, he will die."

Lily briefly glanced around. The street was crowded with shoppers going to the Roman Theater or the mosque. She saw two policemen trying to control traffic, but dared not approach them. The old woman started to move along the street lined with chickens, looking back to see whether Lily would follow. She had the choice not to, but started after the old woman making her way through the crowds.

She did not go far, a block; then she turned a corner into a narrower street made even more crowded by the cars parked up against the buildings on one side. Lily became aware of someone following, but did not look back. The old woman suddenly stopped and turned. She stood next to a car, an old dented Mercedes diesel, beside which were two *fedayeen,* with black *hattas* over most of their faces. One of them opened the back door for Lily. Inside, she saw another man in the driver's seat. The old woman watched her, offering nothing. Lily stepped toward the car and as she stooped into the back seat, the old woman approached close enough to rasp, "My husband, my son, died from the American bullets in Jewish guns, but someday my other son or grandson or great-grandson will return and farm our land in Hebron! Tell them, tell the Americans, we will never give up! Never!"

She was pushed out of the way by the two men, who got in and sat on either side of Lily. The motor started and the back doors closed. Another man, the one who'd been following her, jumped in the front. Instantly one of the men grabbed her arms and pinioned her to the seat as the other unrolled a length of adhesive tape for her eyes. When the car pulled out into the narrow street, the last thing Lily saw was the old woman's face, aflame with rage and certainty.

Lily knew then that she would probably die. Diplomatic immunity meant nothing; being an American meant considerably less. She was shoved down on the floor and ordered to lie quietly. A blanket was thrown over her. She listened for street noises that would indicate where they were taking her, and tried not to panic.

The ride was not a long one. Lily heard nothing to pinpoint her location; the car's labored ascent up steep and twisting inclines could have been on any of the seven *jebels* of Amman. Then, suddenly, the car coasted down a short incline, stopping silently in a place that felt unusually cool. As Lily was lifted up and out of the car, she could smell cement. The men carried her roughly by her arms, and she heard their steps echoing off walls. She guessed that she was in a below-ground garage, an unusual structure in Amman. That would be helpful, if she survived.

They went through several doors. Again she was lifted off her feet and was carried up several flights of stairs, then marched along a length of concrete floor until they all stopped. There was a quick knock on a door, which opened. She was lifted in and placed roughly on a metal chair.

For a moment, there was silence, but Lily was sure there were people in the room other than her escorts. Fingers grasped the end of the adhesive tape and ripped it off her eyes. She shouted with the pain; one eyelid and the hair of her eyebrows felt torn. The room was dark, but as she put a hand to her eyes to touch the damage, enough light leaked around the black paper taped over the windows for her to make out the features of the man who stood above her with the tape in his hand. She stopped breathing.

Abu al-Saffah was wearing a shoulder holster over a stained T-shirt, plain khaki pants, and American running shoes. His hair was much thinner, and when he turned to the other men, she saw that one side of his chin was slick with multiple scars.

"Again you're useful to me," he said to Lily in Arabic, "as I swore you would be."

"How?" Lily asked as steadily as she could.

"You'll see shortly," he answered.

"I was shown a picture of a man and told he'd die if I didn't come. I'm here, so I'd like to see him."

His arm shot out and he grabbed her hair hard enough to force tears into her eyes, but she suppressed a shout and met his look as he said, "We're not negotiating. No clever diplomacy. That's for the weak, who are unwilling to act. We work a different way."

"I know your way," Lily answered, gritting her teeth against the pain. "And tell me of all your success with your people's cause."

Several voices behind him called out for him to hurry.

His wet eyes squinted as he pulled her hair harder and put his face close to hers. "You're a fool," he said fiercely.

"For trusting the terms by which I came here—your terms—yes, I am a fool."

He let go of her hair, almost pushing her out of the chair. "You pampered diplomats, you American hypocrites, preaching peace and selling arms to anyone who will buy."

"Not to you, at least," Lily responded, and braced herself to be hit.

Surprisingly, he laughed. "I will have the best American weapons at my disposal in a year's time. *That* is your diplomacy, your brilliant American diplomacy." To the other men in the room he said, "She is yours. Hurry," he added as he walked away. "I will watch."

Instantly, men surrounded her, held her arms, spread her legs. She screamed, and a wad of material was jammed in her mouth. She saw a dagger, then another as they cut off her skirt, blouse, and bra. She was thrown on the floor and held spreadeagled while hands grabbed at her breasts and the blade of a dagger slipped up her thigh and cut through her panties, which were ripped off and flung into the air. Above her, she saw two men tear open their pants; they knelt.

All of a sudden there was an infuriated growl of disgust. The man already kneeling between her legs said, "Unclean," and quickly stood, pulling up his pants. He'd seen the protruding short length of string connected to her tampon and pointed it out to the others. Then he spat on her, as did several of the others, and released her. Lily rolled over and balled herself up. She was shaking badly. From the floor she saw the American running shoes come toward her. He stood within kicking distance, as several of his men repeated, "Unclean." Others again asked him to hurry, but he interrupted them impatiently with the order "Into the closet." She was lifted by her arms and dragged across the room. Al-Saffah twisted a key in a lock and opened the door, holding a gun in his other hand. He peered inside and spoke to Lily. "Give thanks to Allah it was your time of month."

He grabbed her wrist and threw her into the closet, slamming and locking the door behind her. She screamed as she fell in the pitch-black darkness, not from pain, but because she had landed on a body. When she heard the men outside laugh, she stopped, refusing to contribute further to their enjoyment. Scrambling away from the body, she sat on the floor, her back pressed against the concrete wall, listening, waiting for her eyes to adjust to the new level of dark. Only the slightest light leaked in from the top and bottom of the door. Even that source of illumination and air was being blocked as some kind of material was hammered around the door frame. The space already felt close; she wondered if there was enough air to keep her alive. It was while she listened to the men's hurried departure, and the slamming of another door, that she knew the body must be Moshe's. But she couldn't see even the opposite wall. Her entire body began to tremble; she gripped her knees and tried to control herself.

"Lily," he whispered.

She blurted, "Moshe!"

"Did they hurt you?"

"No. Are they still out there?"

"I doubt it. They were in a big hurry to leave."

"How did you know it was me? Can you see?"

"No. They told me what they were going to do. Al-Saffah knew about us somehow. He thought that instead of just killing me and making me a hero, he could divert attention, maybe even cause a scandal, by leaving our bodies to be found together. Mossad and the CIA would know our background. It'd muddy the blame for murder so it wouldn't be traced to him. 'Two birds with one stone,' he said."

The perversity of al-Saffah's plan appalled her. "Are we going to die in here?" she asked.

"No." He started to move, but groaned from pain and lay still.

"What did they do to you? Can I help?"

"One ankle is fractured," he said. "I think some ribs. Several sodomized me, which is their way of showing contempt. What clothes are you wearing? Do you have on any jewelry?"

"Nothing."

"What about hairpins?"

"Moshe, there's only a piece of elastic holding my hair. They stripped me."

He was silent, then started to move again in the direction of the door, gasping quietly. She could hear his hand move over the surface of the door. He knocked to see how solid it was. It sounded hard, thick. He fiddled with the knob. Then, still gasping, he moved again and, without warning, Lily heard him kick repeatedly against the door with one foot.

"Wait a minute," she said and crawled beside him. Feeling for space with her hands, she lay down on her back beside him and lifted her legs to hit the door. "Together on three, one-two-*three!*" Their feet smashed against the door, once, twice, a third time before they accepted that there was no chance.

"Breathe slowly," he said. "Stay near the floor; the air is better."

"How long will it last?"

"Depends on how much we talk. It's a big closet."

She breathed slowly. "Why did you ask about jewelry, my hair?"

"I could pick that lock with something sharp, a pin, a piece of wire . . . This is a new apartment building, unfinished, being built for the rich. There's a space at the back of this closet for a safe, things like that, the best materials in case of bombs, lots of locks and concrete. By my count coming up here, we're five flights up."

"Then the construction workers will come—"

"No. They have to put in telephone equipment that hasn't even arrived in Jordan yet. Everything waits. Al-Saffah explained all this to me. He wanted me to know."

"Did he tell you what he had planned for me?"

"Yes, and he planned to have me watch. I managed to kick him in the crotch at that point. Stupid heroics. He had them hold my foot down and he stamped on it until it broke. Then they knocked me out and threw me in here. I didn't come around until you landed on me." He coughed, which made him gasp again. She heard him move, trying to ease pain. "Did they rape you, Lily? How badly are you hurt?"

"They didn't."

"That's incredible. How——?"

"I have my period."

"Thank God."

"Al-Saffah suggested I do that." She lay quietly on her back, trying to breathe slowly against a growing sense of panic. She talked to distract herself. "How did they catch you?"

"They didn't. Saddam Hussein's secret police caught me outside Baghdad and gave Abu al-Saffah the job of getting rid of me, not in Iraq of course. They don't want to offend anyone now that they're fighting Iran, not even Israel, particularly not the U.S. So al-Saffah brought me to Amman, the dumping ground of the Middle East. What better place?"

"Baghdad?"

He paused. "I'd been working there," he said, and moved again to the door. She heard the rattle of the doorknob, then the sound of his fingernails scraping over the face of the lock. "We've got to get out of here," he said with intense urgency. He pounded the door with his hand in frustration, then sank to the floor, breathing hard. He choked again, which made him groan. She heard him make chewing noises.

"Lily, I'm getting blood in my mouth. One of these ribs may have gone through a lung. I have to tell you some things——"

"Talking won't do you any good. Let me help——"

"I may not make it. You'll last longer. Someone could come, a watchman, someone. If no one does, what you hear won't matter."

He coughed, deeply, and let himself down on his side, adjusting his position for the pain. "You know about the French selling Iraq a couple of nuclear reactors?"

"Yes, six years ago."

"The one in Osirak is big enough to manufacture atomic bombs.

Saddam Hussein wants two as fast as he can get them, one for Tehran, one for Tel Aviv. We tried to prevent the French from supplying the two cores for the reactor; we blew them up two years ago—"

"La Segne-sur-Mer," Lily said. "We know about that, too. But, Moshe, it's not on line yet. Saddam is years away from a bomb. There's heavy diplomatic pressure on Iraq being planned, by us and the Russians."

"It doesn't matter," Moshe said. "Diplomacy takes time. There's a general election in Israel in four days. Begin and the Likud Party want a big enough win to control the Knesset and the cabinet. The bank crisis has scared everyone—wiped out diamonds, by the way. So what do you do if you have an economic crisis and a tough election? You go to war. If you win it, the voters love you. Begin is an old Irgun terrorist. This kind of tactic appeals to him. I've been in Baghdad and Osirak on and off over the last year, pinpointing and mapping the reactor. Army commandos are on alert, the air force has a full-scale model of the reactor in the desert to practice bombing. In Israel, nothing could distract voters from the economy and get their votes better than blowing up the only Arab reactor in existence."

"You mean they'll attack now?" she asked incredulously.

"When the Mossad realizes that Saddam Hussein captured me, they'll presume I was tortured and spilled everything. Israel will move instantly. Even though I told the Iraqis and al-Saffah that I was in Baghdad trying to locate missile sites, Saddam's suspicion will grow, defenses will be mounted, vital parts of the reactor may be relocated. The difference of a day, an hour, could mean a pilot's life, even the failure of the mission, depending on the missile defenses Saddam redeploys from the Iranian front."

He shifted again, his arm brushing against her leg.

"You should sit up," Lily suggested, "in case your lung is filling."

He struggled to do so, and rested quietly, his labored breathing the only sound. "If you do get out of here," he said, "go to a phone, call sixty-four–twenty-three–eleven, say, 'The raven has fallen to earth,' and tell them where I am. They'll save me if there's anything to save. Say it."

"Sixty-four–twenty-three–eleven. The raven has fallen to earth. In Arabic? English?"

"Arabic." He coughed again and was quiet.

"I'm surprised you're still doing this," Lily said. "When did you start working for the Mossad again?"

"About two years after you left. They're running short of people who can speak Arabic well enough to work in Arab countries. Those of us born before independence learned it from our play-mates. The sabras all learn Hebrew now. Mossad knew the reason I'd resigned—you—and bided their time, then did me a favor to get me back."

"Favor seems to be the currency of choice in both our lines of work."

"This was a big favor. They warned me that De Beers was going to force the Israeli banks to raise interest rates on diamond loans. Then they'd cut off supplies to any dealer in Antwerp and New York who dared to sell to Israeli distributors. I got out before the panic selling started. It wiped out hundreds of dealers."

"That was a very big favor."

"Yes, and here I am with you, repaying it." He snorted, then said, "Life is very strange, Lily. All the times I wanted to make love to you and never touched you—I end up in a closet with you naked, and a lung filled with blood."

"I suppose modesty is ridiculous at the moment, but I'm grate-ful for the small mercy of not being seen. You have clothes on, don't you?"

"Socks, pants, what's left of my shirt—all rather messy."

An idea came to her. Even under the desperate circumstances, it embarrassed her. "How long a wire do you need?" she asked.

"A few inches."

She paused a moment, then said, "Please stay there, where you are. I'll try something."

She felt her way to the end of the closet. Leaning her back into the corner, she slid down, then drew up her legs, and pulled out the tampon. Carefully she moved her fingers inside her vagina, trying to feel the two tiny threads connected to her IUD. She remembered the time they'd caused Worth a startled discomfort and he'd asked her to get them cut shorter. Glad that she hadn't, Lily felt the

filaments in her fingers and tried to grasp them, using her finger-
nail and thumbnail as tweezers. The threads kept slipping, and she
forced her fingers deeper until she had a firm hold. She'd begun to
sweat, and as she started to tug, she felt cramps begin. Quickly she
gave a hard tug, groaned at the sudden pain, but held on as she
drew out the IUD.

"Lily, are you all right?"

"Yes," she said, feeling triumphant as she fought to control the
cramps. She wiped the IUD on her thigh and crawled back toward
Moshe. "Give me your hand," she said.

"What is it?"

"My IUD. It's copper wire with plastic over it, shaped like a
number seven, but I think you can bend it."

He took it and without a word struggled to the door. Lily stayed
where she was, gripping her knees, dealing with the pain. She
heard him working, the bare scraping of the wire in the lock. He
cursed once in Hebrew, worked again, then uttered something in
Hebrew and collapsed with a grunt of pain.

"Moshe!"

"I'm all right. Started to faint. Give me a moment."

She crawled over to him, touched his head, and let her hand rest
on his cheek. His beard had grown in fully. She wondered about
the rest of the burns. He reached up and took her hand, holding it
firmly. Then he took a deep breath, let go, and pulled himself up to
the lock again. Lily lay on the floor, balled up, listening to the
scratching of metal against metal and Moshe's tortured breathing.
Her cramps were bearable. The cement floor was still cool, and she
thought that if they couldn't get out, she wanted to be holding
Moshe's hand when they were found.

There was a click, a thud as Moshe hit the door, then a gush of
air and light. She lifted her head to see Moshe collapsed in the open
doorway, the bare concrete of the darkened room beyond him. She
stood up, oblivious of her discomfort, and went out of the closet.
As she knelt next to Moshe, she saw the remains of her clothes,
rolled up in a corner, her purse spilling its contents on the floor
beneath the window.

"Moshe," she said urgently. When he didn't respond, she felt for
the pulse on his neck, found it regular but weak. She got up and

put on her clothes. Her underwear was useless; the skirt was slashed open on one side. She put the cut where she could hold it closed, and tucked the badly torn blouse into the waistband. Just as she stepped into her espadrilles, she heard Moshe trying to move, and hurried over to him.

"What's the number?" he demanded, coughing again.

"Sixty-four–twenty-three–eleven," she repeated. "Will they come for you?"

"Yes. Lily, don't mention Osirak. Give us a day, twelve hours, please. I won't mention that you were here."

"I can't promise you that, Moshe."

He coughed again. "Hurry," he managed.

"Here, sit up," she urged and pulled him into a sitting position against the wall. Then she ran to the window and peeled away the black paper taped at one corner. The sun was two hours from setting.

"I know exactly where we are," she said. "I can get a taxi downstairs, and I'll phone in about ten or twelve minutes. Will you be all right?"

"Fine, except—"

"What?"

"My anger at passing out and not seeing you dress. After that last night in the hospital, I didn't stop loving you just because you went off and married another man. But we'll talk another time, perhaps."

"I think you'll live." She went over, stooped down and kissed him, hurried to the door, and quietly went out.

She took a cab to her apartment and instantly made the phone call as Moshe had instructed her. She bathed, dressed, and drove to the embassy, where she worked in her office, until the early hours of the morning, on a report of the incident to be submitted to the security office. But even as she typed, she questioned what she was doing. Why was she writing a report instead of going directly to the security officer who would contact the CIA station? The information would go to Foggy Bottom and the National Security Council at the White House. Within the hour, diplomatic pressure could be expected to halt any unilateral belligerence by Israel.

American carrier jets would be in the skies over Jordan in time to prevent it.

She was playing with time, yes, because Moshe had asked for it, but also for something else—a resolution to her dilemma. Where did her duty lie? She thought of her father and tried to answer the question through his perspective. Of course she owed her duty to the State Department of the United States, her government, her country. And Worth would be enormously proud of her. Even Ambassador Hooper would jump on the bandwagon and probably give her a commendation. Her career would soar.

Worth and Hooper. One had traded on treason; the other had bought his piece of American diplomacy.

Abu al-Saffah had said he'd have the best American weapons in a year's time. Iran, which had kept fifty-two American hostages in captivity, was already getting those weapons. If Saddam asked for them, the United States would supply him, trying to buy Iraq away from the Russians. And would the State Department or Hooper or Worth or anyone in the government care that some of those weapons would go to terrorists like Abu al-Saffah?

Duty was different now from what it had been for her father. There were many acceptable choices for a diplomat these days: to serve your country, serve yourself, your career, your ambition. She didn't want to please Hooper or Worth or the State Department. Their ideals were shot to hell. Were there any left? Only her father's—"old-fashioned," "innocent," but probably still imbued with the greatness America once represented. Unlike her father, she'd survived Abu al-Saffah. The choice about her duty was surely hers. Saddam Hussein, a megalomaniacal dictator, wanted to make atomic bombs, which he would use. After reading her report several times, she took it down the hall and fed it into the shredder.

"For you, Moshe," she muttered. "Yes, perhaps another time."

She told no one what had happened.

———

The next day, June 4, 1981, fourteen American-made F-14 and F-15 fighter-bombers of the Israeli Air Force, after being refueled over Iraqi territory while using a chartered Irish airliner as a radar decoy, destroyed the nuclear reactor in Osirak with a precision that was described in the world press as a "surgical strike."

On June 7, Israelis went to the polls and rewarded the Likud bloc with solid support, giving Menachem Begin his second term as prime minister. He immediately elevated Ariel Sharon—the hero of the Yom Kippur War, the champion of the West Bank settlements, and the scourge of the Palestinians in the Occupied Territories—to be minister of defense.

The new socialist president of France, François Mitterrand, chose not to replace Iraq's reactor. The United States and the Soviet Union rebuked Israel for its act of war; however, both superpowers were greatly relieved that Iraq's nuclear potential was destroyed.

In September, a small package arrived at Lily's office, postmarked and stamped in Amman. Inside, wrapped in tissue paper, was a finished diamond, large but unset. There was a note.

> You saw this cut a long time ago. The other two parts were
> sold successfully. I'd been saving this for a special occasion.
> You saved my life again; that's special enough.
> Thank you from me and Israel.

TWENTY-TWO

"H OW'D YOU LIKE to get out of Amman three weeks early?" Worth asked. The call was not one of their regular twice-weekly ones, and Lily was delighted with the offer.
"What will this escape cost me, Mephistopheles?"
"Your soul, your body, and two extra weeks in another town."
"And where in hell could this haven be?"
By September of 1982, Lily thought she'd made it through her posting without too much career damage. As far as she knew, Ambassador Hooper hadn't composed a loaded letter for her Personnel file, and her annual efficiency reports, written by the chief of the Political Section, had been glowing. She had requested that she be posted to Washington next. Since the near catastrophe with Abu al-Saffah, she had lived in a constant state of vigilance, always on guard, never walking alone, driving from her flat to the embassy, alert to any diversion. Washington at least would be safer.

Worth was quite the Foggy Bottom star, appearing before congressional committees on a regular basis as the numerous crises of the Middle East focused political and public attention on his area of responsibility. Sadat's assassination, Lebanon's disintegration into civil war, Israel's extension of law over the Golan Heights, Assad of Syria's slaughter of the Muslim fundamentalist population in Hama, and particularly Israel's invasion and occupation of southern Lebanon the past June, had kept the assistant secretary for Near Eastern Affairs constantly before microphones and cameras. Fortunately he proved to be extraordinarily effective at handling both politicians and journalists, providing them with quick and often witty summations, and inviting the select few to join him at his dinner table in the house on O Street. Around Washington and in the press, he was referred to as "adroit Deloit."

The marriage had continued with two phone calls a week, their anniversary in Paris, another short vacation at Christmas on Corfu, a long spring weekend in Marrakesh after his conference in Geneva. They arrived at each vacation more exhausted than at the last, and their determination to relax kept intimacy as well as arguments at bay. They had never again discussed the meeting of Iranians and campaign officials that they had witnessed at the Raphael Hotel.

"Here's the deal, Lily. The chargé in Beirut—"

"Ah, Beirut, peaceful jewel of the Mediterranean."

"The staff there's been cut to the bone because of the troubles, but at the moment they're desperate for a couple of Arabists and a plumber. We're sending the plumber in from Cairo. He'll be the most important man in the embassy, but you'll get five weeks' danger pay."

"When?"

"Tomorrow. We'll arrange to pack up your apartment in Amman, send everything here to Washington. You'll come straight home from Beirut."

"Will Hooper go along with it?"

"He'll howl, I suppose. I've heard he's planned a goodbye party in the desert for you; he's going to stake you down on an anthill. But if Washington calls you, he has no say in the matter."

"Then call me, call me. After Hooper-heaven, Beirut will be paradise."

––––––––––

In twenty-four hours, Lily was in Lebanon by way of a flight to Nicosia and a helicopter ride to Beirut harbor, then under the control of the recently arrived United States Marine Corps. Lily was met at the dock by a Lebanese driver who took her to the American Embassy. An enormous eight-story apartment complex, owned by and rented from a Saudi, most of the building was empty now, occupied by only the most essential embassy personnel. Determined to give the impression of business as usual, the staff chose to avoid making the building into a fortress. Nevertheless, inside the place was pure siege mentality layered between humor, stress, and harassment.

"Welcome to cosmopolitan Beirut," the remaining political officer said as he greeted her and led her down a hall into which the desks had been moved, away from flying glass. "You could drink the water, but the Israelis have turned it off. However, the fireworks at night are grand."

The chargé was a seasoned senior FSO with much experience under fire—Pakistan, Khartoum, Afghanistan—an insomniac who wasn't helped by "the nightly percussion serenade by the Beirut symphony. No doubt you'll hear it. People will tell you that you'll get used to it. They lie." Then he switched to Arabic, which he spoke well but with an obvious accent. "Why I need you is to help with the game we call negotiations around here. As Nasser said once, 'Arabic is hardly a language with which to urge calm.' I read that you know your way through these parts, which will be useful. Look at what we're doing here as a very bloody Feydeau farce, with a different Lebanese group—Muslim, Druse, Maronite Christian— behind each slammed door. They don't want to talk to each other; they only want to kill each other. We have to talk to them so they won't. This is the beginning of the second act; Arafat and the PLO left just before the intermission, when the marines, American flags waving, showed up to escort them out of here. At the moment, we're popular with the locals. They hated the PLO. But this could change into a tragedy real fast, with the Israelis waiting up in the hills. The two of us are pretty hoarse from talking through the slammed doors, so we hope you'll help us out."

"Glad to, if any of them will talk to a woman."

"Right now, you're America, and this is the only place in the world where the Arabs think *we're* protecting *them* from Israel. Your sex will be overlooked. That's how crazy it is. We're putting you up at the Commodore Hotel, probably the safest place to sleep in Beirut. The only danger is the journalists. They've made it their war club, so be careful who you talk to. Settle in, get some sleep— which around here can result in shellshock—and we'll start you out with the Druse tomorrow. We used to have three armored cars but now only two. I'll lend you mine when you go up into the hills."

As her driver careened through the streets on the way to the hotel, Lily realized that she hadn't been in Beirut since her father's funeral. Her memory was of the chic boulevards with luxury hotels, shops, restaurants, nightclubs, and theaters. In the course of her work in Amman, she'd studied the breakdown of Lebanon since its civil war commenced, in 1975. None of it prepared her for the destruction she saw as the sun went down, illuminating in a burning light the bombed-out buildings, rubble, and decay of a war zone. The streets were cratered, the buildings—those which still stood—were pockmarked with bullet holes, their windows shattered, boarded up, or left gaping like empty eye sockets. The sidewalks were piled with explosions' debris—door frames, plaster board, pipes, concrete abutments—pushed out of the way by bulldozers and left to disintegrate.

She saw that about one in five people on the street carried an automatic rifle, the badge of membership in one militia or another; the uniforms were American jeans and gym shoes. Civilians carried metal containers to collect water. Lily's car had to slow down once to pass around a collection of ambulances and fire trucks standing before the remains of half a building that still stood, the other half having been struck by an unaimed rocket. She saw a bed frame hanging vertically from the edge of a floor. Even with her knowledge of Beirut's anarchy over the past years, Lily was unprepared for the totality of change.

The Commodore Hotel functioned as the mouthpiece for madness. Because it was the international journalistic enclave, all parties in the civil war recognized its value for their own propaganda purposes and aimed their mortars elsewhere, particularly when they went there to talk. The lobby was filled with safari-suited knots of conversation that unraveled through the stuffed couches and frayed into the open bar to one side. Lily's room overlooked the sea, "the quiet side," the bellhop informed her; the other side provided a view of the battle zone in Muslim East Beirut. As soon as Lily showered and changed, she walked down three flights—the elevator didn't work—to find the restaurant. But as she crossed the lobby, she heard a familiar voice call out from the bar, "Hey, Lily, haven't seen you since graduation."

Sitting on a bar stool in full safari regalia, including a squashed hat and desert boots, was Mimi Peters. Her press credentials dangled from a chain around her deeply unbuttoned neck, and her hair was cut short for efficiency. The men on either side of her—wearing similar outfits, although both had on well-pressed slacks and one wore a button-down shirt under his jacket—eyed Lily curiously as Mimi stood down from her stool and approached her old roommate with open arms. "My God, Lily, why haven't you aged? What do you do, sleep in formaldehyde?"

"Yeah, a trick I learned in Cairo. What are you doing here, as if it weren't pretty obvious."

"When there's a war, there's Mimi scooping everyone, but without the requisite balls to get on camera. Come meet these guys. Bill MacLeod of AP, and Andy Donatello of the *L.A. Times.* This is my college roommate, Lily McCann, the last time I heard, a dip. Still?"

Lily nodded and shook hands with the two men, each of whom stood to offer her a stool at the crowded bar.

"I hope," the AP man said, "you'll give us the State Department's vision concerning Beirut."

"I've been here for two hours," Lily said. "Haven't had a vision yet."

"Ah," the *L.A. Times* said. "You've found just the right people to initiate you to Beirut."

"We'll be kind," AP added.

"I've been warned," Lily said.

"Drink?" the *L.A. Times* asked. "The absinthe here is tasty."

"These guys are horny for an easy story," Mimi said. "Otherwise harmless, believe me. Married, children back in Bethesda and Pasadena, *boring.* You don't have a thing to worry about."

"Mimi," AP said, "you just chopped off my other one."

"We're all horny," the *L.A. Times* added, "trying to explain in pithy prose to the American public the difference between a Phalangist and a Druse, as if anyone cared."

"You poor bastards," Mimi said. "When are you going to accept that the American public doesn't read anymore? They just want to see nice wiggly pictures moving around on the tube."

"Watch out for Mimi," the *L.A. Times* said. "She angles her shots straight at the groin."

"You know, diplomats always look blurred on camera," AP said. "Better to talk to us."

"I take it you're on television?" Lily asked Mimi.

"Under it," she said. "I hold it up. I'm a producer, but I won't tell you which network so you won't be overwhelmed by my success."

"So what do you think of Israel moseying up here to Beirut to drive the PLO out?" the *L.A. Times* man asked.

"I'd say that was only half their reason," Lily replied.

"Okay, so I'll delicately ask what the hell's the other half."

"Yeah," the AP man added. "What's the official U.S. line?"

"I haven't been here long enough to find out," Lily responded, trying to keep it light. "I'd say that's just the Lily line."

"And you don't think," Mimi began with quiet fervor, "that after ten years of being attacked by the PLO, who'd set up shop in southern Lebanon with their headquarters in Beirut, that Israel didn't have the right to come in and get rid of them?"

Lily shrugged. "A military invasion of one country by another for whatever reason is an act of war. It breaks international law, the world community condemns it, and in this case, it deepens the suspicion that Israel is set on expanding its territory by military force and occupation. The fact that there are two rivers in southern Lebanon that can supply water to Israel is not lost on anyone. Diplomatically speaking, it's a long-term disaster."

"I suppose you also think that you're being objective," the AP man goaded, "diplomatically speaking."

Lily paused and considered the idea. "In this business, you try to be. But in the Middle East, they say objectivity is the big mirage, surrounded by shifting sand. There are some diplomats out here who followed their personal mirages around the desert and were never heard from again. If possible, you turn into the sandstorm and keep your eyes open to see what you can see."

Mimi smiled a challenge. "Might be blinding. Need a guide?"

"It often is. Maybe I will."

———

The following week, Lily was negotiating in a village in the Shouf Mountains, east of the city, with a representative of the Druse militia. His technique of arbitration had been a long and sometimes mystical rambling over several centuries of betrayal and retribution which Lily had borne patiently. Suddenly the security officer who accompanied her was heard arguing to get into the hut where

the parley was taking place. Such an interruption was highly unusual, so Lily excused herself and went out to discipline the man.
When she confronted him, however, he said in English, "There's an
alert. Come now."

With hurried courtesy, Lily broke off her talks with the Druse
representative and was driven down the mountain back to the embassy. In the front seat of the armored limousine, the security man
cleared an Uzi submachine gun and laid it across his lap. Every few
hundred yards, he spoke into the car radio, giving their exact location to the security office at the embassy. The city was filled with
the noise of many sirens, but other than that, it seemed oddly
quiet, with fewer cars and pedestrians than usual. Not until they
were safely inside the embassy gates did Lily hear what had happened. Bashir Gemayal, president-elect of Lebanon and leader of
the Phalangist Party, had been assassinated by a bomb that exploded in his party's headquarters.

The entire American Embassy stayed on alert. Those members of
the staff already there remained to deal with the crisis. Security
officers were sent to escort others in, or check on anyone, employees
or dependents, who had not called. All Americans were ordered to
stay off the streets, and the senior staff set about reporting events to
Washington, as well as figuring out an appropriate response to the
many variations the crisis might present.

Throughout the night, information filtered into the crisis control
office and was examined, discussed, and disseminated appropriately.
Policy was constantly being adjusted and debated by the embassy's
senior staff, who requested that Lily join them. Although fourteen
thousand PLO guerrillas had followed Yasir Arafat in the recent
evacuation, hundreds were rumored to have remained with their
families in the Palestinian refugee camps of West Beirut. Without
Gemayal, the country would remain fractured and be more open
than ever to the inexorable influence of Syria.

A CIA man hurried in and slipped a piece of paper to the chargé.
He read it aloud. "Gemayal's assassin was a Lebanese agent controlled by the Syrian *mukhabarat*. Comments?"

The political officer broke the silence. "That'll tear this city
apart. The Syrians are obviously making a move. I suggest we

recommend to Washington the marines be sent back in here to establish a neutral order."

"What's the Israeli Defense Force doing up in the hills?" another officer wondered. "They certainly know this news."

"Let's not react to the IDF," the chargé said. "I'd rather react before they do."

"May I respond to the suggestion?" Lily asked, aware of her status as a newcomer.

"Please," the chargé said.

"I'm not as knowledgeable about this place as you all are, but from what I can see, order around here is pretty ephemeral. The possibility of any external force imposing it with anything short of a major invasion is slight. The marines would become another element of the chaos, and might provide a convenient focus of resentment of American interference."

"The Marines were the herders of the week when they ushered the PLO out of here," the political officer said. "They'd bring that status back with them."

"There's a vacuum now," the chargé said, "and either Israel or Syria will fill it. We might need a presence here."

"The Lebanese will cheer the parade when the marines come marching in," Lily said. "But then who do they work with, which Lebanese militia? Whoever they *don't* choose will make the marines their target."

"You have an alternative, Lily?" the chargé queried.

"Stay out of it and hope the Israelis live up to their agreement with us not to enter Beirut. It seems to me too late in the day for the American government to try to impose order here."

The political officer nodded. "I'm inclined to agree with you, if—"

The phone by the chargé rang and he picked it up, listened, said, "Okay," and put it down. "The Israeli Defense Force has moved down from the hills and is spreading out to secure West Beirut."

"That's a direct contravention of the IDF's oral agreement with us not to invade that area," the political officer stated angrily. "We had to guarantee that promise to Arafat because his refugee camps are over there." He looked at Lily, who shook her head and said nothing. A recommendation for the marines' return was sent to the State Department as quickly as it could be drafted.

As a result, nothing happened, or rather nothing happened that the embassy in Beirut heard about. All the conveniences of modern communications meant nothing when Foggy Bottom chose not to use them. After the initial bursts of cable traffic with Washington, the answer was silence. Only requests for clarification came in from the Lebanon desk officer. There was nothing to do but assume that Foggy Bottom and the White House were exerting themselves toward Tel Aviv, where the decisions had to be made. Throughout the morning, nothing unusual occurred. News arrived that the Israeli Defense Force was solidifying its presence and control in West Beirut, as well as reports that fifteen hundred Maronite Phalangist militiamen were being trucked over from East Beirut to the airport, obviously with IDF permission. Still there were no instructions from Washington.

By noon, Lily was too tired to be useful. Since Beirut was relatively calm, she requested leave to return to her hotel for a bath and some sleep. Two hours later, the request was granted on the understanding that in case of a new crisis, a driver would be sent to wake her up, and that in any event she would be the duty officer beginning at midnight.

Once in her bed at the Commodore, Lily had a difficult time going to sleep. The hotel was relatively empty; the resident battalion of journalists was out reconnoitering the new phenomenon of Israeli tanks and troops in West Beirut. Distant explosions and overflights of Israeli jet fighters perforated her descent into slumber. Her own edge of responsibility kept points of analysis churning through her mind. Finally sleep came, although with little sense of rest.

Pounding on the door woke her. She didn't remember where she was; then she saw her clock on the bedside table. Eleven-fifteen. She was due at the embassy at midnight; the car would arrive for her in fifteen minutes.

"Lily, are you in there?" Mimi called through the door and pounded again.

Lily unbolted and opened it. "What's the matter?"

"How long have you been asleep?" Mimi asked as she came in.

Lily had seen little of her since arriving in Beirut; they passed each other in the hotel's lobby at odd hours. Mimi now seemed distraught, unusually tense.

"Since about three," Lily answered.

"Okay. What you say is off the record. I just need to know. Is the embassy involved in what's going on in the PLO camps?"

"I don't even know what's going on in the camps. Which camps?"

"Sabra and Shattila. The Israelis have sealed them off. They're keeping them lit up like Christmas with phosphorous flares. We can't get near them, but the word is the Phalangists are in there." The implication of what she described screwed her face into a grimace.

"When I left today," Lily said, beginning to dress instantly, "the embassy had no indication that anything like that would happen."

"If it's true, it'll be a slaughter," Mimi said through nearly gritted teeth. "The Phalangists want revenge, for Gemayal, for what the PLO did to them here over ten years."

"The PLO has left," Lily said trying to calm her. "Those camps are Palestinian homes for old people, women, and children. Last I heard, Israel doesn't condone slaughter."

It didn't work. Mimi frowned, trying to believe what she heard. Then she said, "I'm going over there. You want to come with me?"

"I can't. I'm due back at the embassy. But I'll tell you anything I can, Mimi, as soon as I can."

"Thanks. Leave me a message. I'll come to you."

She left the room. Lily was dressed, and as she put an elastic in her hair to hold it in a ponytail, she followed her friend down the stairs to the lobby, where her embassy driver was already waiting. She left Mimi at the front entrance negotiating with an extremely reluctant cab driver. The streets of Beirut were empty and dark; the driver used only his parking lights. Lily could feel the compression of an occasional explosion. She looked to the south and saw in the distance a white flare arcing slowly toward the ground.

As soon as she walked into the crisis control room at the embassy, she knew something was more wrong than usual.

"Tell the chargé that McCann's here," the chief political officer said into a phone as he indicated a place for her to sit. There was a new map of West Beirut on the wall behind him. A line of Xs marked the Israeli position; two red circles indicated the Sabra and Shattila refugee camps. Two other members of her overnight watch came in, both in clean shirts, obviously rested. The chargé followed and took his place at the table. The embassy's chief security officer as well as the CIA station chief—an unusual presence—were also crowded up to the walnut rectangle.

"Here's the latest," the chargé began. "Whatever's going on in the Shattila and Sabra camps is being controlled by the Israeli Defense Force. The IDF has sealed off both areas. Our information is that the Phalangists are in there, around fifteen hundred of them. There are sounds of firing in the camps, and the Israelis are keeping them lit up. But as to exactly what's going on, we have no verification, which is what we emphasize, Lily, on anything that goes out of here tonight. When and if verification comes, I'll be the one to authorize its validity. Clear?"

"Yes, sir," Lily answered, noting his cool command. Only his eyes revealed his lack of sleep over the last sixty hours.

"The most pertinent information we do have comes through CIA channels and for the moment is classified. No discussion out of this room. Hal?"

The station chief started reading from his notes. "This morning, Thursday, September 16, 1982, there was a cabinet session at the Knesset, during which the Israeli chief of staff, General Eitan, informed Prime Minister Begin of an operation *already begun*"—he looked up and around the room for emphasis—"concerning the entry of the Phalangist militia into various PLO refugee camps. Our informants say that when General Eitan was questioned, he stated it was a military matter and the operation had been approved by Defense Minister Ariel Sharon. Whether or not Sharon had spoken privately to Begin is not known."

"Does this mean," the chief economic officer asked incredulously, "that the Israeli army is running wherever it wants up here with the bit in its teeth?"

"I doubt it," the chargé answered, "but in the past, Ariel Sharon has often had his own purpose, armed with a full quiver of delusions. The chain of command broke down or was ignored."

"Does Washington know about this?" asked a military officer on

Lily's watch. "And have we heard anything from those environs yet?"

"Yes to the first, no to the second," the chargé replied.

"If the Phalangists are in the camps," Lily said, "there'll be a slaughter. Shouldn't the embassy protest in some way, even without word from Washington, so that in hindsight we won't be accused of remaining blind."

"I share that concern," the chargé said, "and the frustration. But we can't wiggle without Washington. And, Lily, do not under any circumstances dare utter the word 'slaughter.' " He smiled sadly, sharing admission of the probable truth.

"What word is preferred if the circumstances demand one?" she asked.

Before he could answer, suggestions came from around the table. "Mass murder?"

"Too judgmental. 'Extermination'?"

"A little reminiscent. What about 'massacre'?"

"Use 'incursion' if you have to, Lily," the chargé suggested gruffly, uncomfortable with the discussion. "Anything else?"

The meeting broke up after several administrative questions were answered, and another long night began. By the end of her watch, Lily had fielded enough of the incoming information to be certain that the worst fears about the camps were being realized. Before she left for her hotel, she submitted a carefully reasoned memo to the chargé, suggesting an immediate diplomatic meeting between him and representatives of the Israeli Defense Force in order to confront them with the extent of their responsibility. When she returned on Friday night, she found the memo on her desk rejected without further comment. At the crisis management meeting, the chargé did not refer to her, whether from irritation or fatigue, she couldn't tell. The only clear word from Washington was "Wait," which is what her team did through most of the early hours of Saturday.

Exhaustion came early, not so much from long hours and strain, but from frustration and a growing sense of horror at what was going on in Sabra and Shattila. It was already apparent that the "incursion" or "slaughter" or "massacre," whatever the press and history decided to call it, was no aberration by some misdirected military officer who lost control of himself or his men and attacked the helpless civilians in a quick rush to carnage. This was a carefully considered action authorized by the military hierarchy in charge. It had gone on for at least two days by the time Lily finished her Saturday morning watch, and there was nothing to be done. Diplomacy's labyrinth kept the event and a reaction to it neatly separated. Desolated, Lily was driven back to the hotel, furious with Washington's silence, wary of her own emotions, and doubtful about herself.

As the car pulled to a stop at the Commodore's entrance, Lily saw a scene of pandemonium. Crowds of journalists were leaping into cabs before they even stopped moving. Several reporters, one whom she remembered meeting, approached the embassy car, waving twenty-dollar bills and yelling as loud as they could. When Lily stepped out, she heard someone call her name above the yells of bartering and urgency. It was Mimi, who hurried over. "The Israelis have pulled back," she shouted. "The camps are open. You want to come?"

Without the slightest diplomatic hesitation, Lily followed Mimi to a car already filled with her crew and their equipment. Jammed into the back seat, Lily held battery packs in her lap. The mile-long ride seemed longer. Mimi recited instructions to her crew, more out of nervousness than need. As they approached the Sabra camp, Lily noted that there wasn't a single Israeli vehicle or soldier in sight.

The car stopped and everyone jumped out. While the crew assembled the equipment, Lily stood, staring at a pile of bodies fallen on top of one another apparently as they were shot, three women, five children, and a white-haired man. There was such a confusion of arms and legs that it took a moment to realize a number of them were not connected. The rows of corrugated tin huts behind them emitted smoke and wails of terror. A woman sat in the dust before a splintered door, silently pounding her bleeding head with her fists. Down the dusty roadway, a team of Red Cross workers in gauze masks were already digging, and Lily saw that between her and the hole there were more than enough bodies or pieces of them to fill it. Walls were smeared with blood and covered with flies. The stench was sickly sweet and nauseating.

Beside her, she heard Mimi gasp, then cough. "My God!" she cried. "What have we done?"

Then Lily saw something move, twenty feet away, a child covered in dried blood pulling itself out from under two bodies. It was a girl of about six, screaming more with terror than with pain, although one of her legs was obviously useless, dragged lifelessly behind her. When Lily approached, the girl collapsed, fearing assault, and wrapped her arms around her face.

Lily knelt beside her and tried to reassure her in Arabic. After a moment, the girl looked out between her arms at Lily and Mimi, who knelt beside her. Then her eyes turned up into her head and she crumpled.

"Oh, no," Mimi said, jumping up. "I'll get someone—"

"It's too late," Lily said as she picked up the almost weightless body and rocked it gently back and forth in her arms. The memory of holding the dead Jordanian children in 1967 hit like a blow to the head and weakened her so that she sank to the dirt, still holding the lifeless child. "We're two days late," she said, talking in order not to cry. "No tragedy of war here, no terrible mistake. This was planned. The ones who're responsible"—she looked out over the camp—"aren't soldiers or politicians anymore. They're criminals. This is cold-blooded murder, and we—"

She turned to look up at Mimi, who was standing quietly above her, the tears flowing down her cheeks. And just beside her was the black lens and the red light of a television camera.

TWENTY-THREE

THE STORY of the Sabra and Shattila "massacre"—the international press's appellation—broke on the evening of Saturday, September 18, 1982. On its evening news, the BBC broadcast the details throughout the world. Television showed the horrifying images on Sunday as film and tape reached their organization's headquarters. That evening, the film of Lily holding the dead child and accusing those responsible of murder appeared on American network television. She was not identified by name, but her position as a political officer at the American Embassy in Beirut was mentioned.

The moment she'd seen the television camera focused on her in the camp, Lily had tried to explain to Mimi why she mustn't use it. But Mimi was in a rage, which quickly became a personal crusade to condemn those responsible for bringing shame and dishonor on Israel and to drive them from power. Her judgment was instant: Ariel Sharon and Prime Minister Begin were guilty. She directed her crew to film every degree of horror that the massacre presented, and there was no lack of it. She interviewed survivors and recorded details of the Phalangist orgy of revenge and the Israeli Defense Force's protection of it. To Lily, Mimi apologized for the trouble that the film clip would cause, but as a journalist she couldn't allow a personal relationship to interfere with the news. What Lily had said was the truth and was not said off the record. Mimi promised not to use Lily's name, but it would be up to the network to decide how much of the clip was broadcast. In the end, most of it was.

Lily stayed in the camp until early afternoon, helping the survivors and translating for rescue workers. Then she returned to the embassy and reported directly to the chargé. When he heard what she had said on camera, his eyes closed under an exhausted frown, and he sank back in his chair with a despairing sigh. She finished, and he looked at her sadly.

"No chance of your friend burying it?" he asked.

"No, sir. I begged her pretty hard already."

"I'll have to report it, but Washington's busy this weekend. Maybe it'll be overlooked. Go get some sleep; I'll need you at midnight. But you'd better sleep here. Once that clip gets around, the rest of the press will want their pound of your flesh."

"Yes, sir."

"What makes me saddest is what Hooper will do with this."

"I hadn't thought of that."

"Better prepare."

As it happened, Lily was duty officer of the crisis management team when a CRIT cable—labeled "critical" as the highest indication of importance—was brought up from the code room and handed to her at three in the morning on Monday, Beirut time, one hour after she had appeared on Sunday evening network news in the United States. Directed to the chargé, it read,

REGARDING FSO-3 LILY MCCANN, SEE THAT SHE IS OUT OF BEIRUT BEFORE DAWN WITHOUT FAIL, AND PREVENT ANY FURTHER ACCESS TO HER BY THE PRESS. HER RETURN TO AMMAN FOR A WEEK IS APPROPRIATE TO LET MATTERS COOL. SHE WILL THEN RETURN TO WASHINGTON AS PLANNED.

It was signed by the secretary of state. Mimi's film clip obviously had not been overlooked.

Because it was a CRIT cable, Lily had to wake the chargé, who lived with his wife in an apartment on the fifth floor of the embassy building. When he arrived at his office and read the cable, the chargé shook his head regretfully and said, "Sorry, Lily. I'll come down to the crisis room and relieve you. We'll send a driver to the hotel to pack you up, and he'll take you to Damascus, where you can get on a plane to Amman. Understood?"

They returned silently to the crisis room. Lily sat in a chair against the wall. Her colleagues took note of the chargé's unexpected arrival and Lily's displacement, but said nothing. As she waited for the driver, she wondered about Worth's reaction:

whether he would call before she left, whether he and the secretary of state had conferred; whether they had sent instructions to Hooper. In her mind, she could see Hooper's gloating face and hear him recite one of his favorite lines: "Well, honey, this time you put your foot in the shit and sank in up to your eyeballs."

Her career as a Foreign Service officer was effectively over. She knew that she'd spend the rest of her years at the end of some long corridor in the State Department pushing papers. Or if she was lucky, if Worth could pull the right strings, she might be sent as a warm body to fill in at some consulate far from the Middle East. The specter of bureaucratic uselessness until retirement was almost as repugnant to her as a week under Hooper's disdain.

She went over to one of the typewriters on a desk by the wall. On a piece of embassy stationery, she typed her resignation from the Foreign Service, a single sentence with no explanations or excuses. Just after she signed and sealed it, another CRIT cable arrived, announcing President Reagan's decision, to be made public the following day, that the marines would return to Beirut "with the mission of enabling the Lebanese government to restore full sovereignty over its capital." Someone asked how many divisions were being sent in to accomplish such an incredible task.

"No divisions," the chargé said, scowling. "Fifteen hundred is the number."

This information was met with startled silence, during which a marine appeared at the door to say that Lily's car was waiting. Lily left without saying goodbye, only waving as if going out on some negotiation. The chargé accompanied her, and as they stood under the porte-cochère, Lily handed him the envelope.

"If I mailed this, you'd get it at best on Tuesday," she said. "Let it wait until then, all right? I'd just as soon that nobody knew where I was."

He nodded, understanding what the letter said. "Good luck, Lily. You're a fine FSO. I'll say so. As far as I'm concerned, you had bad luck with a friend in the wrong place."

"Thank you, sir. I hope this doesn't bring you any more grief than you already have."

He shrugged. "A drop in the bucket, now that the marines are coming to make Beirut just like America." He shook his head at the folly of it and took Lily's hand. "We'll miss you."

The drive to Damascus took three hours. Lily was able to get a seat on the first morning flight to Athens, then fly directly to Dulles, outside Washington. She slept through much of the trip and was numb for the rest of it, looking at but not seeing a bad movie, eating the forgettable meals, analyzing her colossal failure, the discredit she'd been to her father's memory, the embarrassment she'd be to Worth.

She wondered whether it would be possible for her to be the good Georgetown wife, working at a permissible job that didn't interfere with her shadowed life in her husband's eclipse of light. She cried once, silently, thinking of children, of the dead girl and the others she'd helped in the Sabra camp, of the three in Ammar's picture of his family, of those killed by Abu al-Saffah in 1967, of the children that she, Lily McCann Deloit—she'd obviously take his name now—the children she now would have, obviously to replace the meaning in her life and be her crutch through it.

No, no. She shook her head hard enough to startle the man reading in the next seat. Staring out the window at the vast roiling of clouds beneath her, she swore to herself that she'd never have children for such an invidious purpose.

Her plane landed at Dulles in early evening, Washington time. Intermittent sleep through so many time zones left her feeling more jet-lagged than usual. It was still Daylight Saving Time, so she arrived at the house on O Street in a soft twilight that gave the ivy-covered brick façade an unusually intimate and welcoming warmth. The cab driver put her bags inside the front door when she unlocked it. She called out, but didn't really expect Worth to be there that early. During a crisis like the one in Beirut, he might stay at Foggy Bottom most of the night. She'd wait, although she desperately needed to talk to him.

She dragged her bags and carry-on up to the bedroom. The sheets had been changed; the cleaning woman came on Mondays. The idea that she would soon be in charge of the house depressed her. She didn't unpack, but she took off the clothes she had traveled in for so many hours, wrapped them in a ball, and put them in the bathroom hamper. Then she took a shower, dried herself with the clean towels hanging on the rack, and fell into the bed. Sleep came instantly.

When the front door opened, Lily sat up, wide awake. Worth's radio clock read eleven-thirty. She heard voices in intense discussion, and moved quickly to Worth's closet for his robe. The automatic light went on; the robe was hanging on a hook. As she slipped it on, she saw two dresses hanging next to Worth's suits. She slowly pulled them out, seeing they weren't hers. At the same time, she realized the voices downstairs belonged to Worth and a woman. One dress was an elegant silk print from Bendel; the other was an expensive suit from Garfinkle's. On the floor of the closet she saw a pair of black pumps that went well with either dress.

Carefully Lily put back the two hangers and closed the closet door. The voices downstairs were muffled, but she was sure there were only two. She went into the bathroom, took the ball of clothes out of the hamper, and put them back on as quickly as she could. Her hair was still damp; she didn't look at herself in any mirror. Her shoes made no noise on the carpeted stairs, and before they hit the wood floor of the hall, she heard Worth, in the study, say, "Look, we have a week. I'm not going to send her a cable. I'll tell her within twelve hours of . . ."

After hearing three of Lily's steps, he appeared in the hall. The alarm on his face hardened into acceptance. "Cassie," he said without taking his eyes off Lily, "my wife's arrived—unexpectedly. I'll call you tomorrow." Behind him, the woman glided to the front door and went out without even a glance in Lily's direction. Her hair was black and expensively cut. Her dress was white.

"Why aren't you in Amman?" he asked acidly.

"Who is Cassie?" Lily retorted.

He let out a deep breath. "You'd better come in and have a seat."

He stood aside to let Lily enter the study, where she saw two glasses of port on a side table by the single leather chair. She passed it and sat on the settee across from his partners' desk.

"Cassie's the daughter of Senator Rinckart," he explained as he idly picked up one of the glasses and wandered over to his chair behind the desk.

"Of the Foreign Relations Committee."

"Yes," he said.

"I see."

"What?"

"That you have the Executive and the Legislative Branches of government covered, which leaves only the Judiciary."

"I'll try to avoid being snide if you will. Why didn't you go to Amman as ordered?"

"More reasons than you'd care to know, now all beside the point. I've resigned from the Foreign Service."

His mouth opened; then his jaw set. "Brilliant. And are you planning to hold a news conference here tomorrow, now that you're appearing on television? God Almighty, how did you manage to do that?"

"That's snide. Why don't you tell me about you and Cassie? I take it from the dresses in your closet this wasn't to be a one-night stand."

"You know me better than that."

"Yes, but clearly I've missed something. Look, let's save time. Just tell me what you were going to tell me 'within twelve hours.'"

"She's been around Washington a long time, married a rich drunk-about-town, divorced, oh, two years ago. I've known her for years." He stopped as if all the blanks had been filled.

"When did the affair start?" Lily asked.

"It isn't an affair," he said, irritated.

"Forgive me. Tryst, assignation, liaison. Take your pick."

"You're such a lawyer, Lily. It makes hostility easy. About a year ago, a little longer maybe, we found ourselves out on the boat, becalmed in Chesapeake Bay. We talked for hours."

He stopped again, but this time Lily was glad. That they had begun it on the boat hit her hard and tightened her throat. She swallowed once and said, "About the time you became the assistant secretary?"

"Somewhere in there," he said a little too casually.

"Did her daddy have anything to do with that?"

"Not one damn thing," he said coldly, "and thanks for the implication. I did that on my own."

"Yes, you certainly did, didn't you, with a little help from your friends at the Raphael Hotel. So you and Cassie went sailing around the time you talked to me about home and children," Lily said.

"Was it? Yes, I guess it was," he said with a slight wave of his hand, as if it were beside the point.

"Maybe, in all those hours of talk on the sloop, you discussed the idea of home and family with her, too."

"You're leading the witness, Counselor, for no other reason than to make this more painful than it already is."

"Is it, Worth? I don't see the slightest reaction from you, except maybe surprise at my return."

"I don't like to fail, Lily. I think we've failed, and I regret it deeply."

" 'We'? How am I suddenly involved in this failure?"

"It takes two, Lily. We made some choices that were mistakes— separate lives, a marriage of phone calls and fantasy meetings two or three times a year. It doesn't work."

"It did for years. And you knew I was coming back to Washington."

"It was too late. You wanted your career—"

She stood up. "You bastard! You've worked this out for yourself so that it's my fault to want a career, so that I was the one who left you alone, making it okay for you to bed down Cassie."

He smiled bitterly. "You force me to remind you of your good friend Moshe Levy. And Ambassador Hooper loved telling me of your midnight supper with the Honorable Ammar Ben Ashid."

Lily said, "Ah, yes. I had a funny feeling that you and Hooper were telephone buddies. Well, Ammar and I talked—'for hours and hours.' That was all. And you know nothing about Moshe. That happened before you and I were married, and I didn't hang any dresses in his closet."

"Lily, you're right, I'm the villain, you're a much better person than I am. Now what?"

She was already wondering where to go. The antique clock on the mantel showed her it was almost midnight. "Why don't you tell me what you had planned when I arrived in a week." She sat down again on the settee and faced him directly. "That means, what your plans are with Cassie, and how you planned to handle me."

"With more grace than this, I assure you. I'd have met your plane, brought you here, made sure you had some food, as much rest as you needed. And then I'd have told you I'd moved out, the house was yours, a generous settlement was ready to be submitted to your attorneys, in the hope that you'd go down to the Dominican Republic for a twenty-four-hour divorce, because I'm going to have to marry Cassie as soon as possible. She's pregnant."

Lily didn't move or breathe, but stared until the image of him began to float in front of her eyes. "Call me a cab," she heard herself say.

"That's unnecessary, Lily. Give me ten minutes to pack, and—"

"I'd never stay here. Call me a cab."

"Where will you go?"

"I'll let you know." She started to walk out of the study but stopped at the door. Worth had picked up the phone but held it, watching her. She asked, "Did Cassie plan to get pregnant?"

He glared at her, then dialed. "She offered to get an abortion. I refused. People would have heard, and this administration doesn't look kindly on abortion. It would have ruined her reputation."

"Not to mention yours," Lily said and went into the hall. She pulled herself up the stairs using the bannister, suddenly having a difficult time coordinating her movements. From the bedroom, she dragged the two bags and her carry-on to the top of the stairs. She lifted the heaviest of them and started down but made it only halfway. She had to let the bag fall. Worth came out of the study, saw what had happened, and said, "Let me at least do that."

Lily didn't respond but didn't object, and after he went by her to get the second bag, she took the opportunity to go out the front door to the curb. She suddenly felt incredibly cold and her teeth started to chatter; she fought to suppress that as Worth dropped the two bags down beside her, gave her the carry-on, and stood there, gazing down O Street for the cab.

"I'll cooperate in the divorce," Lily said starkly, "not for your convenience or mine so much as for the child. And I don't want any settlement from you."

"Let the lawyers decide that."

"You'll save time if you don't offer me a cent. You owe me nothing. I had my career, which you saved at one point. We're even except for the deceit, and I figure you'll pay for that with the gossip and the press."

"This isn't an unusual occurrence in Washington. Below cabinet level, it isn't really the public's fodder. It'll cause a ripple for a week."

They both saw the lighted diamond on top of the cab as it came around the corner.

"Where will you be?" Worth asked.

"Pouch everything to the embassy in Cairo. I'll be on the dahabeah."

"But what about—"

"I'll fly to wherever it's necessary to get the divorce. I've told you that. But now I'm going home."

He opened the cab door as the driver came around to load the luggage in the trunk.

"Goodbye, Lily," Worth said. "No parting shots. Certainly we're both armed."

She sat back in the seat and stared straight ahead. "Do you think this would've happened if I'd stayed here in the house as the good wife?"

"That's conjecture, Counselor."

She looked over at him. "What'll the jury say?"

"That you're innocent and I'm guilty."

"Do you agree?"

"I've never cared much about juries."

The driver was back in his seat, and Worth shut the door. The cab pulled out onto the street. "Where are we going?" the driver asked.

"Dulles," Lily said and turned to look out the rear window. Worth had already started back into the house. Lily quickly faced forward. As the cab turned onto Wisconsin Avenue, she knew he regretted nothing.

PART FOUR

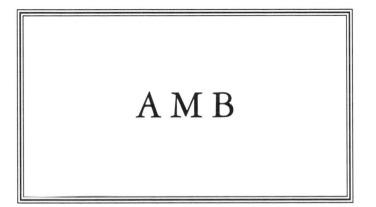

AMB

1992

TWENTY-FOUR

THE MUSIC from the main foyer of the White House could be heard faintly through the door of the small paneled sitting room. Lily sat on a flame-stitched wing chair and the president on a Hepplewhite settee. Every lamp, vase, and bibelot in the room looked as if it had been positioned with a micrometer. The heavy green curtains were drawn, and above the mantel there was a good Ryder landscape, one that Lily had not seen on her previous visits.

"I'd like you to be our ambassador in Cairo," the president said. "You know any reason you shouldn't be?" He was smiling but watching her carefully.

"Well, for starters," Lily replied, "I'm not a Republican, and I am a woman."

"Yes, but we can always hope to change the first one. I guess we're stuck with the woman thing."

It was her turn to smile, but then she said, "We're also stuck with a certain piece of television film where I imply some unpleasant things about certain people in the Israeli government."

He nodded. "I ran that film a couple of times on Tuesday. Doesn't bother me at all. It was ten years ago, and if any of our journalist friends dig it up, that's fine with me. It fits in nicely with what this administration's trying to do about being Israel's banker on demand."

"It might not play so well to the Senate, which has to confirm me."

"The Senate and the public will be made aware of your work as my personal emissary to four heads of Arab states during the Gulf War. You had some connections this government didn't have. That

325

was incredible work, I'd like to say, done quietly, privately, a real sacrifice of time and energy. Even senators will be impressed—particularly the Democrats in this election year." He chuckled in anticipation of their discomfort.

The fact that she had been invited to the White House at the last minute and almost commanded to attend the state dinner had given Lily some warning; she was not totally unprepared for a meeting with the president. An ambassadorship, however, was a surprise, and the idea of returning to Cairo cut many ways through her mind.

"Mr. President, working privately is one thing. A female in the official role of ambassador in a Muslim country might not be able to accomplish as much as you hope."

The president's smile thinned. "Hope isn't a part of my strategy in the Middle East," he said. "I'd just like to keep our head above the quicksand, now that we're up to our necks in this peace process. Look, Lily, you're my choice. I've told State that. I read your book; your ideas about the water crisis and population thing seem right on the money. Your father was over there, you were born there, lived there, you speak the language. The Arabs know all that and obviously appreciate it. I don't know if your family's diplomatic tradition is still there for you, but your earlier career as a Foreign Service officer makes you more of a pro than—well . . ." He dismissed the sentence with a wave. His administration's record of questionable political appointments to American embassies had earned well-editorialized criticism. "Besides that, you went to Yale," he joked, "and being a woman sure hasn't bothered your company's dealings with the gentlemen from OPEC. You sell them half the gas pumps in Europe at the same time you're dealing in Israeli diamonds." He stopped and looked at her in mock fluster. "How the heck did you get away with that?"

She smiled, knowing exactly how carefully the president had been briefed about her, wondering how much he'd been told of her relationships with Ammar Ben Ashid and Moshe Levy, realizing those two names were connected with hers in any number of files around Washington.

"Mr. President, as you know, my former husband is under secretary of state for political affairs. Working directly for you might be different from working in his department. I doubt very much that he'd be pleased with this appointment."

"As a matter of fact, Lily," he said with a shrewd smile, "I can tell you that Mr. Deloit has been informed and was urged to be as pleased as punch."

As she rose, Lily suppressed a laugh. "I'm honored by your confidence, Mr. President. There's a lot to think about. How long do I have to decide?"

"We're moving our man in Cairo to the Philippines. We can't afford to have a long vacancy in Egypt, particularly with all the shifts going on since Madrid. I'm having breakfast tomorrow at seven-thirty to discuss the Middle East with the secretary of state, national security adviser, and the, um, under secretary." A knowing look indicated his anticipation of the personal edge at the meeting. "If you've decided to serve by then, you're invited. If not, well, we'll drink our grapefruit juice and try to think of someone else." He opened the door for her as, outside, a Secret Service agent moved adroitly away.

"I'm not going to give you any of that 'ask what you can do for your country' stuff," the president said, speaking over the band music, which grew louder as they walked down the hall toward the foyer. "We need you, Lily, pure and simple. If there were anyone I thought could handle the situation better, you wouldn't be here tonight."

When they re-entered the crowded main foyer, where the marine band was playing for the dancers, Lily was confronted by the usual covetous looks awarded anyone who had spent a private moment with the president. His chief of staff and the guest of honor were approaching. Lily hadn't had time to have her hair done and hoped it remained at least neat if not perfectly arranged from its hurried brushing and blow-drying at the hotel.

Standing beside the president, Lily knew that her decision was already made. Only the million details had to be worked out. She turned to him and said, "Thank you, Mr. President. I'll see you at breakfast."

His eyebrows lifted; then he gave her a look that seemed to be one of gratitude. "Good. I envy you, you know. The Foreign Service is the last place you can really practice pure honest-to-God patriotism. Sure as heck not in politics!"

He turned away to the other business of the evening. His chief of staff glanced at her but didn't smile as he hurried to say something to his boss before the guest of honor started talking.

Lily stepped back and walked toward the exit, eager to get away without seeing any friends. It was not customary for anyone to leave a state dinner until the president did. She doubted whether her car would have returned to pick her up so early and decided to walk. After being escorted by a White House social aide back to the diplomatic reception room and helped on with her coat by an attendant, she made her way to the guards at the south portico entrance. A marine was ordered to escort her down the circular drive to the southwest gate. She heard their progress reported into the walkie-talkies of White House police posted along the way. Not until she reached the sidewalk and strolled up to Pennsylvania Avenue did she pause to consider what had happened to her.

Oh, Cairo, she thought, Mother of the World, here I come back again, home. Automatically, she checked the street, the cars moving by, as she did whenever and wherever she was alone. But she smiled at her caution. Surely she was safe in front of the White House.

She crossed the street to Lafayette Park and walked quickly toward the Hay-Adams Hotel. Although the international financial community in the last five years had regarded her as the exemplar of Arabic enterprise, Lily was well aware that the true reason for her success was her respect for the inviolate differences between the two cultures. In her book, *Pawns and Dice,* in which she considered both the past and future in the Middle East, she described business with the Arabs as being about chance and the quick strategic moves of backgammon; but diplomacy with them, she wrote, was a timeless chess game played on sand, Arab sand, as fine, often blinding, and as easily disturbed as powder.

Nonetheless, she had not the slightest hesitation in accepting the appointment, certain of only two things, a palpable joy at the idea of returning to Cairo, and an admittedly bitchy pleasure that at that moment, probably at some insistently brilliant dinner party in Georgetown, Worth Deloit was presenting his furrowed profile to an enthralled hostess. If there weren't a journalist within hearing, he was emitting profundity and charm to cover a churning rage that his former wife had been chosen by the president to be ambassador to Egypt. Although the appointment had been a surprise to Lily, she knew what an under secretary could do to quash an appointment once he heard about it. And Worth had heard. He must have worn out the thick carpets on the seventh floor at the State Department, cadging appointments with any power he could find in order to eviscerate, ever so delicately of course, her chances. Lily was glad she had not known she was being considered, and looked forward to breakfast. She hadn't seen Worth in years; she had only glimpsed several recent pictures of him standing, firm and resolved, next to the secretary of state at congressional hearings. He still had all of his hair, she noticed, and looked fit.

Lily walked across H Street to the hotel. At the desk, she asked the concierge to let her limousine know that she had returned on her own. Then she crossed the lobby and took the elevator. Once inside her suite, she took off her coat and dropped it neatly over the couch in the sitting room. At the desk, she sat down, unclipped her pearl earrings, and dialed room service. She ordered a double espresso. In her bedroom, she changed out of her black dress into a flannel nightgown. As she slipped it on, she thought of the first one she had ever worn, a gift from Worth that first winter when they had taken a long weekend from Yale and gone to ski at Stowe. The nightgown had featured the American flag, and when she came out of the bathroom of the condo wearing it, he said again, "As I warned you, I'll seduce you with America."

"Bastard," Lily said out loud as she began to brush her hair, then gave herself a silent lecture about not getting hooked by old angers with Worth Deloit. Too often she had seen him use other people's anger, allowing it to flow, even stimulating it in order to drive the person to almost certain error. "Getting angry with Worth is like throwing punches at Jell-O; it does no harm and you get the mess all over you," a fellow director of Worth's at a Middle Eastern desk had once declared. It was just after the unfortunate man had given in to fury over one of Worth's peccadilloes—and just before Worth suggested to a well-placed superior on the seventh floor that the director in question would benefit from an assignment in the field, perhaps Equatorial Guinea, which had a pressing vacancy, and to which the offending director was soon posted. Worth could work the halls at State better than a senator could work a chicken dinner fund raiser. Being on the scene gave him a formidable advantage over anyone in the field, as Lily knew from bitter experience.

She kept brushing her hair beyond need. She had cut it the day her divorce became final. Until then she'd worn it down to her shoulders, held back by barrettes or tortoiseshell combs, a sun-streaked brown tumble. She had always considered the length to be inconvenient, but Worth had commanded her to leave it that way; and when his commands stopped having an effect on her, he had insinuated that the hair covered an ungainly neck.

There was a knock at the door. The bellboy brought in a tray with her espresso and placed it on the drop-leaf table in front of the sofa. On the tray was a small gift-wrapped box.

"It was delivered earlier this evening," the bellboy said. He received his tip and quickly left the room, closing the door behind him.

Before picking up Worth's card, Lily checked herself to be clear about her feelings. Both professionally and personally, she was pleased he'd sent a gift. There were a thousand ways an under secretary could make life difficult for an ambassador; if she and Worth could remain at least diplomatically friendly, her job in Cairo would be much more enjoyable. She warily gave in to memory, recalling the early years when she had loved him, his immediate appearance when her father was killed, his defense at the department of her dangerous gaffe with Moshe Levy in Tel Aviv, his looks, his brilliance, the fun they'd had in . . . She stopped herself and reached for the card, still wary.

Lily McCann was printed on the blank side. She turned the card over. A single line was drawn through his name and the long title, Under Secretary of State for Political Affairs. The pen had jumped slightly in crossing the thick engraving. Written in his ordered, slanted hand in tall, narrow letters were the words "Welcome back."

Expect nothing and be surprised if it's good, she told herself. She knew this man, had loved and hated him, and had come out of their marriage bloody, unbowed, and better. The rage and fantasies of revenge had faded sometime ago, and Lily could honestly say to herself that she hadn't thought of Worth Deloit for any length of time during the last three or four years; most recently he'd come to mind when Congress made noises of investigating the hostage negotiations during the 1980 election. She hadn't forgotten him, either, and she unwrapped the box with no expectations.

Inside was a three-inch length of braided leather with a swivel snap at one end and a strap handle at the other. It was a leash, a very short leash.

Lily picked it out of the box and held it up. She sensed an echo of the old rage, but then smiled coldly, accepting the challenge and acknowledging the status quo. It was a perfect gift of warning from Worth. She would keep it to remind her of exactly who he thought he was. As she walked over to the window, she threw the box into the wastebasket and pulled open the curtains. Slipping the strap handle onto her index finger, she began to spin the leash around in front of her as she stared out at the White House. A line of limousines was moving down the drive onto Pennsylvania Avenue.

Thinking of the other two men whom she had loved, she looked back at the digital clock on the desk. She automatically added seven hours and wondered where in the world Moshe Levy might be spying at that moment, or whether Ammar Ben Ashid was at a mosque for political reasons, doing penance for his past disbelief, or had slept through the muezzins' call, as he had with her in Paris, then called her Satan and laughed. Both men had done business with her company, Isis International, over the last several years, Moshe dealing in diamonds, Ammar opening the many doors to the world of Arab oil. Working in New York, Lily had chosen to keep them both at a professional and geographical distance. With this appointment, however, she would be in Cairo, where everything was always different.

The phone rang. She went to the desk and answered it. "Hello?"

"Ms. McCann, this is B. Winston Turner, assistant foreign editor of the *Washington Post*. I hope it's not too late to call, but, well, y'know, I'm trying to make my deadline. You apparently had a meeting with the president this evening, and I was wondering whether you'd care to comment."

"No, Mr. Turner, I wouldn't."

"I see. Well, it's fairly well known that our ambassador to Cairo is being transferred to Manila, and I happened to call up your file on my computer screen and it tells me that you'd make probably the most appropriate political appointment to an embassy that this administration has come up with. Any comment on that?"

"I'm not sure that the president reads the same computer you do, Mr. Turner, but no, no comment at all."

His split-second debate of whether or not to continue ended with "Thank you, Ms. McCann. I enjoyed your book, although I'm not sure I agree that water will replace oil as the area's most valued commodity any time soon. May I call you again, when and if appropriate?"

"I can't stop you, and I'm glad you liked the book, although that's not exactly what I said. But I'm afraid I never talk to the press, no offense to you intended."

"You did in 1967. About an atrocity, it says here."

"Good night, Mr. Turner." She hung up before hearing his response.

Nineteen sixty-seven. Twenty-five years ago. Lily took the last swallow of her espresso. It was cold, but still did the trick. The clock read just after midnight, seven A.M. in the Middle East. Lily dialed the hotel operator as she opened her address book to the cross-referenced page labeled CAIRO.

"Good evening," she said. "I'm going to make some calls to the Middle East, so if you're not too busy, I'd appreciate your staying with me. We'll place the Cairo calls first. With their phone system, it takes a while. Then we'll go on to Riyadh. When Cairo comes through, you can break in on me, all right? The first is: code for Egypt twenty, Cairo city code is two, then three-five-four nineteen-forty-two. I want Noorna el-Sadim . . . Yes, you may as well make a list . . ."

While the operator wrote down the numbers, Lily thought about breakfast the next morning. She picked up the leash from the desk and began to spin it around on her finger again. "Honest-to-God patriotism," the president had said, ". . . the last place you can really practice honest-to-God patriotism." He was right, Lily thought in spite of knowing the many diplomatic practices based on less noble ideals. The old platitude came to mind: "An ambassa-

dor is an honest man sent abroad to lie for the good of his country."
She wasn't a man, and she wouldn't lie, but practicing patriotism
for the United States of America in the 1990s was going to be just
what her father used to say diplomacy was—"juggling with mercury."

TWENTY-FIVE

GOOD MORNING, Mr. President," Lily said as she shook his hand. The other men in the president's dining room had not been seated and waited for her to reach her place at the farthest setting from the table's head, as protocol demanded. She'd seen Worth the moment she entered the small formal room with its Revolutionary War scenes on the walls. She felt no sudden sensation when she'd glimpsed him standing just behind the president, neither nostalgia nor bitterness.

"Good morning, Lily," Worth said, as he shook her hand, and—obviously by arrangement—took over the introductions. There were more people present than the president had mentioned the night before. She'd once met the secretary of state when she gave a speech at the Council on Foreign Relations. The national security adviser was a stranger to her, but didn't seem formidable; he greeted her with a kind smile. The deputy director of the CIA nodded avuncularly. The president's chief of staff was perfunctory and apparently distracted by more important matters. She remembered who the assistant secretary of state for NEA was from her time in the department, but had never known him. Each had a staff assistant who sat next to his boss.

When the introductions were finished, everyone sat down and conversation began. Worth held out Lily's chair, then went to his place across the table, next to the secretary of state, as coffee was poured. Lily took little extra notice of Worth, although, after almost ten years, the fact that his British-tailored suit neatly covered tight narrow hips didn't escape her. Nor did she pretend to herself that he wasn't as attractive as ever. He laughed at something the secretary said and she remembered him laughing in a similar way

one night when they'd eaten pigeons for dinner on the Nile. As she
conversed with the NSC aide on her left, she wondered why her
memory, on her actually seeing Worth again, kicked in with pleasant times instead of what she usually recalled.

The conviviality continued until the White House waiters
cleared the fruit cup and served plates of scrambled eggs and sau-
sage. One waiter appeared carrying a jar of instant espresso on a
small silver tray with a silver spoon for measuring. When it was
offered to her, Lily was about to refuse, not wishing to draw undue
attention.

"Go ahead, Lily," the president called from the end of the table,
halting other conversation. "We're only trying to show you we've
done our homework." Several of those in the know chuckled as the
president explained to the others. "Gentlemen, Ms. McCann grew
up drinking Turkish coffee so thick you could stand a spoon in it.
Even the White House kitchens couldn't do that."

"Thank you, sir," Lily responded. "I should have realized by now
that I'd have no secrets from you."

She didn't look at Worth, who led the laughter.

"As you all know," the president continued, "I've asked Ms.
McCann to be our ambassador to Egypt, and she's accepted the
offer. We cabled the Egyptian Foreign Ministry last night, and,
with unprecedented speed, were sent an answer, received about an
hour ago. Seems the foreign minister knew your father, Lily, and
they are all clearly delighted. I'd like to announce the appointment
to the press after breakfast—if those guys are awake at this hour—
so if anyone has any questions or objections, let's hear them now.
We're here because this appointment is a heck of a lot more vital
than most, and I sure don't want any problems with it."

The sound of cutlery on plates indicated that no one had stopped
eating, but Lily saw the national security adviser lean over to
whisper to his aide, who quickly drew a book from inside his suit
coat. It was Lily's book, *Pawns and Dice,* and there was a plumage of
colored markers coming out of the pages.

The first one to speak was the chief of staff. "What's the Foreign
Relations Committee going to do with this?"

"What are we worrying about here?" the president asked.

"Ms. McCann," the national security adviser said as he opened her book beside his plate of eggs, "you've made some rather dire predictions, some that affect Egypt, others that touch on the security of the whole area. For instance, you suggest that a Middle East war could break out again—over water. Can you defend that idea?"

"Yes, sir, mainly with the historical experience that wars have been started over much less." Lily saw several smiles as she continued. "The Middle East is largely desert; to make it bloom, to stay alive, takes a great deal of water. The population bomb has already exploded there. Without expensive imports, the region can't support so many people. In Egypt, in Israel, in Jordan, soon in Syria, perhaps, the populations are already beyond what can be fed from the land reclaimable with present water supplies."

"There's been a drought," the assistant secretary said.

"My conclusions are based on normal rainfall. The few rivers on which each country depends can be and are being manipulated. Ethiopia or the Sudan could build dams on the Nile, affecting water supplies to Egypt. Turkey's Ataturk Dam on the Euphrates will have serious repercussions on Syria's water supply. At present, Israel is getting more than half its water from the Occupied Territories. It remains to be seen whether or not it's been diverting water from the Litani River in southern Lebanon, either by truck or underground pipeline."

"Are you implying," asked the secretary of state, "that Israel may be keeping military control over their security zone in southern Lebanon and the West Bank so that it can keep stealing water?"

"I point no fingers in the book, sir," Lily replied. "I leave the conclusions to the reader. Israel's own Ministry of Agriculture has admitted that the loss of West Bank water would constitute a mortal danger for his country. Another fact is that Israel takes millions of cubic meters of water a year from the Yarmouk River, which originates in the Golan Heights and which Israel has annexed. The Yarmouk then flows to Jordan, where it's a major source of water to that country—or was."

The chief of staff cleared his throat and said, "I'd like to remind everyone here that the Israel lobby is still the most powerful lobby in this town. They read books as fast as they get their PACs to write checks to the congressmen who vote their way. There's a large number of those, and not a few of them sit on Foreign Relations."

"That's right," the president said testily, "and I think it'll be good for them to have to deal with Lily McCann. There's been too much noise in the press about our appointing people with no records that can be examined. Well, here's someone with ten years in the Foreign Service who wrote a book for them and the Senate to pick over, and I'm pretty confident she can defend it very well. There'll be some heat, Lily. You think you can handle it?"

"I was born and raised in the Middle East, sir. I understand the Senate is air-conditioned."

This received an appreciative laugh from everyone except the chief of staff, who said, "I think she ought to be prepped, and very carefully. All we need is for someone to have a reason to make the president's Israel policy an issue during the campaign. Appointing a businesswoman whose company has so many dealings with the Arabs is asking for it. You know how dirty that can get."

There was an unpleasant silence, which the president broke. "I've been called dirty already, and worse, for not automatically doing what Shamir tells me to do. Lily, you want to address that?"

"Certainly," she said, sticking to her plan of careful advocacy. "I'm in the process of divesting myself of holdings in Isis International, all of which will go into a blind trust during my service. But I make no apologies for the company's success. Over the ten years of its existence, we've done business in five Arab nations, eight European nations, four Far Eastern nations, three South American nations, the United States,—and Israel. We have not honored the Arab boycott of Israel, nor have we been placed on the Arabs' list of companies to be spurned for doing business there.

"As to anti-Semitism, I'm familiar with the charge. It's made often and easily as a defense against any criticism of Israel. Being a lightning rod for such charges doesn't concern me, although my not being a Jew has occasionally made me a more convenient target. What I can defend is a consistent criticism of certain Israeli policies—the settlements, occupation, water—policies that no other country in the world can get away with, policies that, if continued, will damage Israel irreparably, from without and within. I've been just as consistent in my criticism of certain Arab countries' policies—the lack of human rights, harboring and promoting terrorism, feudal economics—which my book clearly states with an emphasis approaching neon."

There was another spontaneous laugh, for which Lily was grateful; she thought she might have sounded a little strident.

"We sure do like lightning rods, Lily," the president said, "but we usually keep them as far away from the White House as possible." The laughter continued until he said, "I think some charm school for the Foreign Relations Committee is in order, though. Worth, will you oversee that?"

"Yes, Mr. President," Worth said. Lily didn't see a single knowing glance around the table, and wondered how many things had been decided before she arrived.

"Good," the president said as his plate was cleared and more coffee poured. "Let's alert the press corps."

———

After the press conference, the dignitaries retired from the press room into the Oval Office, where Lily said goodbye to the president and thanked him for his support. The Joint Chiefs of Staff were already waiting to begin a meeting. She wasn't surprised when Worth accompanied her as she was led by a White House usher to the West Wing and out to the alley, between the fence and the Executive Office Building, where her car was waiting.

"We should talk," he said, a suggestion, not an order.

"Fine. When?"

"Are you busy now? We could at least start."

"I have to call the office at ten forty-five."

"I came in the secretary's car. Could you give me a ride over to the department?"

She nodded and stepped into the back seat, sliding over to allow him room. He was being too nice. She remembered the leash.

"Well," he said as the driver shut the door. "Where to start?"

"We'll go to the State Department first," Lily instructed the driver as he took his place in the front seat.

"I suppose," Worth said, "by telling you how impressive you were this morning."

"Thank you."

"Did you get my gift?"

"Yes."

"A joke."

"Of course."

"You remembered, about leashing Ambassador Hooper and all that?"

"I got it."

"Ha ha ha," he said.

"Ha ha," she replied.

He paused. "How's your mother?"

"She died two years ago, as outrageously independent as ever."

"I'm sorry; I didn't know. I'd have written."

She doubted it but said nothing.

The car was directed by the White House police out to Pennsylvania Avenue, where it headed west.

"I have to tell you that I tried to stop your appointment."

"I was pretty sure you would."

"But now that you have it, I promise you that no one will be more supportive than I, including the president."

"Thank you, Worth. I'll need that, and I'll depend on it." She wouldn't until he proved himself, but she wanted the obligation in place. "Tell me about charm school."

"Well, first of all, my staff will prepare dossiers on each of the members of the Senate Foreign Relations Committee. Then we'll take you away for a weekend or two and perform a little mock hearing, with several talented dips playing the senators and you playing the star."

"That'll be fine," Lily agreed. "Please make sure I know which ones received campaign money from the PACs that the American Israel Public Affairs Committee controls, and how much. They're the ones who'll go after me."

"Don't offer that opinion to anyone else, all right?"

"Everyone's scared of them in this town, aren't they?"

"AIPAC is one fact of life in Washington. There are others. We'll try to create an appropriate prophylactic that fits you."

Lily laughed and looked over at him. He, too, was amused, but was gazing straight ahead, his smile more one-sided than before, his head of dirty-blond hair still noticeably larger than the norm. No signs of age were visible except a certain deepening of his eyes, which may have been fatigue. "I wonder who you are now," he said idly.

"Oh, you know . . ." she answered.

"Not really. I read somewhere that you were seeing Jason Wallace, the publisher."

"A couple of years ago. Not now." He was starting to dig. It was too soon. "And you never married Cassie," she said.

"No," he replied. "She wasn't pregnant after all. She lied," he said as if still surprised that such a thing could happen. "The old trick."

"Did you find out before or after our divorce?"

"After."

"You mean my quick trip from Cairo to Santo Domingo was for nothing," she suggested uncritically, keeping the conversation light.

"Oh, I don't know. It was probably time for us to part company," he answered in kind.

They both rode silently until Lily asked, "Do you still have the house on O Street?"

"Um-hmm. Been done over twice since you've seen it; that's easier than moving when I get restless. Maybe you'd like to come over to dinner?—No, no, I didn't say that." As Lily smiled, he said, "I can't believe my mouth would form those words in your presence."

"I'll come when it's on a guided tour." After a moment, she turned in her seat to face him. "Worth, there are all kinds of minefields for us that we don't really have time to map. I'm not suggesting that the past is forgotten, but I can overlook it if you can."

"I think we pretty much overlooked that past when it was the present. We shouldn't have any trouble with it here in the future." The car was pulling up to the State Department. "We'd better not. The president wants you over there fast. Thanks for the ride. Can you come back this afternoon? We'll take you through NEA, find you office space, get things started."

The car stopped at the curb, because the driveway up to the front door was blocked off by vehicles against possible terrorist attack.

"Do I get to see your office? I've never risen to the great halls of the seventh floor."

"I'll give you no-knock privileges," he said and stepped out of the cab.

Over the next several weeks, Lily shuttled between Washington and New York. Extricating herself from the company she'd created and run for ten years was more emotional than administratively demanding. The appointment dance in Washington was more complex. At the State Department, she quietly familiarized herself with everyone with whom she would work in NEA. In trying to pick a deputy chief of mission, she was dismayed by how many of the good people she'd known in the Foreign Service had left it for lack of opportunity. She attended classes and seminars at the startlingly updated and impressive Foreign Service Institute, and studied the voluminous reporting from the Middle East that had accumulated over the last ten years.

More critical were the carefully orchestrated meetings with influential members of Congress, and specifically the senators who sat on the Foreign Relations Committee, particularly those of the Subcommittee on Near Eastern and South Asian Affairs. Sometimes social, usually informal, but occasionally a direct interview in a senator's office, the discussions inevitably drifted away from Egypt and seized on Israel. A few senators had read Lily's book, or at least their staffs had, and she was questioned extensively about it. Lily didn't back away from anything she'd written and was able to counter objections with other quotes from the book as well as her own reasoning, which seemed to appease them. But she knew as well as anyone that a senator's reaction in private was often quite different from what it would be in a hearing room. Nevertheless, the State Department members who were prepping her, some of whom accompanied her to the Hill, reported that she'd done well.

One evening when she returned to the Hay-Adams, where she continued to stay while in Washington, Lily was given a message at the desk from Worth, marked URGENT. She had seen little of him during the past weeks, although she was certain he had been briefed on every step of her progress. When she dialed the number, he picked up. "Deloit."

"It's me, Worth."

"Lily, we have a problem. Come down right away, please. We're meeting in the crisis control room, sixth floor."

"Who's 'we'?"

"Your team, Lily." He hung up.

At that hour, it took fifteen minutes to reach Foggy Bottom by cab. Lily showed her credentials to the guards in the main lobby and took the elevator to the sixth floor. The crisis control room was nothing dramatically different; it was a large office with a table in the center and telephones on desks by the walls. When Lily came in, she recognized everyone there and sat down opposite Worth at the center table. She waited for him to end a conversation he was having with the director of the Office of Egyptian Affairs.

Worth glanced at her and without any preamble said, "There's been an assassination in Cairo, four hours ago, the head of the Muslim Brotherhood. The assassins got away on motorcycles, going against the traffic on the Corniche along the Nile, right downtown, a couple of blocks from our embassy. Very professional, very well planned. No one has claimed responsibility, and the Brotherhood hasn't accused anyone yet. Cairo is calm. The government has proclaimed national mourning, and a state funeral is being planned for tomorrow." He paused for a reaction.

Lily said, "It sounds as if they're handling it very well."

"Very well, indeed," Worth said with an edge the others responded to by glancing uncomfortably at Lily. "In sweeping through the city in search of the assassins, an Egyptian army unit came on a man who for no reason started to run. They were able to catch him, and when he was brought in for interrogation, he was recognized, under the beard he'd grown, as Abu al-Saffah." Again Worth waited for Lily to react.

"Was he involved in the assassination?" she asked straightforwardly.

"The Egyptians don't think so. He still doesn't seem to know about it, and they believe him. It's pure chance that they got him, and we believe that. He wouldn't put himself in jeopardy if he'd known there was going to be any."

"Let's hope the Egyptians hold him longer than the Italians did. Does the problem you mentioned involve more than this?"

"We're not sure," Worth said, watching her carefully, "but we think so. Al-Saffah hasn't spoken much, but he's referred to you a number of times." He reached over a stack of files in front of him for a cable, from which he read aloud. " 'I will speak only to the newly appointed American ambassador,' he demands. 'Be sure to remind her of our last meeting.' " Worth put the cable down and folded his hands over it. "We thought we'd better review that meeting, since senators are naturally sensitive to meetings with terrorists."

"I have a long history with al-Saffah," Lily began, assessing the dynamics of the room and how best to tell the tale. She did not doubt that Worth had received the information after many other people had known of it, and couldn't speak with her privately.

"We were reviewing that history before you came," he told her; "at least the part of it we know."

"I'm not sure which 'last meeting' he's referring to," Lily said. "Three years ago, he said that he met me in Bahrain but that I didn't recognize him. I don't believe that; I'm sensitive to this man's face. But it may have happened, or he could have seen me from a distance. It was an oil ministers' conference, pretty crowded. Even so, there was nothing particularly memorable as far as I'm concerned."

"You say, 'he said,' " Worth noted.

"He writes me an occasional letter."

Worth nodded, indicating that he remembered. "How often?" he asked for the benefit of the others.

"Once every year, just to let me know he's still around."

"You've submitted those letters to security?"

"For a while, when I was still in the Foreign Service. Since then, I've tossed them. I'm not much for leaving intimidation around the house."

She heard some appreciative sounds from those at the table and smiled slightly to acknowledge them. Worth picked up the cable again and said, "It wasn't Bahrain. He said, 'Be sure to remind her of our last meeting—in Amman.' "

Her fury was instant, but so was her control; she knew how Worth could play on anger. "You left that out, didn't you?"

"Forgive me."

"I'm very happy to answer any questions you have," she said evenly, "but if you're going to select the information you give me in order to trap—"

"No, no. An oversight," Worth said coolly, making light of her concern.

"Do I now know everything that Abu al-Saffah has said about me since his capture in Cairo?" For dramatic reasons, she looked at the dozen people sitting around the table, thereby making them witnesses to Worth's reply.

"Yes, Counselor," he said and dared to smile intimately at her. "And perhaps you'll tell us about Amman," he prodded pleasantly.

There were two other women at the table, another sitting at a desk taking notes of the meeting. The rest were men.

"Abu al-Saffah's men picked me off the street in Amman in nineteen eighty-one, June, I believe. I was taken to a construction site, where al-Saffah gave me another dose of his contempt and anger, after which he gave me to his men so that they could display contempt by gang-raping me. Fortunately I was having my period, which is a severe taboo to any Arab man, even to secular terrorists. I was then locked in a closet and left for dead. In that closet was an Israeli intelligence agent whom they'd tortured and left to die. With great luck, we were able to escape."

Worth asked incredulously, "How?"

"He picked the lock with my IUD."

Most of the male mouths around the table dropped open. Astonishment was apparent in the women's eyes. Worth stared at her, astounded, which almost made Lily smile. One of the women, the Egyptian desk officer, said sympathetically, "There's nothing in your file. Didn't you report this to security?"

"No, for many reasons, some of which I'm sure are obvious."

The deputy assistant secretary for the area cleared his throat and said, "Yes, they are. But you were a Foreign Service officer on duty who was attacked by a foreign terrorist. That's a security matter."

"In all candor, I thought of it as a personal matter between al-Saffah and me. I still believe that. Somehow I've become lodged in his imagination as the symbol of America. The psychiatrists call it a compulsive fixation, something to do with his need to triumph —whether as a male or as a terrorist, no one will speculate. But, whichever, I'm inclined to go along with that interpretation. I'd also admit that the intimacy of the situation, perhaps a certain amount of modesty, kept me from the security office. I wasn't severely hurt by al-Saffah. The United States wasn't involved except in his invective. I figured my history with him gave me the right of choice, and I chose to keep it to myself."

She had spoken to the entire room, but ended with her eyes on Worth, who listened intently. When she finished, it was very quiet, with no indication of her team's reaction until Worth said, "I agree that you had that choice." It was said as an official judgment by the under secretary, and the room reacted with nods of agreement and quick whispers of relief.

"How do we handle this on the Hill?" asked the public affairs officer who had helped to prep her. "I expect that Abu al-Saffah's capture and his demand to talk to her will shortly be news. Might even make her look good to the AIPAC people, her confronting a Palestinian terrorist."

His partner in Lily's charm school, a recently retired ambassador called back for this special service, said, "I think the appropriate senators should be told, privately and discreetly, exactly what happened. After the Clarence Thomas hearings, I can't imagine any of them daring to start a line of questions about picking locks with IUDs."

Before anyone had a chance to laugh, Worth said, "Our only worry is whether Abu al-Saffah has any surprises for us." He spoke softly across the table. "Do you think he does, Lily?"

"Almost certainly," she said. "He's a terrorist, and a terrorist's motivation is to get attention for himself and his cause, which in this case I believe are the same thing. He can say anything, and will. It will be reported. The question is whether he'll be believed. If what he says serves someone's purpose, unfortunately he will be."

"Can't the Egyptians keep him buried in a jail until after the hearing?" the public affairs officer asked and was answered with near-unanimous objection. He held up his hands. "Suggestion withdrawn."

Lily asked, "What do the Egyptians want to do with him?"

Worth picked up the cable again and turned to the second page. "The Egyptians are eager to go on record against terrorism, but they have nothing on this particular terrorist. Apparently he and his people never worked from there or caused any damage. He was using a false passport, so legally all they can do is deport him, in this case to the Sudan. But they don't want to do that. And they're not about to extradite him to Israel." He looked directly at Lily. "The Egyptian government has requested our help and advice."

Lily didn't respond, but decided in that moment what she would do. The only question for her was whether her team could be convinced to support her.

"Would the Egyptians try him?" the former ambassador asked. "I mean as a pretext for deportation."

Worth looked for an answer from the deputy assistant secretary, who said, "There are a good many reasons right now that they might—their sense of leadership in the Arab world, their tilt toward us and the West, their past and present experience with assassinations and terrorists. Also, their neighbor to the south, Sudan, is becoming the haven of choice for terrorists. I think they'd try al-Saffah to stick it to the fundamentalist government in Khartoum —*if* they had a very showy, tight case."

"Such as one bolstered by an eyewitness." The Egyptian desk officer, who said this, let her eyes move to Lily.

The deputy assistant secretary added, "Yes, exactly. They'd have a noisy trial, paint him the villain he is, prove his crimes in front of the world, then extradite him to the country where one of the deeds was done so that he could be tried again and perhaps punished. For Egypt, maximum show, minimum blame."

"The question for us, then," the former ambassador said, "is whether—and how—it might be beneficial for the president's choice as ambassador to Egypt to be the star witness, and, if so, would she?"

Lily took a moment before replying. "Probably the first part of the question is for you to discuss and advise. But there's no doubt about the second part. I have no desire to see this man. In fact, the idea sickens me. But if Egypt wants to take on Abu al-Saffah, I'm obligated and willing to help if it's appropriate. I'd prefer to go with your blessing and the understanding of the president, but you should know that I must go, and that if there's a choice between going and being ambassador, I'd have to give up the latter."

The room remained silent until Worth said, "That sounds like an ultimatum."

"It isn't at all. I have no choice in this. The man's a murderer for hire. He's killed children before my eyes, one of the first of many crimes that have appalled the world. He kidnapped me and attempted to murder me in Amman. He gave the order to kill my father. I'm morally and legally obligated to appear against him, and that obligation—which I'm sure the American public, even senators might understand—is greater than my intense desire to be ambassador to Egypt." She let that sink in while she surveyed the room, trying to sense the reaction. Then she said, "Maybe I should get out of here and give you all a chance to work it over. Is the White House in on this yet?"

"About Abu al-Saffah's capture, yes," Worth said, "and his demands to see you. They're waiting to hear from us."

Lily stood up. "I'll go back to the hotel. Worth, may I speak to you a minute?"

He followed her into the corridor as the rest of the team began to discuss the situation among themselves.

As they walked down the long gray corridor, with its purple locator stripe running the length of the wall, Lily said, "One thing I didn't tell the team. The Israeli agent in the closet with me in Amman was Moshe Levy. It was part of al-Saffah's plan that we die together."

They continued a few steps. "You should have reported it, Lily."

"That judgment's easily made by an outside observer more than a decade later. Having been there, I believe I deserved to choose as I did. You agreed with it in there, for which I'm very grateful."

"Anything else I should know?"

"No."

"You'll hear from us as soon as we bring the White House people into the loop." He started back down the hall, leaving Lily to continue on to the elevator. Then he stopped.

He shook his head once and gazed at her. "You amaze me."

Not sure if his comment was a compliment or an irritation, she smiled, shrugged, and walked on.

———

It was one-thirty in the morning when the phone rang in her suite at the Hay-Adams.

"You travel as a private citizen at your own risk," she heard Worth say, his voice the hollow echo produced by a speaker phone, used for the benefit of the others listening. "Both the White House and the State Department will issue statements that you've elected to go on your own, that your legal obligation is respected, but that the appointment process will be put in abeyance until the situation with Abu al-Saffah is resolved. You remain the president's firm choice, but at that point in the future, the nomination may be reappraised, depending on the outcome."

"Or the fallout. I'll go tomorrow. Before I leave, may I have copies of any current CIA and State Department files on Abu al-Saffah that are available?"

"Done. Let us know your flights. The Egyptians want to provide security. They've made assurances that the matter will be handled with the utmost discretion, that perhaps depositions are all that will be needed. You may not even have to see him."

"Thanks for that. What about my getting in touch with the embassy?"

"They'll make contact with you, but as a private citizen."

"Fine. I'll be on the dahabeah. It'll take a couple of days to get the phone connected."

"I took care of that; it's being done. The team wishes you good luck. They want you to know they support you in spirit much more than the situation allows them to demonstrate."

"Tell them I very much appreciate their support, and that I hope to be back with them soon."

"Good night, Lily," he said, paused as if he were going to say something else, and hung up.

TWENTY-SIX

THE MUEZZIN'S RECORDED CALL from the loudspeaker atop the minaret woke Lily before dawn. The mosque was across the Nile from the dahabeah. She had always been able to sleep through the chanted call to worship, but the jet lag of the trip from Washington had left her sensitive to sound.

> God is most great.
> I testify that there is no god but God.
> I testify that Muhammad is the Prophet of God.
> Come to prayer.
> Come to success.
> God is most great.
> There is no god but God.

Lily followed the chant with her lips and, when it ended, turned to look at the dim design of light filtering through the *mashrabiyyeh* screens in her bedroom. The steady honking and torturing of motors came across the river from the already crowded road on the opposite bank. Somewhere she heard the bray of goats, whether from her side of the river or on a barge floating silently with the current, she couldn't tell. A baby started crying, perhaps very near, having slept with its parents by the river, perhaps far, its voice carried on a single errant early morning breeze.

"Come to success," Lily repeated in Arabic, in this country of fifty-five million with arable land the size of Holland. It had taken her only the drive in from the airport to sense once again the fatalism of the city that she loved, the fatigue of those who tried to live here, beating back hopelessness with eternal humor and fantasies of escape, surviving stagnation and time and dust by not car-ing, praying for death's paradise and dealing with life's hell with a shrug and *"malesh."*

She stretched her arm across the bed, rolled over, and tried to sleep again, but her hand felt the fine sand on the linen sheets. It was there even though the bed had been under two dust covers. The night before, she'd been too tired to vacuum. Not moving, trying to forget the noise and sand, she closed her eyes, knowing she needed more rest. But it wouldn't come. Her mind churned over the quandaries she would face that day.

She would have help—help that she could trust. After the early morning call from Worth—and the strange "Goodnight, Lily," of his official role with its intensity of concern that she could not but believe others of the team had heard—Lily had placed two calls to the Middle East, one to Ammar Ben Ashid in Algiers, the other to Moshe Levy in Tel Aviv. They were difficult to reach, but when she got through and told them her plans, they both agreed to meet her in Cairo as quickly as possible.

From Ammar she wanted diplomatic advice on how best to handle a potentially volatile situation in relation to the Arab world. He could be more objective than her many Egyptian friends. From Moshe, she wanted security. Once Abu al-Saffah's terrorist group knew that she was in Cairo to testify against its leader, the possibility of its trying to prevent her was strong. Although Egyptian security was already in place, Lily wanted an element involved that was unknown to the officials.

She had learned from the CIA profiles that had been delivered to her at Dulles that Abu al-Saffah's Palestinian Command Group had dwindled. At its peak, of two thousand well-trained, well-financed members in the early 1980s, it had proven its capability of inflicting terror around the world. Al-Saffah, having broken with the PLO and accusing it of moderation toward Israel, had attracted young zealots whom he trained to go to any extreme to attack and punish Israel or those he judged were deviating from total rejection of the Jewish state.

More recently, because of heightened antiterrorist activity not only by Israel and the Western states, but also on the part of unsympathetic Arab nations, the PCG had lost large numbers of its most effective members; many were either dead or languishing in prisons throughout the hemisphere. The financing that used to come from a cross-section of Gulf oil states dried up as Abu al-Saffah became identified ever more exclusively as a terrorist for hire instead of one who directed his efforts against Israel. He was often found at the center of internecine struggles within the terrorist movement, to the extent that he and the PCG were shunned, if not marked for death, by his natural allies.

The CIA report concluded that at present he had only a hundred and fifty members still under his control. Many were long-time veterans; most were judged to be mercenaries rather than patriots. The group's recruiting had been abysmally unsuccessful for the last four years, owing mainly to a lack of money and the stultifying, often irrational demands of al-Saffah's most recent sponsor, Saddam Hussein. The PCG had been based in the Iraqi desert for seven years, ever since al-Saffah's banishment from Libya and then Syria. During that time, they had attacked an airport, massacred a synagogue's congregation in Italy, blown up a plane, failed to plant a bomb on another, and fought a pitched battle with a rival terrorist group. They had assassinated a number of Saddam Hussein's enemies abroad and contributed violently to the suppression of dissent in Iraq. One fact Lily had not known was that Abu al-Saffah had been personally responsible during the eighties for developing and protecting Saddam Hussein's biological-weapons program, both in Iraq and Eastern Europe.

In spite of the rhetoric that al-Saffah's group repeated in its propaganda and recruitment, as well as in the occasional, carefully orchestrated press interviews given by al-Saffah himself, the PCG had not done an iota of permanent damage to Israel, and in fact had succeeded mainly in gaining ever-greater sympathy for the Israeli cause and ever-greater opprobrium for "Palestinian" terrorism. After the war in Kuwait, al-Saffah had suffered a personal falling-out with Saddam Hussein over money, and had moved his headquarters to Khartoum.

The profile went over the facts that Lily already knew about his past, his youth in a village near Nablus, the loss of his family's farm to the Zionists, his education, including three years at Cairo University when Nasser was preaching pan-Arabism, and his recruitment by the PLO in the early sixties. There was a list of his family members—his father, brother, and two sisters—who had been killed in the struggle with the Israelis. However, the CIA files didn't offer any hint about why Abu al-Saffah had been in Cairo. To Lily, that was a major mystery.

Outside on the river, Lily heard shouts at the same time that footfalls sounded on the ceiling above her. She slipped out of bed and carefully approached a window, where she saw, through the intricate carvings in the wooden screens, a motor boat moored twenty yards from the dahabeah. In it were three Egyptian soldiers with machine guns yelling at the crew of a felucca, ordering them to take their boat to the far side of the river in order to pass. The soldiers on the roof joined their colleagues in the shouted warning. The crew offered no objection, but stared at the dahabeah as they sailed past.

She thought she might have to move. The special security the Egyptians had supplied was good, as Lily knew from past experience in Cairo, but the protection was too obvious for trained terrorists. She would leave the decision to Moshe when he arrived. Lily doubted that many people knew yet that she had come to Cairo, but the White House would make the announcement that day. Before the press found her, she hoped to have arrived at an agreement with the Egyptian authorities about her role in their case against Abu al-Saffah.

Opening one of her suitcases on the bed, she took off her *galabiyya* and went down to the bathroom for a shower, hoping the water pressure was above a dribble. Again she heard the soldiers above her on the houseboat's flat roof. They had been there the night before, when she arrived in Noorna's car escorted by two military vans full of armed troops. Lily smiled, remembering the objection of her *boab,* Karamat, to their presence. He had been cleaning the first floor when the soldiers arrived earlier in the day. As far as he was concerned, they were neither needed nor welcome. He was proudly possessive of his role on the dahabeah over the past several years, even resentful when, on a few occasions, Lily had arrived with a male companion.

Three, actually. As she showered, Lily thought of them, nice men, attractive, successful, attentive, sensitive, lovers but not loved, fillers of time and the occasional loneliness, the required social partners, the companions of pleasure, but eventually either boring or insistent, and soon after, gone. Ammar and Moshe had woven themselves through those years, both temptations but, for professional reasons, rigidly suppressed. She'd accepted that she would spend her life alone, never admitting so to her mother before she died. Helene, in spite of her constant suspicion of Worth, had seemed to miss him once he was gone.

Lily didn't believe that her own independence was an inherited maternal quirk. Marriage just wasn't the completion of self and life to her that Western culture advertised it to be. And not only Western culture. Her greatest objection to Arab tradition was a woman's hopeless role in it, the main purpose of a wife supposedly being to serve her husband, her primary use being to breed sons. For many Arab men, sons were the only solace for the hopelessness of wasted lives, and if—

The water pressure abruptly dropped, leaving her with a weak spray on her back. She didn't notice. The question she'd been asking herself about why Abu al-Saffah was in Cairo suddenly meshed with her rumination. Could there be a son? That would explain it. She dried herself quickly and dressed, suddenly eager to go to her meeting at the Foreign Ministry.

Karamat greeted her gravely, as was his habit, in the sun room, where he brought her coffee and fresh 'aish, the sweet unleavened bread. *"Hamdillah 'alal-salaama,"* he said—thank Allah for your safety—a common Arabic greeting, perhaps used pointedly that morning, what with soldiers on the roof and river.

"Allah yisallimak," Lily answered—may Allah keep you safe also. "Karamat, I'll be expecting guests today. Two men. If I'm out and they wish to wait here for me, please make them feel welcome."

"Yes, Mrs.," the *boab* responded with only the slightest reproach. He had been informed that she was once married, and form of address was important to him. "But no soldiers, yes?"

"Only if there's a need; then they must come in."

"The names of these men, please, Mrs."

"If they come, they'll say in Arabic that they are old, dear friends of mine. 'Old, dear' are the two important words. If they don't use those words, don't let them in, and go tell the soldiers."

"Yes, Mrs.," he answered, but didn't leave the sun room. When Lily looked at him, he asked, "Do you have a special danger, Mrs.?"

Lily smiled at his concern. "Yes, but I have special protection, too." She glanced up, indicating the soldiers.

With a flick of his hand, he dismissed the usefulness of those on the roof. "You will survive it," he pronounced.

"Insha'allah," Lily added.

"With or without Allah, you will survive it," he repeated as if from secret knowledge, "alone."

Outside, there were calls from the soldiers on the road above to those on the dahabeah's roof, and one of them climbed down the ladder on the side to knock at the houseboat's front door. Lily watched Karamat as she stood and finished her coffee. "Thank you," she said, and started out to the car that had come for her.

"Katar khayrku," he said, bowing and backing out of her way— may your goodness grow even greater.

As she climbed the steps from the dahabeah to the top of the riverbank, she wondered about the *boab's* apparent certainty, and what kind of knowing he had brought from his ancient civilization, now largely submerged under a lake created by the great modern advances of humankind. She passed soldiers in full battle gear with automatic rifles guarding the road above the dahabeah, and stepped into the armored limousine, noting the follow-up van filled with Egyptian commandos. It was the kind of security an American ambassador had to have anywhere in the Middle East; obviously the decision had been made to treat her at that level of risk, although officially she was only a private citizen. As they sped down El Gabalaya and across the island to Tahrir Bridge, she was grateful for Karamat's severe prediction, somehow more trusting of it than of the armament and technology that sealed her off from the dangers of the world as would a padded, air-conditioned sarcophagus.

At the Foreign Ministry, she learned that the Egyptians had arranged for her to identify Abu al-Saffah, then give a deposition, which would be used in a trial to be held at a later date—before, they hoped, she returned to Cairo as American ambassador. For political reasons, they would not extradite their prisoner to either the United States or Israel. If they were unable to document crimes against any other Arab state, they would prosecute him for the atrocity he committed that Lily had witnessed and then send him to Jordan.

Lily argued against their strategy. "Jordan is deeply influenced by the Palestinians. King Hussein wouldn't dare to punish al-Saffah. It'll be like Italy and Libya all over again. They'll send him back to the Sudan."

The Egyptian deputy foreign minister, who chose to speak to her in British-accented English, of which he was proud, smiled a sad acceptance. "That may be so, but his usefulness will be destroyed. We plan to describe carefully his murder of *Arab* children, the damage he has done with his crimes to Arab and Palestinian causes. If Jordan were to let him go, he would become a fugitive, one in considerable danger from his many terrorist enemies, we think."

Lily didn't labor the point, for she had no influence on it. "When I identify him, I wish to have time to speak with him."

The request surprised the deputy foreign minister, who removed his glasses to wipe them with a silk handkerchief he took from an inside pocket of his suit. "We understood that you didn't wish a confrontation," he said, a smile still spreading his thin lips. "It would only be painful to you."

Lily recognized the beginning of an Arab negotiation, at which she'd become skilled in her ten years of making deals for her company. It was convoluted, never confrontational—unless a moment of truth was demanded, when either the dagger was thrust or a retreat was made—its terms suggested elliptically through a gauze of pious praise and courtesy. Contradiction was not used. Any concern about time was considered a weakness; a straightforward demand was considered rude, so much so that the negotiation might abruptly wallow into silence, then end.

"Yes, perhaps painful," Lily rejoined, smiling pleasantly, "but without doubt useful to both our purposes. I have changed my mind about meeting him. He has asked to talk with me. Perhaps he has something important to say."

The deputy nodded agreement, which meant nothing. He continued, thoughtfully, "I cannot imagine that listening to his crude rhetoric, the hyperbole about his cause and about you, would be in any way rewarding, to either of us."

"I agree. You're very wise. I don't think you should listen." The

Egyptian diplomat's eyes squinted at her and he quickly replaced his glasses. Lily continued. "If he is assured our conversation is private, that he is not preaching to you and Egypt and the Arab world, he may reveal more than otherwise."

"Surely he might. Your perception is truly keen. But he summoned you. By giving in to his demand to see you, only you, we his captors may be compromised at his trial. He may assume a status, feel a power over events that we don't wish him to feel."

Lily assented gravely. "We share that concern, and you are right to have it. I can only assure you that by the end of our private meeting, Abu al-Saffah will have gained no power from me. You can be certain that he'll feel less. You must trust me on that."

"Our trust in you is very great. By coming so far, particularly at such a delicate moment in your appointment process, you honor us and give us a genuine opportunity to condemn the terrorism that is the great blight of the Middle East. But I cannot help wondering why this is not enough for you. Why would you wish to be involved in a meeting that cannot but be a painful exercise, with no guarantees of any new discovery, allowing this terrorist an access to the future ambassador of the United States of America?"

"Your questions are justified and show great sensitivity to the circumstances in which I find myself. Knowing the history of this relationship, as you've so well illustrated that you do, you'll understand that there is a deeply personal connection between Abu al-Saffah and me, one that predates and supersedes the symbols we've become. I'm sure that you and the foreign minister can understand my insistence. I believe no one else has a better chance of learning, for instance, why the terrorist was in Egypt and what dangers his presence here may represent to your government."

The deputy foreign minister, still smiling his thin smile, licked his lips and nodded, a nervous gesture that indicated to Lily that she'd made her point. "Nothing is impossible," he said.

"*Insha'allah,*" Lily answered.

"May I have the honor of passing on some of your thoughts to the foreign minister?"

"I'm flattered to have you represent me. Please give His Excellency my respects."

He rose. "You shall hear from us."

"I depend on it, and will wait for your call until tomorrow at noon. I'm honored to be able to serve Egypt, for as a private citizen I owe this country a great deal. But I will understand, as I know you will, that because of many considerations, this opportunity might be lost. If so, I wouldn't think of remaining here to embarrass you or the foreign minister, and I would leave promptly." Then she stood.

"Of course we would understand, but I'm certain the details will find their way into a design satisfactory to us both," he said.

With continued reassurances, he showed her to the door of his office, and a guard escorted her back to the car. As she was driven back to Zamalek, she went over what she had said to reassure herself that her message had been clear—"my insistence," "tomorrow at noon," "I would leave promptly"—the implication being that they would not get her identification of Abu al-Saffah or her testimony unless her terms were met.

As she went down the steps to the dahabeah, she saw Karamat waiting, looking up at the soldiers on the roof with undisguised irritation. When she reached him, he said, "Mrs., one of your visitors has arrived."

Lily crossed the small gangplank and went through the kitchen to the sun room. Ammar stood at one of the windows, looking out at the police boat bobbing on the Nile.

"Hello, Ammar," she said as he turned, gazing at her with a look of affection she had caught on numerous occasions over the last decade. They had met each other all over the world on business, he smoothing her transactions with the many Arab governments and entrepreneurs with whom Isis worked. As Algeria's oil minister and respected negotiator of many Arab countries' disputes with the West and with one another, Ammar had been the first to respond to Lily's idea that the Arab oil countries should not simply sell their crude on the open market, but should refine it and retail it, making profits at all the steps along the way.

Working together, they had drawn up a grand plan of which facilities in Europe could be secured, and Lily presented the first simple step—the purchase of eight gas stations in Sicily—to the Algerian Energy Ministry only four months after Isis International was incorporated. The deal was accepted by the Algerian government—Lily and Ammar had celebrated with champagne—and he subsequently adopted the plan as far as his bureaucracy would let him in Algeria, then introduced it to his colleagues in OPEC. Largely as a result, over the next seven years Isis International brokered the sales of refineries, tankers, and gas stations throughout Asia, the Middle East, and Europe, becoming a major player in the global business of oil.

The reawakening of fundamentalist Islam in Algeria had resulted first in Ammar's divorce and more recently in his resignation from the cabinet. His wife had grown increasingly pious and insistent that he join her in the faith, which he refused to do. Their relationship became acrimonious and finally destructive to them and to their children. The divorce was painfully public and served as a notorious example of the conflict between the secular and the faithful. When the 1989 regional elections in Algeria resulted in a wide gain by the Islamic parties, Ammar was a natural target. His resignation was demanded by a shaky government desperate to erase such a visible secular symbol. The more recent suppression of the fundamentalists by the military had made him a political pariah.

"Ah, Lily, why are you always more beautiful this time than the last?" he said without smiling.

Pleased, she tossed off, "I haven't washed my hair in days."

"The sun has already made love to it, I see."

"No, that was done in a beauty parlor on Connecticut Avenue."

He came over and greeted her, kissing her on both cheeks. "You always refuse me my romantic notions."

"It's just all this reality that creeps in."

He said, *"Malesh";* then they sat down facing each other in two creaking wicker chairs, which they drew close together for privacy. Sitting in the sunlight from the windows, Lily could see the boat with the soldiers guiding the river traffic away from the dahabeah.

"I've spoken to my people in Saudi Arabia," Ammar said, getting right to business, as was his habit ever since she'd known him. "And Syria. They are of the opinion that their governments will not object to an Egyptian trial of Abu al-Saffah—and, tangentially, your testifying against him."

"Syria? Are you sure?"

"Hafez al-Assad wishes to appear the civilized man of peace," he said skeptically. "He's dancing as fast as he can toward the West. Israel, being officially at peace with Egypt, will make a noisy demand for al-Saffah's extradition, which they expect will be refused. However, they won't try to kidnap him from his jail cell, or so my Tel Aviv informant believes. By the way, your planned testimony here confuses Israel's motive for opposing your nomination. Even as someone who's pro-Arab, which they believe you are, you'll still have more to do with an anti-Israeli terrorist's destruction than they. But they plan to deal with you politically in Washington, not here."

"I didn't know there'd been a decision to oppose me."

"Nothing official."

"Just pressure in Congress."

"At which they are skilled. I've heard Congress called 'Knesset West.'"

Lily said, "Perhaps that's changed." Ammar sat back in his chair and gazed out at the river. When he spoke, his voice no longer carried the tone of official business.

"I've known you long enough to acknowledge that the danger, the public pressures that will inevitably descend on you now, won't change your mind about doing all this—testifying here, in Washington, discovering the utter frustration of being an ambassador in a government bureaucracy, practicing the diplomacy of the puppet, bearing your many masters' messages. There's an alternative I want you to know about, even if you won't consider it."

"Oh?" Lily said warily.

"I'm leaving Algeria, moving to Switzerland, as an international consultant on oil. My client list will surely be long, but the thought of going alone to my perfect chalet is quite gloomy. Every time I think of whom I'd like to be there with me, you monopolize my imagination. This Swiss alternative is hereby humbly offered."

Lily sat silently a moment, then leaned sideways and reached for his hand. She held it as she spoke. "I can't consider ways out of this right now. I'm going to confront al-Saffah and, if possible, go through with my appointment. But please know how much I appreciate the Swiss alternative."

He leaned forward and kissed her hand. "Perhaps time will do the tempting for me."

The phone rang. Lily stood instantly, pulling her hand from his. "The Foreign Ministry," she explained and went to the telephone on the bar. "Hello?"

"That's a charming little scene you two are playing," Moshe said in English, "but have you considered shoulder-launched rockets from the opposite bank? Al-Saffah's people love to use those."

"Where are you?" she asked, turning toward the windows.

"In one of the apartment buildings you're looking at now. This nice couple let me in here with my amazing lens, which I'm looking through, because they believe I'm a film maker, scouting locations, talking on the phone now with my English crew about this truly fabulous view. This won't do, Lily. If I can see you, so can anyone else with good binoculars. The soldiers are a disastrous advertisement. I want you out of there immediately, with or without the amorous Ammar Ben Ashid."

"Where do you want me to go?"

"The top floor of a building tall enough so that no one can shoot down on you, a hotel, whatever. Then all these soldiers smoking their Cleopatra cigarettes can control the stairs and lobby. Do it now. I must go. English is upsetting these people."

"What about Noorna's eighteenth-floor apartment on the Nile, other side of Zamalek?"

"I'll see when you get there, but go. Make sure the Egyptians haven't bugged the place, and don't say anything over the phone."

"Will I see you there?"

"No. And don't tell anyone I'm here." He hung up.

When she put the phone down, Ammar asked, "Moshe Levy?"

"You're not supposed to know he's here."

"Did he hear us as well as see us?"

"No."

"Allah be blessed for such small relief. Did you have to bring in the Mossad?"

"He's here as a private citizen, as I am, as you are. He wants me out of here. Says it's dangerous." She started out. "And he's right." She was suddenly alarmed, and hurried through the kitchen to the dahabeah's front door. Why hadn't she at least drawn the sun room's curtains? She couldn't afford to be that careless. "Karamat," she said as the *boab* rose from his chair at the door, "I'm going to stay somewhere else. Pack everything. I'll send a car back for it."

"Yes, Mrs.," he said as he stepped up the stairs ahead of her, leading her to the street to call her a taxi, as was his practice. Ammar followed, but at the same moment they heard the whine of a powerful motor approaching. The soldiers on the roof started shouting. Instantly there was gunfire from the shore, then on the river. Lily was far enough up the steps to see over the roof. A small speedboat was heading directly down the Nile toward the daha-beah. Two men were standing in it, firing automatic weapons. As Lily watched, both were shot and collapsed over the speedboat's windscreen. The boat, locked on course, kept coming. Ammar and Lily tried to run up the steps. She saw soldiers jumping off the roof; some on the bank continued firing. The speedboat careened past the soldiers' boat.

The force of the explosion blasted Lily into the bank and ripped through her head; she blacked out momentarily from the concussion. The first thing she heard was Ammar yelling for help. The first thing she saw was Karamat, lying nearby with blood coming out of one ear. When she reached over to touch his face, his eyes moved slowly to her.

"You will survive it, Mrs.," he said, and died.

TWENTY-SEVEN

"LILY, THEY'RE HERE," Noorna said, standing by the bed in an elegant pants suit, her traditionally hennaed hair rolled in a chic chignon.

Lily opened her eyes and smiled at her friend, then patted the bed for Noorna to sit down next to her. "I'll never forget this. Taking in a terrorist target is beyond the call of friendship."

"You and I went somewhere beyond friendship some time ago," Noorna replied as she sat on the bed. The death of her parents three years earlier and her divorce a year after that had saddened her eyes, but they were no less bright with the anticipation and mischief Lily remembered from their childhood.

Through the two nights since the bombing of the dahabeah, Lily had not slept well. In spite of painkilling drugs, the twenty-three stitches in her chin and the deep bruises and cuts on her legs from flying wood had caused enough discomfort to break through sleep. In preparation for her meeting with Abu al-Saffah that afternoon she'd tried to take a nap, but it was no good. The press had swelled in number to fill the lobby of Noorna's apartment building. Her team at State had called four times, but she hadn't heard from Worth. She'd had to reassure Foggy Bottom that she was not hurt too badly to finish what she'd come to do. Diplomatic and political pressures were building all over the Middle East concerning her testimony and the anticipated trial. And in spite of the security precautions, she was gravely apprehensive about her meeting with Abu al-Saffah.

"Are the children all right?" she asked Noorna. Both had been hurried out of the apartment just before Lily arrived from the hospital after the explosion. The daughter, Amina, was now fourteen.

The son, Anwar, named for Egypt's assassinated president, was seventeen, soon to go to university in Europe.

"They're delighted," Noorna said, laughing. "Since the divorce, their father spoils them outrageously and they take full advantage of him. They've all gone to Alexandria until you leave. None of us wants you to hurry."

"Only a few more days," Lily said as she stood and limped over to the full-length mirror to brush her hair and put on her suit. "I'll see him today, and give my deposition tomorrow."

"I wish you'd stay here, use this as your residence when you come back as ambassador," Noorna said. "What a ball we'd have! Talking about everything the way we used to at the club, giving parties, trading beaus, creating scandal—the Wild Divorcées of Zamalek, they'd call us."

"I doubt whether the United States would look kindly on that arrangement. They're spending twenty billion a year on security now. Once they have a cage, they have to keep a bird in it."

"For that they tore down the lovely old Chancellery. Those hideous office towers make your embassy look like an airport. And that grotesque prison wall around it. They say it can stop tanks."

"Remember the parties on the Chancellery's lawn?"

"It's as if the terrorists had succeeded in making you prisoners."

"We'll have fun anyway, if I make it back."

"Is there any doubt?"

"A lot. The kind of show that's going on here doesn't lend itself to objectivity about a nomination. If it goes too far, I may decide it's best to withdraw."

"Never do that, Lily. Stay and fight for it, make them tear it away if they're going to. You're the right person for this position. We need you here. Don't give it up."

Lily saw Noorna's reflection in the mirror. She'd stood up and spoken with the same intensity Lily had seen many times. Lily smiled. "Is that how you got those twelve million condoms from the UN?"

Noorna laughed again. "Exactly right, and you know I still have eleven million, nine hundred, ninety-nine thousand left? My clinics started to pass them out to the wives, but as expected, the husbands were too embarrassed or proud to use them. They gave them away to the children to make water bombs. We'd walk down an alley where we thought we'd had a big success and find exploded condoms all over the place. There was a great joke about the power of Egyptian men's ejaculations."

Lily laughed aloud. "I've got to get going," she said and started for the door, then stopped and reached out for Noorna's hand. "You always make me laugh."

"Don't let Abu al-Saffah touch your life anymore. Leave him to the jackals."

Lily watched the force on her friend's face play across her full cheeks and dark eyes. She tried to take the courage that Noorna offered, but even going out of the bedroom caused her anxiety.

Noorna's marbled, all-white penthouse living room opened on three sides to a wide, flower-filled terrace, where an Egyptian colonel conversed with Ammar. Two armed commandos in civilian clothes were waiting by the front door. No one spoke. Lily and Ammar were led to the elevator, which took them down to the second floor. A woman stepped on with another commando. The woman had on a wig of sun-streaked hair and large dark glasses. Wearing one of Lily's dresses, she was made up to look as much like Lily as possible. Lily reached out to correct a wave of the wig and wished the woman luck in Arabic.

Ammar, who had acted as her press spokesman over the last few days, touched Lily's hand as she left the elevator with one of the commandos. He led her to a back stairway and an exit to an alley. Two black-and-white taxis waited, one filled with more commandos dressed in civilian clothes. Once inside the first taxi, Lily listened for the sirens from the decoy motorcade as it left the front of the apartment building with the disguised woman and Ammar, headed for the central jail. When the sirens reached their peak, Lily's commando driver moved the taxi inconspicuously out of the alley and into traffic.

The technique was of Moshe's devising; he had delivered it to her in the medical facility at the U.S. Naval Observatory Center, where Lily was taken after the explosion. Within an hour of her arrival, he had appeared at her bedside attired in a doctor's white coat laden with the requisite identification tags, which showed him to be Dr. Richard Miano, recently arrived on staff from Walter

Reed in Washington. How he'd managed the disguise he didn't allow Lily to ask, even when he'd pulled the curtains around her bed in order to examine her. He was all business, checking her wounds, asking what the doctors had done, what medicine they'd used, then giving her careful instructions about security. When he was satisfied she had been well cared for and understood the details of what she had to do to survive, he leaned forward, kissed her, and said, "I love you." Then he disappeared through the drawn hospital dividers.

Since then, she'd seen him only once; he was wearing a *galabiyya* and was among the surprisingly large group of mourners who turned up to bury Karamat the next day in the City of the Dead. There'd been as many Egyptian soldiers as friends of the *boab*, for Lily's insistence on being there was regarded by the Foreign Ministry as a serious security risk. From his scowl, she could tell that Moshe was also not pleased that she had chosen to attend, so dangerously exposed.

In spite of everyone's objection, Lily was determined to see the *boab* put in the dusty earth. He had purchased a small walled plot for the purpose. Already someone had set up housekeeping in a makeshift tent against one wall to act as caretaker of the tomb, another Cairo adjustment to overpopulation and housing shortages. Standing in the hot sun as a sheikh read from the Koran, Lily tried to understand Karamat's unlucky fate, the will of Allah, *malesh*. The pride in his reassurance to her was heartbreakingly clear. Lily left the funeral burdened with mourning and guilt.

Now, as her taxi crossed Tahrir Square, the wound on her chin began to throb painfully. The bandages over the stitches had been changed that morning by an American doctor who'd come to Noorna's apartment and later addressed the press downstairs about her condition. He'd explained to Lily that plastic surgery could remove any remaining scar when she returned to the United States. The wound ran from the center of her chin along her left jaw, and the doctor commented, as had all the others who'd seen her, on her being lucky that whatever caused the injury had missed the carotid artery, only inches away. Lily carried pills for pain in her handbag, but she didn't want to take one lest it affect her concentration with Abu al-Saffah. She rubbed her left leg gingerly near a particularly painful bruise below the knee, which, she saw, had turned a deep purple.

The two taxis drove slowly through afternoon traffic and headed south into Islamic Cairo. The Egyptians had chosen the meeting place, which met her demands of privacy and their concerns for security and logistics. Even Moshe had approved, but still had warned her—unnecessarily—to stay well clear of Abu al-Saffah.

As they drove up to the entrance of the Ibn Tulun Mosque, Lily saw several troop transports parked in a line on the street. Soldiers were already stationed every ten feet on top of the walls of the mosque and along its entryway. Accompanied by the commandos from the taxi that had followed hers, Lily went hurriedly to the double door leading into the open center court of the mosque. There, under the scrutiny of more commandos, she relinquished her shoes to a white-robed caretaker, who substituted a pair of cloth slippers, which he tied on behind her ankles. Then, escorted by a single commando, she entered the court.

She saw the figure seated in a chair halfway between the center fountain and the *mihrab,* a niche in the eastern wall that indicated the direction of Mecca. Soldiers were spaced evenly along the crenelated tops of the walls, adding their armed emphasis to the perfect symmetry of the open space. As she walked in, Lily remembered the first time she had come to Ibn Tulun as a child with her father. They had entered at the same door, and she had stopped, transfixed with the purity and magnificence of the mosque's design, amazed at the intricate details of the stucco carvings on the arches of the walls, each different from the other, in contrast to the simplicity of the white stone paths radiating from the center of the open square and the massive stone fountain for ablutions before prayer. She had let go of her father's hand and walked into the court with her arms out, staring at the minarets as if she would fly up to them. In her eight-year-old fervor, she had called to her father, "This is what beauty is, isn't it?" and she remembered his delighted laugh echoing into the same archways that surrounded her now as she limped closer to the shackled form of Abu al-Saffah.

He was bound to a metal chair with handcuffs, leg irons, and chains. The commando who accompanied her motioned for her to remain at a safe distance, then stepped forward and stripped off al-Saffah's blindfold. Walking backward, with his automatic rifle pointed toward the terrorist, he retraced his steps to the entrance. Lily stood alone, beginning to sweat but not from heat. She thought how easy it would be to leave, and how difficult it was to control her fear.

Even though his chair had been placed in the shade of the center fountain, Abu al-Saffah was momentarily blinded as he looked around, apparently unaware of where he was. Lily was surprised by how he had aged. His cheeks were deeply lined, and his hair, once so black, had thinned and turned a muddy gray. Yet the eyes, still dark and moist, stared out with a vicious and feral intent, and his mouth hung open like that of a rapacious predator, revealing his gold teeth. He noticed the soldiers stationed on the walls, and as he turned his head from one side to another, he became aware of the figure standing before him. The old scars on his temple had grown slick and discolored with time. He blinked several times and squinted before recognition suddenly appeared on his face, along with a bitter smile. Then, testing the give of his chains, he looked around again.

"What is this place you've brought me to?" he asked in Arabic.

"You never saw this?" she asked, controlling her voice. "You were a student in Cairo for three years."

"I never went to the Pyramids, either. I had better things to do."

"This is the oldest mosque in Cairo," Lily said, using the details to settle down, watching him as he gazed about, "built by Ahmed ibn Tulun in eight seventy-nine, one of the greatest examples of Islamic architecture, one of the most beautiful buildings in the world."

"And you are my tour guide," he mocked.

"We're here because you can be easily guarded while we talk without being overheard by anyone."

"Directional microphones? Close-up camera lenses? Lip readers? Nonsense," he said dismissively. "They listen to my stomach growl."

"As I remember, you said that in Rome."

"Yes, Rome," he responded with an ironic smile as he pulled at his chains. "A similar circumstance."

"This time I've made sure we can't be overheard. This space is too large for microphones. We can speak softly and turn our heads to prevent any possible understanding. I want privacy because I haven't come to listen to you give sermons. You asked to talk to me. Here I am." She had surprised herself with a steady voice.

They both turned to watch a helicopter fly low over the mosque, its rotor wash buffeting them for a moment before it rose and circled idly northward but remained in view.

When the noise subsided, Lily explained, "That's in case your people come after you by air. A squadron of the Egyptian Air Force is on full alert."

"With all their gleaming American weapons, always given so freely to American lapdogs." He looked at her, taking notice of the bandages on her face. "You are wounded?"

"My dahabeah was blown up by your men."

He said coldly, "No doubt they died. You didn't."

"No. I'm very much alive. The Egyptians have asked me to identify you and testify against you."

He blew his lips together to make a contemptuous, dismissive sound, and asked, "You received my letters?"

"Yes."

"And?"

Lily blew her lips together with similar contempt. "They revealed you as you are." Her anger was finally in play.

"What am I?"

"A man of doubt who needs to yell in order to convince yourself that you're still important, that you've accomplished something to be remembered beyond your bloody acts. You write me sadistic reminders of what you consider your great triumphs over the Satan America, and of the presumption of whorish women like me. You also write to history, to your people, as if they'll read your words one day and give you your rightful place in their heritage. You fool yourself. The letters show you howling on paper with pathetic self-delusion. You should be grateful that I threw all of them away."

His eyes flared. "If I'm so pathetic, look around this most beautiful mosque. Tell me why I'm guarded so, and why the future ambassador from America comes at my bidding."

"Think carefully, Abu al-Saffah," Lily said, furiously calm, eager to destroy his conceit. "The Egyptians would have been happy to have you rotting in a jail cell, listening to the screams in the walls. You're here, the troops are here, only because of me. And I'm here not as the future ambassador, but as a witness to some of your crimes, and the daughter of a diplomat you chose to have killed." She looked away, for her anger had begun to flow too freely, dangerous so early in a negotiation. "I've thought for some time that the murder of my father was when your devotion to any cause became corrupted by your need for political power, aggrandizement, and of course your share of the oil countries' money."

"My cause was, is, and ever will be the destruction of the Zionist state some call Israel, which has for decades ravaged the soul of my people, stealing their land, crushing any hope of survival—"

"Remember, no one else can hear us." Her interruption irritated him and he shifted in his chair, the rattling of his chains on the metal echoing across the open space to the arches around them. "And tell me how," Lily continued, "your slaughter of Saddam Hussein's enemies in Iraq, or murder of Muammar Qaddafi's opponents in Europe served the Palestinian people. That's nothing but murder for money."

"Like all Americans," he said patronizingly, "you can't understand the importance of violence to the Arab mind. There is a respect gained, a reputation enhanced—"

"Not by killing innocent people, the congregation in a synagogue, the passengers—women, children—on an airliner."

"They were Jews in the synagogue," he offered as an obvious explanation.

"There's no respect for slaughter," Lily shot back. "You get only revulsion for your people and a reputation for cowardice."

"The plane," he continued, ignoring her interruption, "all the planes brought attention to a state of horror that the world had disregarded—and still overlooks, wishing the Palestinian people would just go away, as Israel systematically suppresses them, puts them in concentration camps, and tortures them. You know this. It's in your book."

"You're still living in the past. The Palestinian people have gone forward, made you irrelevent. The terrorists can justify themselves only by terrifying their own people now. If Palestine is created," she said, "it'll be diplomacy, not terrorism, that creates it."

"The way Western diplomats created the Middle East so brilliantly after the First World War?"

"We're not here to change each other's mind, are we?"

Neither looked at the other in the silence that followed. Lily shifted her weight from one foot to the other. Her leg had begun to bother her.

"I wish to negotiate an urgent matter of international importance," he said intently, "and you're the diplomat I know best."

"I'm here as a private citizen. I have no authority from either Egypt or the United States. I'm in no position to help you."

"*I* want no help. I need no help from you," he stated angrily. "I'll survive this or not; it doesn't matter anymore. It's about someone else."

Noting his fatalism, Lily seized on the opportunity to chance her guess. "Your son?"

His hands tensed in their shackles and his head moved only slightly from its slumped posture. He stared at her; then fear lifted his brow. "What do you know?" he asked, then choked drily.

She hadn't been sure until that moment that seeing him would have any result at all beyond mutual recrimination. But because of her hunch, Abu al-Saffah's presumption had to be that she knew a great deal about his son instead of nothing. She stood without moving, pain pulsating through her jaw as she said, "Why don't you tell me what you want."

He slumped again and looked around the mosque; the sun had sunk farther to darken the shadow of the center fountain over him. "I want my son to live. Do you have him, too?"

Lily shook her head. "You know there's nothing I can do or tell you."

He pulled hopelessly at his chains, then collapsed against his chair. "I know exactly what you can do. With what I can tell you, you'll speak directly to the president. But you must agree in the president's name to—"

"The United States has a well-established policy of not negotiating with terrorists. I can't speak for the president or the United States, only as a private citizen. And I'll promise you nothing."

"You have access to as much power as you need. Look at all this."

He gestured toward the walls of the mosque with his head. "Use that power to save my son."

"Why?" she said, losing her temper, but not raising her voice. "Why should I make the slightest effort to save your son? I don't even want to listen to you." She started walking toward the entrance, limping, glad for the chance to move, needing the interruption to control herself.

"Then save Israel," he called.

Lily kept limping along the walkway in spite of her alarm at his implication.

"Fool! Bitch!" he yelled, the chains grating on his chair. "You'll be cursed from this day—" He stopped abruptly because Lily had begun walking back to him. She took her time, stretching her legs, letting the blood circulate from the slight exercise.

"How old is your son?" she asked when she stood again at a safe distance.

"Fourteen."

Lily gave al-Saffah a withering look. "For him, I'll listen for three minutes. I'll tell you nothing of what we may or may not know about him."

He nodded as if formal terms were agreed, but hesitated as he made a decision. Then he began speaking quickly. "I was in charge of security for Saddam Hussein's biological-weapons program," he said, as if reporting, "not only in Iraq but in Europe, for supplies and subcontractors. One of those I worked with was an Englishman living in Brussels, Dr. James Rector, a genius of biochemistry, whom his own government at first had acclaimed, but then disavowed. When he lost government support and started a private business, they hounded him into tax court, a short term in prison. He left his country a bitter man, set up in Belgium. There, among other things, he discovered a synthetic hormone. When introduced into a male animal, it enters the bloodstream, interacts in the testes to sterilize, painlessly, with no side effects or interruption of sexual activity. In humans the sterility wouldn't even be noticed until children were not born. By the time Dr. Rector was able to isolate the hormone—he worked very hard to be certain it could be suspended and transported in nothing more complicated than water" —he paused for emphasis—"I'd convinced Rector that Saddam was unwilling to pay him any longer because of the various war adventures in Iran, then Kuwait. I wanted personal control of that particular product. I told Rector that I would find the money for the hormone's further development. I demanded sufficient quantity to prevent the birth of an entire generation of Jews in Palestine. My British genius therefore became financially dependent on me. He was also driven by devils to wipe out the Zionists."

"Why?" Lily asked, regretting immediately any display of interest.

"He was a true British bigot," al-Saffah said and smiled. "The son of a solicitor and an admiral's daughter, had every advantage, was convinced that Jews were the main problem in the world, responsible for his troubles as they began to happen. He had no reason for hate, as we do. He was determined to prove that biology was a greater weapon against the Jews than bombs or missiles—ovens and gas." He smiled at Lily. "His motive was his business, the hormone was mine. It was a brilliant weapon, a powerful hormone in a half-gallon container, easier to transport than an A-bomb or a Scud missile. We could have used typhus bacilli, but they would have been detected instantly when people started to die. With this, suspicion doesn't even begin for nine months." He laughed triumphantly. "There'd be no international reaction, for who would there be to react to?"

He paused, but Lily said nothing.

"Answering your question took my time," he said. "I'll need more."

"You were going to tell me about your son."

"Stop playing this game with me," he shot back. "You want to hear what I have to say. Admit it. This is not diplomacy anymore. It's war."

"No, not yet. It's about genocide, and the life of your son. So get on with it."

He stared beyond her for a moment at the fountain. "My son was born in Beirut. I never knew of his existence until he was seven. His mother—I was not married to her, only saw her on those few occasions when I returned to Beirut. She died in the Zionist slaughter at Sabra, about which I remember you once spoke so eloquently on television. The boy, four at the time, survived. He was cared for

by an aunt who told no one who he was—as his mother had not—
for by then, no one could be trusted with information about me or
such a vulnerability as a son. After three years, his aunt was finally
able to inform me about him, and I arranged for them to leave
Beirut for Cairo. They've lived here ever since."

"A privileged life for a Palestinian boy," Lily said, "a terrorist's
luxury to have his son comfortably out of harm's way, living in
Cairo, like Arafat in his luxury hotel and private jets in Tunis. A
long way from the Occupied Territories, isn't it? At fourteen, most
of those boys have been attacking the IDF with rocks."

"He's been raised for more important work," al-Saffah said sarcastically. "Not for him throwing rocks, then capture, Israeli torture in their concentration camps, which they model on those they
remember so well from Poland and Germany."

"Don't be ridiculous. What does your son have to do with this
hormone?"

He paused before answering. "He and I could have created a
nation of Jewish eunuchs, a withering away of the Zionist population. That, combined with the resulting economic catastrophe and
the present phenomenon of the Jews leaving their promised land of
milk and honey for almost anywhere else in the world they can go
—my son, in his time, would lead a force through a deserted Jerusalem and on to the sea, at last ridding the world of this thieving,
grafted state of Jews called Israel."

Lily let him sail for a moment before saying, "You're as crazy as
your biochemist. And whatever happened to him?"

Al-Saffah smiled darkly. "Always working, aren't you? He's
dead, murdered outside his apartment in Brussels in March, two
shots in the back of his head, the signature of the Mossad."

"You think the Israelis know about Rector?"

"Something. Not as much as you, now. Not that he'd already
produced enough of the hormone to do the job, or that I had it.
Their policy of assassination is either prevention or vengeance. In
this case, they were too late."

"And your son has this magic hormone?"

He watched her carefully. "If you have him, you perhaps know
that. If you don't, you'd better admit it. There is a plan he'll try to
carry out."

Lily met his eyes and came to a decision. "Where is he?"

"Will you save him?" he said without pleading, strictly as a negotiation point.

She felt anger again. Immediately she suppressed it. "The murderer of my father now asks me to save his son. I told you, I'll make you no promises. Obviously *you* can't save him, so you'll have to trust me, won't you? And I can do nothing until I know where he is."

"I don't know where he is."

Lily stepped forward in irritation, but he went on before she could speak.

"I planned this last triumph for me and my son, so that the future would know of us, and his future in Palestine would be assured. But he can't do it alone, though he'll try. He's brave beyond his years, having had no childhood. Without me, he'll be killed. You must stop him."

"How?" Lily asked impatiently.

"When the Egyptians caught me, we had two routes to Israel under consideration. They've kept me incommunicado until today, not even letting Arab League lawyers in to talk with me. I'm sure when I disappeared, my son went ahead. His aunt and he knew all that was necessary. Only the three of us knew of our plan." He looked at Lily again for emphasis, this time smiling maliciously. "Your book, *Pawns and Dice,* I had read to me. Your analysis of Israel's water system gave me the idea of how to spread our biological scourge. Once again, you've been useful to me. I arrived in Cairo overland from Khartoum with the hormone container only a week ago. My son and I mapped three possible locations where we could drop the hormone into the main aqueduct leading south from Lake Tiberias. From there, as your book so magnificently describes, the water flows to eighty percent of the Jewish households—"

"That aqueduct is very heavily guarded, day and night."

"Yes, so my son won't be able to get through without me. You must stop him before he gets there."

"I don't know if you can possibly be this insane," Lily said, "but what about the more than a million Arabs who live in Israel, the Palestinians in the Israeli prisons, in Gaza, on the West Bank?"

"As you well know," he answered angrily, "the Zionists steal all the water from the West Bank aquifers, and the West Bank drinks the damp sand that's left over." He tried to keep his anger, but it wavered. Instead, he became contemptuously off-handed. "About the others—the innocent always suffer."

Lily took several steps toward him, dangerously close, and bent over to look directly into his face. "Don't dare plead insanity at your trial," she said. "I'll make sure they'll never believe it. Have you ever wondered how your biochemist genius tested his hormone, measured the long-term effects you accept? Or was he just feeding you bigotry to your taste, and selling you nothing but a fancy birth control hummus while living the good life on your money in Brussels? You see, no one would consider you crazy—only a fool."

She expected him to rage, yell, or spit at her, try to bash her with his head, the only part of him free to move. But he remained motionless, watching her with bitter fatigue. Before he even spoke, she knew she had to believe him.

"I had his molecular modeling checked by others with computers. If you're very clever, you'll someday discover a small town in West Africa with a single well, where, mysteriously, there hasn't been a birth in three years." Then slowly he leaned toward her as far as his chains allowed. "Save my son," he commanded.

"How much time is there?" Lily asked, again standing back from him.

He glanced at the sun's height in the sky behind the fountain. "If he left Cairo as we'd planned, twenty-two hours."

"What's the plan? Is his aunt still in Cairo?"

"Yes. There's an alley off al Mahatta in Giza—it has no name, the fourth in on the left from the station, a baker at the corner. Walk to the end, there's a building, old green paint. On the third floor, she'll be waiting to hear from me. Her Palestinian name is Zenovialle, which no one knows in Cairo but me. She will listen to you if you don't terrify her. She will be scornfully courageous if you do. She loves the boy very much. The plans, maps, routes, everything is there. I'm sure your diplomatic skills can convince her to share them with you, and tell you which way the boy chose to go."

Lily stood silently, her mind sorting final details.

"What kind of container is the hormone in?" she asked, as if she were an ally.

"A lab vial sealed in a thermos bottle, Scotch plaid, the MacLeod tartan, it says. He picked it out himself at a stand in the Ezbekiah Gardens."

"If I succeed, I'll expect never to hear from you or see you again, no matter what happens at your trial and after."

"You'll just have to trust me, won't you?" he said with a sneer.

"What if I hadn't come? Who would have saved your son?"

"No one!" he shouted. "The Egyptians would botch it; the Israelis will gladly kill him. Remember that, if you're tempted to call them in. Remember that my son will react to any alarm, give up our plan, and make his own. I know how much you'll want to save him; it'll make you feel so righteous, so superior to the man who killed your father. Well, help yourself, but let him live."

"Not superior, only human."

Lily walked along the straight pathway leading from the fountain to the side exit. The commando who had escorted her came forward and asked if she was finished, then hurried past her with Abu al-Saffah's blindfold, rifle ready. At the door, the caretaker had to call to her to remove the slippers and replace her shoes, which she had forgotten. After giving him the customary baksheesh, Lily hurried toward her taxi, accompanied by the phalanx of commando guards.

Then Lily saw Moshe standing behind a barrier set up for the tourists who had been prevented from entering the famous mosque while she'd had her conversation. She spoke quickly to her escorts, who followed her as she approached the crowd. Moshe was alarmed and tried to back away, but when she called him by name and signaled urgently to him, he stepped forward.

"Come to the taxi, Moshe. I need you with me now."

He shrugged but followed her. Once they were in the back seat, Lily began speaking quietly in English so that the Egyptians in the car wouldn't understand her. "Moshe, there's an imminent threat to Israel that I have to deal with instantly. I want your help but only on the condition that you not notify your government or the Mossad until I say so."

The taxi began moving.

"What authority am I dealing with?" he asked.

"None. We'll have to trust each other as private citizens."

"I've done that for years."

"This is different."

"Is the threat catastrophic?"

"Yes."

"Nuclear?"

"No."

"Can I trust you to negotiate in good faith at any time if the circumstances demand notification of Israel?"

"Yes, but my decision is the final one. Otherwise, I'll let you out here."

"You cut a deal like a diamond. I have to agree."

"And nothing personal can be involved."

"Of course not, although an acknowledgment of what I said yesterday in the hospital would be appreciated."

"It's acknowledged, Moshe, but I can't respond right now."

"I look to the future. What'd al-Saffah say?"

As they were driven back to Noorna's apartment building, Lily wrote notes of her conversation with Abu al-Saffah and explained to Moshe with short bursts of information what they were confronting. Again to avoid the press in the lobby, Lily and Moshe went through the back entrance. By the time they rode in the elevator to the eighteenth floor, Moshe was firing questions at her faster than she could answer, and she begged him to wait until they could sit down with Ammar and Noorna. She had decided that official channels, either American or Israeli, would never be able to react fast enough or subtly enough to do what had to be done.

But something was different outside Noorna's apartment door. There were two American security men waiting with the Egyptians already posted there. When the door opened, Ammar held it with a disgruntled look on his face. Beyond him, in the living room, Lily saw Worth looking alert and expectant, standing in the white room wearing a dark diplomat's suit, talking with Noorna, who turned to give Lily her most knowing smile. When Noorna saw Moshe, she rolled her eyes in expectation.

TWENTY-EIGHT

I'M DUE at a disarmament conference in Geneva in three days,"
Worth stated quickly after introductions, not pleased with having to share the explanation with the two men who stood on
either side of Lily. He didn't like Noorna's amused smirk either. "I
flew over early because . . . Maybe we'd better speak alone, Lily."

"There's no time," she answered. His raised brow indicated that
he wasn't used to being put off. "What is it, Worth? Is something
wrong?"

For an instant, she saw a glimmer of his disappointment at not
seeing her alone. Then he went official. "The president is concerned." It was an obvious warning.

Lily disregarded it. "I've just met with Abu al-Saffah. There's a
crisis. We'd like you to be involved."

"Who's 'we'?" Worth asked.

"The four of us," Lily said, looking from Noorna to Moshe to
Ammar, none of whom seemed enthusiastic about Worth's inclu-
sion even in something they so far knew little about. "We may
need your clout," Lily continued, "but you have to agree to say
nothing to anyone outside this room. Otherwise you'll have to
leave."

Worth treated the others to his own version of diplomatic disdain. "Agreed," he said to Lily. "It'll be intriguing to see the inner
workings of Isis International."

"We'd better sit down," she suggested as she led them into
Noorna's dining room. "The first thing we have to talk about is a
Dr. James Rector."

For the next ten minutes, they discussed the dead biochemist
and the viability of a hormone that could cause sterility. Moshe

378

knew a great deal about the man because of the Mossad's careful attention to his activities over the past decade. Whether it was the intelligence agency that shot him was not considered. Surprisingly, Worth was forthcoming with added information that had crossed his desk over the past several years, not as specific as Moshe's, but useful in clarifying the scientist's financial and political ties to Iraq. After Lily's concise questioning, the conclusion was reached that Dr. Rector was certainly capable of having delivered an effective sterility hormone, so the threat could not be overlooked.

For the next half hour, Lily used her notes to re-create in explicit detail her conversation with Abu al-Saffah, pausing only to describe the dialogue's emotional context. They had spoken Arabic and because all her listeners were fluent, Lily used that language in the telling, occasionally breaking into English for some of the details. The effect of her reporting was obvious; they listened with expressions of increasing astonishment and horror.

"That's truly diabolical," Noorna said when Lily finished.

"I don't care what al-Saffah thinks," Ammar suggested; "we have to notify the Mossad, even the Israeli Defense Force, to stop the boy."

"We will if we have to," Moshe said. "But a boy with a thermos is not easily found. A public alarm would be noticed, the boy might panic, do something unplanned and therefore undetectable. There'll be time to notify Israel—to stop drinking water—if we fail. But now we have to find the aunt."

Out of the agreement around the table came Worth's question. "Lily, how great an obligation do you feel to save the boy?"

She faced him and felt the others watching her. It was so like Worth to cut through the surface drama and excitement and get at the emotional vulnerabilities. "He's fourteen," she said, "doing his father's bidding. I plan to get him out of it alive. But I accept that it may not be possible."

"You have a plan?" Worth asked.

"Half formed, but a definite intention. What's your fix on this so far?"

Aware of her parry of his question, Worth replied, "I think Moshe's right about not contacting anyone just yet. Obviously the aunt is next. Al-Saffah warned you against threatening her. We have to think about what her state of mind must be, her relative domestic calm as surrogate mother suddenly obliterated by her brother-in-law's capture, her sending the boy away, probably to his doom. She probably expects discovery, has nowhere to go and little to live for. Under those circumstances, our best bet is a very gentle confrontation. What if Lily and Noorna went over to Giza wearing *abbayyas* so you don't attract attention getting out of here or going down the alley to her apartment. You know her real name. That'll get you inside the door. She'll be more inclined to talk to women than to men. Moshe goes separately and does his invisible security, and Ammar and I stay here by the phone as the crisis team, working on strategy and logistics. We'll meet back here after you've finished with the aunt, ready to move."

No one spoke until Noorna stood up and motioned to Lily, saying, "Come on," and went into the kitchen. Lily watched the three men, who eyed each other but offered no objection. Moshe stood up, said, "I'll be there," went to the front door, and left. Ammar remained seated, took out a small notebook and pen, then slipped out of his suit coat and hung it on the back of his chair.

Lily had to pass Worth on her way to the kitchen. As she went by, she put her hand gently on his shoulder. An old habit; she had done it many times during dinner parties at the house on O Street when they couldn't speak but she wished a touch of intimacy. He turned his head in time to catch her smile of gratitude.

In the kitchen, Noorna was already speaking with her cook and, through an open door, to the woman who did ironing in the laundry room. The two servants stood transfixed, one holding a ladle in midair, the other her iron, as Noorna explained that she needed their clothes, no, not clean, the ones they had on, their head veils and the thick black *abbayyas,* which covered them from neck to foot. Even as the two women objected, Noorna led them with Lily to her dressing room and offered them appropriate, though luxurious substitutes.

Within minutes, the four women had changed clothes. The two servants were still modestly covered from head to foot but in elegant linens of various beige hues; Noorna and Lily, in their black *abbayyas,* had covered their hair with veils. After the servants left, Noorna applied make-up to Lily's face and black kohl to her eyes.

Then, from a drawer she pulled two black silk scarves and fashioned face veils, *nikabs* worn over their noses so that only their eyes could be seen. Returning to the dining room, they interrupted Worth and Ammar and stood silently for inspection.

"Are the *nikabs* too much?" Worth asked.

"These days, more and more women are wearing them," Noorna said.

"Lily," Ammar said, "you're standing too straight. Settle down on your hips. Roll a bit when you walk."

After Lily made the adjustment, Worth said, "You may as well go out past the press in the lobby. That'll be as good a test as any. Noorna, do you have any maps of Israel?"

"There are road maps in the bottom left drawer of my desk in the study. Come on, Lily."

The two friends were silent in the elevator. It slowed to a stop. Lily stepped out into the lobby, Noorna beside her. They averted their eyes appropriately from the inquisitive but momentary stares of the journalists and cameramen who stood or sprawled on the floor of the lobby. The two women quickly padded across the rug to the front door, which a *boab* held open for them. He watched them with too much curiosity, and Noorna ended it with a quick command as she passed him. She and Lily walked down the sidewalk to make sure no one followed, then hailed a taxi.

Neither spoke until Lily said, "You should talk to her first, find out what she thinks of me before she knows it's me. No telling how her brother-in-law prepared her."

Noorna agreed. "I'll try. I just hope he didn't leave her with a gun."

"Nice thought."

They rode on silently and reached the Giza Station at the bottom of al Mahatta in fifteen minutes. There, they dismissed the taxi. Al-Saffah's directions were precise, and they found the alley several minutes later. The sun was setting; darkness had risen to the tops of the alley's buildings. Their disguises were so effective that they drew little attention as they made their way to the crumbling building. Once painted a florid green, it was now faded and flaked, revealing large cloud shapes of sandy stucco. Children, chickens, and fetid puddles made walking in the alley a careful exercise. The noise of people yelling from one window to another, and the blare of radios and tape decks playing Egyptian music or rock-and-roll, made any further talk between the two women impracticable.

The building's doorway was open, its stairs rancid with varied excrements. They climbed the three stories into deepening darkness and reached a small, unlit landing facing an ancient wooden door of heavy splintered molding. After exchanging looks with Lily, Noorna knocked. There was electric light leaking around the door, but there was no answer. Noorna knocked again, then called, "Zenovialle!" She knocked louder and called the name insistently.

"Maybe she's out," Lily said.

"No woman of the alleys leaves lights on when she goes out," Noorna replied and tried the door; it opened without effort. She let it swing open, and both women gasped. Lily stepped in, pulling Noorna with her, and shut the door.

The Palestinian woman, wearing an *abbayya* and head veil, was seated rigidly in a latticed chair standing in a pool of blood. A slashed wrist was hanging down over the armrest. In her other hand was a carving knife, still held tightly, resting in her lap. Her head had fallen to one side, its weight bending her neck into a grotesque angle. Flies were on her wound, her eyes, and the pool of blood. The light, an old brass standing lamp with a naked bulb, had been placed to illuminate her and the wall she sat near. Covering the wall was a message written with a child's multicolored crayons, the remains of which had fallen to the floor, at the edge of the blood. The colors of the Arabic script had changed as crayons and patience wore down.

> Cursed be a world where children must do
>   the work of the fathers.
> Cursed be the Jews who remember their
>   Holocaust while they create ours.
> Cursed be the Americans who pay and pay
>   and pay for it, blind in their paradise.
> Cursed be the Arab nations who use us for
>   their purpose, then ignore us in our need.
> Cursed *are* the people of Palestine who
>   die strangers in every land, even their own.

Cursed *are* the women who raise each other's sons only to
send them to their early death.

Propped against the wall below the script was a cheaply framed
picture of a boy about twelve, with dark curly hair and a scowl of
hate on his taut, narrow face. His eyes, large, dark, and wet, were
his father's.

Lily read quickly, struck by sadness for the dead author of the
words. She forced herself to go farther into the room and began
searching it, careful to cover her hands with the material of her
abbayya.

"What are you doing?" she heard Noorna ask shakily.

"We have to find what we came for. Get the picture. Do it
carefully, no traces of us . . ." It was a simple room, spotlessly
clean, luxurious by the usual standards of alley life, large enough
not only for two beds, but for a dining table. The walls and ceiling
were painted vermilion and pink. There was a stove, refrigerator,
television set, wash basin, and even a bath and toilet in a back
room. All were rusted or stained, but nevertheless unusual in the
alleys of Cairo. Two chests of drawers were next to the beds. The
one Lily searched was filled with boy's clothing. Under a stack of
underwear, she found three loose nine-millimeter bullets.

"Any list, diagram, any piece of paper," she said as she hurriedly
went through torn jeans and T-shirts. Noorna was searching
kitchen shelves when suddenly she grimaced.

"Look," she said, pointing to the dead woman.

Through the latticed back of the chair, they saw papers pressed
behind the woman's back. Lily moved hurriedly, pausing only
when she realized she couldn't reach the woman's body without
stepping in the pool of blood around it. She looked for something
to step on, unwilling to track blood through the apartment as they
left. There was a thick book beside one of the neatly made beds.

"Bring me that," she directed Noorna, who rushed to get the
volume.

"It's the Koran," she said respectfully.

"Bring it. They'll think she dropped it."

Noorna hesitated, then said in justification, "It may help save
the boy's life," and hurried over to Lily.

She placed the book halfway to the chair and stepped onto it. The flies rose momentarily, then sank back to the surface. Leaning over as far as possible, Lily forced her hand behind the body's back, sliding her fingers down the latticework until she could grip the papers. They started to tear as she pulled them, so she pushed the body forward with her other hand and yanked them free. The body, stiff in rigor mortis, remained in place, and Lily stepped off the book. She looked at the papers: one, a map of Galilee; one, a set of scientific instructions in English; the last, two itineraries, in Arabic, from Cairo to Beirut and Damascus, both ending in Haifa. Without a word, she took Noorna's hand and led the way out. As Noorna closed the door behind her and as they started toward the stairs, engulfed in the sudden darkness, they were aware of someone next to them on the landing.

"Any luck?" Moshe whispered.

"Yes," Lily said. "Let's get out of here."

"There's a taxi at the end of the alley," Moshe said, "parked in front of the baker's. Get in the back seat. I'll follow you out of the building."

They hurried down the stairs and out of the alley to the taxi. When they were safely inside, Moshe appeared and took his place in the driver's seat. He started the engine and maneuvered into traffic.

"We have to notify someone about her," Lily said. "She should have been buried by—"

"Buried?" Moshe interrupted. "She was dead?"

"Suicide," Noorna said hollowly.

"You're sure?" Moshe asked professionally.

"Yes," both women said together.

"But you found—"

"Yes," Lily interrupted impatiently, and saw him check her in the rearview mirror. "A map, itineraries, the boy's picture, and these." She handed the bullets to him, and he examined them as he drove. "But I still don't know his name."

Lily turned away, not daring to look at Noorna, with whom she'd shared the sight of that sad room. Remembering the wall's curses, she tried to edge them from her mind by unfolding the papers she'd brought with her, hidden under the folds of her *ab-*

bayya. She examined the map and discovered three small arrows pointing to different locations along the aqueduct—the reservoir at Tsalmon, the open canal north of Beit Netofa, the junction of the Yarkon-Negev distribution system at Rosh Ha'ayin. She knew them well from her work in Tel Aviv when she first became aware of Israel's water problem. Her book had described the water system in detail. The Kinneret-Negev Conduit supplied ninety percent of Israel's available water resources. Its contamination would affect every home in Israel south of Acre.

And if Abu al-Saffah hadn't been captured in Cairo by pure chance, no one would have known for nine months, a year. How soon would suspicion have grown? How long would it have taken for the population to begin dwindling? Could the nation ever have attracted more immigrants? Would the ultrareligious have allowed massive campaigns of artificial insemination?

An instructor at the Institute had said once, "We as diplomats don't think in terms of crimes and horrors of international life, but regard them dispassionately as mistakes, blunders. Our job is to recognize and prevent them before they happen and, if we're really good, without anyone realizing it."

"We have to fly to Haifa," Lily said.

"The conduit? Is that where he's headed?" Moshe asked from the front seat.

"Yes. The map's marked at Tsalmon Reservoir, and the canal north of Beit Netofa. Also Rosh Ha'ayin, but that's too far south. My guess is that it was an alternative in case things went wrong."

"A helicopter from Haifa, then," he suggested as he looked around briefly. "But, Lily, we can't cover the whole reservoir, or the canal, even if we knew the exact time, the exact spot he might appear."

"I know. Both itineraries take him to Haifa tonight, though. There's an address there, probably of someone who'll guide him to the conduit. We have to get there before he leaves."

"If you have an address, I can have it surrounded in the hour." He reached his hand back over the seat, expecting the papers.

"And risk losing him if he's not there yet," she said, holding back the papers.

Moshe looked angrily at her in the rearview mirror and put his hand back on the steering wheel. "We're not going to negotiate about the destruction of Israel, Lily. If we don't get him there, we have to call in the troops." It was a statement, not a suggestion.

"Moshe, any alarm will force that boy to go his own way. We'll lose the best chance we have of finding him."

"If an alarm goes out, with his picture, they'll find him before it's too late."

"And shoot him," Lily challenged.

"Perhaps, but his bomb won't get dropped."

"Listen to me," she said, leaning forward. "I want more than to stop him. I want him alive to manipulate his father. And I don't want that thermos to fall into the hands of the Israeli Defense Force."

She could see his hands grip the steering wheel hard enough to turn white. "You'd use me against my own country?"

"It's not against your country," Lily said, as furious as he. "The Egyptians will be able to get more out of the father about terrorism by using the son than either Americans or Israelis could. And do you want that half-gallon of hormone passed around the right wing of Israel?"

He drove on silently. Lily looked over at Noorna, who was listening, open-mouthed.

"What if I refuse," Moshe said, "get out of the taxi right now and—"

"I can't do anything," Lily interrupted, then said slowly, "except to trust your word."

Again he glanced at her in the rearview mirror, watching her as he said, "Don't try to use echoes of an earlier betrayal in this present negotiation. It won't work, Lily."

"I'm using nothing but the obvious good reasons why I want this boy and his thermos safely out of Israel."

Moshe had to stop the taxi for a red light. As soon as he could, he turned around to face Lily. "Look, can we compromise: if we don't catch him tonight in Haifa, I'll pull the alarm. All right?"

Lily said, "I accept that." He was right. If they missed the boy in Haifa, their chances were nil. The lack of time would necessitate a massive search and a nationwide alarm.

A horn blew behind them and Moshe turned back to drive.

"How much time do we have?" Noorna asked.

Lily looked at the itineraries. "It seems he plans to leave Haifa at dawn and head for one of the three locations—probably one of the two in the north—in time to drop the bomb into the water at noon."

"Then you have until dawn," Noorna said and looked west at the magenta sunset. "How will you get to Haifa?"

"We have to talk to Worth and Ammar," Lily said. "What about departure and arrival in Israel?"

"I know someone in Cairo with a plane," Noorna offered, "that's registered in Switzerland."

"Can you call him?" Moshe asked. "Right now?"

"Yes. But who's going?"

"Moshe and I," Lily said, then added, "and Worth."

"Lily," Moshe objected, "traveling with an under secretary of state gets too much attention."

"If all goes well, I want to be in and out of Israel before dawn. If we run into trouble getting out with an Arab boy, traveling with an under secretary might be very helpful."

"Ammar and I will stay by the phone in Cairo and pick you up at dawn," Noorna offered.

"I'll have to use the Mossad to get us through customs at Haifa. Otherwise, the customs people will alert them."

Alarmed, Lily started to object. "You can't—"

"Don't worry. I'm in a position to do this. Trust me."

Again they exchanged looks in the rearview mirror. Lily nodded.

"All right," Moshe said, "let's do the whole thing on a public phone. Call your friend, Noorna, get the plane set, then call Deloit and Ben Ashid, get Worth out of your apartment without us having to go in and give the press another chance. He can bring Lily's clothes and passport."

Within the hour, they were airborne. The flight to Haifa took an hour and fifteen minutes. The plane was an American Gulfstream owned by an Egyptian industrialist whose family had known Noorna's. Lily changed out of the *abbayya* into slacks and blouse in the plane's opulent mirror-and-marble head. Worth's two security men were in the rear of the plane. Lily, Moshe, and Worth sat around an inlaid table, studying the documents and picture that

Lily and Noorna had taken from the dead woman's flat. Before he left, Worth had called the embassy for a detailed map of Haifa to be delivered to the apartment. Even though he knew Haifa well, Moshe studied the map carefully, locating the address from the boy's itinerary. Worth and Lily asked Moshe questions as they plotted other courses in case the boy was not found, how best to notify Israeli authorities for the quickest response, how to explain the delay in the notification, and, at that point, whether anyone but Moshe should be involved.

After they agreed on the strategy in case of failure, Moshe put forth a preliminary plan for reaching the boy.

"Pray for a telephone," he said as he went over the map of Wadi Nisnas, the Arabic quarter in Haifa. "That way we can negotiate from a safe distance. I've arranged for two cars with telephones. We'll park near the Bet Hageffin, the Arab-Jewish community center. I'll leave you for a time to do my work, find the house—it's two blocks away—and if the boy's there, what kind of arms he and whoever's with him might have, and whether there's a telephone. I'll bet there is. The Arabs in Haifa aren't the usual second-class citizens. It may take an hour. Then I'll come back and we'll go from there. Worth, can your security people be used or are they neutral?" He asked the question offhandedly.

Worth considered before answering. "Not neutral, but passive involvement only. I'm not eager for an American security officer to be put in the position of shooting the fourteen-year-old son of a notorious Arab terrorist."

"What if he comes out shooting and starts to run?" Moshe asked impatiently.

"We duck," Lily said, "start working the car phones, and call for help."

Moshe frowned, obviously irritated. "It'd be impossible for me to let him get away."

"I understand that," Lily said firmly, "but remember—that's the worst thing that could happen. If we save the boy, think what Abu al-Saffah would tell us about terrorist groups around the world in order to see his son—still innocent—go free."

The reasoning silenced Moshe. Worth sat back in his chair with the hint of an appreciative smile. "What do we do with the boy if we are successful?" he asked.

"He'll go to Egypt on this plane with me," Lily said. "You'll call on the American ambassador in Tel Aviv and go back to Geneva. The Egyptians will take official responsibility for the boy, let al-Saffah see that he's safe, and then negotiate for anything the father knows." She faced Moshe. "Can you go along with that, Moshe?"

"I'm sure the Egyptian government will be grateful to the future ambassador," he said pointedly. "But fourteen-year-olds who are let go come back to kill at fifteen."

"Maybe so, but isn't the chance worth taking? Al-Saffah will never negotiate anything if Israel has the boy."

His struggle was obvious, but Moshe finally nodded and immediately stood up, in need of a place to go. The only place available was the head, so he went back to it and closed the door hard behind him.

"Worth," Lily said, "I need to talk to you about Washington."

"Nicely done," Worth said, smiling approvingly.

"What?"

"Cornering Moshe Levy so neatly."

"It's better for Israel this way, and Moshe knows it. It wasn't cornering."

"I had my doubts."

"What doubts?"

"Oh, I worried that the rescue of the boy was some kind of catharsis of your own experiences—the atrocity in Amman, your father's death—with the ironic kicker of his being al-Saffah's son."

"And you think none of that's in play?"

"Is it?"

"Yes, Worth, of course it is," Lily said impatiently. "But I wanted to ask about the president's concern. Is it about my health or about my appointment?"

"Both."

"Am I in trouble?"

"You're getting a lot of notice. Senators go into a frenzy when fame is involved, hoping some of the glitter and light will fall on them." He chuckled. "This administration detests such attention, because it usually stimulates unnecessary examination. What we're doing tonight in Haifa, even if it goes well, could bring you what you really don't want just now."

Lily rested her head on the back of the seat. "I want this job," she said. "But if it goes badly tonight, I'll ask the president to withdraw my nomination. If we succeed—I mean, if we get the boy back to Egypt quietly, with no public notice about the threat to Israel or whatever, and I give my deposition to the Egyptian authorities and leave as planned"—she turned her head so that she could watch him—"what will you do, Worth? You can shoot me down a hundred ways now without my even knowing how it happened."

"I told you that I'd support you as—"

She shook her head. "I've seen you give that kind of support before. You set yourself a kind of quota of favor, which in this case I'd say you've surpassed already. Once you reach that quota, your sense of moral responsibility is satisfied. Don't think I don't appreciate all you've done so far. I'm just curious about where you are now."

He didn't answer right away, nor did he look at her when he started to speak. "This will surprise you, as it did me. When I came aboard this opulent plane and sat down at the table, I saw the picture of the boy. The first thing that somehow crashed into my mind was that he was about the same age as the child we might have had, if we'd had the inclination at the time. Of course, back then nothing could have been further from our ambitious minds, except maybe once or twice."

He looked at Lily and started to smile but changed to a hard glare. "You can't see me anymore. We're blind to each other, I suppose. I regret it. I wonder if you do."

"What am I supposed to see?" she asked carefully.

He replied in an angry whisper, "That I'm aware of certain mistakes, that taking you for granted and letting you get away—*sending* you away—because of the idiotic phony pregnancy thing with Cassie, was genuinely, deeply . . . stupid, for want of a more artful term. That what we saw at the Raphael Hotel in Paris one night, which I've manipulated through two administrations as my job guarantee, is a pretty deplorable shadow in a career. That you're the only woman who's put up with me and never bent. Your independence always irritated me, probably because it threatened me, but it made you the only kind of woman I can stand. And to have lost you—"

Moshe came out of the plane's head, looked startled, then resigned as he took them in, and moved to start a conversation with the security men.

Worth sat back, his pained anger quickly replaced by his familiar look of aloof superiority.

"When was I supposed to have seen all that?" Lily asked softly.

"I don't know," he replied sadly. "It doesn't make any difference now. Just realize that I'm aware of the mistakes. It may all be over soon, and I promise you, I'll support your appointment as long as it can do you any good."

"What may be over?"

"You've read about it. There's going to be a congressional investigation into the Tehran hostages and the 1980 election."

Lily leaned forward. "Would you be involved?"

"There are certain people whom I used for my own purposes. If those people are subpoenaed and testify under oath, their basic defense will be to deflect blame, or at least to dilute it by sharing it. I can't imagine that my name won't be dropped sooner or later. Then I'd be called to testify, too."

"What could they prove?" she asked.

"You're talking like a lawyer again. Thanks. If I deny everything, it'd only be my word against theirs. If they're indicted for treason, or even if the whole thing wallows along to a nonconclusion, which will probably be the case—so much for my distinguished foreign service career. The taint of treason doesn't go away. I may just admit the whole sordid mess, tell them all to go to hell, take a job on Wall Street, and write books about . . ." He would have continued, but he noted Lily's narrow-eyed suspicion. "What is it?" he asked.

"If you denied everything," she said, "and had a witness who could substantiate your denial, someone who was at the Raphael Hotel with you, someone they would believe, for instance your former wife, the current ambassador to Egypt—"

"Lily—"

"Is that why you came to Egypt? Is that why you've been so unstintingly helpful, so movingly eloquent about the child who might have been, why you'll support my appointment as long as . . . ?"

"That's very creative cynicism, Lily. When did that happen to you?"

"I suppose when I got to know you well."

"I came to Egypt with presidential instructions—"

"Drawn up by him or by you? And I can check that."

"Oh, do, Lily. Check it." He shifted in his seat. "But I meant what I said, about the mistakes and the support. Believe what you will. It makes no difference now."

Lily saw the seat belt sign flash on. As she attached the belt across her lap, she began to question her judgment, and blamed herself for being too quick to reach that bitter conclusion. Yet, going over the way he'd presented this latest quandary, so ingenuously, yet with such guile, she doubted that she could ever trust him.

The plane banked and Lily saw the lights of Haifa's port etched into the blackness of the Mediterranean Sea. She thought of the boy, fourteen, and wondered who her own child might have been.

TWENTY-NINE

THE CAR PHONE'S SHORT BEEP repeated itself for a long time. Sitting in the front seat, with the receiver to her ear, Lily saw through the windshield a single light go on behind a window grille in the old sandstone house. Its arched Levantine doorway faced the car from across the street; she and Worth had a direct view. One of his security officers was in the back seat. The second car was in the alley behind the house, where the other security officer listened on his car phone as he watched the back door.

Still no one answered. The streets of Wadi Nisnas were empty and quiet at two A.M., and Lily could barely hear the phone ringing inside the house. There were no streetlights on the corner where the house stood; the only illumination came from a strangely tilted three-quarter moon just rising over the city above Mount Carmel. Fortunately, even that source of light was not present when Moshe did his reconnaissance of the house, discovering that it was occupied only by the boy and a woman.

"What do you want?" A woman's angry voice answered the phone in Arabic. "It's very late; I must work early tomorrow—"

"I have a message for the boy from his father and his Aunt Zenovialle," Lily said quickly so that the woman would not hang up.

There was a pause. "Who are you?" the woman asked.

"Please. Let me speak to the boy."

Again there was a pause, the phone obviously muffled against sounds of argument. At that point, Lily saw Moshe lying on the two-story building's flat roof. He was listening too, having rigged his own receiver on the phone line that entered the house.

393

"Yes, who is this?" The boy's Arabic was pure Egyptian. His voice, newly turned deep, was steady but full of apprehension.

"Before I tell you that, let me tell you what I know to assure you that I come from your father and your aunt."

"You know her name?" he asked incredulously. "You've seen her?"

"Yes," Lily said guardedly. "Zenovialle."

"Go on," the boy said.

"You have a thermos; the MacLeod tartan is on it. You bought it at a stall in the Ezbekiah Gardens. You're planning to pour the contents of the thermos in the Kinneret-Negev Conduit tomorrow at noon, either at the Tsalmon Reservoir or the canal north of Beit Netofa."

"Yes, I will believe you. What do you have to tell me?"

"Your father told me all of this in order to save your life. The conduit is heavily patrolled. Because he is not with you, it's almost impossible that you would survive."

"I'm willing to take that chance."

"He told me you would be. He was very proud of how brave you are. But by telling me of the plan, your father knew he was preventing its success. If you refuse our offer, Israel will be warned. Troops will be brought in. Even if you succeed, the nation will be alerted."

"Where are you?"

"Across the street, behind the house, on the roof."

"You're here?" Panic cracked the boy's voice. "They're surrounding the house!" he yelled to the woman.

"We're not here to harm you or capture you. You've done nothing to warrant that. Listen to me. We're here to save your life, which is what your father wants."

"He'll die in prison. They'll murder him or throw him to his enemies. You're killing my father." He began to sob.

"No," Lily said compassionately, "no, we aren't. We're here at your father's bidding. And if it goes well between us, I promise you that you'll see your father soon after dawn."

The sobbing stopped suddenly and for a moment Lily couldn't even hear him breathe. Then he said, with a voice of hate, "You're the McCann woman. The papers say he asked for you."

"Yes," Lily answered.

"Of all people in the world, how can I trust you?"

"Because your father did."

He paused a moment. "What do you want me to do?"

"First, let me tell you what we hope to do," Lily said. "We'd like you to come with us, not under arrest, but as a free person, back to Cairo. We have a plane waiting at the airport. If you'd like the woman who's with you to come too, that will be agreeable. Whether or not your papers are in order, you and she will be allowed to stay there as long as your father is dealing with his legal problems. You'll be able to move freely, though I'm sure your Egyptian hosts would wish to observe your activities to some degree. You'd have to put up with it. When your father is free to leave Egypt, you will be free to leave with him."

"But now you want the thermos."

"Yes. After all, it's useless."

"What if I refuse?"

"You're in Israel, with a biological weapon designed to destroy this country. That's a serious conspiracy, and it would also be used against your father in Egypt."

He didn't respond and seemed to cover the mouthpiece again. Lily heard no argument, and when he said nothing after a long pause, Lily said, "Hello? Are you there?"

"Yes. Yes. I'll come out, but you must promise not to bother this woman. She's extremely upset. She knew nothing of my father's plan, and wishes to stay here in Haifa. She knew my mother in Lebanon; that's the only reason I came here."

Lily looked at Worth, who took only a second to shake his head.

"I can't make guarantees for the government of Israel," Lily explained. "They'll check her background, and if she is a valid resident, she should have no problems. If she is not, I'll use my influence on her behalf."

Worth scowled disapprovingly as the boy spoke directly to the woman, who apparently agreed to the arrangement, for the boy said, "We accept."

"When you come out the front door," Lily hastened to add, "we'll turn on our headlights. The woman should stay inside, out of sight. Carry the thermos in both hands held at arm's length in front of you. I found some nine-millimeter bullets in your clothes in Cairo. Have the gun in plain sight stuck in your pants at the waist."

"That was my father's gun. He had it with him when the Egyptians arrested him."

Lily looked at Worth again. He shrugged, not knowing whether it was true.

"All right," Lily said. "We're waiting for you."

There were several clicks of disconnection. She saw Moshe move further into view as he looked down from the roof over the front door. The other car was to stay at the rear of the house, in case anyone tried to escape, unless there was trouble up front.

"You'll take the thermos?" Worth asked.

"Yes. Let our people examine it and destroy it."

Lily felt his hand slip over hers and hold it. "Please believe what I said on the plane," he said quietly, aware of the security officer in the back seat.

The front door of the house opened and a figure was outlined in the dim light from inside. The boy took a tentative step, and Lily turned on the headlights. The glare blinded him and he turned his head but held the plaid thermos in front of him. Lily stepped out of the car and stood behind the open door.

"We're glad to see you," she called. "Please walk to the center of the street, put the thermos down, and step back from it to the sidewalk."

He wore jeans, high-topped American sneakers, and a T-shirt with the Palestinian flag stenciled on it. His face looked grim, but the large, moist eyes stared into the headlights with defiance. His mass of curly black hair was tied with a bandanna made of the familiar checked material favored by the PLO. Above, on the roof, Moshe had his revolver trained on him. The boy walked forward slowly, stumbled slightly on the curb, then, more accustomed to the light, stepped into the street and put the thermos down.

"Do I see you now, Lily McCann?" he called contemptuously as he walked slowly backward to the curb, felt for it with one foot, and stepped back on the sidewalk. "I've had nightmares about you all my life."

Involuntarily, Lily tensed and glanced at Worth, who looked back. "Yes," she said, "I'm coming."

As she walked into the headlights, she heard the other car doors open behind her. The boy watched her as if she were an exotic but poisonous animal, a stunned curious smile of recognition appearing briefly before a grimace of hate replaced it.

"You have been the devil of our lives," he said. "My father spoke of you every time he came to see me. He used to rave—" He stopped, suddenly embarrassed by the admission.

Standing in front of the thermos, she said, "I'm surprised to hear that. But it can end here, right now."

"Never. We Palestinians have years, generations of hate for Americans."

"I meant you and me. Your father was as much my devil as I am yours. Did he ever tell you what he'd done to me?"

He hesitated before admitting, "The children, your father—the closet in Amman."

"Does this have to go on between us?"

He didn't answer right away. "I can't see your face in this light."

"I'll pick up the thermos and then you can walk toward the car. There are two men there; one will search you. You'll sit in the front seat. When you're in the car, we'll talk some more. Is that agreeable?"

"Yes." The boy walked into the street, watching her as he moved.

She stooped to pick up the thermos and stood with it in both hands. By that time, the boy was equally in the light and stopped to stare at her. Lily chanced a slight smile.

"Lily, get down!" Worth yelled. As she fell to the street, she dropped the thermos and glimpsed the long folds of a woman's robe sway in the doorway of the house. She held a large revolver.

"No!" the boy shouted. "What are you doing?"

The first shot cracked the street's quiet, hitting five feet wide of Lily and ricocheting off into the darkness. Five other rapid shots were fired from Moshe's silenced revolver from above, but the woman stayed inside the door. Lily felt someone fall on top of her as another shot burst from the doorway through the yells of the boy, who was running toward the woman. But then two shots exploded from the direction of the car, followed by a slow cry. Lily looked up to see the woman collapse into the boy's arms.

"No, no, no, no, no!" he cried out as he sank to the ground under the woman's weight. "She was in Sabra with my mother," he cried as a tearful explanation. "She was in Sabra . . ."

Lily was aware of Worth lying on top of her and of the security officer kneeling next to them, saying urgently, "Sir? Sir?" She felt moisture on the small of her back and tried to roll over. Worth's head was above her shoulder and it didn't move. "Worth?" she shouted, then controlled herself and eased out from under him as the second car's headlights suddenly swept over the street.

"Worth? Can you hear me?" Lily said urgently, lying beside him on the street. The bullet had entered his lower back, and blood was spreading through his dark linen suit. "Call for ambulances," Lily ordered, confronting the devastated face of the security officer. "Hurry!" she demanded. Moshe ran up as the second officer went to the door of the house, his revolver drawn. "I've already called," Moshe said as he knelt nearby.

"Worth?—We've got to stop the bleeding," Lily urged, the flutter of panic beginning to spread in her voice.

Moshe took off his jacket and then his shirt, which he pressed hard on the wound.

Worth groaned, a deep sound that Lily had never heard. She saw his eyes flutter as he recognized her and, his cheek still on the street, tried to breathe.

"An ambulance is on the way," Lily said. "Don't move."

Worth frowned and tried to look up as far as his eyes would let him. "Is the boy—?"

"Yes," Lily said. "He's safe. Don't talk, Worth, please."

"Get him out of here," Worth continued. "Have the security men take him to the plane. Right now! Before—" He shuddered and stopped talking.

Lily looked at Moshe, who bent his head.

"Search him," Moshe called in English to the security officer standing beside the boy and the dead woman.

Lily heard sirens in the distance just as the boy started yelling. "I didn't know she had a gun. She lived alone, a widow, her husband was murdered in Sabra before her eyes—"

Lily stood up and hurried over to the boy. "You have to leave now." To the security officer, she said, "Take him to the plane. If I'm not there a half-hour after you, take off."

The boy yelled, "I can't leave her!"

Lily reached out and shook him by the shoulders to stop him. "You'll be arrested by the Israelis, and they won't believe you as much as we do. I'll see that the woman's buried. Go now and see your father."

The sirens were close. The boy heard them. His eyes wide with fear, he let himself be hustled to the second car by the security officer. Lily returned to Worth and knelt at his side in the street. Moshe still held his shirt against Worth's wound, but it too was soaked. He offered nothing when Lily looked at him. They heard the car turn and drive away, passing an ambulance as it rounded the street corner.

"Worth, they're here. Hang on. Hang on." She reached out to touch his face and was startled by how cold it was. The ambulance crew began working on his clothes, cutting them away as Moshe spoke urgently to them in Hebrew. Lily saw the thermos under Worth; he'd grabbed it as he fell on her. She took it and stayed on the ground, hoping to see a reaction on Worth's face even if it was pain. But she couldn't tell whether he was still breathing.

"I've told them who he is," Moshe said, kneeling next to her. "The hospital's preparing for surgery. He'll be in the operating room in seven, eight minutes."

Lily did not trust herself to speak. She was aware of other vehicles arriving and the noise of a curious crowd. Suddenly Worth was lifted and placed on a gurney, and Moshe helped her to her feet. "I'll stay here to deal with the police," he said. "The other security man will follow in the car. Say nothing about why you were in Haifa. I'll be able to cover it officially and we'll deal with publicity later. Stay very strong, Lily." He was helping her into the ambulance and she turned to him.

"He's not going to die," she said, but watched Moshe as if she'd asked him a question.

Moshe didn't respond; he stepped back as a paramedic slid the side door closed. Holding the thermos, she sat on a jump seat next to Worth, who lay on his side, one arm attached to an intravenous drip, the other to a monitor on the ceiling which beeped irregularly. While the paramedics worked to stabilize him and keep the wound clean, one was conversing in Hebrew with the hospital, describing the patient's condition. The ambulance began to move; Lily looked out the window and saw in the flashes of the emergency lights crowds of curious Arab citizens and Israeli troops controlling them. Briefly she saw a second ambulance backing up to the front door of the house, where the woman's body lay, covered with a white sheet.

"Lily."

She turned and leaned close to Worth's face. "We'll be at the hospital in just a few minutes."

"Take my hand, will you? I'm not sure where it is."

She was able to grasp two fingers of his left hand without disturbing the intravenous needle. "Don't talk now."

" 'Talk when you can or you might lose the chance,' " he responded. "Remember that from the Institute?"

Lily tried to smile for his sake, though she wasn't sure how much he could see. His eyes moved restlessly around the interior of the ambulance.

"I wish to confess my sins," he said in gasped attempts at his usual verbal flourish, "to you, not to anyone else. I wanted you back, Lily. I came out here to tell you, had no idea how, tried to tell you in the middle of all this, ran head-on into your justified suspicion." He took several breaths. "Let me tell you something else. It honestly hadn't occurred to me to ask you to be a witness for my defense. But as soon as you said it, I suspected myself. I wondered whether I could trust any of my motives again."

"You can give yourself more credit than that."

He looked directly at her. "I doubt it," he said. His eyes closed, and Lily squeezed his fingers in alarm.

"Worth," she said urgently.

Without opening his eyes, he said, "There's so damn much I have to do."

One of the paramedics looked over at Lily and shook his head as an order to keep Worth from talking.

"We're almost there," she said, "and being angry doesn't help much. Shut up."

He smiled again and opened his eyes, but looked alarmed. "Where are you, Lily? I can't see."

Squeezing the two fingers, she said. "I'm right here."

"I loved you, Lily, more than anyone else in my life, with the possible exception of myself. And they shouldn't carve my name on the slab at Foggy Bottom. What I did to get shot wasn't serving my country. It was you. Do I get that credit?"

"Yes, but don't talk anymore. You're upsetting the hell out of me."

He tried to smile, but closed his eyes again. "I think your father may have had it right about . . . Damn death. God damn death anyway."

His fingers went rigid, then relaxed as his mouth fell open. An alarm went off on the monitor, and the paramedics moved quickly to give him an injection as the ambulance pulled into the emergency entrance of the hospital. Lily let his fingers go and reached up to close his mouth. She leaned over and kissed his cheek.

"Goodbye, Worth," she whispered and sat back to stay out of the way as the doors opened and they rushed Worth's body into the hospital. She stayed there, without moving, until the American security man appeared, asking what she wanted to do.

"Nevertheless, Ms. McCann, there's still a good deal of confusion—not only among the members of this panel, but with the American public—as to why you and the under secretary of state were running around the Arab district in Haifa in the first place."

Lily didn't respond, aware that the senator was making a speech, not asking a question. Camera people squatted and crouched in the space between her table and the raised dais on which the senators of the Subcommittee on Near Eastern Affairs sat, peering down in their customary posture of superiority. The shutters of the cameras continually whirred, trying to catch a telltale look of fallibility on Lily's face.

"Now, we have been told," the senator continued, "—as this legislative body is so often told—that information is not forthcoming about your visit to Haifa because it's a matter of 'national security.'" His sarcasm oozed through a florid smile. "And we certainly have no wish to delve into anything personal that may have transpired between you and your former husband. But we do have a responsibility, in considering your appointment as an American ambassador, to make certain your actions were at least appropriate and justified, even though they ended so tragically. Can you reassure us about Haifa, Ms. McCann?"

This was it, the question every pundit and interviewer had asked, personally or in print, in the two months since she'd returned from the Middle East. She had to answer it well, for the senator who asked it had been suspiciously silent over the two days of her hearings, and suddenly seemed primed for a showy debate. Lily had been informed by her team at State that this particular senator was the point man for the American Israel Public Affairs Committee and had received $105,000 for his last election campaign from pro-Israeli PACs.

"I very much appreciate your sensitivity, Senator," she began, leaning comfortably into the microphone in front of her. Avoiding the "testimonial hunch," which the witness table and the dais of senators usually caused, Lily sat with a straight back, slightly tilted forward. She had brought no counsel or adviser with her, aware of the effect of appearing completely alone at the huge table at which witnesses were usually flanked by lawyers, aides, and stacks of files.

"I mean your sensitivity about the personal as well as national security," she continued. "Thank you, sir. As you've explained, I'm not permitted to comment in any detail about that trip, except to say that, although Mr. Deloit's death was indeed a tragedy, it was not the only result. In response to your question, I've been authorized to tell the committee that as a direct result of what was accomplished in Haifa, the CIA and Mossad garnered information that enabled them to bring to an effective end the three terrorist groups I'm sure you've been reading about in the papers. Over the past decades, those three groups were responsible for the deaths of some two hundred Israeli citizens, as well as numerous people from other countries, including twelve Americans on a bombed airplane. How many lives have therefore been saved from future acts of terrorism we can only speculate, but it's safe to say that Mr. Deloit did not die in vain."

The reaction in the hearing room was a dramatic silence, which pleased Lily, for her interrogator retreated momentarily from his peering perch in order to ruffle some papers.

"Well, now, that's quite a revelation, isn't it?" he asked. "Who authorized it?"

"The Department of State, sir."

"And how convenient that it could be revealed today."

"Only because of your question, Senator, which surely represents the understandable curiosity of the American public."

"Well, thank you, Ms. McCann, but if you can reveal those results, why on earth can't you and the State Department and, let's be frank with each other, the White House—why can't you reveal how those results came to be accomplished?"

"It's still an area of active involvement, Senator, a situation in progress that may be impeded by public scrutiny. I must add that the easiest way to have obviated further attention on this matter would have been to withdraw my nomination. I'm grateful for the confidence the president has displayed by refusing my offer to do so, but I'm naturally concerned that my presence here may inadvertently cause undue notice to focus on an extremely sensitive intelligence operation."

The senator gazed down at her with open skepticism. "Then we may assume that, by sending you on up here, the president regarded such 'public scrutiny' as this committee represents to be a risk worth taking. The public has a right to know, Ms. McCann, and we are chary of secrets. We are not the Intelligence Committee dealing with spies and agents. Our interest is diplomats, the practice of diplomacy in the interests of the United States of America. I for one fail to see how this, uh, secret mission—no matter the benefits you say accrued—how such an undercover operation fits into the purview of this committee. Perhaps the president, with all his confidence in you, should nominate you to the CIA." He played it for the cameras and for a laugh, but got neither; the TV and press cameras stayed on Lily for her reply.

"It was not a 'secret mission,'" Lily stated with a calm smile. "It was not an 'undercover operation.' It was a diplomatic response to an international incident of great consequence. It relied on qualities of diplomacy that have been practiced for centuries—reacting with a trained instinct to an impending crisis, practicing the art of communication under extreme stress of time and place, preparing the best possible circumstances for a negotiation to succeed, and, finally, avoiding the devastation of a probable conflict while protecting and enhancing the interests of this country to the degree of devotion that Mr. Deloit illustrated."

She sat back in her chair, cleared her throat of the sudden emotion, and leaned forward again. "I cannot tell you the details, Senator, though I agree that the public has a right to know. Yet every member of that public has trusts and promises to keep, yes, secrets they will never tell anyone. Diplomacy is not exclusively about secrets, but it *is* largely about trust, between nations, between people who represent nations. It takes years to establish that trust and more years to learn how best to use it. That's what a diplomat does, and why much of what happened in Haifa is evidence of a trust between nations—in this case, the United States, Egypt, and Israel—that must not be broken."

There was a good deal of low vocal reaction, both from the other senators on the dais and from people in the audience. Lily remained at the microphone, her eyes on her interrogator as the chairman of the subcommittee gaveled for order. The cameras were even more active than before, and Lily remained calm.

If he gets to make a speech, I do too, she thought, but that's enough for today. "Charm the troops," as Worth surely would have advised. She shut her eyes a moment, oblivious of the cameras, missing Worth again, despairing that he wasn't in her life, for better or probably worse, acknowledging the diplomatic edge he forced her to keep, and remembering what he'd done to save her life. None of it was sorted out yet, and she wondered if it ever would be.

"Ms. McCann," the senator said, his tone devoid of his earlier amusement as he held up a copy of *Pawns and Dice* for the cameras, "do you think it's appropriate for someone who has written so forcefully against the State of Israel to be placed in such a position of responsibility as our ambassador to Egypt?" He opened the book and was preparing to read from it.

"I know that book pretty well, Senator," Lily said and got a laugh, which she spoke through. "And you and I can sit here for days quoting it back and forth to each other, which I think wouldn't do much good except to sell more books, for which I'd certainly be grateful." Again there was laughter and again Lily ignored it. "But, sir, why don't I save you and the committee time by admitting to you that my book is critical of Israel. I hereby do so. It is equally critical of Jordan, Syria, Iraq, Egypt, and—in no uncertain terms—the United States, its foreign policy, and the Department of State. I'll admit all of that—if you will. But criticism is not prejudice, Senator. I am not naïve about history's xenophobic, racist horrors, its holocausts and genocides, but history must never preclude or excuse today's criticism, or we in America, in our paradise, will grow blind to the rest of the world. I assure you that if I go to Egypt, it will not be to criticize, but to nurture and enhance the common interests of our two countries, a major concern of both being the furthering of Israel's viability in the Middle East."

Before the senator could respond, the chairman of the subcommittee spoke into his microphone. "Excuse me, Senator. We're being called to the floor of the Senate for a tax vote we dare not miss in an election year. Because it's late in the day, we'll recess until ten tomorrow morning, if there's no objection. And I anticipate a vote on Ms. McCann's appointment sometime before noon."

He banged his gavel before anyone could speak, and Lily watched as most of the senators hurried out with staff aides while others conversed with one another in their chairs. The television lights went off, and Lily rose. The members of the press corps surrounded her, and she fielded their questions as she moved out of the hearing room, joined on the way by several members of her State Department team, who had been observing from the back.

One of them, the Egyptian desk officer, smiling broadly, managed to say quickly, "You've got it! The chairman's move for a vote tomorrow means—" The rest was lost in the barrage of questions. Lily kept smiling at the cameras, hoping that her hair had held and her lipstick was at least evenly worn off.

Then, in the corridor, between hand-held recorders, microphones, and flashbulbs, Lily saw a familiar form leaning casually against the wall. He'd shaved his beard. She hadn't seen him since Haifa. Her smile spread noticeably as she looked away to avoid directing any attention toward him. Moshe gave her a thumbs-up sign; as they'd arranged, he would meet her later at her hotel. They had talked on the phone almost daily to coordinate their own stories as well as their governments' reactions. They had talked about many other things, too.

As she walked down the Capitol's steps to her car, and the members of the press gradually fell away, Lily asked herself what kind of relationship the American ambassador to Egypt might have with an Israeli, a member of the Mossad. None, she answered herself, unless it was acknowledged in detail in at least three capitals of the world. That would be interesting.

Just before she stepped into the car, she caught sight of the American flag, barely moving in a languorous breeze in the Capitol's forecourt. "I think your father may have had it right about—" What was Worth going to say, she wondered. Patriotism? Sacrifice? Duty? Diplomacy? Any or all of them would do. Lily smiled, wished her father could have lived to see this day and those to come, and heard his proud laugh.

"Right principles, consistently applied."

She sat in the back seat and let the driver close the door. The car sped away as she smiled through the window at the last reporters.